Praise for

Body of Stars

"The book's fantastical premise is just distanced enough from reality to make Celeste's story a tantalizing escape, and yet close enough that its implications are convincing. The characters are down-to-earth, average people, and both men and women face real gender challenges and work together to overcome them. The book's palpable anger at injustice is met with love—a fierce, familial, and able challenger. This is an exciting debut."

—*BookPage*

"A story of devastation, rebuilding, grief, and hope—along with incisive social commentary on rape culture and misogyny."

—*Book Riot*

"*Body of Stars* is set in a vividly imagined alternate reality that feels eerily familiar."

—*Southern Review of Books*

"A tender rebuke to the idea that biology is destiny, *Body of Stars* explores the boundaries of family, identity, and predestination. Through the lens of a complex coming-of-age story, Laura Maylene Walter asks us to consider how we can make the future matter when it seems like we already know its outlines, and what the difference is between the destiny of an individual and the fate of a society."

—Adrienne Celt, author of *Invitation to a Bonfire*

"What a gift Laura Maylene Walter has given us in *Body of Stars*. Through the lens of dystopia, this incandescent debut novel holds a critical mirror up to our world's limitations on gender and the violence of those restraints, while it also forges a bold vision for agency, self-determination, and freedom. Through and through, this is a powerful and luminous book."

—Anne Valente, award-winning author of *The Desert Sky Before Us*

"In *Body of Stars*, Laura Maylene Walter has created the kind of alternate reality that feels wonderfully, thrillingly strange, until you realize it's all too familiar. This tantalizing, powerful debut bewitched me from page one and left me unable to see our world—not to mention our collective psyche—in quite the same way again."

—Anna Solomon, award-winning author of *The Book of V.*

"Rapturously written and wildly original, Laura Maylene Walter's debut novel maps the dreams and nightmares of girlhood. Like the best dystopian fiction, *Body of Stars* is both an allegory of our own world and a door that opens to a better one. Our lives may be written on our bodies, but our futures are not."   —Emily Schultz, author of *The Blondes* and *Little Threats*

"In Laura Maylene Walter's *Body of Stars*, women's bodies are their destinies, resulting in a cruel, predatory world for young girls. Yet siblings Celeste and Miles show strength and courage against the malevolent forces surrounding them. Walter writes with tenderness, empathy, and beauty. An unusual, bewitching tale."   —Bina Shah, author of *Before She Sleeps*

"Laura Maylene Walter's *Body of Stars* will be enjoyed as a novel that employs the fantastic to inventively explore both the victimization and the power of women in a world very much like our own, but its central pleasure and achievement may be its depiction of a complicated and extraordinarily moving sibling relationship. In Walter's generous and capable hands, Miles and Celeste remind us that love often means damage, and that the true test of love is not avoiding that damage but repairing it when we've caused it."

—Karen Shepard, author of *Kiss Me Someone*

"*Body of Stars* sparks with tenderness and beauty, and Walter's writing on the female body is genuine art. A thought-provoking exploration of fate and forced binaries, this is a book that lingers."

—Erika Swyler, author of *Light from Other Stars* and *The Book of Speculation*

"Part allegory, part warning, and part celebration of the female body, this is a thrilling and flawlessly crafted debut about the potential women have to hold magic, make magic, and change the course of history with the underestimated weapons of intelligence and love."

—Courtney Maum, author of *Touch* and *Costalegre*

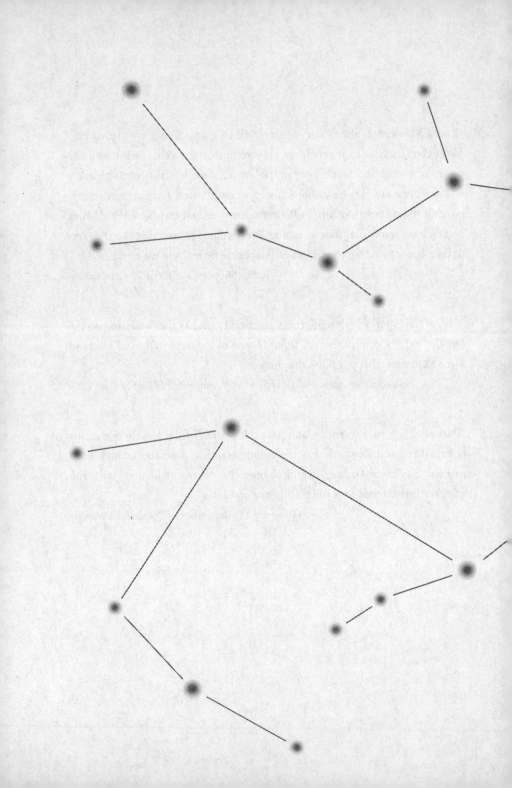

Body
of
Stars

A Novel

Laura Maylene Walter

Dutton

DUTTON

An imprint of Penguin Random House LLC
penguinrandomhouse.com

Previously published as a Dutton hardcover in March 2021
First Dutton trade paperback printing: April 2022

Copyright © 2021 by Laura Maylene Walter

Penguin supports copyright. Copyright fuels creativity, encourages diverse voices, promotes free speech, and creates a vibrant culture. Thank you for buying an authorized edition of this book and for complying with copyright laws by not reproducing, scanning, or distributing any part of it in any form without permission. You are supporting writers and allowing Penguin to continue to publish books for every reader.

DUTTON and the D colophon are registered trademarks of Penguin Random House LLC.

Illustrations by Alexis Seabrook
Interior Art: paper background by MM_photos/Shutterstock

LIBRARY OF CONGRESS CATALOGING-IN-PUBLICATION DATA
has been applied for.

Dutton trade paperback ISBN: 9780593183076

Printed in the United States of America
1st Printing

BOOK DESIGN BY ALISON CNOCKAERT

For Huda and Jennifer

I

Possibility

MAPPING THE FUTURE:
AN INTERPRETIVE GUIDE TO WOMEN AND GIRLS

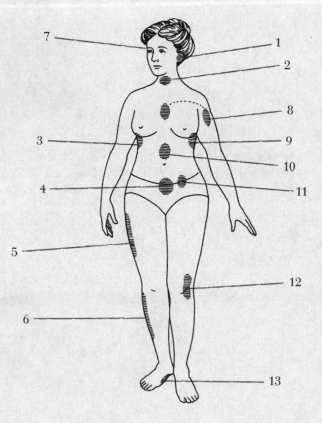

Universal Marking Locations, Front View

1. Mental Acuity

2. Personality

3. Companionship

4. Family, Nuclear

5. Family, Extended

6. Fitness and Sport

7. Academics

8. Matters of the Heart

9. Transition and Change

10. Compassion

11. Perception

12. Method and Order

13. Individuality

1

FROM THE TIME of my birth my brother Miles read me like a map, tracing my patterns of freckles and birthmarks to see my future and to learn something of his own. In those early years, my body was as much his as it was mine. To share meant letting him lift the back of my tank top or sweater so he could search my skin for a hint of what was to come. I never complained because I believed we were the same, that the predictions marked on my body were part of him, too. We were partners working in a discipline that required practice. He'd approach me at the breakfast table or in the upstairs hallway and ask if he could examine me again, as if my markings might have shifted—a phenomenon we both knew wasn't possible. At least not yet.

When I was too old for Miles to see me shirtless, he studied my arms, focusing on the constellation of moles near my left elbow. "You're lucky," he told me. "You know what will happen."

It was true. I did, as a girl, have this blueprint of my life imprinted on my skin. At sleepovers my friends and I stripped to our underwear to read our own futures. We lingered over our lower backs, the place for love and romance. "You'll fall in love more than once," Marie told Cassandra, and Cassandra in turn studied Marie's back and said, with wonder, "You'll live with a woman," which none of us at that age understood. All we knew was that our lives were speckled in advance on our skin, as it had been for our mothers, as it was for our sisters, while our brothers and fathers were left in the dark.

Over the years Miles memorized me, every inch, and documented my marks in his notebook. That notebook was thick, with unlined pages and a pale blue cover. Sometimes I'd sneak into his room and flip through it, the little dots of ink pressed so hard into the pages they made a series of bumps, like a book for the blind. I was nearly sixteen, and the childhood markings my brother recorded would soon be outdated when I matured to my adult markings. Then, I knew, he'd want to study the revised map my body had produced.

That summer and early autumn leading up to my sixteenth birthday was a time of uncertainty, of risk and wonder. All around me, other girls were entering puberty, and before long I joined them. My hips widened, and I grew taller and gained some weight. I understood these changes extended beyond my physical body. Soon, everything would change—my predictions, my expectations, my future. My entire life.

WE KEPT OUR household copy of *Mapping the Future: An Interpretive Guide to Women and Girls*—an ancient, leather-bound edition that had been in our family for generations—on the living room mantel, but Miles often claimed it for himself. My brother's interest in interpretation seemed to me another one of his quirks, like how he was left-handed or disliked chocolate. Interpretation was a female art, and for Miles to spend hours studying patterns and predictions seemed a bewildering choice. His love of interpretation was an obsession, a wildness, a force swelling beyond his control. Watching Miles cultivate a skill he was not meant to have, not meant to love in the first place, was a lesson all on its own.

We spent so much time together then. In August, a heat wave drove us into our basement, that shadowy space with the dirt floor and beams furred with cobwebs. We slipped past stacks of boxes to a tight spot under the kitchen where we could hear snatches of our mother's disembodied voice from above. When we were younger, Miles and I would hide there to eavesdrop on our parents, but on this occasion we were motivated by little more than heat and boredom. We sat on the floor and leaned against the concrete walls, letting the coolness sink into our skin. Much later, I'd recall that afternoon as a dark point in the evolution of our relationship, the start of a chasm yawning open between us. But at the time, we were merely trying to fill a few empty hours.

"Let's play Did You Know," I suggested. The game was our own invention, created on a long-ago summer afternoon much like this one, but we hadn't played it in ages.

Miles rooted in his pocket for a coin. "Call it," he told me, and the coin turned over itself in the dim basement light. Heads or stars. I called heads, but when he caught the coin against his arm and lifted his fingers, it faced stars up. A sly expression crossed his face. My brother was nearly eighteen but could still look impish, like a twelve-year-old boy just coming into his own.

"Ladies first," he said.

Going first was a disadvantage, but I was ready. I turned to write my answer in the dirt behind me, where he wouldn't be able to see it.

"Did you know," I began, "there's a chance the upper school might make gym class coed, like it is in the lower schools?"

He looked amused. "I don't think so, Celeste."

"Just listen. Cassandra's mother is on the school board, which met last night." When crafting a lie in this game, it helped to mix some truth into the matter. I went on to explain that a board member was advocating for mixed-gender physical education to help girls and boys view each other as equals. Combining curricula could also save money.

As I spoke, my brother studied me with one side of his mouth twisted, a sign of his uncertainty. "If that's true," he said, "you wouldn't have waited until now to tell me."

"Saving information for the game is a good strategy. You taught me that yourself." A sense of calm washed over me, an understanding that I could go on lying for as long as it took to win. "Besides, nothing's settled. It's just an idea someone suggested at the meeting."

Miles rolled the coin between his palms. I could tell the implications of coed gym were flashing through his mind—how girls newly matured into their adult markings, and thus at the height of their beauty, would be thrust into closer contact with boys at school. But if this was the allure of my story, it was also its downfall.

"Lie," Miles said at last. "Parents would complain about their changeling daughters being so close to boys during physical activity."

Before I could try once more to convince him, Miles crawled around me to peer at the answer in the dirt. *Lie,* I'd scrawled in looping cursive.

"My point," Miles said. "But that was a good round, Celeste. You almost got me."

I waited as he wiped clean my answer and replaced it with his own. Once he'd finished, he settled cross-legged before me, dust battering his knees and shins.

"Did you know," he said, "that Mom and Dad tried to have another baby after you?"

I worked to keep my face impassive.

"I know what you're thinking—that's impossible, because Mom's markings showed she'd only have two children." Miles lowered his voice. "Here's the thing. They thought maybe the markings left something out, or were unclear. Maybe they indicated a *minimum* of two children. You know how these things can go. For a time, they even thought she was pregnant. Mom started showing and everything." He mimed the arc of a belly over his own flat stomach.

I watched him closely, trying to understand why he would bother with such a blatant lie—was he testing me?

"This was when you were around three years old," he continued, "so I was five. I remember it, but barely. They were thrilled. That's what always comes back to me, this sense of excitement about a third baby. That they wanted more than just you and me."

A muscle in my cheek twitched, but I held my ground. I would not reveal that I was starting to believe his story could be true.

"But it wasn't meant to be," Miles went on. "For a long time, I thought I'd dreamed it. It was outrageous, to think Mom and Dad would believe they could have another child. Then I started to wonder what happened to the pregnancy. Was it a miscarriage? Or maybe it was one of those pregnancies that aren't real. Imaginary pregnancy, I think it's called."

"Phantom pregnancy," I said. "They're rare."

"In any case, I never asked about it. I assumed they wouldn't admit they believed something so foolish in the first place."

"You're right that it's a ridiculous thing to believe."

Miles held my gaze. "This is the deepest kind of truth, Celeste—what seems impossible, what we keep secret. I never mentioned it because I remember how upset Mom and Dad were after it fell apart. They wanted that third baby, even and maybe especially because it wasn't fated, and look what happened."

I let the silence stretch between us. It was untrue, it had to be, and yet I hesitated to give my answer. Miles was a master at this game. He wouldn't propose a scenario so preposterous without thinking it through.

"Time to answer," he said. "Truth or lie?"

I bit the inside of my cheek. Everything in me wanted to say *Lie*, but I couldn't form the word. I was imagining our parents delighting in the possibility of a third child. I imagined them heartbroken when it didn't work out, when they resigned themselves to Miles and me.

"Lie," I said, finally. The word tasted wrong in my mouth.

Miles looked at me steadily. "Are you sure?"

Weak sunlight fell from one of the basement windows and illuminated the dust drifting through the air. When Miles turned a certain way he looked anointed, the dust motes ringing his head like an ethereal crown.

From above, our mother called for us.

"Miles? Celeste?" Her voice had the quality of being underwater. She tapped something on the kitchen floor to get our attention, the legs of a stool, maybe, or else her own foot. "Come up here."

I rose and brushed dirt from my shorts, eager to escape both the game and my brother's scrutiny. A rift had opened between us, the narrowest of fissures that could nonetheless widen under pressure. For Miles to suggest that our parents had defied the facts of fate struck me as sacrilege. Lying for the sake of the game was one thing, but to construct such a shocking detail seemed cruel. It almost didn't matter whether his story was true or false; my distress stemmed from the fact that I couldn't tell the difference.

Perhaps I didn't know Miles, not fully. And if that was so, then I couldn't stand for him to be present when I discovered what he'd written in the dirt. I'd return to the basement later, on my own, when I could confirm his truth or lie in private.

MY MOTHER HAD a novel propped open on the kitchen counter, a thick paperback she was reading as she sliced grapes into a bowl of fruit salad. She glanced up as we came in.

"You two are filthy." She put down the knife. "Go clean up. But first, will you bring me *Mapping the Future*? It's not on the mantel."

"It's in my room," Miles said. "I'll get it."

He slipped from the kitchen, but I stayed behind and studied my mother as she leaned over her novel, her eyes flicking from one page to the next. She wore a teal sleeveless shirt faintly stained with cooking grease, and her hair was pulled back in a clip missing two teeth on one side. A few tendrils escaped and trailed down the side of her neck. When I saw my mother in disarray like this I felt anxious, like I was watching her descend into entropy. She'd had a career in education before marrying and having children, all of which had been outlined in her markings—a future she both embraced and couldn't escape.

"Why do you need *Mapping the Future*?" I asked.

My mother turned another page. "A character in this novel has a marking for vitality in old age. I have a variation of that pattern, so I'd like to look up both versions and compare them."

That marking was on the back of my mother's left thigh. I remembered staring at it as a young child when we were together in a changing room: a line of four moles intersected by two more. It was a lovely prediction to have.

"Miles studies *Mapping the Future* more than any of us," I said, "but he's getting too old to still be so wrapped up in interpretation. Maybe it's time for him to consider what he'll be for real."

"It's hard for boys." My mother turned a page of her book. "Imagine not having the future outlined on your body. I'd feel naked without it, wouldn't you?"

It was easy to forget how lost my brother was as a boy, how he was forced to grasp what he could of the future from me. Our mother's markings were the spaced-out, long-view type, which meant they were too broad to offer much insight into Miles's life. He appeared as a lone dot in the markings on her stomach: the classic triangular cluster denoting family, then a separate cluster showing my father and two children, a boy and a girl.

My juvenile markings offered more detail surrounding my brother. The five moles arranged in a diamond-like constellation on my shoulder blade had prophesized my severe case of the flu at age eight. That pattern indicated that Miles would get sick, too, which he did, despite our parents' efforts to quarantine me. And the cluster of career markings on my right hip suggested that Miles and I might one day work together.

I struggled to see how our future careers could align since I was interested in studying psychology and Miles decidedly was not, but he didn't seem fazed by this. He also chose to overlook the lone outlier marking in my career pattern, the type of mark that offered a rare contradiction—it indicated that I might, in fact, end up working alone. We'd know more once I passed to my adult predictions, but until then, my brother held out hope that this pattern might align with what he most wanted for his own future, which was to become a professional interpreter. His dream was impractical, nearly impossible, and yet he pursued it.

Another impossibility, and one I could not shake: that what he'd told me in the basement could be true. I looked at my mother and tried to picture her belly swelling against her shirt. Maybe Miles and I were two siblings shadowed by the absence of a third.

"Have you ever wanted something that's not in your markings?" I asked. "Something you weren't fated for, I mean."

She slid a bookmark into her novel and looked at me, surprised. "Of course, Celeste. I'm only human."

I studied her, searching for a sign that what she wanted was a child beyond me. But I detected nothing.

Miles reentered the kitchen and placed *Mapping the Future* on the counter. Heavy dark leather, gold text with a filigree design on the cover—a thing weighted with the gravity of truth and time. Our mother gave the text a pat, as if relieved to be reunited with an old companion.

"Thanks," she said. "Now go and clean yourselves up, both of you. You've dredged up enough of a mess for one day."

Miles and I did not return to our game that afternoon. Instead, we passed the hours in a humid summertime blur: we listened to the radio, we let ice pops drip onto our wrists, we sprawled on the living room floor in front of the fan. Eventually, Miles retreated to his room. I sat by the living room window, watching the sky darken to a deep cobalt. Shadows fell on the other houses in the neighborhood, making them appear desolate and gray, as if they'd aged decades in an instant.

All the while, I remained aware of the unfinished game, my brother's response languishing in the basement. Truth or lie. I pictured his answer as a living thing waiting in the falling light, calling for my return. Asking me to bear witness.

MY DESCENT INTO the basement that evening was the first step toward everything else—I can see that now—but at the time, I was simply inching forward in the dark, uncertain and on my own.

At the bottom of the basement stairs, I paused to allow my eyes to adjust. I thought of Miles as I waited, and how he'd grown unknowable during our game. For the first time, I understood he was capable of keeping a real secret, something that carried far more significance than anything we expressed in a game, and I worried what that could mean. There in the cool draft of the underground, an unnamed anxiety stirred to life inside me— alarm for my brother and what else he might one day hide from me.

The basement was lit by a lone, buzzing bulb, its weak illumination barely reaching the corner where earlier we'd sat coated in dust. I crept in that direction, my senses wired and alert. Finally, under the cover of cobwebs, I arrived at the word etched in the dirt. Miles had written his answer in all capitals, a message foretelling his impending deception as well as my own.

LIE, the answer read.

My first glimpse of the truth.

MAPPING THE FUTURE:
AN INTERPRETIVE GUIDE TO WOMEN AND GIRLS

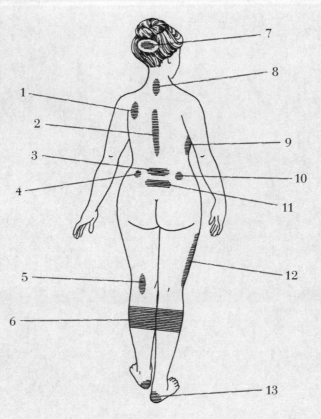

Universal Marking Locations, Back View

1. Disease and Disorder
2. Spirituality
3. Joy and Mirth
4. Finances
5. Aging Process
6. Domestic Matters
7. Emotional Health
8. Intellect
9. Honesty
10. Career
11. Love and Romance
12. Benevolence
13. Self-Esteem

2

By a trick of fate, I was born exactly two years after Miles, giving us a shared birthday. Sometimes I imagined we were twins, that we were separated by neither time nor space. We looked enough alike to make twinhood seem possible: hair the same walnut color, hazel eyes shaded more brown than green, and even the same eyebrows and ear shape, as if I'd been stamped out as his copy two years too late. I was always chasing those two years, trying to catch up to my brother as if I could outsmart time itself.

That year, summer flared into autumn abruptly, moving from heat to frost with little transition. The first cool day in September was a shock, the chill rendering the air unfamiliar. I remember it so clearly because that was the day Miles asked me to walk with him to interpretation class. His teacher, Julia, wanted to see me before I matured to my adult markings. I'd only met Julia once before, but I'd heard things about her—that she was skilled as an interpreter, though her methods were unorthodox—and I was curious what she had to say to me, a near stranger.

It was late afternoon, the time of day when sunlight pooled gold and the trees were alight with bird chatter. Miles walked just ahead of me through our neighborhood, *Mapping the Future* tucked under his arm. I tried to keep up but remained a step or two behind. My legs were long, but his were longer. We were the same, and we were not.

He was worried about being late; I understood that without him having to say so. As the first and only male student in Julia's class, he needed to work twice as hard to be taken seriously.

"We'll make it," I assured him, but we'd only just left our street and had more than a mile to go. We lived in an older neighborhood situated on the edge of downtown. It was a community of sidewalks and hedgerows, but the homes were packed together, and some showed their age. One of the houses neighboring ours dropped peels of paint like a great shedding birch, and another had plywood nailed against its upper windows. Only a few blocks away, the lawns grew green and lush, the houses bearing pillars and turrets and, in one case, a pair of lion statues flanking the walkway, their mouths cracked open in perpetual roars.

We crossed into the downtown city limits, where the streets narrowed and minuscule plants flourished in the sidewalk cracks. Broken parts sprouting new growth, decay layered with whimsy—these were the first signs we were approaching the interpretation district. A wrought iron arch reading *Future as Fate* marked the entrance. Once we passed under it, we entered a maze of cobblestone streets lined with crooked rows of townhouses. The upper floors of these townhouses served as residences, while interpretation businesses occupied the street level, their windows uncovered so customers could peer inside.

The interpretation district was half serious, half farce. Both real and facetious interpretation took place there, with professionals like Julia coexisting alongside pseudo interpreters who hung neon signs and distributed coupons on the street. The crystal balls, palm readings, tea leaves, tarot cards, dream interpretation—they were nothing but theater. Only the markings were true.

As Miles and I made our way down the main street, the contents of the storefront windows flashed in the corner of my eye. Lights, lace, crystals, the cheap rattle of beaded curtains—these were the trappings of fantasy. I found myself telling Miles about the girls I knew at school who patronized these businesses for a laugh. They delighted in the outlandish predictions false interpreters dreamed up: improbable romances, financial windfalls, adventure.

"Some of us are considering coming here for readings after we pass to our adult markings," I said.

Miles shook his head. "Don't waste your money. Besides, visiting the interpretation district as a changeling is dangerous."

"Only at night."

"Maybe. But it's still too much of a risk."

He was referring to how newly changed girls—especially bold girls, or reckless girls, or vulnerable girls from damaged families—were more likely to disappear after dark in the interpretation district. As the only city district zoned for professional interpretation, these streets attracted scores of visitors and were thus a prime target for predatory men. I already knew this, we all did, but like most people, I preferred not to dwell on it. Back then I viewed abductions as I did my own mortality: they were an indisputable fact of life and yet unfathomable, too vast and horrific to hold in my mind for more than a few seconds.

So I didn't. I was fifteen, a teenage girl simply spending the afternoon with her brother. Julia awaited us, as did the whole of our futures. All we had to do was keep moving.

JULIA'S BUILDING HAD no sign out front, nothing to indicate that her home was also a place of business. No neon lights or cheap beaded curtains, and certainly no crystal balls. Miles and I let ourselves into the parlor, a room adorned with an antique couch, a grandfather clock, and wallpaper dappled with a metallic imprint. It was a place, I felt, where the future was taken seriously.

We could see Julia through the glass doors that enclosed the classroom area, where she addressed a half dozen teenage girls seated on the floor in front of her. Unlike the theatrical interpreters who wore scarves and iridescent eyeshadow, Julia dressed in jeans and a fitted dress shirt, her heavy brown hair hanging loose around her shoulders. She was practical but also progressive—which she'd have to be, to teach interpretation to a boy.

Miles hesitated outside the glass doors. "You can join me, you know. Julia would be glad to have you."

I shook my head. "I'd rather wait here."

He slipped into the classroom, leaving me alone in the parlor. I wandered over to the bookcase and scanned the collection until I found it: a heavy hardcover book full of intricate geometric patterns. I'd discovered the book the first and last time I'd been at Julia's. That had been months ago, during an open house for students and their families. My parents and I dressed up for the occasion. A nervous energy hung over us, as if we worried Julia might find us lacking, but she was warm and welcoming. Julia was the one to lead me to her bookshelf, to invite me to browse. Later, when she found me still poring over the book of patterns, she'd looked pleased.

I pulled the book down and cracked it open. The pages revealed a mesmerizing array of shapes and designs found in rugs, paintings, sculpture, mosaics—all the beautiful things in life. Best of all, they had nothing to do with my skin or my predictions. It was my only chance to get lost in patterns that held no larger meaning.

I flipped dreamily through the pages for a long time. When the grandfather clock crept closer to the hour, I replaced the book and peered through the classroom doors. Aside from my brother, the students were all girls. They were a bit older than me and dressed in that effortless way I wished to emulate: sandals in metallic colors, scarves repurposed as belts, and silky, scoop-necked shirts that slipped off the shoulder to reveal a colorful bra strap.

The girls sat close together, their copies of *Mapping the Future* flung to the side so they could focus on the living maps of their skin. Their skin was brown, or olive, or else it was like mine, the color of wheat. All marked with the future. Each girl took her turn holding out an arm for a classmate to read. My brother couldn't offer his own body, but when he leaned closer to interpret a pale-haired girl named Deirdre, he had everyone's attention. He moved his finger steadily across her skin, knitting his brow with concentration. He was careful, and respectful, and serious. If not for his gender, he could have passed for a professional interpreter.

Before long, the clock struck the hour, its deep tones marking the end of class. I stood back while the first girls pushed open the classroom doors and came spilling into the parlor. Julia held a copy of *Mapping the Future* open before her as she exited, explaining a diagram to one of her students. When she noticed me, her expression shifted. It was a subtle, flitting change, but I caught it.

"Celeste," she said. "I'm so glad you're here." She smiled as she approached, then reached forward to tap my left arm. "May I?"

I nodded, and she held my hand in her own, running her fingertips lightly over my skin. I closed my eyes at her touch. Interpretation involved more than sight. Touch could add new depth and layers. Touch was sometimes part of the magic.

"Hmm," Julia murmured. She focused on the cluster of moles near my left elbow, a pattern slightly inconsistent with anything appearing in *Mapping the Future*. Over the years, interpreters had formulated different explanations: A minor illness around your sixteenth birthday, one suggested. A car crash, but not a serious one, another told me. The only consensus was that I needn't worry much, that these juvenile patterns were a mere blip of ambiguity in a lifetime of more certain predictions.

"Miles thinks I'll change soon." I glanced down at the freckles on my forearm. I wanted to memorize them, not as they appeared sketched in my brother's notebook at home, but how they were in the here and now—little pinpricks of the future about to become the past.

Julia nodded. "It's an exciting time, just before you change. The possibilities seem endless."

The time before the transition to adult markings was like watching a wave bear down on the shoreline: waiting for the crash, for the turmoil and confusion, before the sand could be smoothed into a fresh surface again. When it arrived, girls had the benefit of new predictions, but they were also thrown into the chaos of their changeling periods—those risky, unpredictable weeks when they would be irresistible to nearly everyone, but especially men.

"It makes me nervous," I admitted, "how I have no control over what my new markings will reveal. How I'll just have to accept them."

Julia pulled me closer. A faint scent came off her, something with a hint of lilac. I felt embarrassed when I noticed it, like I'd been caught spying. She gripped my arm tighter, and I had to fight not to pull away.

"The future will come for you as it intends," she said. "That is undeniable. With time, however, you'll see that your actions might make a difference. Not a dramatic difference, but even the slightest change might be meaningful. We do have free will, after all. Think of it as wind moving through the leaves of a tree."

Julia released one hand from mine and swept her arm up to conjure a tree in the air between us—her forearm the trunk, her fingers the branches, the thick frenzy of her hair transforming, in my mind, into a leafy canopy. "The tree itself remains the same, but the manipulation of leaves creates altered shapes, shadows, sound. The greater form is unchanged even as it is made anew. Do you see?"

I blinked at her.

"That's all right," she said. "You're a smart girl. You'll understand one day."

Shaken, I rubbed my arms as if to shed my confusion. The entire point of interpretation was to submit to an irrevocable future. Depicting a future as fluid as wind rushing through leaves didn't make sense. Our markings couldn't reveal everything that would come to pass, but seeing even a glimpse was a relief. It was what drove people to interpreters, to study *Mapping the Future*, to plan their careers and marriages based on what was already fated.

If only our markings could reveal the full truth in vivid detail, like a vision. If only I could have seen even a single scene in its entirety—perhaps a day several years in the future, when Julia and I would spend an afternoon together as equals.

This was the future awaiting me, but that day in Julia's townhouse, I couldn't predict it. Maybe that was for the best. We spend too much time either imagining the future, that vast expanse of unborn possibility, or else wandering the past, the land of the dead. And yet I return there, again and again, as if watching it unfold in my memory can affect the outcome. As if the past could ever be as changeable as the future.

I WAS STILL holding my arm, still caught between the present and what was to come, when Miles stepped out of the classroom with Deirdre and I finally saw things clearly: Deirdre was radiant, searing, her skin alive with a faintly ethereal glow. She was changed, newly passed to her adult markings. Glorious.

I watched, mesmerized, as Deirdre crossed the room in a filmy indigo skirt that swirled around her ankles. At her throat, an opal dangled on a gold chain. I'd read a gemstone book not long before, so I knew something about opals. They were delicate, vulnerable stones that could crack if struck or exposed to extreme temperatures. Opals were changeable depending on how you looked at them—they were lightning, fire, the sheen in an oily puddle. With this stone shining against her skin, Deirdre moved as though the atmosphere was thinner around her. Like the rest of us were trudging through water while she breezed through a high, clear sky.

Without intending to, I leaned in Deirdre's direction. I had the sense that if I touched her, I'd feel a welcoming spark.

"Miles, I hope you and Celeste are still able to walk Deirdre home," Julia said. "My car is not yet in working order, I'm afraid."

"Of course," Miles said.

I looked at him, surprised that he'd made this plan without telling me. Later, I'd learn that Julia's car sat in an alley behind the townhouse, its brakes hopelessly worn as she saved for repairs. It was an inconvenience that would come to have graver consequences than I could have imagined at the time.

"Maybe I should come with you, just in case." Julia frowned. We all

knew what she was thinking: if the hour grew too late, she couldn't respon-
sibly send a changeling out into the streets.

"It's still light out," Deirdre said.

"And we'll walk fast," Miles added. "We'll stay together, all three of us.
Celeste will be there the whole time."

Was this the real reason Miles had invited me along, to act as a chaperone so he could spend a few more minutes with Deirdre? For the first time,
I started to view my brother as the rest of the world did: a boy becoming a
young man, and thus a possible threat to girls like Deirdre. It didn't matter
that I knew my brother wasn't capable of harming anyone. It was the possibility, the chance of it, that counted.

Julia was looking at me, awaiting confirmation.

"Deirdre's house is on our way," I said. "It's no problem."

She smiled. "Thank you, Celeste. You're really saving me."

Deirdre and Miles were already heading toward the door. I followed
them outside, down the front steps, and into the street, where Deirdre grew
shy. She positioned herself between Miles and me as if to hide—a fruitless
attempt, since changelings were destined to be noticed.

When we passed a group of men standing outside a corner market, their
collective gaze shot over to Deirdre as if she'd hypnotized them. They
didn't approach her, didn't whistle or call out, but the moment felt turned
on its side regardless. Watching those men gaze at Deirdre was one of the
rare times I let myself feel it: the fear of being a girl.

I didn't linger in that anxiety for long. We turned a corner, the men
disappeared, and I went back to my own world.

AT DINNER THAT evening, when my parents asked about the visit to
Julia's, I told them it was uneventful. That wasn't a lie, but it wasn't exactly
the truth, either. No one pressed the issue. My father simply served cas-
serole while my mother poured herself a glass of wine. The future was not
on their minds.

I went upstairs after dinner to work on my geometry homework. It was getting dark, so I snapped on my desk lamp to illuminate the proof I was working on. Angles, arcs, the unending reach of a line. I was beginning to appreciate the reasoned methodology of geometry, its careful, step-by-step documentation outlining how to solve a problem.

I was halfway through the proof when Miles leaned into my room. He was holding *Mapping the Future*.

"Can I check your markings?" he asked. "I learned something new in class I'd like to practice."

He loomed in the doorway, waiting. He had grown so much in the past year that sometimes I didn't recognize him.

"All right," I said. "But make it quick."

I sat still as Miles took my upper arm in his hands. This I was used to. When it came to my brother, I was his subject, his practice ground, his key to the language of interpretation. This was our oldest and most familiar way of interacting with each other.

While he worked, I stared at the walls my father had recently helped me paint. The hardware store sold gallons of returned premixed paint at a discount, which was how I ended up with a creamy blue color so pale it was nearly white. We spackled over the nail holes, sanded and cleaned the walls, and finally painted. After the second coat dried, I hung my posters: an enlarged diagram from *Mapping the Future* that predicted a life filled with joy, a panoramic landscape of mountains, and a painting of a woman reclining among flowers and jewels. As a finishing touch, I applied a set of tiny sharp stars that glowed in the dark, pasting them on the ceiling above the bed in no particular constellation. I liked to look at them at night and know they were only stars and nothing more.

When Miles finished with my right arm, he came around to my left side.

"If you put the effort in," he said, in an offhanded way, "I think you could be really good at interpretation."

I sighed. This was a mild but long-standing point of contention between us: Miles wanted me to study interpretation with him, and I had no interest in doing so.

"It's not for me. You know that," I said. "Besides, Julia's not like other interpreters. You should have heard what she was saying about a tree, and how our actions can change the future."

"Nothing we do can outright change what has been fated. Influence uncertain outcomes a bit, maybe. Give them a different flavor. That's all she means."

"It's still an odd way to think. I like her, I do, but what she said seems off." I watched as Miles consulted the index in *Mapping the Future.* "What about you—do you trust her?"

He didn't look up. "With my life."

I wasn't sure what to say to that.

"Are you almost done?" I asked instead. "I need to finish my homework."

"Soon." He scrutinized my left elbow. "Besides, your markings have always indicated that you're a strong student."

"Yes, but not if I stop studying." As I spoke, I heard an echo of what Julia had said about the tree, about incremental change. I shook my arm away.

Miles looked up. "You should appreciate what you have. I'd give anything to be marked like a girl."

His words reminded me of how I used to sit on my father's lap and locate the mole on his neck so I could marvel at its meaninglessness. I drove myself half delirious trying to grasp that it was simply a mole, nothing more, and that in fact male markings were not arranged in patterns as they were on women's bodies. They were scattershot, random. Unreadable.

"Deirdre's going back to school tomorrow, you know," he added. His voice took on a practiced, casual tone—so this was his real reason for coming into my room. Once again, he had concealed his motivations. "Since you two have classes in the same part of the building, I thought you might keep an eye on her this week."

"I barely know her." Deirdre was a third-year, a year above me. We did not socialize.

"Just look out for her," Miles said. "Please. My schedule doesn't align with hers, but you'll at least have a chance of seeing her."

He looked so serious, like he had aged many years that afternoon.

Maybe he had a crush on Deirdre. Maybe, I thought, all of this was no more than teenage attraction.

"All right. But she'll be fine."

"Thanks, Celeste. I owe you."

He reached into his sweatshirt pocket and pulled out a handful of wild strawberries, which he shook loose on my desk.

"We forgot to pick them this summer, but there's still some left." He shrugged. "I thought you'd like them."

My brother could do that—disarm me in an instant by conjuring our shared past. When we were children, he and I picked the wild strawberries that grew along the side of our house. Once, we set up a strawberry stand in the front yard, where we divvied the berries into tiny paper cups marked fifty cents each. We didn't make a single sale. At the end of the day, we ate as many of the remaining berries as we could and then smashed the rest onto our arms. Like we were driven to destroy what we couldn't consume.

Once Miles left my room, I popped the strawberries one by one into my mouth. In each berry I felt the slip of dozens of tiny seeds skimming the surface of the pink flesh, just waiting for the chance to come to life.

Mapping the Future:
An Interpretive Guide to Women and Girls

Category—Career

Location—Hip, right

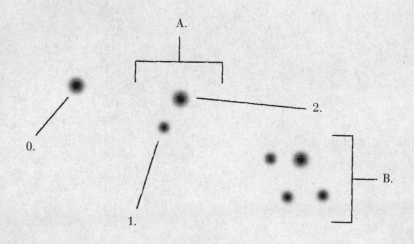

Cluster A: Specifies individuals involved in the subject's future career. **A1** identifies an older sibling, while the position and size of **A2** denotes either a parental figure or mentor.

Cluster B: The downward slant in this classic four-marking career cluster indicates a profession involving intricate work.

Marking 0: As an outlier, this marking suggests the subject will work alone. [See **Appendix C: Contradictions.**]

3

WHEN MY BROTHER made me a promise, he kept it, and I did the same for him. That was our history, and I believed it was our future, too. But fulfilling my promise to look out for Deirdre proved difficult. Deirdre was elusive, unpredictable, a phantom girl slipping from my grasp. I searched for her in the halls after homeroom and again after the first two classes that next morning, but she never appeared. Once I swore I sensed her presence, but when I turned around, no one was there.

The upper school was shaped like a T, an endless hallway for arts and languages capped by a shorter hall dedicated to science and math. The time between classes amounted to a crashing push through the halls, a building of pressure as students jammed together at the intersection. Those flashes of disorder were routine, the kind of adolescent chaos I'd later recall with a tinge of fondness.

Each time I failed to find Deirdre between classes, I returned to my usual routine of walking the halls with Marie and Cassandra. We'd met in primary school, a trio of eight-year-olds drawn to one another by curiosity and fate. What different lives we had back then: lighting sparklers, chalking snail hopscotch diagrams onto the playground, lining our wrists with jelly bracelets. We wore ponytails secured with beaded holders in jewel colors, little treasures we'd later trade, and our skin was touched by sunburn and scabs. We were children. We were girls.

I positioned myself between Cassandra and Marie as we pushed our way through the halls. I'd long been the friend in the middle, the bridge between my two friends' extremes. Marie was the innocent one, the youngest in both appearance and mannerism. At fifteen, she still wore her bangs cut straight across her forehead like a child, still carried herself with a girlish shyness. She seemed a delicate thing compared to Cassandra, who had already begun surging toward risk, adventure, sex. While Marie dressed in jumpers and put her hair in braids, Cassandra wore deep V-neck sweaters and lip gloss, her hair falling freely down her back.

I liked how I was with Cassandra, how I became a bit bolder and more daring. When she and I had gone to the lake that summer, we jumped in the water straightaway and then rose, dripping, to sunbathe on the rocks. Putting ourselves on display. A group of boys on the shoreline watched us, but while I burned with the flickering heat of their attention, Cassandra pretended not to notice them. I envied that of her—maybe I envied everything about her. With her pink bikini and her damp hair fanned across the rock, she looked like a mermaid. When I'd reached for her shoulder her skin was hot and cold, dry and wet, all opposing sensations at once.

"You're giving me goose bumps," she'd said, flicking my fingers away. She turned over, revealing the markings on her lower back. The place for love. "I'm hungry," she added, cutting her gaze toward me. "Celeste. Aren't you hungry?"

I hadn't answered her, just squinted at the sun instead. I wasn't like Cassandra; I wasn't the type of person to announce my desires and expect them to be met. But maybe I was ready to try. Now, around Cassandra, I could admit when I wanted something, whether it was food or adventure or, more recently, the perilous world of boys—their sweat, their wildness, their shattering lack of control. I wanted it all, even if I remained too uncertain to claim it.

I FOLLOWED MARIE to her locker after Cassandra headed for her next class. Marie pulled a sheet of paper from the top shelf and stared at it for a long and wordless moment. I recognized her expression—nerves, uncertainty, maybe a bit of defiance.

"I'm signing it," she said at last. She wasn't quite looking at me, as if making eye contact would weaken her resolve.

She held out the paper for me to read. It was a conscientious objector form that would release her from the markings inspection scheduled that day. These inspections were offered twice yearly in the upper school, the results logged permanently in our transcripts. Submitting to ongoing readings throughout our school years was meant to establish routine, demonstrate obedience, and prevent any oversights related to our markings. Government inspections were usually no more than a mild inconvenience, like getting a medical checkup, but declining to participate was considered taboo.

"Are you sure?" I asked, surprised.

She shook her head. "No. Maybe. I don't know."

I took the form and smoothed it out. The paper felt damp from her hands, but the signature line at the bottom was still blank.

"Just because your mother is modest doesn't mean you need to be the same," I said. "Always covering up, not being able to work with men—it sounds impossible."

"There are benefits, too. Security and protection, for one."

I flattened the form one more time, trying to erase every wrinkle. Marie's mother was one of a dwindling number of women who chose to cover her markings in public. From the onset of the changeling period until the end of their lives, modest women concealed their skin with long sleeves, long pants or skirts, gloves, and scarves. As much as possible, they avoided work or social situations that might put them in close contact with men outside their families. The system was based on a belief that women's markings were private, sacred, and infused with inherent sexual tension, and so concealing them and instituting gender segregation was only proper.

This way of thinking struck me as archaic. The modest lifestyle had arisen from a bygone era when women didn't have the benefit of the same laws we did now—when a woman could be detained by police for an impromptu markings inspection, or when transcripts were public record and thus open to everyone's scrutiny and judgment—and every generation claimed fewer and fewer adherents. As far as I knew, Marie's mother had never pushed Marie to become modest herself one day. Even she recognized how limiting that choice would be.

"I can always change my mind later," Marie went on. "Nothing is permanent."

"But if you go through with the inspection, you won't have any gaps in your transcript. That will make a big difference if you don't become modest. Either way, you'll have to make the choice for good once you change." When a girl passed to her adult predictions, a markings inspector was dispatched within the week to conduct a special reading. Bypassing this changeling inspection was far more meaningful than forgoing one of the twice-yearly obligations.

Marie frowned, but I could tell she knew I was right. None of us wanted to undress at school and allow a federal employee to run her cold fingertips over our skin, but objecting meant forfeiting important opportunities. While our transcripts were confidential, we had to disclose them in order to advance professionally or personally. When I applied to university, I'd submit my official government markings transcript along with my grades. When I looked for a job, that transcript could mean the difference between getting an interview or not. No records meant, in some respects, no future.

I leaned toward Marie. She looked clean, untouched. I felt protective of her and grateful at once. I was remembering the year before, when I didn't have money for the summer festival, and how she asked her mother to pay my admission. It had been a blazing July day, and Marie's mother sweated under her layers of clothing as she counted out the bills for our tickets. I didn't know how to thank her. I simply accepted the money, which felt swollen from the humidity.

There at the lockers, I reached into my back pocket and pulled out the index card I'd received in homeroom. My name and appointed inspection time were typed across the top in a crooked line, the ink fading into almost nothing by the end. I showed the card to Marie.

"My inspection isn't until two o'clock. When's yours?"

Marie hesitated, then lifted the edge of the magnetic mirror inside her locker. She'd tucked her index card underneath, hiding it just behind her reflection.

"Twelve thirty," she said.

I nodded. "Same time as Cassie. You two can go together."

Marie stared at the card until she seemed to reach a conclusion. She took the conscientious objector form back from me. I watched as she folded it on the diagonal, cutting a sharp crease through the paper.

"There," I said, pride in my voice.

The bell rang. Marie slammed her locker, and we headed toward our next classes. On the way, I watched Marie toss her objector form into the trash can. The paper slid in gracefully, almost as if it had soared there itself. As if that's where it always belonged.

To think of how many hours I spent with my friends in that school building, how solidly those walls contained us, how trapped and yet how safe we were—it's remarkable. At the time, that school was everything, the place where we learned and fought and grew. We were challenged, we rebelled, and we looked ahead to when we could strike out on our own as adults.

At school we were tested constantly, on all subjects, including the future. Every year, we received diagrams of a blank female body, that familiar image from the front of *Mapping the Future*, and were asked to label the universal marking locations. By the time I was fifteen I could receive the test sheet, close my eyes, and fill in everything. I earned full marks each time, my teacher decorating the top of my test sheet with a hastily scrawled star. I thought this meant I had it figured out, that the future was orderly and would evolve per my expectations. Now I understand that all I saw or could not see in my skin, all that was predicted or not, was only one part of the story.

The rest I've had to create myself.

AT TWO O'CLOCK, I clutched my index card and walked toward the gymnasium at the end of the science wing. Classes were in session, so the hallways held a ghostly silence. Still, I could sense the activity in each classroom, the energy of students tucked away in that concrete mass of a building. On my way past the chemistry lab, the flare from a Bunsen burner lit up my peripheral vision.

When I reached the gym and heaved open the metal door, I was met with a clash of echoing voices. The inspection line began near the basketball net, where screens had been set up for privacy, and stretched halfway across the gym. We'd strip down in the same space where, on other days, we played volleyball or badminton.

Everything reeked of disinfectant. I cut across the gym, my shoes squeaking against the floor. I already felt washed out, exposed. Windows near the ceiling—windows placed so high it was impossible to glimpse anything outside other than sky, windows that made me think of portholes or prisons—provided some natural light, but otherwise the industrial fluorescents showered the gym with a poisonous glow.

I took my place at the end of the line, behind Anne from my homeroom. She turned to greet me and started gossiping about a mutual friend, but I couldn't focus—because there, just a few spots ahead of us in line, was Deirdre. Deirdre in her rose-colored sweater, her hair in a ponytail to show the back of her neck, the gold chain of the opal necklace clasped at her nape. Deirdre, who stood out from the others like a hot spark. I'd found her at last.

I swallowed, absorbed by desire. It was like wanting to touch fire despite understanding it would burn. For most men, this sensation manifested in a potent sexual desire. But no men were present—the gym was closed to boys and male teachers for the day, out of respect for our privacy. It was just me, just Deirdre. No one else.

"It wasn't fair of him to do that, not when he knew I was already having a bad day," Anne was saying. "Don't you think?"

I blinked, trying to guess what she might be talking about.

"Right," I said. "Completely unfair."

The line inched forward. Whenever a girl finished her inspection, she appeared from behind the partition and streamed toward the exit with a tangible sense of relief. Free, her body her own again. We waited and waited until Deirdre reached the front and slipped out of sight behind the screen. Her absence felt like physical pain. I tried to distract myself by chatting with Anne about her science project—it was something involving cacti and water retention—but I failed. Deirdre was all-consuming. For weeks she would be noticeable in this way, irresistible, until finally her changeling period came to an end. Only then would she be ordinary again.

When Deirdre emerged a few minutes later, her expression was neutral. These government checks were usually anticlimactic, but every now and then a girl received news that her family or interpreters had somehow missed. Not Deirdre, apparently. She proceeded through the gym with her chin held high. An almost imperceptible flutter surrounded her as she went, the energy in the air shifting as the other girls watched her go.

The line crept forward again. "My turn," Anne said. She offered her index card to the inspector managing the line and glanced back at me. "See you on the other side."

Anne vanished. I was left with the government employee, a tall woman wearing a wrist brace. The Office of the Future employed dedicated markings inspectors like her to administer official government readings in schools. The nongovernmental counterpart to this position was the humanitarian ambassador program run by the Humanitarian Global Alliance for Women, an international entity that promoted the advancement of women and girls. Of the two, humanitarians had the more glamorous positions—they were sent abroad to help underprivileged girls in other nations who were denied education or equal rights, they met with international representatives, and they were rewarded with high pay. Federal inspectors, meanwhile, received full government support, faced less strenuous work demands, and were not obligated to travel or endure long stretches of separation from their families. While this inspector didn't make as much money as a humanitarian, at least she could return to her family every night.

Anne breezed out from behind the partition, giving me a quick smile.

"Next," the inspector said. I handed her my card, glad to be released of its slender weight, and she waved me in.

Once concealed in the screened area, I changed into a gown and waited for the inspector to join me. She knocked on the partition in two quick raps and then stepped inside, her attention focused on the paperwork in her hands. She wore a conservative navy suit with a red pin—a tiny, shining square—on her lapel, standard attire for an Office of the Future employee. Her skin was dark, the markings contrasted in smatterings of deep amber.

"A juvenile reading, I see," she said, giving me a quick glance. She made a check mark in her paperwork. "Looks like it might be your last one before you change."

"Probably," I agreed. I fell silent, both wanting the reading to be over but not particularly wanting to submit to it. As routine as these inspections were, I felt something bigger might be at stake for me. I just couldn't say what.

The inspector gave me a nod, her signal to begin. I stood with my legs planted firmly on the floor, my arms held straight out to the side. After the inspector checked my arms, legs, and face, she carefully shifted the gown out of the way so she could inspect my chest, my stomach, my buttocks and back.

"Everything looks in order," she said as she jotted down a few notes.

"Do you have any idea what my aptitude might be?" I asked.

The inspector's gaze drifted my way.

"I couldn't imagine," she said.

"But you see a lot of girls. Surely you could at least guess what I might turn out to be, even if my career markings are vague." Those markings suggested Miles and I might work together, while an outlier marking also indicated I might work alone—it didn't make sense.

The inspector turned back to her clipboard. "I suggest you at least wait until your change before you get all worked up about the future. At this stage in your life, it doesn't hurt to try to live in the present now and then."

She flipped past my paperwork, signaling that it was time for me to leave. I dressed and ducked out of the changing area. The line had grown longer during my inspection, snaking all the way to the doors. To leave the gym, I had to walk past the end of that line, looping back to where I'd started. A beginning and an end all at once.

ON MY WAY back to class, I stopped in the bathroom tucked away near the auditorium. The door was marked *Women*, not *Girls*, and when I pushed through it and rounded the corner inside, I found Deirdre. She stood at the last of the three sinks and was leaning toward the cloudy mirror to apply lipstick. She paused when she saw me, the bright red lipstick hovering in midair.

"Hey, Celeste," she said.

I nodded at her, but my heart was thrashing. I went to the middle sink and rooted in my bag for my hairbrush. As I fixed my hair, I glanced at Deirdre from the corner of my eye. She smacked her lips together, testing the lipstick's hold. As I watched her, I felt a low-frequency shimmer, something akin to the shock of static electricity.

"What's it like to change?" I asked in a quiet voice.

She glanced at me. Even the whites of her eyes were brilliant.

"If you're talking about the high lucidity, that's not something I can explain."

"No, not that." I knew all about the heightened senses that accompanied the changeling period. Girls like Deirdre could see more, hear more, feel more. It was something I'd have to wait to experience myself. "I'm talking about everything else. It seems intimidating."

"Do you mean getting your adult predictions, or the way men will look at you?" Deirdre smiled. "Or do you mean the abductions? Because I don't worry about that."

"Oh, I don't, either." I tried to say this casually, to sound mature. Besides, most girls who disappeared came from rocky families, or were homeless or on drugs. That was what I believed at the time.

"Here's a secret." Deirdre leaned in. "Being a changeling is incredible. There's so much power. People look at you, I mean really *look*. They want you, but they also respect you." She shook her head. "Adults tell us how to behave so they can keep us in line, to make us afraid. Because if we're afraid, maybe we won't use this power to our advantage."

"What advantage?"

"To make our own choices. To take control for once."

I remembered how those men had stared at Deirdre in the street the other day. Like they wanted to destroy her.

"You should be careful," I said. "Changelings are vulnerable."

Deirdre dabbed at her eyeliner with her pinkie. I could tell I'd lost her attention. I grew ashamed, convinced she could see every plain, timid part of me.

"You don't need to be so serious, Celeste." She stepped closer, and I felt the pull of gravity, the revolving weight of a moon. She reached out and took my chin in her graceful fingers. It was an adult gesture, infused with intimacy and confidence, and at the time it dazzled me. Deirdre touched me as though she wanted to tilt my face toward the sky. To show me the vast unknown.

Before I could stop myself, I fell forward, unable to resist the pull any longer. I collapsed against Deirdre, pressing my face to her neck. She was all vibration, a tingling siren call. The moment was infused not with sex but with something grander—the whole of the universe and our tenuous place in it.

After a few moments, Deirdre gently detached herself.

"Everything will be fine," she assured me. "Remember that."

She gathered her things and left. I watched her swing out the door—*Women*, not *Girls*—before turning back to the mirror. I saw an uncertain girl reflected there, young and unknowing. Barely more than a child. Gingerly, I touched my fingertips to the glass as if I could conjure Deirdre's reflection instead of my own. I felt like a failure, like I'd just wasted something precious.

That was the last time I would see Deirdre in school. By nightfall, she was gone.

MISSING GIRL

[ALTERNATE TITLE: LOST]

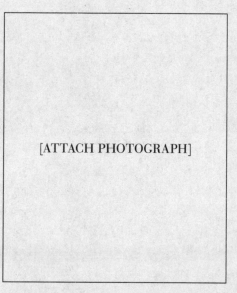

[ATTACH PHOTOGRAPH]

[LAST NAME, FIRST NAME]

AGE:

HEIGHT:

HAIR COLOR:

EYE COLOR:

SKIN COLOR:

DISTINCTIVE MARKINGS:

DATE/LOCATION LAST SEEN:

CIRCUMSTANCES OF DISAPPEARANCE:

CONTACT [NAME] AT [TELEPHONE NUMBER] IMMEDIATELY
IF SEEN.

4

THAT EVENING, MILES and I headed to the backyard to play brick-ball, a game we'd invented as children. We took turns slamming a small rubber ball against the back of the house, which the other person had to catch after no more than one bounce. It was a brutal game, spare and vio-lent, and playing it in the final darkening moments of the evening felt right. As the light dimmed and the shadows lengthened we only played faster, as if railing against the loss of the day.

Miles played hardest, I noticed, when he was frustrated, and what most frustrated him was his unattainable dream of becoming an interpreter. I, too, threw harder when I was angry, but it was difficult for me to name the root of that anger. At fifteen, I struggled to process how I felt about the rules I was expected to follow, the risks that were mine to bear simply by nature of being a girl. Anger simmered beneath the surface, driving my gameplay. After a few rounds of brickball, my palms burned and my shoul-der ached, and sometimes I walked away with bruised shins.

As we played, I thought of the markings inspector, and Deirdre's lips,

and I threw hard, hard, hard—hard enough for my mother to open an upstairs window and complain about the noise. Her silhouette against the
yellow light inside drove home just how dark it had grown, and how we'd
need to abandon our game even if she hadn't ordered us to.

Miles had possession of the ball. He held on to it as our mother shut the
window, her shadowy form vanishing from sight. I watched as he hesitated,
his biceps flexing, and I thought he might throw it anyway. He scowled at
the back of the house, and then I realized he was counting.

"Four to three," he said, lowering his arm. "You won." He tossed the ball
into the weeds near the fence, where it was instantly swallowed by the
shadows.

We headed inside to find our mother standing in the kitchen with the
phone pressed to her cheek. Her hand lifted halfway to her chin, fingers
trembling. Her face a mask.

"Miles," she said in a low voice. "It's Deirdre. She's gone."

Gone where? I thought at first.

My mother swiveled toward me. Red splotches bloomed across her
cheeks, the first sign she was about to either yell or cry. "Celeste, you
shouldn't be hearing this."

"Why not? I want to know what's happening."

Miles put a hand on my shoulder, a tenderness that felt jarring after the
violence of brickball. "She's right, Celeste. You should go."

"But I just saw Deirdre this afternoon in school."

My mother wasn't listening. She'd brought the phone back to her ear to
conduct a whispered conversation. Finally, she hung up.

"It's official." She left her hand on the receiver and leaned into it, letting
it bear her weight. "Her parents have already gone to the police. Apparently
someone reported seeing Deirdre on the street talking to a man."

"She'll be fine," I said, but once the words were out, I wasn't sure why
I'd said them. The moment felt fractured, like reality was dismantling itself
piece by piece.

"Please, Celeste," my mother said. She blinked to hold back tears. "Go
to your room. I've already said too much."

I left, dazed by the sight of my mother crying, and stumbled upstairs. Without thinking, I climbed into bed and under the covers. I was shaking. First it was just my legs, but soon it spread throughout my body: a violent tremor I could not control. I pulled the blankets tighter and clenched the side of the mattress as if that could provide the mooring I needed. I squeezed my eyes shut and counted to ten. When I opened them again, I was still shaking.

I knew what was happening to Deirdre, and I did not, both at the same time. Deirdre was a changeling, and she had disappeared. That meant a man had taken her. That meant she was ruined. Like all girls, I'd grown up with an inherent understanding of that concept—if a girl was taken against her will, she came out on the other side changed, damaged. Never to be the same again.

Downstairs, the phone started ringing again. I held my hands to my ears and squeezed. I pressed so hard I created a roaring sound, like the echo of the ocean inside a seashell. Crash after crash after crash.

I STAYED IN bed a long time. I was staring at the stars on my ceiling— staring until they blurred, multiplied, birthed themselves anew—when a knock sounded on my door.

"Come in," I called.

The door eased open. Miles entered, our parents just behind him. My father had come home and I hadn't even noticed. He'd been putting in a lot of time on a new account at work, an advertisement for a banner downtown that he said would shake up the industry, so it was a shock to see him home so early. Or maybe it wasn't early. Was it possible I'd fallen asleep?

"I'm sorry, Celeste." My mother wrapped her arms around her sides, holding herself. "I should have told you about Deirdre in a better way. I was in shock."

I sat up and pushed the blankets away. "Is there any news?"

"An official alert has gone out," my father said. "I heard it at work."

"It's awful." My mother shook her head, still holding herself. "Just awful."

Miles scanned my room as though he might find Deirdre hiding among my things.

"What exactly did she say to you this afternoon?" he asked.

I could feel everyone watching me.

"I just saw her for a minute in the bathroom. We talked about when I might change." I didn't mention the lipstick, or how she'd talked about power and choice. I was afraid to make the case that she'd brought this on herself.

But it was already too late for that. All over town, as parents and teachers and students heard the alert, they were imagining how Deirdre went wrong. It was a certain kind of girl who let herself get caught by men: the rebellious kind, the flirty kind, the kind who flaunted her future. I had grown up believing that. We all had.

Miles slumped onto my bed. He smelled faintly of sweat from our brickball game, a sour smell that reminded me he was nearly eighteen, nearly a man, and not the boy I pictured in my mind.

"I shouldn't have let her out of my sight," he said.

"You can't blame yourself, Miles." Our father held up his hands, as if absolving us all. "Deirdre must have behaved recklessly for this to happen."

I thought again of the lipstick, the way Deirdre reveled in her newfound allure as a changeling. Maybe my father was right. Maybe it had been her fault.

"What I'm worried about is how her family didn't consider this a real threat," my mother added. "Here we are, living our lives as though everything is fine, but it's not. It's truly not." She broke off with a strangled sound in her throat.

"She'll be back before long," I assured everyone. This was a simple fact. Once a girl's changeling period ended, she was less desirable. Abducted girls were set free at this point. Years ago, there had been a smattering of murders, girls whose bodies turned up under a soft layer of loam in the forest on the outskirts of the city, but that was an abomination, the result of one sick man. He'd been caught and placed in prison for life. Justice served, everyone said.

So much about abductions was predictable, even though a girl's markings never revealed that particular fate. First, Deirdre's abductor would certainly be a man. I'd once heard a rumor about a woman who took changelings, who couldn't resist them just like men, but this was urban legend. For men, it was about more than sexual attraction; it was about their need to read our futures, to take something of what they'd never have themselves.

Next, we could anticipate what Deirdre's return would lead to—gossip, whispers, isolation. She could never get a good job or go to university if she'd been ruined. The best employers didn't hire women who'd been taken, and no university would admit them. To be abducted indicated a moral failing, a lapse in judgment and restraint that pointed to more serious deficiencies. As a result, her abduction would follow her always.

The shaking returned. It started in my stomach, a fluttering as if something alive had been placed there.

"I'm not feeling well," I said. "I think I'll go back to sleep."

My mother came forward to kiss the top of my head.

"I'm sorry," she said again. "We'll leave you to rest."

Once everyone had gone, I closed my eyes and tried to imagine what Deirdre might be enduring at that moment—locked in a room with a man, curtains pulled shut, shadows everywhere. A man might drug her and keep her for weeks, until she passed out of her changeling period. When she stumbled into the light again, she would no longer be her same self.

The story was an old one. The best we could do was warn changelings not to go out alone at night, to stay within the safety of a group, to dress chastely during those dangerous few weeks. Girls were considered women as soon as they changed, so we were expected to shoulder that responsibility, to put forth the effort to protect ourselves.

In health class at school that year, Mrs. Ellis had digressed from her lesson plan to give us a lecture about returned girls. Mrs. Ellis was short, with broad shoulders—built like a bull, the boys liked to say—and in her gentle way, she explained that most abducted girls didn't stick around for long once they returned.

"If they have access to money, they could go to the Mountain School," she said, though we all knew most people weren't that wealthy. Others, she continued, moved in with relatives out of town. But if the returned girls didn't have connections elsewhere, things were more difficult. Maybe they hitchhiked to someplace far away to find work as waitresses, or maids, or strippers, or worse. Maybe they lived on the streets, or stayed in shelters, or found companionship with other lost souls.

This type of life might be preferable to returning home, where the abducted girls would discover everything had changed. Their families were theirs but not. Their communities rejected them, as would universities and most employers. The stigma followed abducted girls forever. Not to mention that the girls' markings—their very futures—might have been stolen, marked down and duplicated, then sold and transposed onto illustrated cards or books, all so collectors could have the thrill of owning the image of a real girl's markings.

"Once those markings are recorded, they could end up anywhere," Mrs. Ellis said. She illustrated her point by jabbing her finger at the world map rolled down over the chalkboard, as if the potential for our ruin—for the shame of having our bodies exposed to all who cared to look—lurked everywhere. I understood what Mrs. Ellis was really trying to say: that the world did not belong to us.

I burrowed deeper under the covers and reminded myself that the terror and risk we experienced was nothing compared to what girls faced elsewhere: openly thriving sex tourism, changeling river cruises, or the equitorial beach resorts where changelings were booked as just one more luxury accommodation. The information we gleaned from other nations was often vague, but we were taught in school to be grateful for our own progressive government. Our country had rape laws, antidiscrimination policies in workplaces, birth control, and the chance for most women to access the same education as men. Here, women could not be arrested based on suspicious markings. A woman fated to become a homemaker could still choose to attend school and might even be admitted to one of the lesser universities. We authorized the access of our transcripts. In short, we had rights, legal protections, and at least some degree of privacy.

We could convince ourselves we were safe.

MILES AND I walked to school the next morning through thick fog. Droplets stuck to my eyelashes, and I felt covered, as if the fog could shield us from the signs of Deirdre's disappearance that blinked into view all around us.

Overnight, Deirdre's parents had plastered MISSING GIRL signs on every telephone pole within a three-mile radius. They'd photocopied Deirdre's photo onto the flyer, and the repeated image of her smiling face took on a ghostly, otherworldly expression, the staples gleaming in the paper like little silver stabs. Already her pre-changeling face seemed a shadow of her more brilliant self. The girl in the flowing skirt in Julia's classroom, the girl applying lipstick from a gold tube at school—I couldn't find her in the photocopied flyer. It was like two versions of Deirdre had disappeared at once.

When I glanced at Miles, he was staring straight ahead, avoiding Deirdre's image. Maybe he was thinking that the MISSING GIRL flyers were a futile effort. The police would give the appearance of searching for Deirdre, but they already knew she was with a man who'd set her free soon enough. The worst had already happened, they probably told Deirdre's parents. Now it was time to wait for her to come back.

I could only wonder what my brother might be thinking because he was quiet and withdrawn that morning. Holding his secrets close yet again.

When we arrived in the schoolyard, Miles and I separated. I found Cassandra and Marie by the flagpole, their hands in their coat pockets. The top of the flagpole disappeared into the fog.

"You okay?" Cassandra asked. She wore a chic black raincoat I'd never seen before. She looked like she was in mourning.

"No," I said. "Are you?"

Cassandra shook her head, as did Marie. We hugged, one by one, and turned to face the school's entrance.

"Let's get this over with." Cassandra tightened the belt of her raincoat. "They'll lecture us, I'm sure."

Marie nodded. "This school hasn't had an abduction in a long time. I saw the paper this morning. It's been a decade." She gazed at the building. "We don't want to get a reputation like the city district."

"We're still a long way from that," Cassandra told her. "I heard the city's upper school stopped taking attendance this year because the skip and dropout rate is so high. And they have the highest rate of abductions of anywhere around."

"This one abduction is enough to draw comparisons," Marie said. "Don't you agree, Celeste?"

I didn't answer.

"Celeste." Marie touched my wrist. "You're really pale."

I blinked at my friend. She wore a red headband, the skinny plastic kind with teeth that dug into the scalp. Those headbands hadn't been in fashion for a long time. On another day I might have felt frustrated with Marie for making such a childish fashion choice, but in that moment, it comforted me.

"I'm fine," I told her. "Cassie's right, let's get this over with."

We headed inside and were swept up at once in a flood of students moving toward the auditorium. Our teachers stood grimly in front of their open classroom doors, watching us pass. When I accidentally caught the eye of my homeroom teacher—her expression projecting undercurrents of horror—I averted my gaze and kept moving, letting the crowd carry me forward.

DURING THOSE DAYS I was a good student, but I tended to view my teachers with detachment. I did not imagine my teacher's inner life, her future or her past or her private goals and dreams. Instead I was impatient to leave the upper school for university, where I would at last have professors instead of teachers, new opportunities, freedom. It was, I believed, where I could develop into the person I was destined to become.

To be a school-age girl, meanwhile, was to be constrained and controlled, to receive lecture after lecture about appropriate behavior and the rules of our sex. Even the assembly following Deirdre's disappearance was a variation on the same safety talk we had endured for years, often read aloud directly from *Mapping the Future*: never go anywhere alone, but especially not at night; never enter into a discussion with strangers about our markings; never wear short skirts, plunging necklines, or other provocative garments; and never be alone with men we did not know. These precautions were necessary precisely because the markings never predicted abductions, making that bit of fate unknowable to us.

While boys weren't included in those safety lectures—they were sent out of the classroom for free periods, or even went home early—they were compelled to attend the assembly. I resented having them there that day. They fidgeted, knocking their knees against the seat backs, and the auditorium felt too small to contain them. I was jealous of their freedom, their easy way of moving through the world. Boys could afford to not pay attention to the assembly: how Principal Radshaw had placed an oversized photograph of Deirdre onstage, how he gestured to her portrait as he talked, how he warned us against repeating her mistakes.

The photo was the same one from the *MISSING GIRL* poster, an image already seared into my mind. I stared hard into Deirdre's photocopied eyes, willing her to become unlost and whole once more. This was no more than a fantasy, but I couldn't help myself. For the rest of the day I wouldn't stop thinking of Deirdre, not for one minute.

Her face haunted me right up to the final bell.

MAPPING THE FUTURE:
AN INTERPRETIVE GUIDE TO WOMEN AND GIRLS

Category—Misfortune

Location—Ankle, left

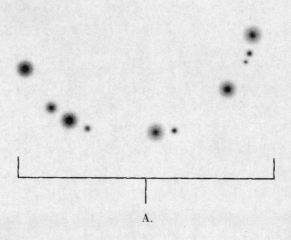

A.

Cluster A: Here, the meanings of individual markings mean less than the whole. The arc of the pattern, and the way smaller markings orbit the larger, indicate multiple losses. This is a marking of grief, yes, but also strength. This is a marking to endure.

5

When Deirdre disappeared I felt the world should operate differently, that the days should be longer or shorter, the skies brighter or darker. I expected food to taste hotter, oxygen to pierce sharper in my lungs. If I pricked my finger, I believed the blood wouldn't stop. I thought everything would hurt more.

I was wrong, but also right. The world kept turning same as ever, night to day and back again, but I noticed a shift within my family. Miles began shadowing my every move. He insisted on walking me to and from school, and more than once I turned from my locker to find him watching from across the hall.

Our father, too, grew more protective in the days following Deirdre's abduction. He ate breakfast with me before school each morning, a new routine for us. He showed up to the table freshly shaven, still adjusting his tie; sometimes he wrenched it so furiously it looked like he was punishing himself.

"You're growing up so fast," he said once, without warning. My father was not a sentimental man, and this comment caught me off guard.

"You could pass to your adult markings any day now," he added, "and then you won't be my little girl anymore. You'll be a woman." He said this with a sincere sense of loss.

By the third morning at the breakfast table, I noted the stress in my father's shoulders and jaw, the way he clenched the fork in his fist. I worried he was coming undone. He was busy, I knew, preparing for the installation of the new banner advertisement at work, a project that consumed him. At the time, I was only aware that the ad was expensive, and important to his career, and that it would soon hang on the bank building downtown. I knew it was coming, we all did, but that didn't mean I was prepared for the disruption it would cause.

In hindsight, it's clear the timing was all wrong for the ad. If its debut had been delayed by a few weeks or months, things might have gone better for my father, for our entire family. But on the morning of the fourth day of Deirdre's disappearance, the banner went up as scheduled. It appeared quietly, in the earliest light of the day, and waited for the city to take notice.

The ad showed a drawing of a naked woman—that was all I heard, at first, through the rumors already circulating at school. I couldn't imagine it, couldn't see how my father had a part in something so scandalous. I might have ignored the gossip had my brother not appeared at my locker that afternoon. He put a hand on my shoulder, tightly, like he was trying to hold me in place.

"After school," he said, his voice low, "we're going downtown to see it." And then he was gone, flowing like water through the crowded hall, the lingering pressure on my shoulder the only sign he'd been there at all.

MILES AND I walked downtown that afternoon without saying much, without even looking at each other. We were on a mission. When we reached the bank building, we stood side by side for a long time, staring. So this was what our father had brought to life.

That banner was a marvel, a catastrophe—a triumph and tragedy at once. It showed a woman drawn in black ink strokes on a white background, a body defined in lines soft as a new star at dusk. She was stylized, which meant she had no markings, the details glossed over. Her face, turned in partial profile, featured an aquiline nose and half-lidded eyes. Hair billowed in clouds around the woman's cheeks, her breasts drawn full and round with frenzied swirls for nipples. Her waist drew in sharply, the belly button a smudge, and beneath that, a shadow between her legs.

MORE THAN A PRETTY FACE, the banner read. It was an ad for skin cream. The jar could be spotted in the lower right corner, but even I understood that wasn't the point.

"I can't believe he really went through with it," Miles said at last.

I looked at him. "You knew about this?"

He didn't answer. I didn't tell him what I was thinking, which was that I couldn't understand how our father had created this, or how he could have told Miles but not me. How people harbored secret parts of themselves. My brother and I just looked straight ahead, embarrassed by the woman's nakedness. But I was also drawn to her—maybe because she was so clearly a woman, not a girl. Maybe because she seemed to have chosen this nakedness, to revel in it, and I couldn't imagine growing up to become that confident myself.

Or maybe I admired her simply because she had no markings, no future, no dark realities awaiting her. Because she was free. Because her body was her own.

MILES AND I returned home to find our mother sitting alone in the kitchen. She'd cracked the window and pulled her chair close. She was holding a lit cigarette, a little brown one that smelled of vanilla and cloves.

"You don't smoke," Miles said.

She exhaled. "He's going to get himself fired. I warned him."

"It's not so bad," I assured her, but that was a lie. People were already connecting the ad's obscenity to Deirdre's abduction. They said the public display of such scandalous material was cosmic retribution, or else a warning. The city was becoming increasingly depraved, they claimed, which could lead to more abductions, and this monstrosity proved it all. Rumor had it the skin cream company already regretted signing off on the ad and was going to pull it.

"He took too much of a risk." The cigarette smoke rose to trace my mother's cheek. "Now we'll have to deal with the fallout."

My father had worked for the advertising agency for ages. It was small and family-run, but the skin cream company was only one of his many accounts. Even if he lost this one, I reasoned, he had others.

My mother leaned forward to stub out her cigarette.

"This smell will stay in your hair for hours," she said, and started fanning the air to send the smoke away from me. I told her I didn't mind, but she only waved harder, creating a space for me that was clean and pure.

THE DAY AFTER the banner appeared, Cassandra and I sat next to each other in health class for our annual lesson on the passage to adult markings. This, too, was so familiar it was embedded in our memories, but we were asked to endure it again regardless. "You can never be too prepared for such a monumental change," Mrs. Ellis said, and she started the filmstrip outlining how we'd change overnight while we slept. Our childhood markings would vanish and be replaced by more detailed, mature markings. It would be a painless process, nothing extraordinary. It was, droned the narrator's authoritative voice, perfectly natural.

When the filmstrip ended, Mrs. Ellis lectured us on the high lucidity we'd face during our changeling periods, and how we could control the flood of new sensory awareness with breathing exercises. We practiced together as a class, breathing in and out, loud and slow, until a girl in the back row broke into laughter.

Mrs. Ellis marched over to her. "Do you think this is funny?" she asked, meaning our bodies, our lives, our futures. The girl fell silent.

Cassandra and I shared a glance. Outside of class, we didn't always take our bodies so seriously. We delighted in discussing rare cases, like the boy someone once knew who tattooed marking patterns on his body because he felt he was meant to be a girl. Likewise, we heard of girls who identified as boys and tried to scar their predictions out of existence. These were stories adults chose not to address, but privately, we reveled in sharing them. They hinted at a broader, more complex world that expanded beyond the rigid male-female gender roles we lived with every day.

"Girls," Mrs. Ellis said, "if you learn only one thing today, I hope it will be to respect yourselves."

That day in class, Cassandra and I passed notes back and forth. We wrote to each other in bubble letters and folded slips of notebook paper into tighter and tighter squares until they felt thick, indestructible. But in reality, our notes were no more than paper, easily torn or crumpled or otherwise transformed. They were as fleeting as our girlhood, which I could feel ticking toward its conclusion. And Cassandra, I predicted, would pass to adulthood before me. I could sense her impending change, could feel it approaching with every passing hour.

That was Friday. By Sunday, when my mother woke me in the blue light of morning to tell me Cassandra had called, I knew I'd been right. I rose and followed my mother to the kitchen, where I pressed the receiver to my ear. Through the trick of the phone line Cassandra still sounded like my friend, but something was different. She was changed.

CASSANDRA LIVED SIX blocks away on one of the more prosperous streets in our neighborhood. I put on my tennis shoes and headed out, planning what I'd say once I arrived. *Be serious*, I imagined telling her. *Be careful. You are entering a delicate and dangerous time.*

By the time I arrived, I was sweating. I paused on the flagstone pathway to wipe the moisture from my temples. Cassandra lived in a Colonial with a perfectly landscaped lawn. Her parents were divorced, but even so, her family was well-off, and they had the time and inclination to keep up a meticulous appearance. I had often envied this about Cassandra, but on that morning I was too distracted by worry to feel jealous. I let myself in, as usual, and hurried upstairs before Mrs. Hahn could intercept me. This was no time for adults. This was a time for girls—or, in Cassandra's case, girls who'd just become women.

I flung open Cassandra's door to find her waiting in the center of her pastel bedroom. My friend, newly changed, stood with her palms held forward like she was making an offering. She was naked. It had been a while since the three of us had stripped down to look at our markings, so the sight of Cassandra—her defined waist, her hips, her developed breasts—was a shock. Her body revealed the truth I'd long known but had never witnessed so intimately: that once a girl passed to her adult markings, she was transformed.

Marie was there, too, standing pressed in the corner of the room as if trying to contain herself.

"We were waiting for you." Cassandra gazed down at her own body, but in a detached way, as if it had nothing to do with her. "Let's do my back first. You know how hard it is to interpret markings in a mirror."

I approached Cassandra and lightly ran the tip of my index finger from mole to mole, like I was playing a connect-the-dots game across her shoulder blades and down her spine. Cassandra's skin shivered beneath my touch. She let out a nervous laugh and pulled away.

"Sorry," she said. "I'm still getting used to how this feels."

"I won't use too much pressure," I promised.

Cassandra's new markings looked like they'd been there forever. She'd woken up that morning and there they were, with no fanfare, just as they'd been fated. It was both a mystery and a fact of life. Whatever her juvenile predictions had revealed about her adult future would still hold true, even now that those markings were faded and gone, but this passage to adulthood pulled everything into focus.

Marie joined us in trying to decipher the markings. I watched her trembling fingers and thought back to the summer festival, when she and I ran straight to the last deep stretch of park until we reached the Ferris wheel. We pushed past the creaking gate to enter a car that swung wildly when we stepped inside. As the ride jolted us into the sky, we leaned forward to view the fair from above. Instead, we saw our classmate Veronica in the car underneath ours, at an angle that allowed us to see straight down her dress to the pale moons of her breasts. Marie gave a start and sat back so hard she made our car sway. When I looked over at her, she was blushing deeply.

It was that same way in Cassandra's room. Marie stared at our friend's body, transfixed, her face flooded with color.

"This is good, Cassie," she said at last. "I don't see any illnesses, and you'll be happily married one day."

"Look at this." I pointed to the bunch of pale moles on her hip. "You're going to have a very successful career."

"Yes, but in what?" Cassandra craned to see for herself. "My mom couldn't figure it out, and neither could I."

Marie and I studied Cassandra's skin for a while longer, but it was no use. The patterns meant nothing specific to us, only something vaguely good. My own juvenile career markings were similarly ambiguous—aside from suggesting I might work with Miles one day, and that my profession would involve intricate work, they didn't reveal much. Of course, I could look forward to future clarification when I passed to my adult markings. Cassandra no longer had that luxury. Now that she was a woman, these markings represented the last predictions she'd ever have.

We consulted the gilt pages of *Mapping the Future* to look for career constellations that resembled Cassandra's, but we couldn't find a perfect match. I pressed my finger against Cassandra's right hip and closed my eyes. I waited to feel the low vibration that the best interpreters experienced during readings, but I felt nothing. I was talentless.

I turned to the guide's index, tracing my finger down the list until I came to the entry for *Expectations, Subverted*. We'd all heard the tales of a couple who married based on the woman's markings only to divorce years later, or the woman who gave birth even after her markings labeled her barren. Usually, all one had to do was return to *Mapping the Future* and re-map those markings to discover their true interpretation.

While I read, Cassandra seemed distracted, gazing at her arm. Getting new markings, it appeared, was a bit like falling in love with yourself. I thought again of Deirdre in the school bathroom, how she leaned in close to the mirror to apply that lipstick. She'd been confident and bold, just like Cassandra was now. And then she was gone.

I dropped the book and grabbed Cassandra's shoulder. "You need to pay attention."

She blinked. "To what?"

"Everything. I don't want you to end up like Deirdre."

Cassandra waved her hand, and her dismissal felt all too familiar. She was a changeling, but she was also the same girl who raced me to the dock at the lake and leapt in wildly, determined to make the bigger splash.

"You need to see a professional." I gathered Cassandra's clothes from the floor and tossed them at her. "Someone who knows more than we do about what those markings might mean. And we should go now, rather than wait for your government inspection. That will take too long."

Cassandra hesitated, holding the clothing to her chest like a shield. Then, slowly and with care, as if each layer against her skin was a weight, she dressed.

DOWNSTAIRS, MRS. HAHN waited in the foyer, blocking the door. She wore an immaculate white tunic and a jade necklace, but her polished appearance was marred by her tense expression. She was like a wire strung too tightly.

"You can't possibly think you're going out so soon after changing." Her eyes, red-rimmed, tracked her daughter. "It's too dangerous. Especially after what happened to Deirdre."

"We already talked about this," Cassandra told her. "Remember? It's daylight, and I'm with my friends. It's fine."

"I'll come with you, just to be safe."

"Mom, you promised. You gave me your word you wouldn't lock me up once I changed, or follow me around like I'm a child."

Mrs. Hahn paused. "That's true. Girls need their independence. Your father always said that the second you passed to your adult markings, that was it. No more school, or parties, or anything until the danger passed. But I won't have my daughter kept a prisoner."

"Exactly." Cassandra put a hand on her mother's arm. "Besides, Deirdre stayed out after dusk, and I heard she flirted with men. You know we're smarter than that."

Ms. Hahn's gaze flitted around the room to the granite-topped console table, the coat tree, the polished floors. She took in these things of beauty and then turned to look at me.

"We're going to see Julia, my brother's teacher," I said. "She might have some insight into Cassie's future career."

That did it, this reference to Cassandra's mysterious career markings. Mrs. Hahn took a deep breath and moved away from the door.

"Stick to the busy streets. Right to Julia's, and then straight back afterward," she said. "If anyone comes near you, don't be afraid to scream. Go for the groin if it comes to that. Do you understand, girls?"

We agreed. As we headed out the door, Cassandra and Marie began chatting about various career options. This was, I realized, the first time I had ever known Cassandra to take such an active interest in her future career. Maybe I didn't know her as well as I'd thought. I certainly didn't know, not then, that she'd go on changing until a time came when I couldn't recognize her at all.

WE KEPT A brisk pace all the way to the interpretation district. After we passed under the *Future as Fate* arch and hurried through the cobblestone streets, Julia's townhouse came into view. Red brick, three stories high, the narrow facade—a place where the future was made an ordered thing.

When Julia opened the door, I pushed Cassandra forward.

"This is my friend Cassie," I said. "She just passed to her adult markings."

"I can see that. Congratulations, Cassie." Julia wore a soft gray robe over her clothes, and she fidgeted with its belt as she considered us. "But I don't work on Sundays, and this isn't an emergency."

"Please? We need a reading."

Julia took in my expression and softened.

"All right," she said. "I'll do a quick reading and then have you on your way."

Julia led Cassandra to her office while Marie and I waited in the parlor. I passed the time by twisting my hands together in my lap.

"You're panicking," Marie said in a quiet voice. She reached over to rest her hand on mine. "Cassie will be fine."

"But you know how she is." It felt traitorous to describe Cassandra as I sometimes saw her—impulsive, wild, boastful—so I didn't. "I'm worried about her, that's all."

"She'll be fine," Marie repeated.

She was too naïve to understand the risks. It was probably due to being sheltered by her modest mother. I knew I wouldn't be the same if my mother had always covered every inch of her skin and refused to work or socialize in a mixed-gender environment. While Marie's mother didn't compel her to dress modestly, other aspects of the lifestyle, such as the focus on traditional gender roles, crept into my friend's daily routine. Marie attended a domestic arts club at school, and she could do things I couldn't, like follow sewing patterns or set a table with formal place settings.

"I just want things to stay the same," I said.

Marie shook her head. "It's already too late for that."

I fell silent. From the corner of the parlor came the ticking of the grandfather clock. I focused on that sound, waiting and waiting until the office door opened down the hall and Cassandra reappeared, her eyes shining.

"Julia says my career will be something high-end, most likely in medicine," she told us. "She thinks these markings can make a case for me to get into medical school."

"That's great." I'd never known Cassandra to dream of becoming a doctor, but if her markings suggested she could, that changed everything. "Did she see anything else?"

"Nothing we didn't already find on our own. My future husband isn't anyone I know yet, so I'll have to wait for that."

I looked at my friend and pictured the life she believed she had coming to her—professional success, financial security, the love of an as-yet-unknown husband. Cassandra would surely take that future for granted. She wouldn't think twice about whether it could be ruined.

"Wait here," I told my friends. "I'll be right back."

I walked down the hallway to Julia's office. She was at her desk, staring at the doorway like she'd been waiting for me. Maybe she could sense my nerves, how my heart beat hard and fast.

"Celeste. Please come in."

I took a seat. "Cassie seems happy. You told her exactly what she wanted to hear."

"I told her the truth."

"Maybe you should also ask her to be careful." As I spoke, my gaze was drawn to the framed document hanging behind the desk. It was written in Latin.

"What's that?" I asked.

Julia glanced over her shoulder. "It's my degree from university."

"I didn't know you went to university." While professional interpreters had to be licensed and adhere to a set of guidelines, they didn't usually pursue higher education. Interpretation was an art form that didn't fit into a specific academic discipline.

"I once thought I'd be something else. Maybe an engineer. That's what my father hoped I'd become." She laughed a little. "And before that, my mother wanted me to be a homemaker like her. I have five brothers and sisters. Can you imagine? But that future died once I passed to my adult markings. It was marked on me plain as anything: no marriage, no children."

"That's awful." I estimated Julia was in her mid-thirties, still within childbearing age, but I'd never wondered whether she was fated to have children. I supposed I'd assumed it just hadn't happened yet for her.

She didn't seem moved by my concern. "The right future found me," she said. "I can help people, especially young girls, as an interpreter. And in any case, motherhood was never my dream."

"I guess." A note of doubt had crept into my voice.

"You know," Julia went on, "I learned a long time ago that I could live the life that best suited me, not anyone else. One day you might learn that, too."

I felt insulted, though I wasn't sure why. "I already know what I'm going to be. A psychologist."

"Of course. I only mean that sometimes, our true abilities surprise us. Like your brother and his gift for interpretation. No one could have predicted that."

"Maybe, but he's still a boy. There's no use teaching him in the long run."

"He has real talent, Celeste. You might be surprised."

But I saw no surprises in the future. Not even for me, someone who was a mediocre reader of markings at best.

"Here," Julia said. "I'll show you."

She came around to my side of the desk and propped her left foot on the edge of my chair. She rolled up the bottom of her pants leg to show me her ankle, which was encircled by a set of markings like a bracelet. I held in a gasp.

"Oh, Julia." I leaned in closer. I was looking at a constellation that spelled misfortune. "What exactly does it mean?"

"Look at the variations." She pointed to the tiny markings orbiting a set of larger ones, the pale markings joined up with the darker. "That many variables make specific predictions almost impossible. All I can determine from *Mapping the Future* is that this pattern indicates future loss." She looked at me. "The first time your brother saw this, he sat down for a good long look. He couldn't figure it out—this kind of prediction needs time to come to light—but he's smart, with excellent instincts, and he's not intimidated by a challenge. He's a natural, Celeste."

"But he's still a boy. He has no future in interpretation."

"I trust him, and I trust that he'll find a way. That's what matters." She covered her ankle and removed her foot from my chair. "You're a lot like Miles, you know. Once he sets his mind on something, that's it. From what I hear, you're the same about your future career." She peered at me. "If I may, what attracts you to the field of psychology?"

I looked away, thinking. People didn't generally ask me why I wanted to be a psychologist. Whenever teachers or my friends' parents learned what I wanted to become, they usually just smiled as if I'd said something amusing. Sometimes they'd make a joke about psychoanalysis, like how they should be careful about what they said around me lest I uncover their secrets.

"I knew a psychologist once," I said. My voice was tentative. "She was my mother's friend. This was a long time ago; I was very young. When we went to her house, she'd let me play with her impression cards."

"I remember those. They were once quite popular. Each card had a different image, just a simple line drawing in ink—is that right?"

"And only two colors: red and black." I nodded. "I loved those cards. My mother's friend explained it all to me, how she gave them to patients and asked what they saw in the images. Everyone had a different answer, she told me, because it wasn't about the image so much as what each person projected onto it. I found that fascinating—that our minds work so differently, and that we reveal the psyche merely by describing what we see in a picture."

Julia was watching me closely. "When you put it like that, it sounds like you're talking about the art of interpretation."

"It's not the same at all," I said quickly. "The skill in interpretation is in figuring out what the prediction means. Like the marking on your ankle—it refers to one set future, even if that future is unknowable to us right now. But psychology is more open-ended." I paused. "I like the thought of choices. Of there being a larger puzzle with more than one answer."

"That makes sense. Still, everything you say suggests that you could make a great interpreter, too. Just like Miles."

It would always come back to interpretation for Julia. She and my brother both saw the world in the same way: as one long stretch of predictions just waiting to be understood.

Slowly, I stood. "I should go. My friends are waiting, and Cassandra's mother is expecting us."

"Of course." Julia stood, too. "If you girls would like an escort back to your neighborhood, I'd be happy to walk with you."

I shook my head, letting Julia know we'd promised Cassandra's mother that we'd stick together, and that we weren't afraid. It seemed important to say those words to Julia, to stress our courage. As if by convincing her we were strong and clever and safe, I could also convince myself.

My friends and I left and made quick progress through the streets, crossing under the arch and passing into the heart of downtown: the courthouse, the old stone church with the crooked cemetery stones, the bank headquarters displaying my father's ad. I noticed a flurry of activity around the bank, a gathering of men, and on instinct I froze.

"It's okay," Marie said. "They're not here for us."

I looked again. One of the men held a ladder against the wall while another climbed. I was still standing there, gaping, as the first corner of my father's banner came loose and flipped over itself. Then the entire top half went slack.

"Come on, Celeste," Cassandra said. "We don't need to watch this." She and Marie gently pulled me away and placed me between them, like I was the one who needed protection.

They told me not to look back, but I did anyway. I watched my father's advertisement crumple. I watched the beautiful face cave in on itself, watched the torso stand bare and alone until it, too, was folded away. I watched until the banner was dangling, about to drop. I watched until my neck hurt, until my friends urged me on and I turned around.

Behind me, I could hear the banner fall.

MAPPING THE FUTURE:
AN INTERPRETIVE GUIDE TO WOMEN AND GIRLS

ADDENDUM IX, GENDER AND SEXUALITY

Following numerous inquiries surrounding the shifting perception of gender and sexuality, the authors hereby enter into this edition of *Mapping the Future* the following addendum:

For the purposes of sanctioned interpretation, any romantic relationships referenced within these pages assume lawful sexuality, i.e., one man paired with one woman, as is consistent with cultural and social decency. Those who act on attraction to the same sex should not expect to benefit from government support. Additionally, the descriptors "man" and "woman" refer exclusively to sex assigned at birth. Any interference with natural marking patterns—by tattooing, scarring, or other methods of self-inflicted deformity—in an attempt to alter the natural sex state is considered a misdemeanor under the law.

As the government agency responsible for all matters related to markings and interpretation, the Office of the Future maintains control solely over this nation's official editions of *Mapping the Future* and bears no responsibility for addenda published in other countries. Citizens are forewarned that foreign editions may be incomplete or inaccurate, either by error or by intent.

6

CASSANDRA SHOWED UP at school the next day with a stack of pink invitations. Thick pearl card stock, embossed lettering. *Your presence is requested this Saturday at the coming-out party for Miss Cassandra Hahn.* My invitation was addressed not only to me but also to my father, mother, and brother, our full names rising from the paper in relief.

Cassandra stood by my locker sorting her remaining invitations. She was excited, jittery, energy coming off of her like steam rising from the street after a summer rain. She wanted things to be perfect. She wanted her party to be about her, not about my father's banner or Deirdre's abduction or any other distractions. I supposed that was her right. This was her time.

I didn't want a coming-out party of my own, which was for the best considering my family could never host an elaborate event like Cassandra's. It had always been that way for us. Thanks to our shared birthdate, Miles and I had joint birthday parties as children. Our mother bought blank invitations at the drugstore and wrote out the details by hand. Every year, it was a battle to decide the theme of the invitations: Miles wanted robots, I wanted dragonflies. Usually we compromised and got the balloon design. It never occurred to us to ask for two sets of invitations, or, for that matter, separate parties. My father's job didn't pay as much as he seemed to think it should; plus there were debts and other adult matters Miles and I didn't understand at the time. We just knew our family lived on the line between having enough and not.

That day in school I marveled at the sheer number of invitations Cassandra handed out. Olivia, the fourth-year who played the female lead in every school musical, slowed her pace as she passed us in the hall. Cassandra dug through her stack of invitations and thrust one toward her.

"It's on Saturday," Cassandra said brightly. "Come celebrate with me."

Olivia smiled. She was our school's rising star, the kind of girl beloved by all and invited to everything, but she'd be sure to grace the party with her presence. I knew this just as I predicted the boys would trail Cassandra all day at school as though she were their queen.

My friend's invitations were coveted, a symbol of social success. To be invited to her party was to be welcomed into her world of beauty, and wealth, and the promise of a bright future. Throughout the day I caught glimpses of that card stock everywhere—carried in plain sight through the halls, conspicuously exposed during class. I tucked mine inside my history book, but sometimes I cracked the spine and reached in to touch it. The paper felt shimmery, solid. Even hidden away in the dark, it had worth.

I RETURNED HOME to an empty house. My mother had a doctor's appointment, and my father was still at work. Miles was at Julia's for a private lesson. I wondered where the money came from for this education, what he had to do to earn it.

A few years ago, when he'd been invited to take a photography course and needed to pay for film, paper, and chemicals, Miles got creative. He made flyers advertising a dog-walking service and hung them around the neighborhood. He tried babysitting, but not many people wanted to hire a boy. One weekend he and I went door-to-door offering to mow lawns or weed flower beds, but that ended after I got a sunburn so severe my skin peeled for weeks.

Miles refused to give up. He was devoted to that photography class, and he was going to find a way to fund it. He enlisted my help again, this time to participate in the neighborhood yard sale. Together we spent hours sorting through our old toys and dragging unwanted household items outside to sell. Miles's biggest offering was the croquet set he found in the garage. It was a nice set, real wood, heavy, the balls with a heft like weapons. He placed the croquet set prominently in our front yard and sat for hours in a folding chair while no one bought it. Eventually I took a break and walked up and down the street, examining our competition. By then the day had become about more than Miles and raising money. It became about my curiosity, my nascent wonderings about the human mind.

That neighborhood yard sale was where I found my first psychology book: *Principles of the Mind*. The author, Dr. Lauren Kisterboch, was pictured on the inside back cover wearing a black skirt suit, her arms crossed with authority. I bought the book with the loose change in my pocket. When I returned home, Miles was angry. He said the point of the yard sale was to make money, not spend it, but I told him the book had only cost twenty cents, which was basically nothing. Plus it was mine, first the money and then the book, which I placed in a prominent position on my bookshelf. It remained there still, its red spine setting it apart from all my other books.

After school that day, I slid Cassandra's party invitation on the kitchen counter and went to my room. I headed straight for my bookcase, resolved to stop worrying about how Miles might pay for his interpretation classes. He'd find a way—he always did for what he most wanted. It was time to direct my attention to my own interests instead.

I pulled down *Principles of the Mind* from its place on the shelf among the other psychology books I'd collected: old textbooks I'd found in the used-book store, the remaindered copies of lesser-known professionals touting some theory or another, the biographies of the greats. They were mostly written by men, with the author's photo printed across the full back cover. Gray hair, beards, suits, shiny knotted ties. It all meant nothing to me, not just the authors but the books themselves. Even Dr. Kisterboch's *Principles of the Mind*, which I'd devoted the most time to studying, only made sense in flashes. The material was too advanced for me, impenetrable, and I waited to grow older and have it all make sense. I thought life was like that: reach a certain milestone and poof—complete understanding.

For a while I sat on the floor flipping through *Principles of the Mind*, reading snatches of Dr. Kisterboch's dryly balanced analysis of the human psyche. Before long, I found myself thinking of Miles instead. I thought of the game we played in the basement, how he could look me full in the face and withhold the truth about something so grave. I worried what else he might conceal, what secrets were yet to come between us.

I abandoned my books on the floor and snuck into Miles's room. It was a tradition for me to hunt through his things when he wasn't home. I picked my way over the clothes and books strewn across the floor to reach his desk, where an envelope caught my eye. It was addressed in my brother's handwriting to the Office of the Future, and when I picked it up, the paper seemed to slip out and unfold in my hands as if of its own accord. That was how snooping worked for me: it was an out-of-body experience, something for which I believed I bore no blame.

I was holding a Petition for Addendum form. I skimmed its contents, expecting to read a mundane technical request, but soon I felt blood rush to my cheeks. My brother was petitioning the Office of the Future to create special interpretation training programs for men. The interpretation field was female-dominated, my brother argued, only because it was considered women's work, which caused men to dismiss it out of hand. As a result, the strict gender line held, potentially robbing the world of men's talents.

"Just as our government forbids explicit discrimination against women in the workplace, men should receive rights equal to women in pursuing the profession of interpretation," he'd written. "To discourage men from this line of work reinforces outdated gender politics, and it unnecessarily restricts gifted men from making valuable contributions in the field." He went on to suggest that to alleviate fears of men taking advantage of girls, each male interpreter could be accompanied by a female assistant during readings. Like a chaperone, or like the nurses who stayed in the room while male doctors examined women and girls.

I lowered the letter but didn't let go of it. It struck me as a hopeless thing. The *Mapping the Future* authors and editors were exclusively male, but that didn't mean they would be sympathetic to my brother's request. The editorial panel was notoriously conservative, and they made updates to *Mapping the Future* only rarely. The latest addendum, which purported to focus on gender and sexuality, barely acknowledged the reality of same-sex attraction and relationships. Miles was asking the authors to take too great a leap. He was also being unreasonable, in my view. Girls could never truly be comfortable with male interpreters. It was just common sense.

Back then, my teenage self did not understand the distinction between official channels and the underground, the place where real progress was born. A *Mapping the Future* addendum would eventually be published, yes, but not for what Miles had originally petitioned. In the years to come, I'd buy the revised edition not for myself but for all the girls who had a different sort of future—one I could hardly begin to imagine back then.

I WAS STILL holding that form when Miles returned home, when he bounded up the stairs toward me. He took one step into his room and stopped when he saw me.

I held up his letter. "What are you thinking?"

"I'm trying to change the system." He came forward and snapped the paper from my hand. "It's a waste to keep good men out of the profession."

"You know what *Mapping the Future* says about male interpreters." I walked over to his bookcase to locate our family copy of the text. I plucked it down and paged through until I came to the section "On Men and Interpretation."

"'A woman is marked by nature, but a man is naked, unreadable,'" I read out loud. "'For this reason, men are dissuaded from pursuing interpretation professionally. No man is as gifted as a woman in the interpretive arts, and he should harbor no illusions concerning the scope of his abilities. A man's role is to guide society, set laws, and accept responsibility for the larger arc of the future. The realm of the domestic and individual, meanwhile, falls to women.'"

"I know what it says." Miles looked flustered. "You have to see the bigger picture, Celeste. Maybe men aren't considered skilled because they haven't learned properly, or they never thought to try. And maybe the Office of the Future hasn't seriously considered this because no one has fought for it. I'm willing to do that."

Like my brother, I understood what it felt like to be held back based on gender. My bookshelf full of psychology books written by men was proof enough of that. At the same time, I'd never want to undress for a male interpreter, with or without a woman chaperoning him. We'd never even met a male interpreter in real life—the few men who did practice lived in bigger cities. Even then, their work was considered a lark.

"Did Julia have you do this?" I asked. "I told you something was off about her."

"No. This was my idea, but Julia supports it. She knows I'm talented. She knows what I can be."

I scanned the final sentences of the "On Men and Interpretation" section, which I read silently, to myself: *Our stance on this issue is clear and concrete: It is the female sex that bears the burden of interpretation, and thus it is women who are best qualified to study the finer parts of this art form. A man, in this case, is no woman's equal.*

"Anyway, that doesn't matter right now," he said. "I have to go."

"Where?"

Miles didn't answer me. He reached down to dig through a pile of clothes on the floor. When he found his navy zip-up sweatshirt, he tossed it on. I noticed for the first time that his hands were trembling.

"Miles. Tell me what's going on."

He wouldn't look at me. "It's Deirdre," he finally said. "She's back."

The book grew heavy in my hand. "She is?"

"I just heard. I'm going over to see her."

"I'm sure she doesn't want to be alone with a boy right now. I'll come with you."

"That's not a good idea." Miles adjusted the sweatshirt. "Trust me."

For a moment I worried the shaking would start again, that I'd be so stricken with terror that I would not be able to move. But no. I had to see Deirdre, to face what had happened to her.

"I'm coming," I said firmly, and I replaced *Mapping the Future* on Miles's bookcase. The gold-embossed letters on the spine glinted dully. Not like stars but like a pair of eyes watching me. Remembering where I'd been and where I'd yet to go.

ACCORDING TO MILES, Deirdre had been found unconscious, dumped in an alley somewhere. Paramedics lifted her body and took her to the hospital, where she spent four days recovering in the Reintegration Wing. Only then was she sent home. There was no public announcement, no parade or welcome-home party. It was almost as if she were still gone.

Deirdre lived at the edge of our neighborhood, about a mile away, in a modest brick bungalow covered in overgrown vines. We crossed the uncut lawn, passing a rusted birdfeeder hanging cockeyed from the pine tree out front, to knock firmly on the front door. Deirdre's parents invited us inside at once. They were probably grateful their daughter had any visitors at all.

Upstairs, we found Deirdre in bed. She looked smaller, as though she hadn't eaten for many days. Her hair was chopped off at her chin, which I found odd—did her kidnapper do this? Maybe it was her parents, in an attempt to conceal her identity, or perhaps it was the nurses at the hospital, or maybe Deirdre did it herself, precisely because she knew she wasn't the same person anymore.

Miles took a seat at the desk while I sat cross-legged on the floor. I noticed Deirdre wasn't wearing her opal necklace—just one more bit of brightness wiped away.

"How are you?" Miles asked.

Deirdre fixed him with a blank stare. "The only thing I have going for me right now is that I can't remember anything."

Miles and I nodded. Kidnappers drugged abducted girls to keep them quiet and under control. It was a fortuitous side effect, some people said, that the drugs also erased memory.

Deirdre shifted her gaze my way. I had so many questions for her, questions I knew I could never ask out loud. What her body felt like, her skin, whether she could still smell him. If she had a sense of who he was, how he hurt her, what he did. It was too horrific to imagine, and yet I was imagining it: A man making Deirdre exposed, vulnerable, raw. Breaking the life she'd known. That her hair was cut short seemed appropriate, making her a pruned thing, snapped off at the source. These thoughts collided in my mind, a mess of salacious details, but I could not stop myself. I felt like a monster for even thinking of what Deirdre had gone through—and for the tiny part of me that desperately, nakedly, wanted to know more.

Deirdre was still watching me. I worried she sensed the grotesque scenes blooming to life in my mind.

"I brought you something." Miles pulled out a plastic bag containing two red pills. They shined like spots of blood in his palm.

Deirdre leaned forward on her knees in bed, allowing her comforter to fall away. I couldn't help but look at her body—her thin, bruised body, no longer glorious because her changeling period had passed. She was a woman now, a dull copy of the girl I'd seen in the school bathroom just a few weeks ago, but she was also something else. She was strong. She had to be, I decided, to live through that violence.

"Bloodflower," she said, reverence in her voice. Miles spilled the drugs into her open hands.

"Where'd you get that?" I asked him. Bloodflower was illegal. I knew it was fairly easy to obtain, and possession only amounted to a misdemeanor, but still.

"I know a guy," he said, as though that was enough.

Several years ago, our school brought in a recovering bloodflower addict as a speaker. The man was skinny all over, with ropy tendons visible in his arms and neck. He told us how his use of bloodflower over the years made him disassociate from reality. How he went from living an average, productive life to living one built on fantasy and delusion. He lost weight, lost friends, lost his job. All he wanted was to swallow those red pills, to float himself onto another plane of existence. And for returned girls, bloodflower had an additional effect: it could help recover memories from the abduction.

Deirdre set one of the bloodflower pills on her bedside table. She swallowed the other one dry. I wanted to protest, to point out that the drug would make Deirdre hallucinate or lose herself in a dreamworld or break into an uncontrollable sweat. To remember what might best be lost forever.

I was so young then. I had no idea what people did to carry on.

When Deirdre raised her eyes again, she focused on me.

"You haven't changed yet." She said it like an accusation. "Who else has, since I've been gone?"

"A few girls in your interpretation class," I said. "Khalia and Yvonne. Their parents are keeping them at home. And my friend Cassandra."

Deirdre considered this information. "Is Cassandra stuck at home, too?"

"No. She's going to school, spending time with friends. Like everything is the same."

"It's not the same." Deirdre pulled at a loose thread in her comforter. "But listen. I'm not going to tell you to stay locked in your room when your time comes. You can't let what happens in the worst cases prevent you from living your life. Do you understand?"

I nodded, but Deirdre was already looking over my shoulder, into the distance.

"This was meant to happen to me," she said. "That means it has to be okay."

I didn't know what to say, or whether I believed a girl's fate could truly be that bleak. In so many ways, Deirdre was trapped, her future cut off before it began.

I let my gaze wander around the room until it landed on the bureau. A brochure lay there, its cover displaying pine trees and horses. I went over to it and picked it up.

"Is this for the Mountain School?"

"One of my aunts sent me that," Deirdre said. "As if there's any way my family could ever afford that place."

The brochure was glossy, thick. Full-color photos of classrooms, a science lab, stables, tennis courts. Teenage girls flung their arms over one another and beamed. Those girls had to be the richest of the rich. No one else could pay for such a reprieve from the real world.

"It was from the aunt I always suspected secretly hated me. She must have sent it as a form of torture." Deirdre paused, putting a hand to her forehead. Her eyes were unfocused. "Wow. I can really feel it kick in."

"It will help you relax," Miles said.

Deirdre gathered up the comforter and rolled onto her side. "I have to face it anyway," she said. "Might as well start now."

Miles and I waited, as if Deirdre might pop up in bed at any moment and return to her old self. Instead, she closed her eyes against us and lay silently, without moving.

After a long moment, Miles and I shared a wary look and got up to leave.

DURING THE WALK home, I asked Miles again where he'd gotten the bloodflower, and how, and whether he ever took it himself. He told me not to worry about it. He said this without breaking stride, his eyes not meeting mine. This only confirmed he was capable of keeping more secrets than I'd imagined.

We arrived home to find our parents sitting at the kitchen table. My father was dressed in jeans and a T-shirt, definitely not work attire, and he was drinking a beer.

"God forbid someone takes a creative risk." He looked right at us while saying this, as if we'd been following their conversation. "These people can't even articulate why they're so angry. Some say it's because it's a lewd image, others because the woman in the drawing has no markings." He shook his head. "What a crime, to ask people to use their imaginations."

"So Mom was right." Miles reached behind me to slam the door shut. I'd left it hanging open, like I'd forgotten we needed to keep the inside separate from the outside. "You got fired."

"No." Our father took a swig of beer. "Suspended. And removed from three of my best accounts."

"A demotion," our mother explained.

"It's not a demotion, Paulette."

She shrugged. Her hands were empty, but I saw her fingers twitch. I wondered if she was thinking about cigarettes, the papery drag against her skin.

"Kids," she said. "Give us a few minutes, will you?"

Miles pulled me from the kitchen and led me upstairs to his room. He closed the door and turned to me.

"This is serious. We were already only scraping by, did you know that?"

"Yes," I said, but maybe I didn't. I looked more closely at my brother. His expression was tight, frightened. "Hey." I put a hand on his arm. "It's okay. He didn't get fired. He'll get those accounts back before long."

He nodded. "You're probably right. I'm overreacting." He started to move toward the door but stopped. "I can't shake it."

"Shake what?"

"The thought that something terrible is going to happen." His eyes searched my own. "I think about it all the time. Sometimes I can't even sleep because of it."

I stared back at him. Much later I'd remember his words as a clue, a prophecy unto themselves, but in the moment I only felt compassion. My older brother was afraid. He was weak and uncertain. He was human.

From downstairs, we heard our parents' voices rise and grow louder.

Miles looked at me. "Not a word," he mouthed. He waited until there was a break in the argument downstairs, until a heavy silence settled over the house, and only then did he push open the door.

ON THE DAY of Cassandra's party, my father put on his suit as though nothing were wrong. I stood behind him to help brush the lint from the back of his jacket. *This suit will have to last him,* I thought when I touched the fabric. That was a surprise, to have words like my mother's arriving unbidden in my head.

I wore my best dress: dark blue, tea-length, with a full skirt that flared out from my hips. Miles put on pressed khakis and a collared shirt. I watched him slick his hair down in the bathroom with a tub of product I didn't recognize. I wanted to tease him for trying to look nice, but at the last second I lost my voice. That was how it was for me back then. One moment I'd be focused on something insignificant, like Cassandra's party or Miles's tentative pride in his appearance, and the next I was jarred by all that was wrong. Our father's demotion. Deirdre lying broken in bed. My brother's secrets and his impending sense of disaster.

My father knotted and reknotted his tie while waiting for my mother to finish getting ready. She wore an older dress, a red one that was too tight around the waist, but I told her she looked nice. My father didn't offer any compliments. He just stood jangling his keys, waiting to leave.

We walked to the party as a family, crossing onto Cassandra's property in the same order our names appeared on the invitation. *Neil, Paulette, Miles, Celeste.* An attendant directed us to follow a trail of rose petals into the backyard, where a pink-and-white-striped tent sheltered stations for fruit, appetizers, desserts, champagne, a butterscotch fountain, and the traditional rose sherry. Pink balloons bunched like grapes in the trees.

"This is obscene," my father said.

"Look," my mother murmured. "There's Cassandra."

My friend appeared like a mirage in a crisp white dress laced through with pink ribbons. Her eyes had a certain shine I attributed to the flute of rose sherry in her hand. Behind her, a group of boys and men gathered like a cloud.

When it came to changelings, men could not control themselves. That was what we were told. And yet not all men were monsters. My father, for example, would never hurt a changeling girl. Miles wouldn't, either. I believed this to my core. Sometimes I studied men on the street and thought, would he? What about him? Who in this crowd would take advantage of a darkened sidewalk, the broken streetlamp, the girl out alone after dark?

Most days, I couldn't imagine any man capable of such crimes. Other times, I viewed every man as a threat. Just as girls held within their bodies a great capacity for the future, men, I suspected, carried the curled beginnings of violence. In the right circumstances, maybe anyone could strike.

Cassandra was too busy greeting other guests to pay much attention to me. I sat at a party table sprinkled with pink flower petals. My mother got herself a glass of rose sherry and, as an afterthought, brought me one, too.

"It's almost time for you, anyway," she said.

I accepted the tulip-shaped glass and took a sip of the pink liquid. As I swallowed, I had to struggle not to make a face. Rose sherry did not taste as pretty and pale as it appeared—instead, it was a sharply sweet drink with a bite.

I turned to see my father tucked in the far corner of the yard with a few other neighborhood dads. Their eyes followed Cassandra wherever she went. Her own father was among them. After the divorce, he'd moved to the next town over with his new wife. Cassandra didn't see much of him, especially not after her first stepsister was born, so it mattered that he'd shown up for the party. Later, I knew, he'd take Cassandra upstairs alone to inspect her markings. This father-daughter ritual was an honored tradition, but there at the party, it made me sick.

"Everyone wants to devour her," I said to my mother. "It's disgusting."

My mother sipped her rose sherry. She was stoic at that party, so calm and in control. I'd later realize it was an act. She didn't want to let on how afraid she was for me, how afraid all mothers were for their daughters.

"These parties are practice," she said. "They show us how to maintain decorum even and especially in the face of what courses beneath the surface."

As she talked, we watched a group of boys approach Cassandra. One boy reached for a ribbon on her dress while another touched her hair, an act that seemed to make him shiver.

Another boy backed out of the circle and stood to the side. I squinted and saw it was Anthony from my homeroom. I'd noticed him sitting in the shade earlier, glaring at the ground as if he could will the party to disappear. As I watched his strained face, I slowly grasped the source of his discomfort. He wasn't interested in Cassandra, just as he wouldn't be in any changeling girl, or at least not in the desperate sexual way the other boys were. Like me, he surely felt a pull toward Cassandra, wanted to envelop her in his arms, press his skin into hers. And yet boys of his age had an extra desperation in their desires, a telltale gleam. No matter how hard boys like Anthony tried, the lustful pull toward these girls could not be faked for long.

I felt an overwhelming sadness for him, a kind of grief. While boys like Anthony could go on to share their lives with male partners if they wished, they could never marry or receive partner benefits or full support from the government. It was perhaps even more difficult for girls—as it would be for Marie, I was starting to realize. The official stance in *Mapping the Future* asserted that her predictions of love and romance pertained to men, not women. It didn't matter that the markings on her lower back indicated she'd one day live with a woman; the Office of the Future rejected that such a romantic pairing could be fated. Instead, the sanctioned interpretation might suggest that this woman in her future would be no more than a roommate. Like Anthony, Marie was destined to spend her life halfway in denial.

I turned away from Anthony, my eyes stinging. What a dangerous time we were all living through. It was a time for girls and boys my age to be exposed for who they really were.

For the rest of the afternoon, I sat sourly next to my mother. I watched Marie play with children near the butterscotch fountain, but I did not join her. I watched men ogle and caress Cassandra, but I did not intervene. I sat, watching the party carry on before me, and I silently begged Cassandra to be careful. She was a wholly different person now, and the world was filled halfway with men.

*   *   *

THE NEXT MORNING, and the one after that, and the one after that, I woke up the same: marked in my juvenile predictions. My parents bickered about money. Miles continued his interpretation studies and checked the mail every day for a response from the Office of the Future. Marie visited me a few times, and together we sat on my bedroom carpet and played board games like children.

Miles had given up on his blue notebook. There was no need for it now that my juvenile markings were all but expired. In its place he had bought a hardbound, unlined artist's pad with thick, heavy pages. It waited, clean and professional, for my new future to reveal itself, to submit to being recorded.

I had grown up hearing rumors of a girl born completely blank, without a mole or mark on her body. Everyone claimed they had a friend of a friend who had a cousin who knew this unmarked girl. The truth was that no girl like this existed, no girl ever. Girls with albinism were marked in tiny pale dots. Dark-skinned girls bore markings that shined the color of honey or amber in the sun. The girl without markings was as unreal as a shimmering unicorn.

Cassandra was like a mythical creature, too. That was how I saw her, now that she had changed: beautiful, ephemeral, untouchable. At school, Marie sat on the other side of the cafeteria so she could eat in peace instead of reaching toward our friend with quivering fingers. I stayed with Cassandra to keep her company, but it felt bitter, this preview of what was to come for me. I was impatient and angry all the time. I woke up sweating under the covers, and every morning I stood in the shower, willing the water to wash off my childhood markings just to get it over with.

In reality, my change would happen as it happened for nearly everyone: in bed, silently, while I slept. A natural wonder. Later I'd think back and try to remember my dreams from that night, but I came up empty. I was a big dreamer, the dreams elaborate and long-winded; someone once told me this meant I didn't sleep well and that I must be walking around in a state of perpetual exhaustion. This I would not disagree with. But when I think back to the night of my passage to adulthood, I can only imagine myself lying still in bed, everything inside of me taking its slow shift, regular and careful as a clock. When the clock's hands had ticked their way to a predetermined hour and minute, it happened:

At 6:48 A.M. on Monday, October the second, I woke up changed.

II

Changeling

Mapping the Future:
An Interpretive Guide to Women and Girls

METHOD FOR CONDUCTING A READING

Breathe. Steady yourself. Rely not purely on sight but also on touch, on instinct. The task you are about to complete is both a gift and a responsibility. Respect it.

Once the subject has disrobed, take her left hand in both of your own. Hold her wrist fast with one hand while your other skims the length of her arm. Study the diagrams in this book, but also allow yourself to move by instinct. Allow the electricity to jolt straight through your bones.

Left shoulder, right shoulder, then cross over to the back of her neck. Lift your subject's hair and read her scalp as best as possible. Move to her temples, her forehead, her cheekbones and collarbone. Cross now to her right arm and right hand before moving down: breasts, ribs, stomach, pubic area. Then upper back, lower back, hips, buttocks, the legs and ankles and feet.

Markings in this text are arranged by category, location, and pattern. Follow the index to find the applicable part of the body, the number of markings, and the precise arrangement. The diagrams are intuitive, designed for laymen and professionals alike, but this alone does not ensure accuracy. Some patterns are ambiguous, and others reveal more than one interpretation. Pay attention. A star is not a circle is not an arc is not a ring. A pale mole is not the same as a minor one. Remain open, therefore, to professional assessment. Be willing to reveal yourself.

To read and to be read is an act of trust. A true reading is an offering, a question, an act of surrender. And so we ask you to breathe again. Move your finger from the page to the skin. Touch, hold steady, tremble. Release.

7

I KNEW BEFORE I opened my eyes. A gentle tingling radiated through my limbs from a deep and secret source. It was subtle, like catching the glimmer of a faraway wind chime and wondering, after the sound faded away, whether it had been there at all.

The night had passed in chills and drafts, the quilt a heavy weight on my body. I did not want to lift it away. I did not want to see what had changed. I lay there, feeling my skin touching my pajamas, which touched the sheets, which touched the blankets, which touched the quilt. I could hear the beating of my heart. It was the day before my sixteenth birthday. Time was moving forward, the future shifting, and there was nothing I could do to stop it.

I pushed off the quilt and stood. Slowly, shivering with the cold of morning, I dropped out of my pajamas and my underwear. I avoided the full-length mirror, since reflections could distort markings, and looked down at the new future made manifest on my body.

My skin flashed before me, a swerving wreck of predictions. I shut my eyes, disoriented. The morning sun seeped brassy and strong through my eyelids. I could feel it—thermal energy, the hot center of the earth. I cracked open my right eye to see the sunlight shimmering between the slats of the closed blinds, a wavering vision of heat and salt and painful bright.

So this was high lucidity. I sensed the blood moving through my veins, spreading outward like the branches of a tree. I could hear it, too, along with the thrumming of my heart, the rustle of leaves outside, the wind coursing over grass. This was survival-level hearing, the kind meant for wild animals, for the hunted and the primeval. And then came the smells: an egg frying downstairs, a wisp of old bleach in the bathroom, the spots of dried toothpaste on the medicine cabinet mirror. I bent forward, gasping for air. Which I could feel moving in and out of my lungs, every ragged desperate gulp. As if someone had turned me inside out.

I remembered the breathing exercises I'd been taught to dampen the lucidity. A breath in, a breath out. Slower, then slower still. It worked, my senses narrowing to a dulled pinprick of their former strength.

With new confidence, I began my reading as I should have from the start: slowly, carefully, an inch at a time. First my left fingers, hand, and wrist; then the left forearm and upper arm. The vague markings by my left elbow were gone, replaced with nothing. How strange to see blank skin in that spot.

When I reached my stomach, I paused to marvel at the constellation meant to predict children. The open configuration indicated that children were a possibility in the coming decades, but that was it. The pattern was not specific enough to spell out the number of children or their genders, as my mother's markings had for Miles and me, but I wasn't bothered by this uncertainty. Future children were not something I fixated on.

My right hip, the place for career. I scrutinized those markings for a long time. The juvenile pattern indicating I'd work with Miles, along with the lone outlier marking, had disappeared. My career cluster still slanted downward to suggest an intricate, detail-oriented profession, but that could point to so many careers: dentist, horticulturalist, bead artist. Or a psychologist, I decided, since nothing was more intricate than the workings of the mind.

For the lower back I had to use the mirror, which resulted in many jumbled predictions about my future love life—an eventual marriage, perhaps preceded by two failed loves. Finally, I checked my sides. The skin of my right rib cage remained blank, but when I crossed over to the left side of my body, the prediction there stopped me short. It showed a diagonal, an arc, a pattern of stars.

A sound like static foamed in my mind, which fizzled into a faint ringing in my ears. I almost cried out. I almost burst into tears. *Mapping the Future* couldn't have been clearer about this arrangement of markings: two diagonal moles for *brother*, a starlike pattern for *death*, and an arc of three moles descending in size to indicate three years.

According to the markings on my ribs, Miles only had three years left to live.

I drifted across the room as if underwater. For a second I pictured my brother's face, just a flash of it, like a haunting. But I refused to give in to panic. I was going to dress myself, cover those markings, and from that moment on keep them concealed—from Miles, from my family. Maybe even from myself.

The clothes hanging in my closet seemed unfamiliar. I ran my hand over a row of shirts and considered the cloth, the distinction between each type of fabric. Every detail now was a distraction. I pulled down a turtleneck. From the shelf I selected a pair of gray corduroys, the ribbed cloth like a protective covering of tree bark against my legs. As a final touch, I wound a scarf around my neck. The knit was loose and soft, the color of blood.

A time would come in the future when I'd see changeling girls wearing knee-length skirts, short sleeves, even blouses cut to reveal a sliver of midriff. Unthinkable during my days as a changeling, when we were advised to cover our bodies for our own safety. I'd want to tell those girls what it was like for me: how I relied on layers, spreads of cotton and wool I pulled harshly across my skin. These were natural fibers, breathable but heavy when wet, and it was only when I piled them on that I felt safe. As a new changeling, I dressed without imagining the lightness girls might one day experience, or how their likeliest threat of exposure was skin growing hot from the pounding force of the sun.

MY MOTHER CAME to my room to make sure I was ready for school. She was still wearing her nightgown, and her feet were bare.

"Celeste." Her voice sounded sharp at first, but then she looked closer and understood. A fleeting range of emotions crossed her face—sorrow, fear, love—and I saw her for all she was, every part of her. She wasn't just my mother standing in my doorway but a whole woman with a past and future. When I thought of her losing Miles in only a few years, I was so grief-stricken that I got up and hugged her.

Once we pulled back, my mother touched my cheek. I thought she might cry.

"I don't know why I'm so emotional. I knew this would happen soon enough." She forced a smile and sank into the desk chair. Her nightgown, patterned with tiny bluebirds, bunched around her hips.

I got into bed and pulled my knees against my chest.

"I'm supposed to look now," she told me, but neither of us moved.

"What would happen," I said, "if I didn't show you?"

She laughed gently. "I suppose the longer I wait, the longer you're still a little girl."

"I mean, what if I didn't show anyone at all." I paused. "Ever."

She didn't laugh this time. "That's not possible."

"I don't see why not. They're my markings."

"They are, but they aren't." She sounded weary. "It's odd—I don't even wonder what your markings say about me. It seems unnatural, to not be curious. Maybe I've lived too long with the weight of a future I ultimately can't control. Not as a woman, anyway." She paused, as if startled by her own words, and I seized my chance.

"It's possible for you to not know. Just don't look."

"But there's Miles, and your father. And the government check. You'll only have a week or so before they get to your changeling inspection."

I sat up a little straighter. "I'm sure Miles and Dad will accept it eventually. And I can sign the conscientious objector paperwork at school."

"You'd only damage your own future. You won't get into university without transcripts."

She was right. If I decided to hide myself forever, I would amount to nothing. Still, I refused to give in.

"Maybe I can at least keep things private here at home."

She shook her head. "I might be willing to go without knowing, but not your father or Miles. Men are different, you know that. They're greedy for it. It's biological."

I was close to tears. My body had changed overnight, my senses were prickling, and I had no control over what was to come. "I want to keep my future to myself."

She peered at me. "Are you hiding something, Celeste?"

"I just want privacy. It's exhausting, being on display all the time."

My mother met my eyes. She not only believed me, but she agreed with me, too—I could read it right there in the worried set of her mouth, the tiny wrinkles sprouting near her eyes. With a sigh, she moved to the edge of my bed and put her hand on the back of my neck.

"I'll do my best with your father and brother." Her voice was low. Everything we did from that moment on was secret. "But we will fail in the end. We'll try, but we'll fail."

She drew me closer and kissed my temple.

"We should get you the birth control shot," she added. "Just in case."

"I can't believe it's time for that already."

"Me, either. But we're fortunate to have access to birth control, and we need to take advantage of it." I knew she was right, that unrestricted access to the shot was a luxury that women in rural areas didn't have.

I waited for my mother to say more, to reassure me or express hope for the future. Anything. But her face remained impassive. I felt I was watching my mother at a funeral, or in the aftermath of some spectacular accident. The light of the tragedy casting shadows across her face.

I STAYED HOME from school that first day. Miles woke up late, as usual, our mother pressing him to hurry. I could hear their conversation from behind my closed bedroom door, just as I could hear Miles rustling the covers, stumbling out of bed, and getting dressed. His motions were heavy, as though part of him was still asleep. I imagined all the ways he might die: Car crash. Leukemia. An accidental fall from a great height. Undiagnosed heart defect. Aneurysm. Random act of violence.

Any option was too terrible to contemplate, so I wondered instead how Miles would react if he learned the truth. To know your life would be cut short before the age of twenty-one—it was too much. I knew all about fate, how it could not be changed or escaped, and how we exercised free will as a thin layer atop a larger destiny. All I could do was wait for his future to unfurl. If I kept the prediction from Miles, at least he wouldn't have to bear the weight, too.

By the time Miles headed down the stairs, he was too rushed to notice I was still in my room, that I had transformed overnight. He must have assumed I'd already left. When I heard the front door close behind him, I let out a breath and nestled deeper in bed.

I'd forgotten about my father. It was his first week back at work following the suspension, but he hadn't left for the office yet. When he passed my room in the hall a few minutes later, he paused. I sensed him standing there, breathing, before he knocked.

"Yes?" I worked to keep my voice steady.

My father eased the door open. He was ready for work: dress shirt, striped tie, his hair damp and combed back. I smelled a jab of aftershave.

"Celeste?" he asked, a note of surprise in his voice.

"Hi, Dad. I'm sick."

Then I burst into tears.

He came over to my bed and sat down, reaching out to stroke my hair. He'd barely made contact when he pulled back sharply, like I was electric.

My mother appeared in the doorway, and he turned to face her. "What do they say?" he asked.

She didn't answer him.

"Paulette?" He looked bewildered. "All right. If you don't want to tell me, that's fine. I need to look for myself anyway."

"Not now." My mother came inside and took his arm, gently pulling him toward the door. "Give Celeste some space."

My father glanced over his shoulder at me. Flustered, flailing. I reminded myself that he had no sisters. This was new to him, too. When he met my mother in university, the story went, she knew right away that he was her future husband. She said her markings pointed to him as her match. My father, meanwhile, was skeptical. He thought her markings could be interpreted in more than one way, and he worried about making a mistake. But my mother was certain. She wooed him, determined, until my father gave up. "I did love her, right from the start," he always said when telling this story. "I just didn't know how to trust it."

"Please, Dad," I told him. "I'd like to be alone."

He hesitated. His eyes flicked to his watch and then back to me. He wouldn't risk being late for work.

"We'll discuss this later." He hovered in my doorway for another moment, staring at me like I was a problem he could solve. Finally, he gave up and left.

After he'd gone, my mother brought me a dry bagel and some orange juice. The bagel kept me busy for a while. I ruminated on every crumb in my mouth, considering the dense texture of the dough, the slick crust of egg wash, the yeast and the salt. Some girls couldn't stand to eat the first day they'd changed, but I finished the whole bagel, letting each ingredient become a part of me. I followed it with a swig of orange juice. That first sip was like a slap, the liquid thick and vivid in my mouth. Too sweet, too bright—it was like swallowing the sun. I waited for the sugars to dissolve on my tongue before taking a second, more tentative sip. If I focused, I could dull my senses enough to handle it.

After I ate, I tried to read. I wanted to distract myself, to pretend I hadn't seen those markings on my left side. But I saw the prediction every time I turned a page, my mind drawing connections between the letters of each word and the constellations on my body. This form of apophenia was why some changelings struggled in school: the hyperfocus that came from high lucidity could mislead, could make us see things that weren't as meaningful as our brains believed they were. Maybe that was what happened with the prediction on my ribs—I'd overthought it, drawn too many connections.

I got up, slipped out of my clothes, and went to the full-length mirror. While my body had been maturing for months, all the developments came into sharper focus at the onset of the changeling period. There was my new body: the fuller breasts, the curve of hip, the soft hair between my legs. I was a woman.

Downstairs, the front door slammed shut. I felt it more than heard it, a physical blow that echoed through my body. It was still ringing inside me when I heard Miles's voice. I dove for my clothes and covered myself as quickly as possible, wondering how he'd found out. I was barely dressed by the time he'd bounded up the stairs and rattled the doorknob to my room.

"Celeste, it's me."

I said nothing.

"Celeste!" He was desperate, not himself. I was not myself, either. I put my hand to the doorknob but did not move. I was afraid that once I came face-to-face with Miles, he'd look different to me. I couldn't imagine him being my same brother, not anymore.

"Please show me," he said. "I need to know."

"Miles, stop. Give her time." My mother's voice, soft and low. I listened as she pulled him away from my room.

Not long ago, my brother had confessed he worried something terrible would come to pass. I couldn't bear to tell him he was right.

*   *   *

MY MOTHER REPORTED my change through the official channels by calling a local outpost for the Office of the Future, where she was told that due to a backlog, it would take nearly ten days for a government inspector to visit our home to complete my changeling reading. While I was relieved to be gifted this extra time, gossip at school moved more efficiently than the government ever could, so news of my change spread rapidly. By the time the school day had ended, Cassandra and Marie called to check on me, a bit bemused that I insisted on a phone call instead of an in-person visit. This was not an easy choice. I wanted to show my friends my new markings—I wanted to show them so much I felt shaky inside—but the prediction on my left ribs held me back.

I passed the afternoon in my room, gazing out the window. I couldn't read, couldn't study, couldn't think. At last, the sun tracked across the sky and my mother knocked on my door and told me it was time for dinner. I asked if I could eat in my room instead.

"You can't hide forever," she said. "Come downstairs."

I dragged myself from my desk and added a cardigan to my layers of clothing. I pulled my hair from its ponytail and brushed it, willing the fine strands to expand and conceal every inch of my neck. Finally, I took a breath and went downstairs.

My mother had lowered the lights in the kitchen and placed a candle in the middle of the table. Dim lighting, a relief from the newly bright world. Still, my eyes went right to the candle. The flame glittered, whole worlds and reflections contained in its teardrop shape. I fixated on it until my eyes hurt, and then I looked away, blinking.

Through my spotted vision, through the light trails and inky blots, my brother appeared. He sat at the table, next to my father. I took my usual seat across from him.

"Stop staring," I told him.

"You're not yourself." His gaze remained rooted. "You're different."

"Some would say Celeste is more herself now than ever," our father added. He was smiling. "My daughter, all grown up—it doesn't feel real."

I wouldn't turn sixteen until the next day, but that didn't matter. By virtue of passing to my adult markings, age was inconsequential. I was a woman.

My mother brought a pitcher of water to the table along with a loaf of my father's homemade bread. "Homemade" meant he dumped the ingredients into our automatic breadmaker and hit start. He didn't mix them first as the recipe recommended, so the loaves usually came out uneven. Whenever any of us complained, he laughed and said he clearly wasn't fated to be a great cook. But on that night, none of us said much of anything. We ate in heavy silence.

Boiled peas popped against my teeth like starbursts, the butter an oil slick on my tongue. The water had a chemical tinge to it, a pungent bite from the treatment plant. This would take some getting used to—and once I did, my changeling period would end and my senses would dull again. I didn't see the point.

After the meal, my mother stacked our dirty plates. Each clatter felt like a drill bit held against my skull.

"Miles, why don't you get your sister's present?" she said. "Every girl should have a gift on the day she changes." Her voice sounded falsely formal, as though she were reading aloud from an old etiquette book.

Miles gave her a mildly annoyed look but pushed back from the table and left the room. When he returned, he held a package wrapped in plain brown paper that he'd decorated by drawing a scene reminiscent of a fairy tale. Two children—a boy and a girl—stood next to an intricate house, the shadowed tops of trees towering over them. I wondered if the house was made of gingerbread, if the children were lost or in danger. About to be devoured.

I ripped off the paper to reveal an astrology book with Orion on its cover. I knew the story of Orion, how he chased the Pleiades sisters through the sky. I traced his stars with my finger—the bright Betelgeuse, the astonishing Rigel—and imagined other worlds in the unbearable expanse of space.

There was comfort to be found in that book, a nostalgia that Miles clearly valued as much as I did, despite his current disdain for false fortune-telling. When we were kids, he and I read the horoscopes together, laughing at their foolishness. Horoscopes, prophetic dreams, the movement of the stars: what strange fantasies some people entertained about the workings of the future. And not just men, either. Women were susceptible to fantasy, too, though I supposed that made sense. What better way to escape your reality than to imagine your way out of it? Back then Miles and I could afford to pretend the future was no more than another game, something we could create and change at will.

After opening my birthday gift, I thought it only fair that I gave Miles his. I was proud of the present—a set of watercolor pencils, which I bought after months of saving the modest bit of chore money our parents could afford—but when Miles opened it, he fell silent. Only later did I see the implication of my gift. Those pencils, when used in his new, blank notebook, would be perfect for mapping my markings.

"Thanks, Celeste," he finally said. He looked at me, and I tried to imagine what he might be seeing. Surely not a sister capable of both bearing and concealing his ruin.

Mapping the Future:
An Interpretive Guide to Women and Girls

ON FATE AND CERTAINTY

The future is not a heavy, settled thing like a stone, but rather
more like a riverbank: carved by the weight of moving water.

That a woman's predictions are not always *predictable* is a
common source of frustration, but we implore readers to maintain
patience in the face of uncertainty. Some markings, it is true, provide as many questions as answers. A thoughtful interpreter knows
to absorb those inquiries, layering them into her final reading. She
is thorough and careful and slow. Most of all, she respects the few
mysteries available to her.

We ask all readers to be as wise as this learned interpreter—to
remember that fate will unfold regardless of our demands, and that
knowing a great deal about our futures does not entitle us to know
it all.

8

THAT NIGHT I locked my door and wrapped myself in blankets. I pictured our cobwebbed basement, the word *LIE* etched into the dirt. Of the two of us, Miles had always been better at keeping secrets, but it was time for me to learn. I'd have to be careful, and smart, and I could never slip up. Not even once.

Sleep came in spurts, in drifting periods of shallow unconsciousness. When morning finally broke, I waited until I heard Miles leave for school and then got in the shower, running the water as hot as I could stand it. Afterward, I wrapped myself in a towel and stepped into the hall. My mother had agreed to let me stay home for one more day, but she'd gone to the store and the house felt too quiet and empty.

When I passed Miles's room, I noticed his birthday presents lying on the bed. There, right on top, were the watercolor pencils I'd given him. A few spilled halfway from the opened package. Red, purple, green, brown. I let my gaze linger on the brown one. It was a fawn-colored shade, the color of my markings. I grabbed it and took it back to my bedroom.

Down went the towel to the ground. In front of the mirror, I pressed the pencil to my cheek. When I pulled back, a perfect dot floated on the surface of my skin. If I only gave it a passing glance, I couldn't distinguish this mark from a real one.

I placed my index finger on the fake mole, applying pressure. When I lifted my finger the counterfeit mark remained, unchanged. I rubbed at it lightly, but still it endured. A tissue dampened in my water glass and more furious scrubbing finally erased it.

With the thrill of blasphemy, I examined the moles on my left side. Adding a single dot in the star-shaped cluster would change its meaning. I lowered the pencil to my skin.

"Celeste?" My father called. "Can I come in?" He was just outside my closed door. I jumped and grabbed the towel from the floor. I had been careless; I should have remained dressed and in bed until he left for work.

"Not now," I called back, tucking the towel securely around my body. "I just got out of the shower and I'm not dressed."

An uncomfortable silence. "That's all right," he said at last. "That's actually why I'm here. I'm coming in. Okay?"

I watched in horror as the door started to unlock. Our parents had keys to our bedrooms, for emergencies, but they'd never used them before. I tossed the colored pencil into the space between my dresser and the wall and clutched the towel to my body as my father stepped in the room.

It looked like he had dressed in a hurry; his shirt was half untucked, his hair uncombed, the shadow of stubble still drifting across his jaw. He shut the door behind him with a click.

"This isn't an ideal situation for either of us," he began.

"Later. We can do this later." My voice was shaking. My legs were shaking.

"Your mother told me you plan to hide your markings." He looked at me sadly. "I know this is difficult, but I need your help, Celeste. The whole family does. Your future is ours, too—surely you can see that."

Tears filled my eyes. I could only shake my head.

"Dad." I hated the high pitch to my voice. "It's my birthday. You can wait until tomorrow, can't you?"

He took a step closer, then reached into his pocket and pulled out a camera. "We should have done it yesterday."

"You're going to *photograph* me?"

He looked embarrassed. "This is to prevent Miles from wanting to do a reading, too. Don't worry, I'll only photograph your markings up close. Now please, Celeste. I'm scared, too, but let's get through this together."

With a pained expression, he moved closer. I heard a ticking that I thought was my heart but turned out to be a steady drip coming off my wet hair. All around me, the inevitability of my life and future churned. There was no escaping it. So I gave in.

I looked off to the side, away from my father, and I let my towel drop to the ground.

MILES WOULD HAVE known. My mother would have known. Anyone except my father would have known that one of the moles nestled among the others was fake.

"That's interesting," he said. He picked up the camera and focused it on my ribs. I stood rigid with my arms crossed over my breasts, trying not to breathe. He didn't notice anything was amiss. When he moved on from my left side to focus on another pattern, I could finally exhale. But he needed to check every marking, and to do this thoroughly, he had to touch. Hands on my back, my calves, the pulse at my throat. We didn't make eye contact. I didn't utter a single word.

Afterward I swaddled myself in blankets and lay on the bed, staring at the ceiling. I couldn't stop thinking of my father's shaking hands, how he positioned the camera close to my markings and made the shutter click. As if I weren't a person but a map.

Wearily, I slid from bed and dressed. Now that it was over, I knew I could survive it.

Once my father left for work, I retrieved the pencil from behind the dresser and returned it to Miles's room. My mother still wasn't home. For a while I wandered the empty house like I was looking for something I'd lost. Eventually, I gravitated toward a window and looked out toward the mailbox. Bringing in the mail—that was a simple, concrete task I could accomplish.

The front door opened with a slow creak. I poked my head outside. The air felt fresh and pure, and the sun shined on. I stepped outside and paused, listening. It wasn't that I expected someone might appear and attack me right there, in daylight in front of my own house, but rather that anything seemed possible. The world buzzed with uncertainty, with risk.

But I was also at home, in my own neighborhood, and it was a glorious day. The leaves of the red maple across the street trembled in the breeze. A patch of clover sprang back into shape after I stepped on it. When I looked up, I saw the whole of the sky at once, all those layers of blue.

At the mailbox, I sifted through a magazine, the electric and water bills, and a soft, cream-colored envelope embossed with a red square—the official insignia of the Office of the Future. I tore into the envelope. Inside was a form letter, two sentences long, denying Miles's request to revise *Mapping the Future*.

I lowered the letter and stared out at my neighborhood. I observed only invisible things: wind, the rising chill in the air, a sour odor leaking from the sewer. My high lucidity gave me beauty but also vulgarity. As I stood with my brother's letter in my hands, it was the ugliness that consumed me—as though something ominous had taken hold there in my front yard, had burst to life as surely as the envelope's red square imprinted a dull mark against my palm.

MY MOTHER CAME home with a bouquet of orange and red poppies. She'd chosen poppies because they were scentless; she still remembered her own changeling days, when her father gave her daisies that emitted an odor so strong it turned her stomach. I thanked her for the flowers and watched as she sorted the mail I'd left out on the counter—everything except Miles's letter, which I'd delivered directly to his desk.

I was admiring the rich saturation of the poppies when the doorbell rang. I already knew it was Marie and Cassandra. It was just late enough for school to be out, and besides, I could hear their notes of laughter outside, the rustling of their clothing and hair. This was what high lucidity was meant for: to eliminate the element of surprise.

When I opened the door, my friends stared, their eyes sparking.

"You look so pretty," Marie said. She didn't try to hide the wonder in her voice and hugged me hard, as if we'd been separated for ages.

I turned to Cassandra. When she and I embraced, I felt our hearts beating together, as if they were syncing. Maybe they were. Back then I believed my friends were the center of my universe, the sun that all else orbited. With them, I had always been able to reveal my full self. Until now. To successfully conceal Miles's fate, I had to hide it from everyone, including Marie and Cassandra. I didn't relish lying to my friends—I considered it a deception, even if only a lie by omission—but it had to be done.

I took my friends up to my room, where Cassandra flung herself on my bed.

"All right," she said, "let's see it."

I took a step back. "I've decided not to show anyone."

My friends exchanged a glance.

"Surely you've shown your mother," Marie said.

"No."

"Miles?"

I shook my head.

"But your father." Cassandra narrowed her eyes. "Did he?"

I turned my face away. "Yes. He looked this morning."

The room was silent for a long stretch. Cassandra picked at the bedspread and wouldn't meet my eyes. I thought back to her coming-out party, when her father had led her away to her bedroom. When Cassandra returned to the party, she refused to talk about it, said it was something every girl went through and that it was too embarrassing to dwell on.

"Give us a hint about your marriage prediction, at least," Cassandra said. "Will you end up with someone good?"

I had to think. Aside from the prediction about Miles, my future appeared perfectly ordinary.

"There are no details," I said. "Just that I'll marry at some point. I don't
know who it will be, or when. The markings for children are vague, too. A
family is a possibility, but I see nothing concrete." This was all true, and
with each word I spoke, I felt a bit more dejected.

"No illnesses?" Marie asked. Her father's death had been predicted in
her own childhood moles. As a baby and toddler, she carried the mark of
his fate on her body. Then he died and her markings endured, a reminder
of her grief until they could be replaced upon her change.

"None that I can see." Nothing aside from Miles, dead by twenty-one.

"Then we should celebrate," Cassandra said. "To your long and
happy life."

My expression must have given something away, because Marie grabbed
my hand. She looked so concerned that I teared up. Not only was Miles in
danger, but my friends and I were facing one another across a gulf growing
wider by the moment.

"I think I understand what you're feeling." Cassandra patted my arm.
"The high lucidity is disorienting at first. But don't worry, you'll get used
to it."

Marie didn't say anything more, but she kept watching me. Like she
thought I might self-destruct right there in front of her.

It was only later that my friends reminded me it was my birthday. Marie
presented me with a card she and Cassandra had both signed, and as a gift,
they gave me a framed print of one of the old impression tests that psy-
chologists once used. The image consisted of a black teardrop shape with a
red smudge in the middle.

"My mother ordered it for us," Cassandra said. "It was in a catalogue of
curiosities."

I brought the frame closer and stared deep into the red heart of the
drawing. The whole point of impression tests was to encourage each viewer
to project their own ideas and realities onto a drawing, but this one felt
so certain to me. It was a flame, it was fire—there could be no other

interpretation. I stared for so long my vision blurred, and the frame grew hot in my hands. It was a gift, I reminded myself. It was art.

It was my future, burning and bright and encased in breakable glass.

AFTER CASSANDRA AND Marie left, my mother took me to the doctor's office for my birth control shot. She held my hand while the nurse slid a needle into my arm. At first the shot burned, like a splash of poison had been put into my veins, but within a few seconds I felt fine. Already it was behind me.

"There," my mother said. She stood up and gathered her things. "Now that's done."

At home, I found Miles alone in his room. He was studying the photographs of my markings and copying the patterns in his new notebook. He used the brown pencil to dot out the markings and the periwinkle to lightly trace constellations between moles. I watched him work and thought about stars, galaxies, the entirety of the observable universe. The mystery of what might lie beyond.

When Miles noticed I was in his doorway, he picked up his letter from the Office of the Future and waved it at me.

"You were right." He tossed the envelope down again. "Denied. But it's okay. I'll think of something else."

"Like what?"

He ignored that and stared intently at the photographs. "I have to say, I'm surprised by how uneventful these markings are." He held up the photo showing the cluster of moles on my left side. "This is the one that catches my attention. What do you think it means?"

I took a moment to pretend to study the prediction. "It seems to indicate a big life change for you just before you turn twenty-one. If I had to guess, I'd say a move."

"Yes." He frowned at the photograph. "But it doesn't quite add up."

"Maybe you'll go to graduate school."

He squinted. "It's not that."

"You might study abroad, or join the military, get married and buy a house," I said, rattling off all the events that could possibly line up with my altered markings.

"Perhaps," he said, deep in thought. "Or maybe it's related to your childhood prediction, the one about us working together one day." He looked up from the photographs. "Remember? It's gone now. I don't see anything in your new markings quite like it."

I kept my expression neutral. "That prediction had an outlier marking. And now my career pattern is so open-ended it's like everything's canceled out."

"I suppose. But something's not adding up."

I tried to appear uninterested, but inside, I knew the truth. My juvenile career marking wasn't wrong—a girl's predictions could not be contradicted, even after the passage to adulthood—but now that it was clear my brother only had three years to live, we simply didn't have much time to work together. As a result, that particular prediction did not shine through in my adult markings. It seemed the outlier marking from my childhood days had been the dominant one after all: I'd end up working alone.

"If you let me see that pattern in person, I'd have a chance of figuring it out." He looked up at me hopefully. "You've always shared your markings with me. Besides, it's my birthday today, too."

"I'm sorry, Miles. But no."

He stared down at his drawing pad, resigned. "It doesn't make sense," he muttered. I couldn't tell if he was talking to me or himself. "It's not here. I expected it to be here."

"What do you mean?" When he didn't respond, I took a step into his room. "Miles. What did you expect to see?"

His eyes fluttered up to me, then back down to the copies of my markings. "I told you I've always felt something awful might be coming."

I felt chilled. I crossed my right hand over to my left elbow, where I'd once had that vague set of markings. No one had known what they meant, but maybe Miles had an inkling. Maybe he saw in those childhood markings what no one else could: a hint of his own fate.

"You worry too much." I tried to keep my voice light, but my throat felt scratched, every word a choke. It was not in my nature to lie to Miles.

"Maybe." He looked up once more, and our eyes locked. We were in the basement again, down in the dirt. We were playing the most important game of Did You Know in our lives. I told myself to keep it up, to conceal the secret at all costs.

"The trouble is," Miles said at last, "that the future is the future. It cannot be stopped. So even if we knew that something terrible was coming, it couldn't be prevented."

My heart, my lungs, my entire body: I felt it all under strain, the blood rushing in a panic. He didn't know. He couldn't. The way his face grew puzzled when he considered the image of the altered marking on my ribs—he had no idea what was coming for him.

"Exactly," I said, and this time I succeeded in sounding calm. "The future is set."

Miles turned back to his drawings. The more he studied them, the more his concern washed away. I saw it happen, watched his body language relax into complacency. I was relieved and guilty and proud, because everything I'd told him was a lie. And every lie was practice.

ON HIGH LUCIDITY

Through this natural wonder, changeling girls are gifted the strength and advantages they need to move safely through the world. A changeling in the throes of high lucidity is, in fact, living out the beatific potential of her sex. She is experiencing one of nature's most glorious privileges while benefiting from an ancient form of protection.

How any changeling can protest, experience fear, or permit herself to be damaged while in this state is a mystery not to be examined by this panel of authors. Time is too fleeting, and the state of lucidity too brief, to waste with such concerns. We direct changelings to be grateful for this phenomenon, and to respect it as one of nature's forms of grace granted only to women. What a blessing to receive this gift. How astonishing to be a woman in this world!

9

To be a changeling was to be exposed, peeled back and laid bare. At school, I could no longer slip by as an anonymous girl. I startled people, making them jump like they'd just heard a clap of thunder. My history teacher cocked his head whenever I passed his classroom, and outside, the boys running on the athletic field shifted simultaneously as I walked along the fence line.

That morning, I turned from my locker to find myself surrounded by boys. They appeared as if from nowhere and fanned around me, creating a barrier too strong to break through. Dirty blue jeans, untucked shirts, ragged haircuts, shoes streaked with grass stains. They were earthy and unapologetic in their disarray as only boys could be.

"Can you give me some space?" I asked.

The boys leaned forward a few degrees, and I clutched my geometry book to my chest like a shield. I was protecting myself, but I was also holding myself back. I saw my male classmates in a new way that morning. They were thrilling and raw, bodies driven by want. New thoughts drifted into my mind: thoughts of kissing and contact, of those flat boy chests pressing right up against me.

The boys drew closer. My back was against the lockers. A wanting started to crack through my body, a surge that broke off in pieces like a glacier calving. I desired power, I desired control, I desired freedom. I desired.

One boy reached out, his fingertip inches from my shoulder. *Keep going,* I thought, while also thinking at the same time: *Stop.*

My homeroom teacher, a woman of cardigans that smelled of mothballs, was the one to save me. She hurried up to the boys and startled them, made them scatter like birds taking flight. When I caught her eye, she smiled.

"Boys," she said simply, like that was explanation enough.

I MOVED FROM class to class in a blur. I was getting better at controlling my senses, at tamping down the sensory data flooding every moment. Some girls fell in love with their high lucidity and went through a depression once it came to an end. Others tried to make money off it, by hiring themselves out to chefs to be expert taste testers, or by creating new color palettes for designers. But not everyone trusted high lucidity. Some people considered it false, a form of hysteria.

Cassandra was the type to embrace her heightened senses. We met in the school bathroom and stood in front of a single mirror, our hip bones jutting against the sink. Cassandra leaned in close to study her pores. She said it was like seeing straight into her body. I opened my mouth wide and peered at my molars, my uvula, the soft tissue under my tongue. I laughed a little. It was nothing short of bizarre, all that was inside us.

I took off my sweater, relieved to feel unburdened of the hot material for at least a few moments. Underneath, I wore a sleeveless undershirt, and Cassandra reached out to touch my upper arm. She ran her finger up and down, calling the tiny hairs along my arm to attention.

"Your skin is so soft," she said. "Was it like this before your change?"

"I have no idea." I reached for her hair, all gloss and velvet. It felt heavy, like I could weigh the protein in each strand.

So much of what people said about changeling girls was urban legend. If someone had burst into that bathroom right then, they might have started a rumor about Cassandra and me, how we turned to each other out of sheer, mindless attraction. But this wasn't about sex for us. It was about wonder, and mystery, and the joy of feeling the slightest touch to the core of your being. It was the kind of connection only possible between changeling girls.

The bell rang, signaling the start of the next class. I slid my sweater back on and we headed to Cassandra's locker. Our teachers would forgive us for being late. They made allowances for changelings, understanding it was difficult for us to be in school in our state.

I leaned against the wall of lockers as Cassandra searched for a book. She was stretched up on her tiptoes, rooting through the top shelf of her locker, when Jonah appeared behind her.

Jonah was a fourth-year, like Miles. He was on the baseball team and also on the drum line, a rare combination, and some mornings he showed up to school without bothering to shave. There in the hallway he crept silently toward Cassandra, shooting me a sly look like he expected me to keep his secret. He edged so close that his breath was probably on the back of her neck. She surely sensed him there, surely heard him and smelled him and even felt the draft of air moving around his body, but she pretended not to. A game.

When Cassandra finally whirled around to face Jonah, he didn't back up. Not one inch. Instead he laughed and reached for a strand of her hair. I'd held her hair only moments before, which had seemed right, and harmless. This was something else.

Cassandra smiled at him. Jonah tugged the lock of hair a little, bringing her closer. If I weren't standing right there, maybe he would have kissed her. Watching Jonah and Cassandra together made me think about the guidelines for appropriate behavior for changeling girls outlined in *Mapping the Future*. For the first time I wanted more rules, a whole host of them, anything to keep my friend safe. I didn't like how she was looking at this older boy, how she was leaning closer every second.

Jonah finally acknowledged me.

"Celeste, wow," he said. "Being a changeling suits you."

Cassandra shut her locker, hard. "Being a changeling suits everyone."

I looked around the hallway, which had emptied completely. The silence felt ominous.

"I need to talk to you, Cassie," I said. "Alone."

"Are you sure?" She was still gazing at Jonah.

"Yes. Right now."

"Go ahead," Jonah told Cassandra. "We'll meet up later." He squeezed her shoulder, and I felt something like static go through the air. He walked backwards for the first few steps, keeping his eyes on us, before he turned and disappeared around the corner.

"You shouldn't get that close to a boy, Cassie," I said after he'd gone. "It's risky. Even if you trust Jonah, it might give the wrong idea to other boys. Or men."

"We're in school. Public places are safe." She put a hand on my arm. "Don't be paranoid."

"I'm just saying it's better to wait until your changeling period is over before getting mixed up with Jonah."

"I can't wait." Her voice started to rise. "New girls start changing all the time. I have to catch his attention now."

"At least promise me you won't go anywhere with him alone."

Cassandra looked exasperated. "You need to relax. No one's getting hurt here." She bent down to zip her backpack, pulling the metal teeth together with a swift flick of her wrist. "No one else will tell you this, so I will," she added. "You're becoming a bore."

"Cassie. Don't."

"I'm serious, Celeste. If you're not careful, no one will want to bother with you. You make things too difficult."

She grabbed the bag by its straps and turned to leave. I waited, stunned, but she didn't apologize. She didn't even look back.

*　*　*

AT THAT TIME in my life, I experienced the possibility of losing a friend as a trauma. Friendships were important to me, *Cassandra* was important to me, and the prospect of a rift in our relationship just then, when I needed her most, was agonizing.

On that day, I worried I'd already lost her. When school let out, Cassandra was nowhere to be found, Marie was in her domestic arts club, and Miles had headed straight downtown to Julia's. I walked home with a group of girls I didn't know well. Elissa, Janet, and Ali. They adopted me, moving in a protective formation that placed their bodies between mine and passersby. Later I'd learn that Miles had set it up, insisting on a small crowd to walk me home even though it was daylight, hours from dusk.

A few times, I glanced over my shoulder to see if Cassandra would appear. She didn't. I hoped she'd found someone to walk home with, anyone aside from Jonah.

"Look," Elissa whispered. She had red hair and freckles spelling a flurry of predictions across her cheeks. "That man across the street—he can't stop staring at Celeste."

We turned to see a young man, dressed for a workout in running shoes and athletic shorts, gawking at me. When he saw us looking he turned away abruptly, stumbling over his own feet.

The other girls clutched one another and laughed.

"Good thing we were here to save you," Janet said. "He might have dragged you off somewhere so he could pretend you were his girlfriend."

She and the others kept laughing, but I felt sick. The gentleness in that man's expression, his sheer embarrassment—it was wrong to lump him in with monstrous men.

"It's not funny," I said. "Think of Deirdre."

That quieted them down. We walked in silence for a while, passing neighbors raking leaves, biking, painting shutters. I smelled the paint, registered the tick-tick of a piece of plastic in bicycle spokes, could practically feel a yellowed leaf crushed by the rake. These were the everyday parts of life, lulling me into a sense of normalcy even as they were heightened, warped, made dazzling by my change.

When we reached my house, I cut through my front yard.

"Thanks," I called back. The girls waved and carried on. I watched them for a second from the front stoop. It struck me as natural that there were three of them, a trio of friends traveling in a pack. I looked forward to calmer days, when Cassandra, Marie, and I could return to our old ways of being with one another.

I fumbled for my key. We kept the house locked all the time now that I was a changeling, even in daylight and when everyone was home. My father insisted on it. I followed his rules even if he often wasn't present to enforce them—we were both so humiliated by his marking inspection that we'd begun avoiding each other. I was starting to wonder how, exactly, the father-daughter inspection ritual had persisted over the years. Women were superior at reading markings, after all, and mothers could read their daughters more freely, with less embarrassment.

But had my mother inspected my markings, she would have known the truth about the prediction on my ribs. In that sense, I was lucky it was my father. The tradition, as humiliating as it was, had helped me.

Inside, I dropped my backpack and climbed the stairs. My mother was in the upstairs hallway, laboring under the weight of shopping bags. I followed as she dragged them into her bedroom.

"I thought we had to watch our spending," I said.

She hefted the bags onto her bed and swept a few sweaty strands of hair from her temple. "I'm going back to work. For a full position this time, not just contract work."

I grabbed one of the bags and peeled it open. It contained neat stacks of dress pants, skirts, and collared shirts. My mother's career markings were incomplete; they indicated success in a career path that helped others but otherwise provided few specifics. She had become a teacher and then worked in education policy. After she quit her job to have Miles and me, she occasionally worked on a freelance basis for her old employer, a charter school consortium, but never anything long-term or full-time. These clothes represented something different.

"Can you believe I didn't have anything professional to wear that still fits? It just goes to show that there are still some surprises in life." She gave my arm a playful jab. "Even for us."

"When do you start?" My mouth felt dry, scaled over.

"Next week. I tried to negotiate a later start date, but they needed someone immediately." She began pulling out her new purchases and smoothing them on the bed. "I'm looking forward to getting back to it."

Before I was born, she'd won a Teacher of the Year award, and a regional magazine published a profile about her. That magazine issue sat by itself in the top drawer of one of the end tables in the living room. I once heard my father saying we should frame it, but my mother refused. She believed in modesty and sacrifice. When she was a new graduate, she worked for Teachers of the Nation, a program that placed young teachers in inner-city schools. She still spoke of her experiences there, usually when she wanted to make a point to Miles and me that we were spoiled.

She took my hands in her own. Her skin was cool and dry and familiar. "Something bothering you?"

I could only think of the markings on my left side, and how they foretold part of the future that perhaps shouldn't be predicted at all. Certain predictions were too severe, too grief-filled, to be laid bare on our bodies. And yet there I was, with this marking unveiling my brother's fate.

"Mothers almost never know," I said slowly, "if their children will die young. Why not?"

Her expression morphed into alarm. "Why are you asking that?"

I gently pulled my hands away. "I was thinking of Donny Rheinholdt."

She softened. "That was horrible." Donny and Miles had been friends. A few years ago, Donny rode his bike across an intersection without looking and was hit by a car. Donny only had brothers, no sisters, so no one had the chance to be marked with his death.

"His mother didn't see it coming. Why didn't her markings give a hint of what would happen? Girls get marked with bad news all the time. Marie knew her whole life when her father would get sick and die."

"I don't know, sweetheart. For a mother to lose a child is one of the worst tragedies imaginable. Maybe we aren't given what we can't handle."

"But why? Our markings give us so many clues about the future. They'll indicate whether we'll get sick and die young. They usually say if we'll have kids, and whether the family will be a happy one." I thought of the pale dots on my mother's stomach, her shining stars of two children situated close together to indicate closeness in real life. "But certain things never appear in the markings. Like suicides, murder, abductions. Sometimes I'd rather have no predictions than an incomplete view of the future."

"Oh, Celeste. I know it can be torture to know a little but not everything. It's especially hard right after you change, when your future has been upended." She stopped to look at me. "What I'm trying to say is that it's normal to feel a little depressed right now."

"I'm not depressed." I stood and moved out of her reach. "I saw Donny's little brother at school today, that's all. It made me think of them, and how sad the funeral was. Remember?"

"I do. You were brave to come with us to support Miles." She paused, her expression thoughtful. "I admit I'm relieved. I know we have your father's reading, but I thought you were trying to tell me you'd seen something terrible in your future. A disease, an accident, a short or painful life."

I forced a smile. "Of course not."

I could never let my mother know what was coming for Miles—that was clear. The truth would be too much for her to bear.

IN MY SHORT time as a changeling, I'd already developed a few coping mechanisms for the high lucidity. One was to close all the blinds in my room and lie in the dark while listening to *Top of the Hits* on my portable radio. I loved *Top of the Hits* because it was more or less the same every day. I lay on my comforter in the dark and listened, my eyes tracking the dull glints from the plastic stars on the ceiling. Every song was about one of three things: unrequited love, lost love, or fated love affairs that had not yet begun.

A ballad in which a man sang about the journey to find his fated wife had just wrapped up when my mother knocked on my door to tell me Cassandra had called for me. I headed downstairs to the phone, squinting against the lights. In my mind I kept seeing Cassandra, only hours before, insulting me by her locker.

"I need you to meet me at Marie's house," Cassandra said. Just like that, as though our encounter at school had never happened.

I glanced out the window. It was growing dark, the treetops in the backyard turning black and tangled. I'd need to convince my mother to drive me.

"I thought Marie was busy tonight," I said.

"She is. That's a cover. Rebecca Delbanco is having one of her parties, and we're going."

Rebecca was a fourth-year. She and Miles attended the art camp together every summer. For the past few years, she'd hosted parties in honor of newly changed girls. Other girls were invited, too, including those who still hadn't changed, but I had never before been included among them.

"I don't know," I said slowly. I wanted to tell Cassandra that going out at night was a terrible idea, but I stopped myself. The word *bore* reverberated in my mind.

"We're only keeping it a secret because of what happened to Deirdre, to prevent our parents from worrying." Cassandra paused, her voice turning gentle. "Celeste, please. I need you there. Besides, these parties are a tradition."

We were meant to revere tradition, especially when it came to our markings. The readings, the professional interpreters, the rose sherry at coming-out parties, the connections shared among girls and women—it was all hallowed ground. I remembered that moment in the school bathroom with Cassandra, how in love we were with our newness and each other. She was my best friend, and I needed her more than ever now that I carried the burden of Miles's fate. What she had said to me in the hallway at school was just an outburst, I decided, a symptom of this tumultuous time in her life.

"All right," I told her. "I'll get a ride."

I hung up the phone and dressed in a long-sleeved shirt and a thin black scarf stitched through with silver thread. I added a dab of lipstick and studied myself in the mirror. I felt covered but visible. Protected yet accessible. Yes and no, bright and dark, pleasure and pain—all of it waiting within the universe of my own body.

MAPPING THE FUTURE:
AN INTERPRETIVE GUIDE TO WOMEN AND GIRLS

ON HISTORY AND TRADITION

In the beginning, when the body of woman was first understood to bear the future, the interpretative arts were a rolling dark sea. Prophesies emerged as stars in the night: separate points capable of telling a greater story when viewed as one. And so women were anointed. And so flesh became future.

Our modern traditions illuminate our rise from that shadowy past. Coming-out celebrations for newly changed girls acknowledge the profound way young bodies are gifted with prescience. The father-daughter inspection ritual recognizes that fathers, while unmarked themselves, gave their daughters life and thus the future. Daughters, in turn, carry the responsibility of sharing what is to come with others.

But traditions among women are perhaps the most powerful. Mothers and daughters, sisters, female friends—when women and girls gather together, they speak their own language of the future. For this we must be grateful. It is women alone who bear the truth and weight of prophecy. It is women who offer this gift to the larger world.

And it is women we thank, through tradition and ritual, for enabling us to spread the sacred word of the future, the truth, and the light.

10

MARIE AND HER parents were visiting her aunt across town that night. I'd gone there with Marie once before, to the stuffy house with aqua carpeting and a screened-in porch patched with duct tape. The aunt lived alone, a single woman whose markings indicated she'd never marry or pursue a lucrative career. She chain-smoked on the porch, stabbing her cigarette butts against an antique ashtray shaped like a fish. The aunt wasn't a modest dresser like Marie's mother, and when I'd been there, she wore a camisole that showed stretched-out bra straps the color of dishwater. I could picture Marie sitting in her aunt's house that night, picking at a stale piece of coffee cake and watching the clock tick its way toward the time she could leave.

My mother seemed in a good mood as she drove me to Marie's house. I felt guilty for betraying her, and nervous that I'd be exposed, and afraid for what the night would bring if I succeeded in this deception. But when we arrived, I saw that Marie's family had left lights on in all the windows, making the home look bright and safe. That, at least, was a relief.

I unclicked my seat belt and hurriedly thanked my mother for the ride. I worried she might insist on walking me to the door. Thankfully, Cassandra appeared in the driveway just then, illuminated by the headlights. She wore a red maxi dress with a long-sleeved cardigan. My mother waved to her.

"Cassie looks lovely," she said. "Chic but covered up. Just the way she should be."

For a moment, I felt guilty. My mother trusted me, would never suspect that I'd conspire with Cassandra in this way. There was so much she didn't know about both of her children now. Again, my mind filled with visions of what might happen to Miles: An overdose. A respiratory infection. Slipping on ice and hitting his head.

"Have fun tonight, and be safe," my mother added, but her words sounded automatic. She believed I would pass an uneventful evening inside Marie's house. She couldn't sense that something had changed, that I was capable of deceiving her.

I slid from the car before she could change her mind. Cassandra hurried over to me and, after one final wave for my mother, pulled me around to the back of the house. My mother, no doubt, assumed we were going straight inside the back door. Instead we stood hidden in the shadows, our backs pressed against the aluminum siding. The neighbors next door were having a party. Twinkle lights buzzed in soft focus along the fence, and the faint sputtering of jazz drifted our way. Against this backdrop, I listened as my mother's car pulled away and took off down the street.

"What are we doing?" I asked Cassandra. We stood on wet grass, the dampness seeping through my shoes. When I exhaled, pale puffs of air floated away from my body.

"Our ride will be here soon. We just need to make sure your mom is gone."

A pair of headlights shined into Marie's backyard. We peered around the corner to see a blue sedan idling in the driveway.

"That's him," Cassandra said.

"Him?"

Without answering, she took my arm and led me to the car. Cassandra threw herself into the passenger seat, but I stood frozen, staring at the driver. It was Jonah. He leaned forward, his left arm draped across the steering wheel. As I watched, his fingers curled halfway into a fist and then flared open again.

"I told you she wouldn't like this," he said.

Cassandra turned to me. The passenger-side window was open, placing her within my reach.

"Get in," she said.

I stood motionless in the driveway.

"If you don't get in, where will you go?" she asked. "You'd have to walk the whole way home in the dark."

The neighbors with their jazz and lights, the clink of glasses. I didn't know those people, but I could go to them, could submit to their mercy.

"Celeste." Cassandra leaned halfway out the window. "This party is safe. I promise. Do you really think I'd let anything happen to you?"

Cassandra was my best friend. My foolish, vulnerable best friend sitting alone in a car with a boy. In a dreamlike state I moved to the back door, watching myself reach out and hook my fingers under the handle. That handle was slick to the touch. It flashed silver in my eye, blinding, a pierce as sudden as a needle. It reflected all the reasons girls did things they never imagined doing.

The door heaved open with a creak. I slid onto the seat and shut myself in, away from the night. Before I was fully settled, Jonah reversed out of the driveway, shifted into drive, and pressed hard on the gas, jolting us forward and back again. I wondered how long he'd had his license. Boys could drive at sixteen, but girls had to wait until they were eighteen—the older age assured that we'd be out of our reckless changeling periods before operating vehicles.

"Your problem is that you take all this too seriously." Cassandra leaned forward in her seat to peel off her cardigan. The dress underneath was sleeveless with a V neckline. Jonah swiveled his head to look, the car drifting in response.

"Girls have been changing since the beginning of time," Cassandra went on. She rolled the cardigan into a ball and stuffed it into the space by her feet. "If things were as bad as you like to imagine, then women would be an endangered species."

"I'm worried, Cassie." My voice was small. "I'm afraid."

Cassandra turned around and gave me a pitying look. "Poor Celeste." She reached over the console between the front seats to touch my cheek. I felt a spark crackle between us. "Don't you trust me?"

I turned my face to the window. We sped on toward the party, the night slipping past in pulses of light interrupted by long stretches of vacuous black.

WE ARRIVED AT Rebecca's house as if in a flickering dream, everything emerging through fog: a side door with a split screen, a staircase leading to a basement, brown carpeting underfoot, voices drifting up from below. On our descent into the basement, Cassandra held my hand and squeezed, her palm damp and hot as a fever.

When we reached the bottom of the stairs, we stood in a cheaply finished room. The walls were covered in paneling that made hollow sounds when I tapped it with my fingernails. About twenty students were gathered in the basement, both girls and boys ranging from first-years to fourth-years. Most were my classmates, but even so, they looked newly unfamiliar in this environment. Many of them turned to stare when Cassandra and I made our appearance. My government changeling inspection was still days away, but entering that basement and having all those eyes on me at once was an exposure as intense as standing naked before a government employee.

I scanned the room. In the far corner, I caught a glimpse of the person more known and yet unknown to me than any other: Miles, my brother, my false twin. He wore the same collared shirt he'd put on for Cassandra's coming-out party, but this time it was untucked, making him appear careless. He was staring straight at me, his jaw set. I could tell what he was thinking, how furious he was that I'd risk coming to this party, but I only gazed back at him wordlessly. Sometimes when I looked at my brother his image seemed to waver, my imagination conjuring blank space instead. Like my subconscious was preparing for the future without him.

I turned to see Rebecca Delbanco at the top of the staircase, the triangle shape of her tea-length dress flaring out to fill the narrow space. She was leading three girls down to join the rest of us: Janine Cotto, who was in my year and had recently changed, and two third-year changelings. Janine stumbled to a stop once she reached me. Her eyes pooled dark, and wet enough to make her blink. She might not have mastered the high lucidity yet. I reached for her hand and pulled her closer.

At the refreshments table, Rebecca loaded a tray with rose sherry poured into the traditional tulip-shaped glasses. She brought the drinks our way and handed the first one to Cassandra.

"Don't," I whispered, but Cassandra jerked her shoulder, like she was brushing me off. She accepted the glass. Janine took one, too, as did the other changelings. When Rebecca offered me a flute of the pale pink liquid, I made no move to accept it. She waited. She did not lower her arm.

"It's just rose sherry," Janine said.

Cassandra lifted her glass. "You drank it at my party."

"That's right." Rebecca smiled, relieved. "This is like any other party." She pushed the glass under my nose.

I took a step back. "I think I'll pass."

"Take it," Rebecca said evenly. "You don't have to drink it, but at least hold it. You'll draw less attention to yourself this way."

I relented and accepted the rose sherry. Rebecca let out a breath, like she'd just accomplished a major goal.

"There now," she said. "We can get started."

I adjusted my flimsy scarf while Rebecca told us why we were there, in a basement with boys during the most dangerous time of our lives.

"Diffusing the tension can help," she explained. "That's why coming-out parties came into fashion. Those parties might have been enough a few decades ago, but now things are a little different. Now we need to do something on our own."

"Like a ritual," Janine said.

"Exactly."

I set my rose sherry down on a ledge near the basement window. I was trembling.

"Relax," Cassandra said quietly. "You don't want to be like Marie."

I picked up the glass again. When I glanced to Miles, he looked away, as if he were too ashamed to meet my eyes. I watched him, fixating on the line at the back of his neck just above his collar, where hair met skin. He struck me as defenseless.

Rebecca was still speaking, but I'd stopped listening. I felt far removed from the others, even the other changelings. They might be new like me, and they might feel just as raw and wild and vulnerable, but they didn't have predictions mapping out their brothers' deaths. I was alone.

"All right," Rebecca said at last. "We're ready."

She shook the last drop from the rose sherry bottle before setting it on its side in the middle of the floor.

"It looks like Spin the Bottle," I said, dismayed.

"Not exactly," Cassandra said.

"Good." I was relieved. "No kissing?"

She didn't answer. The boys edged closer to the bottle, and one reached down to give it a spin.

The girls around us erupted into laughter. I glanced up to see the boy who'd spun—a handsome, older boy with dark skin—standing over the bottle like he owned it. I felt sick as I realized what was happening.

He was staring right at Cassandra and me.

MAPPING THE FUTURE:
AN INTERPRETIVE GUIDE TO WOMEN AND GIRLS

SEX AND THE CHANGELING

A changeling girl may be at her most alluring, but she is also vulnerable. Her body is raw with possibilities for the future, her emotions are erratic, and she is charged with a new sex appeal when she is still too young to bear the sexual burden older girls and women can withstand. For these reasons, the changeling should refrain from intercourse.

To bear the future is to bear the sacred, and as such, changeling girls are tasked with guarding their own bodies from sexual or physical threat. Those who behave appropriately should expect little to no difficulty in avoiding sexual contact during this time. Caution, prudence, and restraint are three of the most important qualities these girls can possess.

Above all, we implore changelings to recognize that the burden of maintaining purity rests on their own shoulders—it is the first grave responsibility they must face in their adult lives, and a modest price indeed for the privilege of holding the future in their skin.

11

For a moment I could only focus on that bottle, how its open mouth was still damp from rose sherry and how it gaped in our direction, an endless dim cavity. It made me remember.

When I was a young child, my mother and I came upon a pair of teenagers wrapped together in the park. It was dark, and they were half hidden under the feathery branches of a willow tree. I could hear their breathing, hard and fast. There was a muffled fumble, the sound of cloth rubbing against cloth, and, just before my mother hustled me away, a delicate, feminine moan. It was my first sense of what people might do together when they were alone, how they could turn into something frantic and primal.

That night, as a boy stood staring at Cassandra and me in Rebecca's basement, I felt the same mixture of fear and excitement that I'd had in the park. I was repelled, and I was attracted. I wanted to look away, and I wanted to step closer.

Once I finally realized the bottle was pointed not at me but at

Cassandra, all those sensations rushed out of my body at once, leaving me
drained and airless.

"Good turn," one of the boys said. "A changeling on the first try."

Cassandra ran her hands over her hair. "Two minutes?"

"Two minutes," Rebecca confirmed.

I watched as Cassandra picked her way through the crowd, which
parted in waves to let her through. Jonah frowned as she passed, but Cassandra ignored him and headed straight for a closet built under the stairs.
The boy followed her inside, then pulled the closet door shut to close them
in. Rebecca turned up the music and set a timer.

I turned to Janine. "What exactly is going to happen in there?"

"I think it's up to Cassandra. But don't worry, Lewis is perfectly decent."
She looked around the basement. "I hope I get your brother when the time
comes. He seems like the type who will just stand there and wait it out
with me."

I glanced at Miles. He stood apart from the others, his arms crossed.

"There are more girls than boys," I said. "Maybe we won't get chosen
at all."

The corner of Janine's mouth twitched. "We're the changelings. The
game goes on until all of us are chosen."

I fell quiet. I was thinking that it was good Marie wasn't at that party.
She would never go into a closet with a boy. I understood without anyone
telling me that girls could not go in the closet together, just as boys couldn't.
Young people might be more tolerant of same-sex relationships than adults,
but even we had limits.

The timer finally dinged. When Cassandra emerged from the closet,
her cheeks were pink and her hair shaken loose, but she didn't seem un-
happy. Lewis came out after her, his eyes shyly fixed on the floor. They
separated; Lewis went to his friends while Cassandra headed to the refresh-
ment table, where she poured herself another glass of rose sherry from a
fresh bottle. She looked flushed, thrilled. I could see the pulse jumping in
her throat as she drank.

The game went on, the bottle making its lazy turns to land on girl after girl. My brother did not take a turn, which the other boys did not comment on—they were too eager to spin for themselves.

The next boy leaned into the circle to send the bottle whirling. He was a fourth-year, tall with a pale complexion. I didn't know him. Around and around the bottle went, spinning in a drunken wobble. When it stopped, it landed on me.

My first instinct was to look not at the boy who'd spun but to Miles, to glimpse his reaction. I knew he'd be upset, and maybe angry, but I also thought he had no right. He'd kept this party from me, making it one more of his secrets, and it wasn't fair. As a boy, he was allowed to come here at night, to mingle with whomever he wanted, while I was meant to be trapped at home. But if I wanted to go into the closet with a boy, as the other girls had before me, that was my choice.

The boy who'd spun for me waited, a patch of red spreading slowly up his neck and cheeks, from either embarrassment or excitement or both. I took a tentative step toward the closet while he held back, letting me take the lead.

Waves of energy rolled off the other girls as I passed them. They chose this ritual. Maybe not every one of them, maybe Janine or I would never have dreamed this up, but some girls chose it. They wanted to dispel the tension, to plunge off a cliff and land in water deep enough to hold them. The other side of the closet door contained a party of their friends, and besides, not much could happen in two minutes. The time it took my father to check my markings was far longer than that—the length of entire days, it seemed, compared to this.

The closet door loomed closer now. I glanced back at the boy following me. He was blond, and as he came closer I saw that he had fine silken hairs sprouting just above his eyebrows, thin cobwebs of hair that made him look delicate and soft.

I didn't remember opening the door or taking the first step inside, but somehow those things must have happened. The boy entered and I focused on the green of his shirt: new-day green, fresh-lawn green. Then the door shut, and we were enveloped. My back to the wall, our breath between us.

"I'm not sure I want to be here," I whispered. The music on the other side of the door swelled louder.

"We don't have to stay." He paused. "Not if you're scared."

"I'm not." All at once, that was true. He had made it so by offering a way out.

"Good," he said. "Because I won't do anything you don't want."

I considered him. "You've been in here before, I bet."

"Yes, but not like this. You're my first changeling."

"I'm not your anything."

"I know. I'm sorry, I know."

A deep silence, the rasp of his breath. My eyes had adjusted and snippets of light crept in—not only from the crack beneath the door but from all around us, as if minuscule holes had been poked into the closet from all sides to shine through with light, like the mechanical star ball at the planetarium. With my high lucidity, it was enough to let me make out the outline of this boy. I could see his chest rising and falling. Time was slipping away, and he knew it. Every second must have been agony for him.

Maybe this closet was safe. He hadn't tried to touch me yet, and time was dropping down second by second. I took a step closer. Now I could both see it and feel it: his shaking. His entire body trembling for me, or for the idea of me, or for every newly changed woman who had ever crossed his path.

I eased forward until my body brushed against his. I felt the jerk go through him like he'd been shocked. I held still, unable to press on and yet unwilling to pull back. Gently, he snaked an arm around my waist. We fell together at once, and it was impossible to say who advanced first—I just knew that one moment we were apart, and the next we were kissing. He was a soft kisser, and his hands were broad and warm on my arms, my sides, my back. I felt his lips shake, felt the beating in his chest.

It felt good to press up against a boy, or at least this boy. Perhaps all the stories I'd heard growing up—the ones warning me about men and boys, as if they were a different species—weren't true. Girls were meant to wait until they'd passed out of their changeling periods before entering into relationships for safety's sake, but how astonishing to experience these sensations now, in high lucidity, when the world was bright and better and full of pleasure.

When the two minutes were up, we forced ourselves to pull away from each other and stumble back into the light. The bottle was already spinning again. My eyes were still adjusting when Cassandra appeared at my side.

"See?" she said. She smiled, and I studied the sheen of her lips, their spark and fullness. I was pulled taut, humming with energy.

"It wasn't bad," I admitted.

She gave me a sideways look. "His name is Owen."

"Thanks. You're right, I didn't even know his name."

She laughed. "I had a feeling you two weren't having a conversation in there." She paused, turning serious. "You're allowed to enjoy yourself, Celeste. It's powerful, isn't it?"

I couldn't help myself. I nodded.

Behind us, the party continued, but the tension felt deflated. Owen had drifted back into the crowd. Everyone felt far away.

"I'm getting more rose sherry," Cassandra said. "You want some this time?"

I shook my head. When she left, I found my gaze wandering toward Miles again. To look at him was to be snapped back to reality: my markings, his final three years of life. I wondered if it would always be like that for me, those bursts of awareness of his fate. How I'd have to constantly remember his future like it was the past.

Cassandra rushed past Miles toward me, her eyes lit up. She was carrying what appeared to be a pack of playing cards.

"Look at this." She presented the deck like a treasure. "I've never seen this kind in person."

I looked closer. She was holding not playing cards but a tarot deck—an erotic edition.

Miles appeared and grabbed the deck from Cassandra.

"You shouldn't have these." But he cracked open the deck and poured the cards into his hand. Instead of standard-issue tarot cards, which were illustrated with trees, rivers, mountains, and animals, erotic cards showed the bodies of girls. They were a thing of great and terrible beauty.

I watched as Miles began placing the cards one by one onto the table. Each featured a drawing of a naked girl, her markings drilled through the paper in pinprick-sized holes. When he held a card up to the lamp, light sprinkled his face in minuscule, illuminated specks. Though the bodies on those cards were illustrated, they were real. They were girls like Deirdre, changelings from all over the country who were caught and recorded against their will. Seventy-eight girls pressed into glossy card stock and shot through with pricks of light.

"Put that down," I said. "It's disgusting."

I didn't mean it, not fully—the cards were gorgeous, a work of true art. Hand-drawn images with intricately sketched borders of woven garlands. Detailed, delicate. For as long as I could remember I had always been drawn to patterns, fractals, the designs found in nature: snail shell, snowflake, fern frond, lightning bolt. This pattern worship was the closest I got to religion. How much easier everything would be if the tarot contained only patterns on their own, designs disconnected from the bodies of girls. But those bodies were the entire point of the erotic tarot. The girls' skin shined slick-bright and bold, and the markings were pierced through with the utmost precision. The future revealed.

As girls and women, we spent our lives marked in our own private futures, but those futures were never fully our own. Family members, spouses, employers, and others made unceasing demands on what our skin foretold, and our only defense was the choice of whether to reveal our markings, and when. Yes, we needed to sign a transcript release form when applying to university or for a job, but it was our choice to apply for those jobs, our decision about who would access our transcripts and when. These cards represented anarchy, a world like the old times when women had no say over who looked and when. These cards reduced girls to mere objects to be collected and consumed and stored in a box.

Miles continued flipping through the deck as Rebecca veered toward us.

"Give those to me." Her voice sounded strained and raw. When she held out her hand for the deck, her fingers shook.

"These cards are beautiful," Miles said, "and the people who illustrate them earn a lot of money. But it's wrong, and you know it."

"I just wanted to see how they were made. I'm not going to keep them." Rebecca's face was red. "Now give them back."

Miles handed the deck to Rebecca but retained a single card that he held to his chest, the side with the girl pressed against his shirt. We could see the arrangement of her markings on the other side. We could see through her.

"Like I said, I'm taking them back the next chance I get." Rebecca's hand was still extended, waiting for the last card. She looked hopeless like that, and it didn't help that we all knew she couldn't return the cards. She must have purchased them on the sly from one of the back-alley vendors outside the interpretation district.

Miles flipped the card around so we could all see it. The girl had short brown hair, green eyes, skin dappled with tight clusters of markings all over. My brother gripped the card so tightly his whole arm was trembling.

"That's Elizabeth," he said.

"You knew her?" I asked, surprised.

"I had pastels with her my first year at art camp," he said. "She lived on the far east side of the city, so she had to take two buses to get to camp. She even went to one of our school dances. But then she disappeared."

Rebecca snatched the card from Miles.

"I didn't realize that deck had a girl from town when I bought it," she said. "I'm not a monster—I love the cards for their art. That's all."

A commotion in the corner of the basement drew our attention away from Rebecca. Jonah was circling Janine, grabbing her lightly around the waist. Every time she stepped back from him, he came closer. Meanwhile, another boy began chasing a third-year changeling through the basement. They were both laughing, but the girl was red in the face and out of breath, her eyes startled.

"Stop it," Rebecca called. "We have these parties to prove we can be trusted with one another. But we can't, can we?" She crammed the tarot cards back into the deck. "No one can be trusted. Not a single one of us."

I glanced reflexively at Miles, but he didn't react. When I turned to Cassandra, she looked worried. That shook me more than anything—that the behavior of those boys frightened even my boldest and bravest friend.

Rebecca wiped her eyes. "All right," she said. "The party's over. I've had enough."

No one said anything.

"I said the party's over," Rebecca repeated, louder this time. She picked up an empty bottle of rose sherry. "My parents will be back soon, anyway. It's time to leave."

With some reluctance, we started edging toward the stairs. Cassandra and I stuck together, so close our arms were touching.

"I don't want to go home yet," I whispered.

"I knew it." She was smiling. "I knew you hadn't lost your fun side."

We joined the crush of bodies moving up the stairs and flowing out the side door. Once outside, everyone stopped, as if unsure how to make use of this unexpected freedom. Maybe we thought Rebecca would follow and tell us what to do. Maybe this was all part of the plan in the first place, a sort of initiation.

But it wasn't. Rebecca shut the door against us, and then she locked it.

ON PRIVACY AND SHAME

Girls and women alike may maintain their privacy by disclosing their markings only to those of their choosing. Unfortunately, some changelings are reluctant to reveal their markings out of a misplaced self-consciousness over their newly developing bodies. For these girls, we offer the following consolation: shame and the changeling have been intertwined since the beginning of time. Girls should not strive to eradicate shame but rather embrace it as the price paid for the gift of being marked for the future.

In some cases, shame arises from nefarious forces. In particular, we highlight the trend of markings thievery, a crime against privacy that the Office of the Future denounces. The production or sale of books, tarot cards, comics, or other printed materials displaying a girl's markings is unlawful. Regardless, girls who find themselves victimized in this way must acknowledge their complicity in failing to protect themselves. While the shame from such unfortunate cases may not fade, girls can take heart that illicit materials tend to run their course quickly and become defunct. Before long, these materials will fade away.

The passing of time, in this case, is on a girl's side.

12

WE MOVED LIKE a pack, beasts in the night. Boys, girls, changelings, all together. The boys who'd driven to Rebecca's house offered rides to as many people as they could fit in their cars, but the other girls and I knew better than to accept. After witnessing the scene in the basement, Cassandra even refused to ride with Jonah. She'd planned for him to drive us back to Marie's house, where my mother would eventually pick us both up, but now that was all ruined. Now we were set loose into the night instead.

"You need to stay with me every second," Miles said. He was on foot like the rest of us, with no choice but to join the crowd. We moved as a group from Rebecca's house to the safest place we could think of: the First Friday celebration in the interpretation district, which was less than a mile away and would be our best chance of finding taxis driven by women. As long as we walked there together, we'd be protected by our numbers and by the First Friday festivities. This was the night interpreters cracked open their finest editions of *Mapping the Future,* wiped their crystal balls clean of fingerprints, and lured in customers with brie and chardonnay. The event would be crowded, electric, alive—a haven for changelings.

All my life I'd been told to never venture out at nighttime once I changed, and yet there I was, doing it anyway. It was thrilling. Only hours before, I would have been terrified by the mere prospect. Now, excitement zipped along my body like a live wire. Maybe that time in the closet with Owen, those two minutes of security and desire, had changed me. Maybe Cassandra had been right about everything all along: being a changeling was powerful, and beautiful, and alluring. Fear was nothing but a distraction from the wonders newly available to us.

The larger group from Rebecca's party broke apart when we approached the crowds of First Friday. Janine and the other two changelings set about finding taxis they'd feel safe in, but Miles, Cassandra, and I continued on foot together.

"We're heading straight to Julia's," Miles said. "I don't care if it's First Friday. No detours."

The night did feel harmless, robust with activity. Once we'd crossed under the *Future as Fate* arch, the streets grew thick with tourists. We sidestepped street vendors and shrieking children and the out-of-town fathers who swiveled their heads in our direction. It was like being at the summer festival, an event that felt safe and familiar with a touch of dark allure. The colors, the sounds, the laughter, the fizz of champagne—it was a brilliant place to experience through the lens of high lucidity.

We found Julia standing on the sidewalk outside her townhouse. When she caught sight of us, she tilted her head and gave Miles a questioning look.

"Isn't this a surprise," she said as we approached.

"Our plans tonight changed last minute," Miles said. "First Friday was our safest bet."

"Why aren't you inside, giving readings?" Cassandra asked her.

Julia tugged at her sweater. "I don't participate in First Friday. It's a bit vulgar, isn't it? I just stepped out for some air and got lost in people-watching."

Cassandra eyed a family of four gathered around a storefront. "Seems like giving readings on First Friday would be a good way to make some money."

Julia smiled wryly. "Ah. An opportunist." Her gaze wandered from Cassandra and reached mine. Her eyes looked gray in the dim light of the street lamp. Unflinching.

"We need a ride home," Miles said.

Genuine concern crossed Julia's face. "My car hasn't been fixed yet. I'll have to call one of your parents to come get you."

"No," Cassandra said quickly. "We can find a taxi driven by a woman."

Julia frowned. "No taxis. Let me ask a friend of mine to drive you home instead. Someone trustworthy. Come on inside while I call her."

I glanced at the crowds over my shoulder, drawn to the activity and the hint of wonder in the air. I was still carrying the energy from my time with Owen, my newfound strength and sense of control, and I wanted it to last.

"Maybe we could stay out a little longer," I said.

Julia was already on the stoop. She looked back at me, alarmed. "You still need to be careful, even on First Friday."

"Please." I worried that if I stepped inside Julia's place, I'd lose myself— that I'd succumb to a reading, that she would learn all my secrets. "We'll stay on this street and come back within a half hour."

"There's no risk," Cassandra said. "There are children everywhere, families, lots of women."

"That's true," Miles added. I looked to him with surprise. "And I'd be with them every minute. I promise."

Julia gave Miles a long, shrewd look. "Fine. Thirty minutes, then straight back here for your ride home. But you should cover up, Cassie. Here, take my sweater." She started to shrug out of her baggy gray zip-up, but Cassandra shook her head.

"No, thanks," she said, and I thought of her cardigan still crumpled on the floor of Jonah's car. "It doesn't go with my dress."

The sweater was already halfway off Julia's left shoulder. She let it hover there for a moment before pulling it back on. She did this so casually that

I thought she must have known from the start that Cassandra would reject her offer. I imagined Julia as a master reader, someone who had access to a set of markings more detailed than any that could exist on a single woman: a whole universe of markings, a multiverse, every moment of every day plotted out in a map only she could see. It was an impossible fantasy, but being around Julia knocked my sense of reality off-kilter.

"Don't leave this street," Julia said. "Stay in busy areas, and don't get separated."

That simple expression—*don't get separated*—was enough to remind me of my brother's fate. I studied Miles as we headed back into the crowds and thought he seemed healthy and self-assured, at the start of a long adult life. It was agony to be the only person in the world to know the truth. More than that, it was lonely—a pure, cracked-open loneliness that came not only from carrying this secret about my brother, but also from knowing there was nothing I could do to save him.

THE THREE OF us gravitated to a storefront across the street. The neon sign read *Chloe's Interpretation*, and in the window, a novelty crystal ball glowed a garish blue.

"I love it." Cassandra brightened. "Let's get readings."

Miles shook his head. "Frauds like this have no respect for the art of interpretation."

"That's not what this is about," Cassandra told him. "This is for fun. It's entertainment, and it's perfectly allowed."

It was true. *Mapping the Future* even included a brief section on the matter, titled "On Charlatans," which issued warnings about false interpreters while acknowledging that not all such interpreters were of malicious intent. Instead, their businesses amounted to a fantasy, which some customers were happy to pay for. "On Charlatans" explained that scarves, costumes, crystal balls, scented candles, and other such frippery signaled interpretation services designated for entertainment value only. The ridiculous glow-ing ball in Chloe's window was a clear sign that this was not an authentic interpretation business.

Cassandra was already opening the door, making the chimes jangle. Inside, we were met by plumes of incense smoke curling from the mantel. The room's décor matched that smell—candelabras, scarves, crystals dangling from the fireplace. The proprietor, Chloe, was nowhere to be seen, but a handful of customers waited for her services: three women, one man who stood upon our entrance and planted himself in the far corner, and two boys too young to react as men would to our presence. But like all children, they gravitated toward us. With gentle hands open like starfish, they patted our legs, our hips, our stomachs, anything they could reach. Their mothers stood back, watching wearily, and when one of them met my eyes, she looked away, like she was ashamed for the both of us.

Miles studied a long strand of crystals and frowned. It mattered to him, that there was a dividing line in the world between the real interpreters, like Julia, and the charlatans, like Chloe. The sheer scarves tossed over lampshades, the incense, the set of runes on the mantel—it was all an affront to his own aspirations. As a boy, he couldn't even rise to the level of Chloe's false work.

I had long ago accepted that the interpretation district was a place of contrasts: light and dark, virtue and greed, beauty and terror. So I was not surprised when a young girl of about twelve appeared from the back rooms projecting both innocence and calculation. She wore a lavender dress with a broad ribbon tied around the waist, but she also carried a clipboard and cast a shrewd gaze upon the customers.

The lone man waved to get the girl's attention.

"Is my wife about finished?" he asked.

The girl checked her clipboard. "Soon. Aunt Chloe is just being thorough, I'm sure. It's important to be thorough in a reading, isn't it?"

When Miles heard this, he laughed.

"In the meantime," the girl continued, "I'd be happy to bring you some tea. Just give me one moment." She looked over to Cassandra and me, her eyes narrowing. "What about you?" she asked. "Will you be joining Ms. Chloe for a reading?"

I shook my head, but Cassandra's response was immediate.

"Yes," she said. "I'd love a reading."

The girl pulled a pen from the top of the clipboard and held it poised over the page. "What do you prefer—tarot, crystal ball, palm reading? Focus on love, health, financial success?"

"Isn't it obvious? I'm a changeling. I'd like a reading of my markings."

The girl gave a slight nod. "Good choice. We prioritize changeling readings. Chloe will be ready for you soon. If you need anything in the meantime, please call for me. My name is Angel—I'm Chloe's niece." She turned to leave.

As soon as Angel disappeared into the back, I pulled Cassandra toward me. I had a bad feeling, something creeping along the edges of my mind like a lingering nightmare.

"Maybe this isn't a good idea," I said.

Cassandra gently shook me off. "Celeste, it's packed in here. There are witnesses all over the place. Nothing could happen."

"She's right. There's less risk for you here than out on the streets," Miles said. He paused. "Maybe you should get a reading, too, Celeste. It wouldn't be real, not like if Julia did it. This could be for fun."

"I don't want a reading tonight, Miles."

"Fine, I'm sorry. It was just a suggestion."

Angel reappeared carrying a tray containing a teapot, several thick clay cups, and a stack of ginger cookies. She set the tray on the coffee table and offered tea to the man waiting for his wife. She held out the next cup for me.

"Here," she said, and this time her smile felt genuine. I brought the tea close and inhaled. It smelled sweet and mild. It made me think of meadows and sunshine and childhood.

Cassandra and Miles both turned down the tea, though Miles accepted a cookie, which he ate in three bites. Angel left the room again, and I took a tiny sip of tea. It tasted marvelous, like honeysuckle and fresh rain, and its warmth spread through my body.

Feeling relaxed, I wandered over to the couch and sat. The cushions were worn and well used. I sank down and sipped my tea. I could taste everything, from the earthy scent of the soil the tea grew in to the sunshine that dried the leaves. When I blinked, tiny blond sparks lit up near my eyelashes. Cassandra was right to tell me to stop worrying and enjoy this time. Being a changeling truly was astounding.

I closed my eyes. A moment later, the couch shifted, sinking a little deeper. When I registered the new smell—a pungent soapy scent, with a dash of cologne—I opened my eyes.

It was the man from the corner. He blew gently across his cup of tea.

"Just keep looking straight ahead," he said. His words were so slow and deep I almost didn't hear him. "How does five hundred sound?"

"For what?" My voice faltered.

"One hour," he said. "We'll get a hotel room. It will take a little planning to make sure my wife is distracted elsewhere, but I can handle that."

I swallowed. "What do you think I am?"

"I know exactly what you are." Slowly, gently, in a way that I wasn't even sure it was happening, his left hand shifted to brush against my thigh. I was wearing long pants, but I felt his hand like a jolt anyway. "You're ripe," he said. "I know how you girls are. When it comes down to it, you want it as much as us."

"Five hundred?" I repeated. I was thinking of girls who had lost their way, girls without homes or parents, girls who were compelled to accept offers like this. If everything went quickly, they would never have to file a report or go to a hospital. If they were careful, their records would remain clean.

"Okay," he said. "Six fifty." His hand was hot against my leg. "But I won't go higher than that. It becomes a bad deal. Some girls go as low as three hundred, you know."

I trained my eyes on Cassandra and Miles across the room. They were talking intensely. I noticed how Cassandra moved in front of my brother, how she leaned forward and smiled, how her skin glowed in the low light of the shawl-draped lamp. I saw the way my brother's left hand reflexively curled in a fist every now and then, an unconscious resistance to her charms.

The spots in my eyes exploded into color, streaks of rainbow blotting my vision. I blinked hard, but the colors remained. I was hearing things, too—distant bells, the sound of the ocean, a far-off door slamming shut.

"If you're not looking for business, you'd better leave. This is no place for changelings." The warmth from the man's hand traveled even farther up my thigh. "But you know what I think? That you need the money, and that the two of us are in a position to help each other."

I wanted to call for help, or slap his hand away, or at least form the word *no*, but my body felt too heavy and slow to take even the simplest action. Breathing was all I could manage, and in this way I felt newly awakened as a changeling once more: fresh, raw, and out of control.

A woman stepped into the room then from the back. In the time it took her to appear in the doorway, the man's hand miraculously lifted from my leg and he shifted away from me quickly, as if I might burn him.

"I had the most wonderful reading," the woman said. She came toward the couch to address the man next to me. She had vivid, deep-black hair pulled into a tight ballerina's bun. Her skin was smooth and young-looking, her neck dotted with jewels that sparkled when she moved. She was radiant. Chloe had told her so many wonderful things, she was explaining to her husband. She felt, at last, that she had a good sense of direction.

When the woman's gaze drifted my way, she stopped smiling.

"Glad it went well," the man said quickly. He stood. I could smell his sweat, his fear. I could see a bit of red creep up his neck. "Let's go," he added, and started pulling his wife away. She gave me a long, deadly look before they clattered out the door.

I was still holding the teacup, my hands trembling. Miles crossed the room and pried the cup from me. "Relax," he said.

I didn't know how to tell him what had happened, how that man had propositioned me and how I'd felt unable to stop him. Already guilt was creeping in, the realization that I was failing to protect myself. So I didn't tell Miles. I didn't say anything.

Angel appeared in the doorway and looked across the room toward Cassandra. "Chloe will see you now, miss."

Cassandra smiled and smoothed her hair. She might have still been half drunk on rose sherry. She was probably not herself. I wanted to reach out to her, to touch her skin—to comfort myself with the reality of her body, as if this alone could keep her safe.

But I made no move, and Cassandra followed Angel, disappearing into the darkness.

Mapping the Future:
An Interpretive Guide to Women and Girls

ON SUFFERING AND HOPE

And here we must acknowledge that the future is sometimes too vast, too heavy with grief or guilt, for a woman to bear alone.

It is a grim truth that girls and women throughout history have attempted to alter their markings, whether through tattoos, scarring, bleaching, or other mutilations. Others dress modestly to keep their truths private, and yet others refuse to acknowledge their bodies at all, as though ignorance might prevent the future from unraveling. But the future cannot be escaped, dear reader. The future is a force, a steady unrolling of time and truth that presses on regardless of mortal whims. We advise the girls and women reading this text that such fate has played its hand in the life of every female human who has lived upon this earth—and it will be no different for you.

The future is built not only on shadow but on light. To roll back the centuries is to reveal baby girls born with pinpricks of predictions, young girls entering their spectacular bloom, and old women whose thinned skin still carries the weight of prophecy. In that sisterhood can be found suffering, yes, but also endurance and strength and, when all else is washed away: hope. That hope is part of every woman alive, and that hope is what allows a woman to withstand the worst of her fate.

No future, dear reader, can break a woman on its own.

13

ONCE CASSANDRA WAS gone, Miles examined my teacup. He turned it around and around in his hands, rolling it between his palms, inhaling the lingering scent of tea. A single speck of a tea leaf clung to the inside of the cup; he caught it on his fingertip and brought it close to study it.

"Did Cassie drink any tea?" he asked.

I shook my head, feeling dreamy and small. "Just that man."

"Celeste. Listen." His voice sounded stern. "I think you might have been drugged."

I laughed.

"It's not funny."

I laughed a moment longer before the sound splintered and broke.

Miles watched me closely. "You're not acting like yourself."

"I should find Cassie." I rose to my feet unsteadily.

Miles was at my side, letting me lean on him. "We need to go." His voice was so very quiet, but I heard it. I felt I could hear everything, all over the world. I just needed to tune in.

"We can't leave her here," I said, and I veered toward the hallway where Cassandra had disappeared. Miles came with me, holding on to my elbow. I knew as if by instinct where to go: to the door at the end of the hallway, the door that was open just enough to reveal cracks of light around the edges. When I put my hand on this door and pushed, it opened at once.

Miles and I found ourselves in a well-appointed office with floor-to-ceiling bookshelves and antique furniture. Chloe, a middle-aged woman wearing a barrage of costume jewelry, sat at a table before a spread of tarot cards. Cassandra stood in front of her. She was fully dressed, her arms crossed in defiance. My throat hitched at the sight of my friend, how alive and strong she appeared. Some part of me must have sensed the coming separation, our future breach already growing like a crack on an iced-over lake.

"You're not listening. My markings indicate I'll get into medical school," Cassandra was telling Chloe. "Julia said so, and she's a much better interpreter than you'll ever be."

Chloe blinked. She wore so much eye makeup I could see clumps of mascara even from my position at the door. Her face appeared lined and worn, exhausted.

"This is ridiculous," Cassandra went on. She smacked her hand against Chloe's table. "Are you even listening? You're wrong, and I want my money back." Her voice broke, and she turned to face Miles and me. "Will one of you please tell her what Julia said—that I'll get into medical school and become a doctor. It's fated. It is. Tell her."

Miles held up his hands. "Cassie, please calm down."

"Would someone like a reading?" Chloe asked. She was staring, crestfallen, at the table before her. One by one, she slid off her clunky rings and left them glittering against the velvet tablecloth. "I offer tarot, crystal ball, palm. Love, happiness, financial success." Her last few words ran together like smeared ink.

"This is a waste of time." Cassandra headed for the door. "I'm going back to Julia's. At least she knows what she's talking about."

"We're right behind you," Miles called after her, but I couldn't move. I stared at Chloe.

"What's wrong with you?" I asked. My tone was not unkind.

Chloe wouldn't meet my eyes. She was deflated, undone. She stroked the table in front of her as though petting an imaginary animal. Her fingers trembled. I noticed every last detail, my high lucidity alerting me to a threat. Chloe was guilty. She was a criminal. She was not working in service of girls.

"When I was a child," she began, "my markings suggested I could be something real. A lawyer, maybe."

"We need to check on Cassie," Miles said in a low voice.

I brushed him off. I didn't turn around even when I heard Angel enter the room and ask us to leave. I kept my focus on Chloe. That empty teacup waiting by her side. Her rings in disarray all around her. I could have snatched one up and taken it away with me. I was sure of it.

"What have you become instead?" I asked her. I felt sleepy but careful. Whatever had been in my tea made me unsteady but also, miraculously, confident. I was on a balance beam. I was walking a tightrope. I was leaning over the edge to face great danger.

"This is unacceptable," Angel said behind me. "Chloe, do something."

Chloe raised her eyes. "You know what I am." She waved her hand in a dismissive gesture. "It's too late for me. This is who I've become."

"You two need to leave," Angel said to Miles and me. "Now." She walked over to Chloe and stood close to her, as if she needed protection. Chloe blinked. With a vacant smile, she reached up to stroke Angel's hair in a loving, distracted kind of way.

"Come on," Miles said from behind me. He took my wrist and pulled me away, dragging me back to the waiting room. That was when I remembered Cassandra.

"She's not here." I ignored the handful of waiting customers who watched me with concerned expressions.

"She went back to Julia's," Miles said. "Hurry."

We were out the door, the chimes rioting behind us. The street was bright and full of tourists. It would be no risk for Cassandra to cross the street and make it into Julia's townhouse. She had to be there right now. She could already be safe.

"Celeste, wait." Miles steered me away. "We need to check something before we go to Julia's."

This seemed odd, but I felt so cloudy and tired I didn't question him. He took my hand and I let him. He was my brother, my halfway twin.

Miles made a sharp left turn and pulled me into an alley. I stumbled against the rough brick wall, and it took me half a second to realize he had pushed me there.

"Are we hiding from someone?" My tongue felt thick. He must have known something I didn't. Maybe Chloe had sent men after us. Maybe I was in danger.

"Shhh." Miles put his hands on the hem of my shirt and started to lift it. I squirmed away, confused, but he held me tighter. He pushed me against the wall, his body pinning me in place.

"Stay calm," he said. "And keep still. This will only take a minute."

I slapped at his hand, but he already had my shirt halfway up. He was reaching for my left side.

"Please," he said as I struggled against him. "Those photographs aren't good enough. I need to see your markings in person."

I was shivering and furious and terrified, but I felt too compromised to stop him. I tried to slap him again, but it was like a slow-motion dream where fighting was impossible.

"You can't imagine what it's like having this gift no one believes in," he said. "I see things no one else does. If I were a woman, I'd be a revolutionary, but because I'm a boy, I'll never be heard."

He ran his fingers over the markings on my stomach. Just enough light from the street entered the alley to allow him to make out my predictions. It was a frantic reading, so fast and heated I couldn't imagine he was gaining any real insight. It was more like he was staking his claim, remind-ing me that the future wasn't wholly my own.

"One day you'll understand that I'm doing this for you," he said. "To protect you. I'm so sorry, Celeste. I don't know another way."

His hand inched closer to my left side, those fateful markings on my ribs. I twisted violently. Miles held on tighter, but I was still strong.

As we struggled, silhouettes flitted past the alley, then doubled back and approached. I looked up to see two men. They were holding hands.

"What's going on over here?" one of the men asked.

Miles was still pressed against me. The heat of his right palm rested directly on the markings that spelled out his own fate. I held my breath. He hadn't had time to look at that area; it was only his hand flat against my skin. He didn't know.

"Let her go," the man said. He came closer.

Miles released me and took a step back. Shaking, I smoothed my shirt down. When I looked to my brother again, I saw a new expression on his face, something I had never seen before: pure, unmasked fear.

"Who taught you to treat girls like that?" the other man said.

I couldn't understand why Miles looked so distressed. These men were normal-looking, innocuous, and anyone could see they were no threat to girls. I had been far more afraid in Chloe's presence than in theirs.

"You okay, miss?" the first man asked. He had dirty-blond hair and a close beard that made him look bookish and gentle. I nodded.

"Good," the other said. He was taller, with darker skin, and when he smiled, I thought he might have been the most beautiful man I'd ever seen. He held out a hand to me. "Let's get you out of here. This is no place for a changeling."

Without thinking, I stepped forward and took his hand. The blond man appeared on my other side and put a hand on my back.

"Don't touch her," Miles said.

I twisted back to face my brother. "I don't want you anywhere near me." I paused, choking for air. "You make me sick."

"You'll be all right," the bearded man whispered. Gently, and so softly I could barely feel it, he began rubbing my back. "You deserve to be taken care of."

"I said don't touch her," Miles repeated. He rushed to keep up with us, trying to pry the men off me. They barely broke stride when they pushed him back. No matter what angle Miles tried, I turned my face from him.

"We'll make sure you're safe," the second man told me. His voice was smooth and seductive. I thought about Owen and felt the soft press of need. I squeezed this man's hand and he squeezed back.

"Celeste," Miles said. "Celeste, listen to me. I think these men might work for Chloe. You can't go with them. You have to fight back."

I heard my brother's words, but they sounded far away, like he was on a boat receding into the sea.

"Celeste," he said again. Then he gave up on my name and started to scream. He screamed, "*Help*," and I marveled at the strength in his voice. I held on to that single word until it, too, started to slide away, until the bearded man disappeared from my side. Somewhere in the far-off distance I heard a scuffle, and after that the screaming stopped. The man returned and grabbed hold of my arm again.

"Let's go," he said to his partner.

My feet felt heavier with every step. The men gripped me, holding me up. At one point I tried to turn to look for my brother, but I saw only a vast alleyway, empty.

After what felt like a long time, we stopped walking. The man in the brown jacket let go of my arm and knelt to unlock a pair of storm cellar doors. Distant alarms sounded somewhere in my mind, telling me to run. I jerked my shoulder and tried to take off, but the bearded man wrapped his arms around me. He held me still and sighed against my neck, but there was no desire in it, just weariness. When the storm cellar doors creaked open, he gently pushed me forward.

"I'm scared," I said.

The blond bearded man patted my arm. "You're here now," he said, "and you'll be all right in the end."

He stepped into the dark and waited for me to follow him. The other man stood just behind me, his body a solid wall blocking my way out.

I stumbled and hesitated, but when it came down to it, I did not claw or scream or cry. I was caught, the game already over. And so I stepped down into the stale black air. It was so dark I felt bodiless, floating through space.

I took a tentative step deeper into the black, then another. Again and again I pressed forward until I was consumed. Until I was lost.

III

Awake

Strategies for Reintegration:
A 7-Stage Guide for Recovery and Rehabilitation

Stage 1: Acknowledging Your New Future. On behalf of the Office of the Future and the staff of this federally accredited medical institution, we welcome you to the reintegration program designed to address the aftermath of your trauma event. In the days to come, hospital staff will assist you in your recovery journey and ensure all your physical and emotional needs are met.

Your first step is to recognize your new reality. Please note that acknowledging this reality is not the same as overcoming it. In this initial stage, your priority is simple: to survive.

14

I WOKE IN PAIN, on my side, on a mattress that was both narrow and cheap. A coil pressed into my hip. Once I forced my eyes open, I found myself staring at a wall the deep gray of wet pavement. The trim running along the floor and around the doorway was blood red.

"Celeste?"

I rolled onto my back and turned, blearily, toward the sound of my mother's voice. She took my hand.

"I've been waiting for you to wake up," she said.

I blinked away from her, focusing my gaze upward. The ceiling was also painted gray, just a few shades lighter than the walls. Why would anyone do that? I wondered. To purposefully make a place dreary.

"I feel strange," I told her. My head pounded, my vision blurred, and a slick pit of nausea pooled in the back of my throat. I grappled for the plastic bin next to the bed, but I was too weak to hold it. My mother took the bin from my trembling hands and positioned it under me just before I vomited.

The taste in my mouth was unfamiliar. What and when had I last eaten? I had no idea.

I didn't remember anything.

My mother smoothed a strand of sweaty hair against my temple. I looked down. The sheets were gray. The pillows were gray. The blanket, blood red. I was wearing a hospital gown, the strings tied securely at my back.

"Where am I?" My voice was thick.

"You're in the hospital," my mother said. "You're safe here."

"I want to go home."

"Soon. In just a few days."

She handed me a plastic cup of water with a straw poking out of it. I sipped. The water was so cold it stung the inside of my mouth. My stomach turned.

"I have to go to the bathroom."

My mother's face registered worry. "Can you hold it for a little bit? They'll be here any minute."

"Who?"

"The police."

I didn't allow myself to absorb that information. I was focused on my piercing headache, the dizziness, the fabric of the hospital gown that I did not recognize and could not remember putting on. I wanted to be in my own pajamas and in my own bed.

"I really have to go."

Resigned, my mother helped me scoot to the edge of the mattress. My hips hurt. My muscles felt sore all over. My throat was raw, as if I'd been screaming.

Together, we worked my feet into a pair of slippers.

"The bathroom's in the hall," my mother said, gently pulling me up to stand. "You can lean on me."

The hallway was bright, painted dove gray and blasted with fluorescent light. It held about a dozen rooms and, at the end, a nurses' station. The bathroom was two doors away from my room.

"I'll wait out here," she added. "Unless you want me to come in."

I shook my head and limped into the bathroom, closing the door on my mother's anxious face.

Once I was locked inside, I shambled to the toilet. When I peed, it burned. I rose wearily and flushed, then washed my hands with pink soap I worked into a violent foam. Finally, I raised my eyes to the mirror.

My face looked puffy. I touched my fingertips under my chin, just like my mother had the time my lymph nodes were swollen from strep throat. I leaned closer. My pupils were dilated, and my eyes appeared blank with an odd sheen, as if someone had scrubbed them clean. How badly I wanted to be in my own bedroom, gazing instead into the full-length mirror my father and I had installed next to the closet. This bathroom mirror was hung at an angle, the top tipping forward drunkenly to provide a full-body view.

Slowly, I untied the strings of my hospital gown and let it fall away.

My body was covered with bruises.

A kaleidoscope of contusions, from black to muddy brown to sickly yellow, anointed my upper arms, my ribs, my thighs. Acorn-sized bruises lined my shoulders, plums and grapes and currants scattered up and down my torso. A delicate bracelet of bruising along my right wrist carried the faint imprint of someone's fingers.

Some of the bruises partially concealed my markings. This was the case on my left side, for the prediction about Miles—the pattern was obscured, altered, temporarily unreadable.

I stared at my damaged skin in the mirror for a long time. I stared until a realization struggled to the surface, kicking, to illuminate my new reality: I was no longer a changeling. No longer did I have a faint glow, that magnetic dazzling pull. I had been gone long enough for the transformation to complete itself, and now I was a regular young woman. No special allure, no heightened senses, no outrageous beauty.

I gathered my hospital gown and put it on. As I tied the strings behind my back, I caught sight of a brochure waiting on the side table, next to the extra toilet paper and a bottle of crusted-over hand lotion. *Strategies for*

Reintegration. A photograph of a depressed-looking teenage girl appeared below the title.

My mother knocked on the door. "Are you okay?"

With shaking fingers, I added another knot to my hospital gown. I couldn't be in the place that brochure described—it was impossible. If I could only remember what had led me here.

I'd gone to a party with Cassandra—that was certain. I remembered the bottle spinning on the floor, the boys, the closet. Rose sherry, the smell of pine, the inside of an interpreter's storefront. A girl in lavender serving me tea. A man on the couch, his hand hot on my thigh. My brother pushing me into an alley. Two men holding me up.

After that, my memory was blank.

My mother knocked again. When I opened the door, I saw the gray space behind her with new eyes: I was in the Reintegration Wing of the hospital, where abducted changelings were sent once they were returned. I could no longer pretend otherwise.

"Come along," my mother said, taking my arm. "We don't have much time."

I walked as if in a daze. "I can refuse the exam. I'll say I don't need it."

We reached my tiny gray room again. I dragged myself into bed.

"You have bruises, Celeste." My mother's face was strained. "Injuries. Nothing that won't heal, but you needed medical attention. They examined you when you were first brought to the hospital."

"While I was asleep?"

She held up her hands, an apology. "They did it before I made it here. We got the call that you were returned, and we rushed right over, but they'd already gone through with it. We couldn't prevent an exam, anyway. You were gone for more than two weeks."

I turned my face away, the gray entering my vision like a slap. That was the moment I started to disengage, when I began to view my body as a thing outside of myself. It had been wounded and then examined, and I had no memory of either violation. Not to mention the agony of having known high lucidity only to have it ripped away. I should have appreciated it more during that scant time I'd had it. I should have embraced so much else, too. Things like safety, family, the promise of a future.

My mother was holding my hand. She was asking me not to cry. I told myself I couldn't be crying because I couldn't feel tears on my cheeks. I felt no pain, no sensation at all. Even my bruises had evaporated in my mind. I was blank. I was nothing.

THE POLICE CAME in a pair, two men who didn't bother to sit down or take off their hats. I sat up in bed and crossed my arms over the insufficient fabric of the hospital gown. I had no idea where my clothes were.

"Can you describe the events of the night you disappeared?" the first officer asked. He'd either forgotten to shave that morning or else his stubble grew back fast. From his pocket he produced a small notepad and a pencil. It wasn't even a full pencil with an eraser; it was one of those mini pencils, the kind meant to be disposable.

"I don't know," I said. They stared at me, but I couldn't make myself go on. My mother came over to sit on the side of the bed. She squeezed my shoulder.

"We spoke to your brother," the officer continued. "He told us you were downtown at night, that you were drugged."

"Though we found no evidence of illegal substances at the interpreter's place of business," the other put in. He had a big belly, a strain against his belt.

I felt hot all over. "I definitely wasn't myself. I wouldn't have left Miles otherwise. I felt out of control."

"Well. You *were* a changeling," the first officer said. He made a mark in his notebook.

I turned to my mother. Her jaw was set.

"Where are Miles and Dad?" I asked her.

"They were here earlier, before you woke up." She wouldn't look at me.

"Miss, we need to finish this interview. What can you tell us about the two men who led you away?"

The trappers, those men who were kind to me. Or at least I'd thought they were being kind to me.

"One had reddish hair, I think," I said. "Or maybe it was blond. The other had darker skin."

"Age? Height?"

I tried to remember. "Maybe they were in their thirties, but I'm not sure. And one was definitely taller than the other." I paused. "I think the other one had a beard."

The officers glanced at each other.

"They may have worked for Chloe," I added. "The interpreter. She was acting strangely."

"Yes, your brother mentioned that as well," the officer said. "We've questioned her, but we didn't find anything that would warrant an arrest. Based on your brother's statement, it sounds as if you may have gone with these men willingly."

"I wasn't willing," I said, but then I remembered pushing Miles away. Holding hands with one of those men. Feeling, for a few moments at least, safe in their presence. But that didn't mean I'd gone willingly. Did it?

"I wasn't thinking clearly, but I didn't want to go with them." I could feel my mother looking at me, but I refused to meet her gaze. I was ashamed of myself—for getting trapped in the first place, and for not fighting back.

"Can you tell us anything more about the trappers?" the other officer asked. "Any tattoos, scars, or identifiable marks?"

How much easier it was, I thought, for a man to point to a particular woman. *Officer, she had a triangular pattern of markings on her upper arm, the kind that indicates a broken heart. Officer, she had a large birthmark on her cheek, which I remember because, my god, what a shame.* But men, whose bodies were not documented in transcripts that could be subpoenaed in criminal investigations, were so much more difficult to identify.

"No," I said. "Nothing I can remember."

"All right. And during the time that you were missing—any memories?"

I bit the inside of my cheek. I bit it hard enough to draw a sharp pain, as if that could bring something back, but it was useless. Most girls who were abducted didn't remember. They were drugged, continuously, until the moment they were set free again.

"No. Nothing. I remember the men and then waking up here. That's all."

He flipped shut his notebook. "All right. You let us know if you think of anything else. In the meantime, focus on healing. The worst is behind you now."

Both men turned to leave.

"Wait," I said. "What happens next?"

My mother gripped my shoulder harder.

The second officer paused at the threshold of my room. "We'll finish writing up the paperwork. Then we'll coordinate with the doctors to add everything to your transcript. And we'll keep an eye out, of course, for those men. But trappers tend to move around. Without any concrete leads, it's unlikely we'll find them—the trappers or the man who held you."

For a moment I imagined the gray walls crumbling around me, that I was sinking into some nightmarish quarry.

"You know, I feel perfectly fine," I said. "So maybe you don't need to add anything to my transcript."

"Celeste," my mother said softly. "You were missing for weeks. You had a full medical exam. It's too late."

"I won't press charges, even if you find him," I went on. "I don't need to bother with the paperwork. Maybe we can let it slide."

The officer with the stubble lifted his cap a few inches, giving me a glimpse of his sweaty hair. "We can't do that, miss. Not when a federal crime has been committed. But like I said, you should focus on your recovery."

I waited until he left before I curled onto my side.

My mother patted my back. "Celeste. You'll be all right. You're back, and you'll heal. That's all that matters."

"Not if my transcript reflects this. I won't be able to go to university. My friends will go off to school without me. I'll be alone, and I won't be able to become a psychologist. My life is ruined."

"It's not ruined. It's just changed."

I didn't want to hear it. I asked her to turn out the light and let me sleep, and she obliged. Sleep was my last refuge.

But once I was alone, I dwelled on how I'd lost the last few weeks. That time was gone, disappeared, and I could only imagine what unspeakable things had happened to me. Every now and then a streak of pain hit my body, a sizzling wave of discomfort. And I kept picturing Cassandra, kept daring to think it should have been her, not me, lying broken in this hospital bed.

I covered my face with my hands and cried—out of guilt, and shame, and humiliated disbelief—until I exhausted myself. I eventually must have drifted into a light sleep, because one minute I was alone and the next a strange woman was standing over my bed. She wore a navy skirt suit with a little red pin on her lapel. I gazed up at her, convinced I was dreaming.

"Celeste Morton?" she asked. She held a file in her hands. It was my government file, a stack of papers so slender it seemed to have almost no substance at all. She flipped it open to a diagram of my juvenile markings and tapped the mystery pattern on my left elbow.

"Those are gone now," I said, holding out my arm. I still believed I was asleep. "You're a government inspector, aren't you?"

She gave a curt nod.

"Did you ever consider becoming a humanitarian ambassador instead?" I paused, gazing at the woman dreamily. "I was thinking maybe I'll try for that career one day. I can't be hired as a government employee, but I could become a humanitarian. Assuming they still hire women like me."

"It is an equal-opportunity profession," the inspector confirmed. She kept looking back and forth between me and the diagram of my juvenile markings.

"If I became a humanitarian, I'd make good money, plus I'd get to travel." I let my gaze wander over the woman. The red pin shined on her lapel like a prize.

"And I could help people," I added as an afterthought. "Humanitarians do good work for girls. That's what they tell us, anyway. But I'm not sure about inspectors." I squinted at the woman. "Are you here to help me?"

The inspector reached for my left arm and held it in her cool hands.

"I'm here to confirm," she said. She pulled out a penlight and shined it on my arm, then ran her fingertips lightly over my elbow. The contact lasted only a moment before she dropped my arm and made a note in the file.

"Thank you, Miss Morton," she said. "That will be all."

She withdrew from my bedside. A moment later, she was gone.

I blinked, uncertain whether she'd really been there or if I'd dreamed it. She left no trace, not even a lingering scent. I lay on my side, facing away from the door that was always kept open a crack, and stared with wide eyes into the dark. All around me, I felt the press of night.

DURING THOSE EARLY hours in the hospital, the inspector's visit blended into everything else, making a dark smear of confusion. Years later I would struggle to remember her face. I'd study diagrams of the human brain, focusing on the parts responsible for emotion and trauma to better understand my compromised memory from that time. I read about the almond-shaped amygdala, the seahorse-shaped hippocampus. "Hippocampus" as in horse, as in sea monster, but I lingered on *monster*. I was consumed by a monstrous force in that hospital. I carried the wounds from a battle I couldn't even remember.

On the first night of my stay, I waited alone in the dark until Miles snuck in to visit me. I heard the door ease open, heard him slip into the chair next to my bed.

"Celeste," he breathed. "Hey."

He waited. When I did not respond, he tapped my shoulder.

"Mom's been in the family waiting area for hours," he said. "She thinks you're asleep."

I rolled over. "Did you see her?"

He paused. "I just told you. Mom's waiting down the hall. She didn't want to wake you."

"Not her. The inspector." I sat up.

"What are you talking about?"

"An inspector came to visit me. She looked at my arm. She had my file."

Miles reached over to flick on the lamp by my bed, and for a few seconds we blinked at each other. He had a shadow over his left eye. No, not a shadow—the remnants of a black eye. A whole bruise of his own.

"I think I'm confused," I said finally. "Maybe I dreamed it." I was too weak to comprehend the true meaning of that woman's visit, or to grasp the forces at work in our world—how the future churned on and how our vulnerable, mortal bodies struggled to control it. A dream was the best escape I could imagine.

"It's my fault," Miles said.

My first instinct was to comfort him. But then I swallowed, and my throat felt sharp, and I recalled my final memories of that night: How he pushed me into an alley to view my markings. How he was no longer the brother I'd known.

"Chloe may have had a hand in this, too," he went on. "She probably tips off the trappers whenever she has changeling girls in her office. I'd heard of that type of arrangement, but I never fully believed it." Miles paused. "Still, I didn't see her as a risk. And I thought that moment in the alley might be my only chance to look at your markings."

"You put me in danger."

He wiped his eyes. "I was selfish and stupid, and I'm sorry."

"An apology isn't going to give me my life back." I turned onto my hip, facing away from him. I saw our history unspooling, all the time we spent together: The game in the basement, the summer evenings of brickball, the strawberry stand. How, in the end, he betrayed me.

But I had betrayed him, too. Miles had only a few years to live, and I hadn't told him. I couldn't do it, not even then, after my ruin. Maybe I was the stronger liar of the two of us after all—both better and worse.

Miles pulled his chair closer to my bed. I heard the chair scrape against the floor, a grating sound drawing closer, like a threat. I worried he might touch me—I couldn't bear to be touched, I even jumped when a nurse took my pulse—but he did not.

"I'm so tired," I told him. "You should go."

"I'm not leaving you. I won't do that again."

I closed my eyes. Despite my reservations, I fell asleep. I was too exhausted to hold it off. When I startled awake about an hour later, Miles was still sitting by my side. A nurse bustled in to take my temperature, and then another entered to give me pain medication. My brother sat through it all, watching me. As if he alone could make me whole again.

Stage 2: Withdrawing and Mirroring. During your time in this rehabilitation program, you will interact with fellow patients during meals, therapy, and structured social time. Be aware that these relationships may prove complex. Some girls withdraw by initiating arguments or avoiding their peers. Others find comfort in their fellow victims and cling to one another, a process known as "mirroring." Either strategy is part of a normal recovery, and many girls cycle through both at different times.

Expect to revisit this stage in various ways in the days, weeks, or even years to come. Your evolving relationships highlight a fundamental truth about recovery: it is a process with a beginning but no end.

15

THAT FIRST FULL day in the Reintegration Wing, my father did not show up. Miles and my mother sat with me while I ate breakfast—limp toast, a plastic cup of orange juice, gelatinous oatmeal knotted with raisins—until the nurses ushered them out so I could begin the day's programming. "Programming," that's what they called it, and families were not allowed to attend.

When my mother and Miles left, I was relieved. I'd been embarrassed for them to see me in that state: the bruises lining my arms, the thin hospital gown I constantly pressed against my sides to make sure it kept me covered. My hair was greasy, but a nurse told me I'd have to wait until that night for someone to help me wash it in the sink. The only relief came in the form of a pair of gray cotton pajamas. Finally, I could cover up. The pants were a touch too short, and the bright red stitching down the legs reminded me of a surgical scar, but I was grateful for the clothing.

Once dressed, I combed my hair as best I could with the flimsy plastic comb and followed a nurse down the hall to a meeting room. I already knew what I would find there: other girls like me. Girls in gray pajamas, girls with shattered expressions, girls who were bruised. Girls who slept or couldn't sleep in their own gray rooms, who pressed their cheeks into their gray pillowcases and dreamed of safety, of home. Just the thought of them made me miss Marie and Cassandra.

The nurse took my elbow. She was gentle, but I couldn't meet her eyes. I wanted a nurse who knew exactly what I'd been through, but that was impossible because ruined girls didn't grow up to become nurses.

"Come on, dear," she said, and guided me toward the room. "It's time to begin."

I dropped my gaze as I shuffled through the doorway, focusing on the sight of my feet in those gray slippers. My ankles were bare, and I was cold all over, and I could sense the other girls in the room even before I raised my eyes.

There were three of them, all roughly my age. Two had been gone long enough to have grown out of their changeling periods, just as I had. But the last girl had miraculously been released after only a handful of days. She was still bright and vivid, still a changeling, still desirable. I could sense her spark immediately. When the nurse asked me, again, to take a seat, I knew I couldn't sit by that girl. Next to her I would feel extinguished. It would be like sitting next to a warped reflection of my former self.

It would be like watching my own body rise from the dead.

I CAME TO know those girls in the way all girls are first known: through their appearance, the physicality of their presence. One of the girls was tall, with pale skin and brown hair shot through with reddish highlights that looked natural, like they'd come from the sun. She had a narrow face and thick eyebrows and wasn't particularly pretty, aside from her hair, and she had a habit of picking at her fingernails. The next girl was plump with a tawny complexion, her markings so light I had to squint to find them. The last girl was the changeling—black hair and dark skin, with a slight frame and intelligent eyes. Her markings shimmered under the industrial lighting.

I did not recognize these girls. The city hospital ran the only Reintegration Wing in a seventy-mile radius, which meant my fellow patients could have come from anywhere: a faraway suburban town, an adjacent but smaller city, or even a country hamlet. Even so, I couldn't stand to look any of them full in the face. I turned away as I did from my own reflection whenever I glimpsed it in the bathroom mirror: hollow eyes, broken lips, an expression revealing anxiety and rage. During my stay in the hospital, I was actually grateful for the loss of my high lucidity. To feel more than I already did in that place would have been a curse.

"Allow yourselves to comfort one another," a nurse told us that first afternoon. "You've all been through the same trauma."

We ignored her. We tried not to look at one another. I longed instead for Marie and Cassandra. I fantasized about returning home, how our threesome would resume as though nothing had interrupted our friendship.

"Girls," the nurse continued. "You are going to be all right."

As a rule, the nurses didn't address us by name. They called us *girls*, *dears*, *sweeties*, *loves*. If I ever learned the real names of these girls, I forgot them at once. We chose pretend names instead, names we invented and whispered into being that first night over dinner. The girl with the brownish-red hair named herself Aurora, the girl with pale markings was Moxie, and the changeling was Glory—though it seemed unfair, for her to choose a name that flaunted her current state. I was the last to say my new name aloud because I was ashamed, both for how quickly it had come to mind and how unlike me it was: Violet. Delicate and feminine, a name that conjured the sensation of velvet. All the things I wasn't, or no longer believed I could become.

WE GATHERED THREE times a day in the meeting room. We ate meals together in a cafeteria at the end of the wing. We played silent games of checkers in the game room. We barely spoke in our therapy sessions. Instead, we waited.

We would be held in the Reintegration Wing for four days, which happened to be the same length of time women who gave birth remained in the hospital. The girl we knew as Aurora whispered that our wing was adjacent to the maternity ward. She said this quickly and then fell silent, like she'd left us a gift that she refused to watch us open. We were unable to confirm her information, since we were forbidden from wandering beyond our single hallway, but it made sense to me. I could imagine babies being born—half of them girls, born with tiny sets of predictions—while, only a few hundred feet away, a group of teenage girls tracked the ends of the lives they'd once known.

A nurse confirmed this reality of our new fates during the second day of programming, when we discussed our educational options.

"Most girls don't reenroll in their old schools once they've returned," she told us. "It's too stressful. You might find it easier to pursue a different path."

"But I want to graduate," I said, and I heard how petulant my voice sounded. My dream of becoming a psychologist was now impossible, though it still hovered like a mirage just beyond my grasp.

"You're allowed to return to school," the nurse assured me, but she said it like that was a choice that would result in regret. "Just be prepared for the social fallout."

The other girls remained silent. As far as I knew, none of them had any intention of returning to their schools. But they were from smaller towns, I reasoned. While my hometown wasn't exactly a metropolis—larger cities elsewhere were considered more sophisticated—it was surely more progressive than the rural areas these girls were from.

"Returned girls have other options," the nurse continued. "You might consider a correspondence course. It takes longer to earn your diploma that way, but many girls have made good use of it. Alternatively, you may wish to enroll in a local trade school."

"That's what I want to do," Aurora said. "You can study to be a manicurist, or a domestic employee, or even a culinary artist." She said *culinary artist* with reverence, as if it implied working as a chef in a fancy restaurant, but we knew what it really meant: being trapped in steamy kitchens attending to vats of reeking soup and never-ending piles of dishes.

The nurse turned to Moxie, who said she'd go the correspondence route and earn her diploma that way. Finally, the nurse looked to Glory.

"What about you, love?" the nurse asked. "What might you do once you go home?"

"I want to go to university," Glory said, without hesitation.

"Oh, darling." The nurse sat back in her chair. "You know that's impossible."

Glory's face crumpled. I silently willed her the strength to not cry.

After the session, I caught up with Glory in the hallway and reached for her hand. I suppose I thought I could comfort her. She wrenched away from my grasp.

"Leave me *alone*," she snapped. She disappeared into her room and shut the door fully behind her, which was against the rules. I waited for a nurse to rush over and crack the door open again, but for the moment, no one noticed. Glory had won a rare bit of privacy.

For a long while, I stayed in the hall, staring at the closed door. Maybe Glory knew better than the rest of us how to survive.

THE NURSES EXPLAINED that time wasn't what we thought it was. They assured us that even if it seemed we'd been gone forever, even if it felt as though this incident would loom large for the rest of our lives, it wasn't so. We'd eventually view the experience as a blip in the long continuum of our lives. It would become like a bad dream, they said.

They said nothing more about our transcripts, or university admission, or our future careers. Maybe they believed we could begin to forget these things if they stopped speaking of them.

On that second night, I lay on the hospital mattress, so thin its coils pressed through the fabric like bone. The *Strategies for Reintegration* brochure sat on my bedside table, placed there by a nurse with good intentions. Aside from our group therapy sessions, when we were asked to take turns reading it aloud, I didn't touch the brochure. I couldn't face it, especially then when I was freshly returned, broken and bruised. Many years later I'd find that brochure in a box of my old things, and I'd hold it up to the light with a sense of awe. I couldn't believe I had saved it. I couldn't believe it had followed me that far.

The nurses had assured us that if we focused on other things, on the small wonders and happiness even girls like us could achieve, we could begin to forget. I wanted to forget, and yet there in bed that night I also wanted to remember—because to lose that span of time forever made me feel shadowy, dead.

What I needed was a written record of my abduction, a document outlining just how I'd ended up there. The full account of what happened to me might not exist, but there was always my transcript. All I had to do was seek it out and read it.

I sat up and swung my legs over the side of the bed. I put on my slippers. The hallway outside my room was bright but quiet, and when I peered around the doorframe, I saw the nurses' station was empty. This didn't surprise me. The Reintegration Wing wasn't a high-priority area. Once girls' initial injuries were tended to, the nurses mostly waited it out with us. They led us to programming; they offered us therapy. Doctors didn't bother to check on us after the initial exam. It was possible, on that night, that the nurses of the Reintegration Wing had been called away to other parts of the hospital where they were needed more. Where the injuries were purely physical and easier to understand.

I skidded down the hallway in my slippers. The sliding motion reminded me of ice skating, which I'd only attempted once, a few years prior. I'd fallen hard and bruised my knees, which put me off it. Now it seemed silly, to be afraid of falling. The ice was hard, but it was just water. It was there to hold us up.

At the nurses' station, I ducked under the desk and found the drawer marked *Transcripts*. I slid it open and rifled through the thick manila folders inside, letting the names—the true names—of the other girls wash over me. I did not know them. They were not real. I stopped only when I came upon my file, my name written in thick black marker, the word *CONFIDEN-TIAL* printed on the front. When I opened it, pages scattered across my knees and fluttered to the floor. I grabbed at them and started to read.

First there was the police report. *Victim unable to provide sufficient description of perpetrator. Victim has no memory of the crimes. Victim appears to have gone willingly with a pair of trappers; trapper identities and whereabouts unknown. Victim claims she was drugged (unconfirmed).* At the bottom of the page, in red ink, was one final line: *Case suspended barring further evidence. Recommendation for closure following a sixty-day period.*

I set the police report aside, turning instead to the medical report. No one had briefed me on this. No one had briefed my family, either. These cases were confidential, which meant that neither the hospital nor the police would turn over my records to anyone, including my parents, without my consent. The nurses had explained it all during our first therapy session. But when I applied for jobs in the future, or if I had the audacity to apply to university despite all of this, I'd have to sign a waiver granting access to my file. The same would go for the courts when my future husband and I applied for a marriage license—because I was still fated to one day marry, even if just then I couldn't stand the thought of being close to a man. Any time I tried to take a new step in my adult life, this file would be opened, my secrets released.

But for now, no one aside from the doctors, police, and nurses had seen my file. No one else could see the description of my injuries (*extensive bruising on arms and legs, minor internal injuries consistent with sexual imposition*), which I flipped through slowly, in wonder, as if I were reading about a stranger. I studied the list of medications I'd been given, the record of the programs I attended within the Reintegration Wing, and the recommendation for release following the minimum four-day period (*no additional therapy is anticipated or recommended*).

When I arrived at the final pages in the back of the file, I was confronted with drawings of my own markings. My adult markings, including the moles on my left side. While I'd never had my changeling inspection, my body had been recorded upon my arrival at the hospital. During my entry examination, the doctors used a special light to see beneath the bruises, and an inspector must have been on call to record my predictions. Nothing was a secret from the people who worked here, not even my brother's fate.

My hands started to sweat. I shoved the papers back into the manila folder, which I held to my chest like a shield as I hurried back to my room. My first thought was to lock myself in the bathroom and flush the pages one by one down the toilet, but I worried the noise would draw attention. Maybe I could pass the night carefully ripping each page into tiny pieces and then toss those pieces out the window, like little bits of snow. I even considered swallowing the records. I could consume my ruined future bit by bit, making it more a part of me than ever before.

I sat on my bed with the folder. I was still thinking through my options when a nurse swung open my door. She panted slightly, as if she'd run a great distance to reach me.

"Good thing I was the one to see you." She paused and gulped for breath. "If security had been watching the cameras like they're supposed to, you wouldn't be talking to me right now. You'd get the police instead."

I had forgotten about the video surveillance. How foolish I must have looked on camera, lurking behind the nurses' station in my pajamas.

The nurse held out her hand. "Come," she said. "Give it to me."

It was over, and yet I couldn't make myself hand her the file.

"Maybe you can pretend you didn't see me," I said. The nurse's expression—sympathy, anguish—made me push on. "If you helped me, you could change my entire life."

The nurse let out a breath. She came over to the bed and sat with me. I didn't flinch. I didn't move the file out of her reach. I thought she might offer to help.

"You know that's not the only copy, right?" she said. "Even if I wanted to change it, or throw it away, it wouldn't do any good. What's marked down is forever. I'm sorry."

I knew she was right, but I still wouldn't let go of the file. I clutched it desperately, molding the manila folder into a new shape.

The nurse put a hand on my arm. "You'll be all right," she said. "Really. I see a lot of girls come through here, and it's always bad at first. But then they grow up. They get married and even get jobs, sometimes. Not the best jobs, but jobs. They live their lives. They have babies. They find a way to be happy."

As she spoke, I loosened my grip on the folder. When the nurse finally reached for it, I gave it to her without argument. Afterward she stroked my hair, helped me into bed, and promised she wouldn't tell anyone what I'd done.

I curled into the fetal position. The mattress was so uncomfortable; the hospital saved the real bedding for the other wings, for the patients who were actually ill. I believed, then, in that line of thinking. That I wasn't sick. That once my bruises healed, I'd be fine, more or less.

That once my mandated days in the hospital came to an end, I could go home as though nothing had changed. Not even myself.

Stage 3: Confronting Family. Prior to leaving the Reintegration Wing, you will have the opportunity to meet privately with your family. Expect this meeting to be tense, perhaps even unpleasant, as your family members struggle with the new reality thrust upon them. Be patient and deferential during this meeting. You are the victim and catalyst alike of this new dynamic, and as such, you owe it to your family to confront their grievances.

16

BY MY FINAL morning in the hospital, the last of my bruises had paled
to a sickly yellow. They faded from the inside out, leaving dark rings that
made me feel dirty, like my skin was covered in stains I couldn't erase. Each
bruise still ached if I pressed it hard enough, which I did, several times,
during the special last-day breakfast I shared with the other girls. We sat
in the programming room and watched without joy as an orderly served us
waffles on paper plates. The waffles were lukewarm and rubbery, but there
was coffee, plus a plate of succulent red grapes. I popped a few grapes into
my mouth, only to discover too late that they were full of seeds, a swarm of
daggers piercing my cheeks.

After breakfast drew to a merciful conclusion, we headed back to our
rooms. A new girl arrived just then, so we paused in the hallway to watch
her roll past. She was strapped on her back on a gurney, and although her
eyes were open, I got the sense that she was not awake. Her parents trailed
behind stiffly.

Next to me, Glory watched this scene with intensity.

"Are you all right?" I asked her.

She kept her eyes fixed on the gurney, which the staff was maneuvering into an empty room.

"Something is wrong with that girl," she said.

"Of course something's wrong. She was abducted."

Glory shook her head. "I think maybe she tried to hurt herself."

I took a step back, like what that girl had was catching.

"When I was a kid, I knew a girl who tried to end it after she was returned," Glory said. "She managed to get her hands on a bottle of pills while she was still in the hospital. The staff must have been so lazy to let that happen. It's not a surprise, though, is it. That they don't care."

Her eyes had a shine to them, a greedy look, like she delighted in the possibilities of destruction. I knew nothing about her—not what kind of life she had before she was taken, or what she had to return to. I didn't even know her real name.

"That girl's the lucky one, if you ask me," she added, nodding to the end of the hallway, where the new girl had disappeared from sight. "She's not awake to face all this."

Without waiting for my reply, Glory offered a vicious half smile and retreated to her room. For a few moments I stood there, stunned, until my shock solidified into a desire for control—for the power to stop at least one of the disasters careening toward me.

I went to the nurses' station. My legs were shaking, and I had to steady myself by leaning on the counter. I explained to the nurse that I was worried Glory was thinking of harming herself. The nurse narrowed her eyes as I spoke, then called two more nurses to the station. They huddled together, whispering. I would learn later they were making plans to ensure Glory wouldn't be left alone for the rest of her stay in the hospital. But I didn't need to know the details—it was clear that they intended to protect her, and that was all that mattered to me.

I watched the nurses work and told myself that order was being restored. Maybe, I dared to imagine, my actions had shifted a tiny bit of fate. I thought of Julia's metaphor with the tree and imagined roots deepening, branches growing, leaves unfurling. By ensuring Glory received help, perhaps I'd directed her toward a brighter path. The mere prospect was intoxicating. I felt dazzled, like I'd just pulled off a magic trick.

Maybe I could do it again.

IN THE HOURS to come, we were meant to gather our things and wait for our families to arrive for our final therapy session. Back in my room, I found one of the battered suitcases from home on my bed. Inside was a set of clothes: jeans, a pink V-neck T-shirt, canvas sneakers, socks, and a bra and underwear. My mother had delivered the suitcase to the front desk the night before in preparation for my last day.

I dressed. I combed my hair one last time with the plastic comb, and then I threw the comb away. After a moment of hesitation, I bunched up my pajamas and shoved them in the trash can, too. Maybe the staff planned to wash those pajamas and give them to another girl later, but I hoped not. Every girl in that place deserved something new and untouched.

Following an interminable wait, a nurse knocked on the door and peered inside. I was sitting on the edge of my bed, fully dressed and packed, waiting for all this to come to an end.

"It's time," the nurse told me. She smiled a little.

I stood up and trailed her down the hallway toward one of the small meeting rooms. When we arrived, she paused with one hand on the door.

"Are you ready?" she asked.

Before I could respond, she pushed the door open.

I TOOK IT all in: the overhead lights, blazing fluorescents that made everyone's skin burn. The plastic chairs arranged in a semicircle. My family in those chairs, alien, sickly.

Miles wore a shirt I didn't recognize, which was disorienting; I wondered if he'd gone shopping while I was missing. He sat with his right ankle crossed over his left knee, and I tried to puzzle out his expression: distant, aloof, maybe angry. His black eye was nearly gone, but because I knew where to look, I could still see the faint ring of it.

Next to Miles, our parents waited stiffly. My father sat forward on the very edge of the chair. My mother was in her professional clothes, with her hair arranged into a bun at the nape of her neck. She appeared polished, everything neat and tucked away. I realized she must have needed time off from her job to be at the hospital for visitation hours.

The nurse stood behind me and placed her hands on my shoulders.

"Sir?" she said to my father. He was the only person not looking at me. "Sir, you should greet your daughter."

My father raised his head but did not speak. His hair was trimmed and damp, and I could smell his aftershave. I leaned slightly into the nurse's hands so she could support me.

"You should say something," the nurse suggested. I didn't know whether she was talking to me or to my father, but either way, I couldn't stand it anymore. I sat across from my father and leaned toward him.

"Dad," I said. "You need to talk to me."

He brought his hands to the lower half of his face, as if he couldn't bear for me to look at him full on.

"I'm so ashamed," he said at last. "Miles told us, Celeste. About those men in the alley, and how you went off with them."

"They took me, Dad. I didn't want to go." As I spoke, I wasn't so sure. Hadn't I pushed Miles away? I remembered what the police had said, about how I'd gone willingly. Maybe that was how the world would see it.

"We know about that party you went to with your friends, how everyone was drinking rose sherry." My father waved his hand through the air, like he was conjuring a vision of that night. "So maybe you went out, had a little something to drink, and two handsome men come your way, start giving you attention. Or maybe they gave Cassandra more attention than you, and you felt you had something to prove. It's natural for a young girl just coming into her own to want to feel special."

"That's not what happened." I glanced at the nurse, hoping she might defend me, but she only gave me a tight smile.

"Your mother and I should have known not to trust you," he went on. "Girls run off all the time after passing to adult markings. They lose control. I should have kept that in mind and done more to protect you. Instead, I let myself get distracted by work."

"What about Miles?" I asked. "He led me into an alley. If he'd taken me straight back to Julia's, this wouldn't have happened."

Miles looked stricken, but my father frowned.

"You were responsible for yourself," he said. "You have free will, just like everyone else. You made your own choices that night."

There was no way for me to win—I could see that now. The hospital was the first place where I glimpsed the truth of how things worked, not just within my family but on a far larger scale. The world was a sharp place for girls and women.

"Celeste, your father loves you," my mother said. She put a hand on his forearm, as if he were the one who needed comforting. "He was so distraught when you disappeared."

"She's right." My father's voice cracked. "I regret so much, all the ways I could have done better by you. I was too wrapped up in my own problems. If I hadn't been demoted, your mother wouldn't have had to return to work, and we could have paid more attention to you. But you also should have been more careful, Celeste."

He took my hand and pulled me toward him. I let him hug me. I let him cry against my neck and hold me like I was something precious and vulnerable. But I did not feel breakable. I was stone.

"It's always the most difficult for fathers," the nurse said. "They tend to experience great anger and great shame after abductions." She stood up and drew a stick-figure family on the chalkboard, making the father oversized and placing him in the center. "Sometimes it might seem that rage is directed at the daughter, but that's not the case. Their reactions are always, always based in love. Please remember that, Celeste. Let your father feel what he needs to, and stay strong. Things will get better with time, I promise."

My father pulled back and wiped his eyes. The session carried on, a stumbling, halting endeavor. Most of it washed over me in an amnesic tide.

Finally, from the corner of the room near the door, a timer dinged. We all turned to look at it. It was a little brass timer sitting on a table behind the nurse. I hadn't noticed it when I came in.

The nurse reached behind her and turned off the alarm. "Unless there's anything more you'd like to discuss, you're free to go."

No one said anything. I supposed there was good reason for the thirty-minute limit. The staff in the Reintegration Wing saw hundreds of families a year; they'd probably given up trying to resolve anything a long time ago.

We stood and marched from the room: my father first, then Miles, and then my mother, who held my hand but let me drift back a bit. We followed the nurse down the hall to the checkout desk. I looked for the other girls along the way, but they had vanished. Maybe their family sessions weren't so disastrous and they were already on their way home, back to normal lives. Or maybe not.

At the checkout desk, the nurse handed me some paperwork and a pen.

"You're almost free," she said brightly. The form she gave me to sign was insultingly simple. It stated the date and the time and that I would be leaving of my own will.

"Does this mean I could have left earlier, if I'd asked?" I was embarrassed that I'd never thought of it. Adults had placed me in this hospital, had told me I was injured and had to stay. It didn't occur to me that I might have refused.

"Well," the nurse said. She seemed as staggered by my question as by my realization that I could ask it. "We've never had a girl leave before her four days are up. It's a federally sponsored program, you know. We're here to make sure girls recover."

I stopped asking questions. I signed the form.

DURING THE DRIVE home, I sat in the back seat, next to Miles, and leaned my face against the window. I watched the world pass by: the trees changing color, the houses still standing. The hospital was located on the opposite side of town, so we had a long drive.

We were about halfway home and passing through a part of the city I didn't recognize when I saw it: a flyer dangling from a telephone pole. One of its staples had come loose and it flapped desperately in the wind, but I could still make out the photocopied image it bore.

It was my face, a picture I didn't recognize. I was not smiling. And above my head, the single word printed in all caps in a thick, choking font: *LOST*.

Stage 4: Going Home. Following your successful completion of the rehabilitation program, you will be rewarded with a clean bill of recovery and discharged. While most patients are eager to return to the comforts of home, be advised that this transition can be emotionally taxing. In fact, many girls only begin to face the irrevocable changes in their lives after they've retreated to a familiar environment. This reckoning is not always welcome, and as a result, some patients choose to begin their lives anew elsewhere.

No matter your personal circumstances, take heart in knowing it's normal to feel anxious upon being discharged. In many ways, your struggle has just begun. To endure this struggle is the only way to reach the greater future that awaits you.

17

AT HOME I showered, shampooing my hair twice. The suds rained down my body, making me feel clean at last. Afterward, I felt much improved. I was no longer sore, and the steam obscured my remaining bruises. I was even getting used to the lack of high lucidity.

Downstairs, I found my mother drinking coffee in the kitchen. I slid into a seat at the table and asked for a cup. The coffee was hot, bitter, strong. As I drank, it made a burnt path along my tongue.

"Anything you'd like to do today?" my mother asked.

I paused, considering. Routines had vanished from my mind; I struggled to even remember what day of the week it was.

"I think I'll just stay in." The thought of leaving that familiar space to confront the greater world was overwhelming. "But I'll be fine on my own if you want to go into the office. They must be missing you at work by now."

She emptied her remaining coffee into the sink. "That's not necessary."

"Really, Mom. You should be at work."

She began washing the mug.

"Mom?"

She glanced over her shoulder with a quick, tense smile. "I don't work anymore."

"I can't believe you quit because I was gone. You knew I'd come back."

"That's not exactly what happened." She dried her hands on the dish towel, then folded and hung the towel on the peg by the sink. When she finally turned to face me, her expression was inscrutable. "My boss told me that he understood this was a trying time and that I needed to focus on my family."

"But you told him you wanted to stay, right?"

"The board members had already made up their minds."

I finally understood what she meant.

"Maybe I can talk to them," I said, "to show them things are back to normal."

"It's too late, Celeste." My mother crossed the kitchen and put a hand on my arm. "Besides, I don't need that job. We'll be fine."

She was lying, and we both knew it. She'd taken that position for a reason. Not only did we need the money, but she'd been excited about returning to work. I remembered all those clothes she'd bought, how flushed she looked at the prospect of working again.

"I'm sorry."

She squeezed my arm. "You have nothing to feel sorry for."

This, too, seemed a lie. But I forced myself to smile at my mother before I returned to my room, where I climbed under the covers again.

I listened to the quiet of the house. My father had left for work once we'd come home from the hospital, and Miles must have gone to school. I lay there and allowed a series of horrifying images to appear in my mind. My brother falling from a bridge. His body crushed in a train collision. Lying still and pale beneath a paramedic pumping at his chest.

I draped an arm over my eyes and pressed down hard. These morbid

thoughts could neither save my brother nor help keep the prediction a secret. And yet I carried on as if my betrayal—the greatest lie of my life—
might erase what was coming.

CASSANDRA SHOWED UP on my doorstep that afternoon after school
let out. She wore a red sundress and carried a blended coffee drink topped
with whipped cream. I thought, at first, that the drink was for me. I was
about to reach for it when Cassandra lifted the straw to her own lips and
took a sip.

"You seem all right," she said. "But you look older, now that you're not
a changeling anymore."

"You're not, either," I pointed out. Cassandra did seem more adult now
that her changeling period was behind her. Her glossy hair was pulled into
a complicated braid, and she wore a touch of eyeliner and red lipstick. I felt
I'd missed out on years of her life, that she had grown and changed in un-
imaginable ways.

Once inside, she dumped a heavy backpack on the floor.

"What's in there?" I asked. Unbelievably, I still thought Cassandra had
something for me, as though she could apologize for her part in my abduction by bringing me a gift. Not that Cassandra seemed to consider herself
culpable in any way. The fact that she'd been the one to invite me to the
party that night, or that she stalked out of Chloe's office without waiting for
me, didn't seem to weigh on her in the slightest.

"Textbooks," she said. "My mom signed me up for a study group so I
can work through the premed curriculum."

"You must hate that."

She shook her head. "I plan to live up to my markings and become a
doctor. I'm thinking either cardiology or oncology."

I felt a pang. It seemed a cruel trick that Cassandra had a career to pursue while I had nothing. If I tried to imagine myself as a psychologist, the
image clouded over at once.

Marie arrived next. As soon as I opened the door, she embraced me.

"I'm so glad you're back," she said. "I missed you, and I worried about you. I thought about you every minute." I thanked Marie but could only think that she looked astonishingly young—she still hadn't changed. She'd remained a girl while Cassandra and I had become women.

I led my friends into the living room. In the time before I'd been taken, we would have gone up to my room, but now I refused to take them upstairs. I worried I'd crawl into bed and look to them as Deirdre had to me after her return.

"I'm doing really well," I said, though no one had asked. "I don't remember anything, but that's for the best anyway. The hospital was strange—I wish you could have visited, but I know that's not allowed—but maybe it was good, to be there for a few days before coming home. Now I'm ready to go back to school and have everything return to normal."

I realized I was rambling, so I stopped myself.

"Are you sure coming back to school is a good idea?" Cassandra asked gently.

"I never considered not coming back, to be honest."

My friends shared a look.

"It's just that most returned girls don't reenroll in their old schools," Marie said. "Deirdre didn't. It's too hard. We've missed you, and we'd like you to come back to school with us. But we're worried about you."

"Well, don't be. I'm perfectly fine."

Cassandra shook her head. "Celeste, look at yourself. You're covered in bruises."

I glanced down at my arms, which were still marred by faint blotches.

"You said earlier that I looked okay."

"I was being polite."

We sat in silence for a few moments. I felt uneasy, like they were judging me.

"Neither of you has any idea what I've been through." My voice edged toward desperation. "You can't even imagine."

Marie offered a kind expression. "Then tell us."

I thought I might cry. "I don't know how."

"That's the problem," Cassandra said. "You're all mixed up. That's why girls don't come back to school. It makes everyone else uncomfortable. No one wants to be around a girl who's returned. It's too strange."

"So you don't want to be around me?"

"I didn't say that."

"That's what you meant."

Cassandra looked off to the side. "I feel bad for you."

"We feel terrible about what's happened," Marie amended. "You didn't deserve it."

"No one does." I looked at Cassandra, right into her beautiful face. In that moment, I wasn't seeing the friend before me but the entirety of my ruin. "You're lucky you're not in this same position. You were the one flirting with boys and sneaking out at night."

As I spoke, I started to feel angry. It was a relief, to feel something so strongly again. It didn't matter that I also felt a distant but growing sense of unease. Part of me understood that what I was saying to Cassandra wasn't fair—but I pushed that thought away and kept talking.

"In fact," I continued, "it's partially your fault that I was taken in the first place. If you hadn't left me and run to Julia's, I wouldn't have tried to follow you and ended up in an alley. A real friend would have stayed, but you thought only of yourself."

"You don't know what you're talking about, Celeste. It wasn't my decision to go to Julia's. Miles told me to head over there."

"You're lying. He wasn't even with you. When you got upset with Chloe and ran out, he stayed with me." I shook my head. "I can't believe you'd lie to me, on top of everything else."

"I don't have to listen to this." Cassandra stood up. "Unlike certain other people, I have a future. I'm going to be a doctor."

She headed for the door, moving with such self-possession that I was nearly frightened of her. I stayed in the living room, listening helplessly as she collected her backpack, opened the front door, and slammed it shut behind her.

"That was bad," Marie said in a low voice. "It didn't have to get ugly like that. She wouldn't have come here if she didn't care about you. And it wasn't Cassie who hurt you, Celeste. It was a man."

"I don't know why you're acting like you know everything." I looked at my hands as I spoke. "You're basically a child. You haven't even changed yet."

"Celeste," she said. "Don't."

"You've never had much common sense," I went on. I hated myself, I didn't recognize myself, and yet I couldn't stop. "Cassie and I have always taken care of you. It's pathetic."

Marie was quiet for a stretch, letting my words settle.

"I'm surprised," she finally said. "I didn't think this would change you."

I refused to look at her. "I don't see how it couldn't."

"Whatever you say, Celeste." She stood. "I'll leave you alone. That's clearly what you want."

Marie made her way to the front hallway and I followed her, as if driven by a final, clumsy urge to be a good hostess. At the door, I thought something would happen. I thought I might spontaneously apologize, or she would tell me those concerns about coming back to school were unfounded, or we would both agree to move past this and never speak of it again.

What happened instead was Marie put her hand on the doorknob and pulled. What happened was she walked down my front steps and along the stone pathway, and she didn't look back once. I watched her go, following her progress to the end of the walkway, where she turned into the street and proceeded past an idling car.

The driver in that car—female, blond, face crossed by shadow— hunched low over the steering wheel, staring in my direction through the open window. I leaned closer, squinting. I knew who she was even before I got a full view of her face. She and I were, after all, the same now.

Deirdre cut the engine. She climbed out and turned toward me. I had only one wish: for her to disappear, taking her reminders of what I'd become with her.

*   *   *

DEIRDRE'S HAIR, STILL short, was bobbed in the style of an older woman. When she approached and met my gaze, her eyes were watery, vacant. I could not look away. She was a flame snuffed out but then reignited in the deepest reaches of my mind. For years to come I'd rise sweating in the night, jarred awake by a dream I could barely remember save for flickers of gold hair, the creamy richness of lipstick. But I didn't know that yet. Instead, seeing Deirdre up close gave me resolve. It made me want to make the world easier for her, even if only in the smallest, slightest way.

"It's good to see you," Deirdre said. Her voice, at least, sounded the same.

"How were you able to drive here?" I asked, looking with bewilderment at the car she'd abandoned by the curb. "You're not eighteen yet."

Deirdre glanced back, as though surprised to see the car there, and to hear that she'd been the one to drive it. "My aunt lets me take it sometimes." She shrugged. "It doesn't matter for us much anymore, does it? It's not as though our records can be tarnished any more than they already are."

"I hadn't thought of it that way."

She took a step closer. "I never would have guessed you'd be taken. You seemed too good." She paused. "Or careful. You always seemed so *careful.*"

"Looks like you were wrong about me."

She brightened a bit. "I've been wrong about everything."

I studied Deirdre. She still seemed damaged. Angry, sullen. Consumed. I hoped I didn't look like that.

"How have things been for you?" I asked her.

"I moved in with my aunt and uncle, down in the suburbs south of town. It's quiet there. Boring."

"Did they find the man who took you?"

"Of course not. Be realistic, Celeste. Don't tell me you have fantasies of catching who did this to you."

"Not really."

Without warning, Deirdre took hold of my left arm. She pushed back my sleeve and stared at my inner elbow.

"See?" She held her own arm next to mine in comparison. "No markings on either of us in that spot. It's like we're sisters."

I pulled my arm back and rubbed the skin she'd just touched. I didn't believe in connections based on lack.

"Have they come looking for you, too?" she asked. When I didn't respond, she leaned in closer. "The Office of the Future. A markings inspector visited me. She had my childhood file, and she wanted to see my arm, right there in that spot."

My mind turned back to that confused first night in the Reintegration Wing. How I'd told myself that the inspector's visit might be a dream.

"She asked about Miles," Deirdre added. "They wanted to know when I last had contact with him, and what he said." She narrowed her eyes. "They didn't seem happy with him."

Her words reminded me that the events of the future might appear separate but were really interconnected, like cells in a body or a line of dominoes ready to collapse. One thing affected another and another. My brother, sending a letter to the Office of the Future. My brother, predicted to lose his life.

Deirdre glanced behind her. "Sometimes I worry they're following me."

"Who's following you, Deirdre?"

She was sweating. "What?" Her eyes shifted back and forth. "I don't know."

When I placed my hands on Deirdre's shoulders, I could feel her trembling.

"You're fine," I said. "No one is following you."

"They're not?"

"No. Come on, I'll help you to your car. You should go home and rest."

Deirdre leaned against me, promising she could make the drive back home, while I told myself I was nothing like her. I was determined, smart, stubborn. The same person I always was. I'd make my way out of this without falling apart like Deirdre.

At her car, Deirdre stopped and reached into her back pocket.

"I brought you something," she said.

She was holding a plastic bag that contained a bloodflower pill. A single spot of red as shiny and appealing as a berry fresh off the bush. She rattled the bag as if to entice me.

"Take it," she said. "It will make you remember, but in a way that dulls the edges. No one wants to remember, not really, but you have to. In order to move on."

I hesitated only a moment before accepting the bag and slipping it under my sleeve.

"It wasn't easy coming back to this neighborhood," Deirdre added as she climbed into the driver's seat. "It reminds me too much of life before I changed, when I still had my whole future ahead of me." She paused to buckle her seat belt. She moved like a much older person, like everything hurt.

Deirdre put the key in the ignition and looked me right in the eye. For the first time, her expression was sharp.

"That's my only advice for you, Celeste," she said. "Leave. If you stay here, you'll drown."

ONCE DEIRDRE WAS gone, I took the bloodflower up to my room and shut the door. I felt so shattered by what had happened with my friends that I was glad to have the bloodflower to distract me. I held the pill up to the light and turned it from side to side, marveling that it had come from nature.

Bloodflower grew wild all over in the warmest weeks of the year. It grew tall, a scraggly plant full of thistles and thorns. Only in the last days of its short life did the red bloodflower itself bloom, half hidden in the twisting stems. The flower opened, released its potent nectar, and then folded over itself and died. It took a significant effort to combat those thistles, to harvest the nectar at just the right stage, to boil and process it, to dry it into a powder and turn it into a pill. Every bloodflower pill was born of sunshine and heat and determination. Every pill had surely, at some stage, drawn blood.

I slid the pill from the bag. I knew what bloodflower could do, how it could make me remember. If I remembered, then I might have something to share with the police. But I was scared. To remember would be to experience horror, to see something I couldn't ever take back. Bloodflower could be dangerous, too. Addictive, unpredictable. I didn't want to lose myself to it.

And yet there I stood, pill in hand. The air in the room felt heavy, my senses battering against the decision I'd already made. I could do this. I could be strong.

I placed the pill on the center of my tongue. At once, the taste of pine and snowy woods filled my mouth. I was so surprised that I closed my mouth and swallowed.

My body tingled with light, with euphoria. I was energy itself, alive and singing.

All at once, the aftertaste in my mouth changed. Instead of snow and pine needles, I tasted burning. The coals at a bottom of a grill. The ash from a campfire. The dank sharpness of singed hair. I gagged and coughed, but it was too late. The bloodflower had dissolved, leaving a lick of fire to drift through my veins.

And I started to remember.

Stage 5: Grappling with Memory. Now that you've graduated from the reintegration program, you may find yourself distracted by the question of what happened during your trauma event. While many patients are tempted to unearth their memories, this is an ill-advised strategy. Such memory mining results in pain and nothing more. Patients are advised to let the past go and to focus their energies on recovery and rebuilding their futures. Leave the darkness behind.

18

THOSE MISSING WEEKS shot past me in slips and flits, little pieces of memory as rough and sharp as the very pill I had swallowed.

First I saw the shadows of the underground hiding spot I'd been led to, followed by a glimpse of the two men who had brought me into the basement. They pulled away quickly, leaving me standing alone in a cavernous space. I moved forward in a slow, floating gait. Before long, I found a doorway with a strip of light showing at the bottom. I drifted in that direction and pushed open the door soundlessly.

Inside, I found a room with threadbare carpeting and wood-paneled walls. No furniture except a narrow bed pushed against the far corner. A young girl lay on that bed. She was thin and pale, her eyes hollow, but the rest of her glowed.

I stepped forward. I was thinking back to that day Cassandra had changed, how much I'd wanted to touch her. I came closer, then closer, until I was nearly at the bed. The girl sat up to face me. Her hair was mussed around her face, her expression unknowing. She stared right through me. I was finally close enough to make contact with her, but the moment I grazed her skin I leapt back, feeling stung. My fingertip hummed with recognition.

The girl on the bed was me.

I blinked and found myself lying on that same bed. I wore a thin cotton tank top but nothing else, my legs curled to one side. I propped myself onto my hands and stared down at my changeling body. I was beautiful, a wild thing trapped underground.

The palest light pooled into the room as someone entered. A man shut the door behind him and stood at the foot of my bed. This was it. A far-off voice in the back of my head urged me to look up, to study his face, to recognize him, but I couldn't do it. I stared at the man's gut, refusing to raise my eyes.

He joined me on the bed. A patient tiredness overcame me, like this was so routine, so ordinary, that the event barely registered. When he lowered himself to me, I turned my head to the side. I felt ancient inside my own body.

The light flickered. Time stretched to accommodate this moment, as if it were a horror wholly without end, but I refused to acknowledge it. I worked to erase what was happening, what was changing me every second.

It went on until it didn't. The sound he made at the end was one of agonized loss, and I lay still beneath him as he labored to catch his breath. By the time he finally moved his body from mine, I was so far outside of myself that I barely registered the lift in the mattress when he stood.

"That's too bad, about your brother," he said as he began to dress. He nodded toward the markings on my ribs.

I hated him, he disgusted me, I wanted to burn him alive. I fixed my gaze on his face and stared hard, memorizing every wrinkle, every flaw in his skin.

"What do you think you're looking at?" he snapped. His hands were shaking; his zipper jammed. "I'm not attracted to young girls—only women, after they've changed. That's important. I don't feel this way about my students."

So he was a teacher. I told myself to file that information away.

"You can't know how difficult this is," he went on. "It's like being a prisoner. Once you girls change, you're irresistible."

I shifted on the bed so I could look at him. His face was bland, expected, universal. He was just a man.

"Poor baby," I said, my voice velvety. "Imagine the struggle."

He leaned down and wrapped his hand around the back of my neck, pulling me close. "I would stop if I could," he breathed against my neck. "But I can't. I'm human."

"You're not," I said.

Later, when he came back into the room and pushed me down, I looked off to the side and pretended I was somewhere else. I was good at pretending.

When I raised my eyes again, I saw a massive blueprint pinned to the wall. It was not a blueprint of a building but of my body: a more official and intricate version of how Miles had drawn me when we were children. All my predictions were there, including the ones on my left side.

I was shaking. Even in that hallucination, I understood that my markings were no longer my own. I pressed my fists against my eyes and realized, with a start, that I had begun praying. My family was not religious, and we did not attend church. More surprising was that I was not praying to God, but rather to something I feared did not exist: the mythical blank girl. She appeared before me, flashing her hair, filling the room with a luminous glow.

I stretched out my arms to make contact, but it was too late. That girl, if she had ever been real in the first place, was gone.

I JERKED AWAKE. My head was swimming, my eyes watering. I struggled to stand and fell into a heap on the floor. After a few dizzy moments, I managed to make my way out of the room and crawl to the bathroom so I could vomit into the toilet.

I threw up once, twice, three times, then jerked with dry heaves. I could

still feel his skin against mine. I heaved and gagged, as if by emptying myself I could undo the past. Because what I had seen in that dreamlike state
was true. I was confident the bloodflower hadn't made me hallucinate or
invent a false account—those images were unearthed memories, no more
and no less.

From my place on the bathroom floor, I lifted my head to gaze out the
window. Hours had passed and now it was night, the stars visible because I
hadn't been able to turn on the bathroom light. In my imagination, the stars
morphed into marking patterns and the sky flattened into a blueprint. My
markings had been stolen. Who knew where they'd turn up: on flyers in sex
shops, in an erotic comic book series, in the tarot. Men bought these items
for the voyeuristic thrill of viewing real girls and their real markings. It
only took a bit of money to claim the body of a girl.

I was sick one last time. Once I finished, I rose to my feet. My body felt
creaky and broken. I washed my mouth out in the sink and drank a glass of
water. Finally, I swatted my hand along the wall until I found the light
switch. At the sudden brightness, I lost sight of the stars outside. They remained only in my memory, arranged and unchangeable in their constellations.

"Celeste?" Miles was outside the bathroom, knocking. "Are you all
right?"

I opened the door and looked at him blearily. He was holding *Mapping
the Future* but lowered it once he saw my face.

"Come on," he said. "You need to sleep this off."

He led me to my room, where he stood to the side as I crumpled
into bed.

"Some people take to bloodflower more than others their first time," he
said. "Don't worry, it will wear off soon. Where'd you get it, anyway?"

"Deirdre stopped by today." I licked my dry lips. "She was acting
strange. She thought she was being followed, and she had the idea you
might have something to do with that."

An expression I couldn't quite decipher crossed my brother's face: Concern? Frustration? It vanished before I could decide.

"Deirdre is troubled," he said.

"She said an inspector came to look at her arm," I went on. I kicked the sheets around my feet to get more comfortable. "Which I found strange, because an inspector visited me in the hospital. Remember, I tried to tell you? She had my childhood file, and she examined my arm. I was halfway convinced it was a dream."

For a few seconds, Miles and I stared at each other. I was glad to see that his black eye had paled nearly beyond recognition.

"That's odd," he said finally. "But maybe that's the protocol with returned girls."

"Maybe."

I looked at *Mapping the Future,* which he had tucked under his arm. "I suppose you're still taking interpretation classes with Julia."

"It's more than that. Julia made me her apprentice. I never told you this, but she hasn't charged me for classes for ages because she thinks I can actually make a career out of it." He glanced at me, a quick self-conscious look like he expected me to laugh. "I know it's unlikely, but I believe I'll find a way to make this work. As long as I'm persistent."

I nestled deeper under the covers. "I wish I felt that way about my chances of becoming a psychologist." I didn't even try to hide the bitterness in my voice.

"Hey," Miles said. "You still have a solid future. You do. Remember that." He touched my arm, but for once, this didn't make me flinch. His touch felt respectful, professional. I could picture him in the future, working as an interpreter to help girls and women find their way.

But that would never happen. He would barely get to be an adult, much less have a career. He would miss out on everything, and he still didn't know. Surely I was doing a good deed by not telling him of his fate. By concealing the pattern on my ribs, I was protecting my brother and our family from the coming years of agony. It was better to have the grief arrive all at once in a single shock wave rather than in a slow, unbearable crescendo.

"You should sleep," he said. "Sleep is the best thing for you right now."

He pulled the quilt over my shoulders and snapped the light off, leaving me in the dark.

IN THE MORNING, I stayed in bed for a long time after I woke, watching the sun grow brighter and brighter against the curtains. When I finally got up and showered, I scrubbed my skin, hard. I looked down and tried to grasp that this was the same body that existed in that wood-paneled room, that lay under a strange man. It seemed a terrible, unreal story I'd told myself, something completely beyond belief.

My bruises continued to fade. Soon they would disappear entirely.

I dressed in a dark, ankle-length dress topped with a black cardigan. I dried my hair and brushed it. I did not apply makeup. I buttoned the top button of the sweater, gave myself a last look in the mirror, and went downstairs.

My mother was in the kitchen holding a banana with its top half peeled open. She watched as I slid into my shoes in the hallway.

"I'm going to take a walk," I said.

She looked concerned. "By yourself?"

"Mom. There's nothing to worry about anymore."

She gazed at me unhappily. "I suppose you're right." She walked over to the trash and dumped the banana in, even though she hadn't finished it. The sound it made when it landed echoed inside the trash can, the kitchen, my head.

"I'll be back soon, I promise."

I left. Outside, I felt my family and friends following me like phantoms. My parents would surely condemn what I was doing, but Marie might have offered her support if I hadn't pushed her away. I wasn't sure how Cassandra would respond; I was starting to wonder if I'd ever known her at all.

I walked until the police headquarters loomed ahead of me, a blond-brick building with a maroon roof that looked like rust. Inside, I signed the log, writing *New information in abduction case* in shaky handwriting as my reason for the visit. Then I waited alone until an officer called my name. As he led me through the maze of cubicles, the other officers—all men except for a lone woman—glanced curiously at me. As if I were a lost child in their midst.

I was seated at a table near the back of the room and left to wait again. The table was piled high with various documents: financial forms, school registrations, tax booklets, and both federal and nongovernmental employment applications. I sifted through that last stack until I found an application for the position of humanitarian ambassador.

It was a simple application, front and back of a single sheet of paper. Any woman over the age of eighteen could apply, even those who'd once been abducted. The Humanitarian Global Alliance always needed more women willing to give up their personal lives to contribute to this cause, and it was an open secret that ruined women might be naturally inclined to help vulnerable girls.

"Isn't it wonderful," Mrs. Ellis once told my health class, "isn't it a *relief* that women in this country aren't subjected to mandatory police inspections, and that they in fact have this choice to work for a global organization? We have truly come far."

At the bottom of the application, the annual salary was printed in tiny type. I stared at the figure, which seemed astronomical to me, and then folded the application and placed it in my bag. I did this covertly, quietly. It was a time when everything I did seemed tinted with shame.

A detective finally strode in and greeted me. The best way I could describe him was that he was soft—pillowy stomach, doughy hands, broad face. His eyes were not unkind. He took a seat next to me.

"What do you have for us today, Miss Morton?" he asked.

I cleared my throat. This moment would have to make up for the university admission interviews I'd never have. This was my opportunity to be grown up, to showcase my worth.

"I'm here about my case. I was abducted last month, and I was released from the hospital this week." I paused, waiting. The detective did not have my file open before him. He was, in fact, empty-handed.

"Go on," he said.

"Well. I thought you should know I have a new lead on the case."

"Is that right?"

"Yes. I recovered some memories. I was kept in a basement room with wood paneling. The man who held me there was a teacher. I remember his face."

The detective offered a sympathetic smile. "That's very impressive, Miss Morton. And how, exactly, did you manage to recover these memories?"

"That's not important. What matters is I remember."

He was still smiling. "Let me guess. Bloodflower?"

"I'm not so great at drawing," I said, "but if you take me to a sketch artist, I could describe him."

He eyed me steadily.

"Or we could do a lineup," I suggested. "He's a teacher for students about my age, maybe younger. If you round up some male teachers and bring them in, I could tell you if he's there. I'd remember his face. I'm sure of it."

"Miss Morton." His voice was gentle. "Memories recovered artificially, via illegal controlled substances, are not admissible. We can't arrest someone based on that."

"But I'm telling you that I remember. I can picture his face right now."

"That's not proof. I understand how you must feel. Helpless. Angry. You've had a lot taken from you, and it can't be easy to accept. It's not fair, certainly." He nodded sagely, as if it was a big sacrifice for him to admit how unjust my situation was. "But don't drag yourself through even more emotional turmoil over this. If you were to enter a bloodflower memory into the official record, I'm afraid that would just embarrass you."

"Embarrass me?" My hands felt numb. I wondered if I was having a stroke, if I was about to die right there in the police station.

"Let me tell you something," he said. "These cases are horrible for us, too. To see girls ruined and not be able to do anything about it." He shook his head. "But we can't allow unreliable evidence. Can you imagine if we started locking up men left and right based on false accusations?"

"They're not false. They're real." I began to cry. "At least look into

Chloe, the interpreter downtown. She works with trappers, she tips them off. If you investigate her, you might find this man."

"I'm surprised, Miss Morton, that you'd blame a woman in all this. Chloe isn't the one who ruined you, is she? Blaming her won't help." He shook his head. "My advice is that you go home and get a good night's sleep. Let your body and mind heal. You've been through a lot."

He stood up. The overhead lights reflected briefly off his badge, blinding me. I knew I was supposed to get up, too, to follow him out the door, but I couldn't do it. I slumped deeper into the chair.

"You're making this harder on yourself," he said in a low voice. "Come along now. I'll walk you out."

I let him. I let him lead me by the elbow all the way through that maze of cubicles, where I refused to look at any of the other officers. The room was deadly quiet.

Outside, the midday sun blazed; that year, the autumn turned unseasonably warm off and on for weeks. I peeled off the black cardigan and marched home at a brisk pace. Anytime I encountered a neighbor or passerby, I lifted my chin a bit higher. By the time I made it to my house, a jabbing pain shot through my neck.

At home, I waited for Miles to return. Once he did, I rushed into his room. I didn't even knock, I just ran in, and he jumped at my sudden entrance. I wrenched a sketchpad from the pile of books and papers on his desk.

"Here," I said, and thrust the pad and a charcoal pencil at him. "I need your help."

I sat on the edge of the unmade bed and described the face of the man that had materialized during my bloodflower vision. Miles listened, the pencil clenched in his fist, but he remained motionless.

"What are you waiting for?" I asked. It was only when I looked closer that I saw his eyes were red and unfocused. He must have been on bloodflower himself, must have turned to the drug as an escape. I pushed that knowledge aside. "Miles, please. *Draw.*"

And he did. My brother drew the face I described. It took a long time, and it wasn't easy for either of us, but we worked at it together. Miles focused so intently on the task that he didn't seem to understand the implications of what I had asked of him. He sketched as if in a fugue state, with faith and without fear.

When we finished, I pulled the drawing from his grasp. I held the paper so tightly I thought I might grind it to dust in my hands.

"Celeste," Miles said. "What have we done?"

I lifted the sketch. "Everyone acts as though I'm the only one who played a part in my abduction, that it was my fault I was taken. No one ever talks about the man who did this to me. But here he is. He exists, and I just proved it."

My brother's face went white. "You know the police won't accept this, right?" he asked.

I shook my head, disappointed that my brother had missed the point. But then I looked at the drawing again and felt sick, like I'd done something unholy. I had brought to life in the physical world what was meant to stay concealed in murky memory.

Miles reached for the drawing but stopped before touching it, like it might burn him. I wanted my brother to keep going, to tear the drawing to pieces and swallow them whole. To obliterate this man's face and what had been done to me.

But I knew he would not. What I held in my hands was my weight alone to bear.

"Promise me you'll get rid of that," Miles said.

I left my brother and floated toward my room. The drawing was mine. I had birthed it, and I would be the one to destroy it.

Stage 6: Bargaining and Denial. By this point in your recovery, your physical injuries have healed and your mental and emotional states grow stronger by the day. Once you have fully regained your strength and have faced reality, you may engage in the fantasy of returning to your former life as though nothing has changed. Perhaps you're convinced that if you say or do just the right thing, you can return to school, rekindle old friendships, or resume your role as the favorite daughter at home. Do not fall victim to this line of thinking.

As in the other stages, you may return to bargaining and denial many times throughout your recovery, but you must be vigilant against it now. Repeat to yourself: *Nothing is the same, and everything has changed, and I am incapable of altering the tide of fate.*

This is the first step toward acceptance.

19

My mother took me to school on Monday morning and joined me in the principal's office, where we sat before a stack of paperwork. As a returned girl, I had to complete admission forms as though I'd never attended this school in the first place.

Mr. Radshaw stood facing the window while I worked. From time to time I glanced at his back, so straight and stiff and unpleasant. I thought I sensed discomfort emanating from him. I thought he didn't want me there.

I filled out the final form and passed it to my mother to sign. She held her pen poised over the signature line.

"Are you sure you want to do this?" she asked.

I didn't hesitate. "I want my diploma."

She signed the form. The ink of her signature looked a bit shaky, but it was there.

"Thanks, Mom." I looked at her expectantly. "You can go now."

She worried her fingers along the strap of her purse. "I don't know about this."

"I'll be fine. Just go, please. I have class."

She stood, and Mr. Radshaw came over and shook her hand. I braced myself for the adult conspiracy, a whispered conference about me, but it didn't happen. My mother just asked Mr. Radshaw to look after me, and then she left.

"Am I free to go to class?" I asked.

Mr. Radshaw lowered himself into his chair. He placed his elbows on the desk and leaned forward, showing me more of his balding head. Instinctively, I shifted my weight back in my chair.

"It takes courage to come back," he said. "Most girls don't."

"Like I said, I want my diploma."

He nodded, but his mind seemed elsewhere. "Let me know if you have any trouble out there. You can come to this office at any time. Understand?"

I agreed. I was ready to burst out of that office, to succumb to the relief of crowded halls and gossiping students. I was in such a hurry to leave Mr. Radshaw that I didn't dwell on how he described the school. *Out there,* he'd said. A wild landscape, vicious and raw.

That was exactly what I found. In the hallway, where I stood before my open locker, a boy ran by and slammed the locker door shut so suddenly he nearly caught my fingers inside. He was a brown-haired blur, a rush of rage.

"Slut," he said. He hovered there for a moment, full of righteous energy, before he banged a fist against the row of lockers and took off again down the hall.

I stood with my mouth agape. The girl next to me—Trish, that was her name, an alto in chorus—had watched this scene with a disapproving look.

"Can you believe that?" I said.

"Sure I can believe it," Trish said. She leaned in close. Her tone was hard, and although some prehistoric part of my brain was sending out warning signals, I couldn't make myself move.

"You disgust me," she added. And then she spat in my face.

AFTER A SOLID twenty minutes in the bathroom—five of those minutes spent washing and rewashing my face, then another fifteen hiding in the far stall to cry—I wiped my eyes and stepped back into the hallway. As much as I wanted to run home, I had to stick it out. A little spit was nothing compared to what I'd lived through.

I proceeded to history class, which was already half over. No one looked at me when I came in and took a seat in the back, not even the teacher. I didn't bother to open my textbook or take notes. When the bell rang, I walked heavily down the hall toward my science class. This was what I'd been dreading all day: Cassandra and Marie were in this class. I was afraid to see them, afraid I'd ruined everything between us forever.

Like a coward, I entered the room and immediately ducked into a seat. I stared down again, not looking up even when I heard whispers rising around me.

"I can't believe she came back," someone said.

"It's revolting," someone else responded. "Can you imagine where she's been?"

Another student, a boy, laughed.

I took out a pen and pressed it hard into the desktop. I didn't draw anything, just kept forcing the pen down into that one spot. As if I could drill through to the other side if I only used enough pressure.

"Celeste?"

I looked up. Marie stood before me with her hands clasped in front of her, like she was about to pray or beg. Cassandra waited next to her.

"Hey, guys," I whispered. "I'm sorry, you know. About what I said at my house."

"Never mind," Marie said quickly. "We know you've been through a lot."

"And we think it's brave that you came back," Cassandra added.

I smiled, fighting the tears that threatened to start at this show of kindness. "I want to get my diploma."

Cassandra nodded. "I can respect that."

Marie put a hand on my arm. "Really, Celeste. It's good to see you."

I was about to say something more, maybe blurt out how relieved I was that they didn't hate me, but the bell rang, signaling the start of class. My friends returned to their seats and, for the first time that day, I managed to pay attention to the lecture. Afterward, Marie and Cassandra waited for me and we spent a quick moment together in the hall between classes, huddled close like old times.

Throughout the rest of the morning, I floated from class to class. Most teachers treated me as though I'd never left, which I found preferable to the few who made a point of welcoming me back. By lunchtime, I felt a little better. I took my bagged lunch to my regular table, where Marie and Cassandra were already eating.

"Oh, you're sitting here?" Cassandra asked as I sank into the chair next to her.

I looked around. The table sat four people, and we were the only three there.

"It's just that Jonah and Anne have been sitting with us sometimes," Marie said. Her face was red.

"You don't want to sit with me?"

"That's not it," Cassandra said, but she wouldn't look me in the eye. "We'll pull up an extra chair when they get here."

"This table's too small for five." I shoved my sandwich back into the bag. "I'll go."

"Celeste, stay," Marie insisted. "Besides, it won't be like this for long, anyway." She glanced at Cassandra. "Cassie's leaving us."

I stopped gathering my things. "What do you mean?"

"I got into Laurel Haven," Cassandra said. "I start next quarter."

"That snobby private school across town? You'll have to wear a uniform."

"If I want to get into medical school, I need to be serious. I need a school that will look impressive on my transcript, not one that has a reputation."

"A reputation," I said slowly.

"It's complicated," Cassandra went on. "Think of it from the perspective of a university admission panel. Two girls from the same school taken within a few weeks of each other does not look good. I'm sorry, but it doesn't." She leaned over and put a hand on mine. "It's nothing personal, Celeste."

I pulled my hand away. "I'm sorry I've been such an inconvenience to you."

My chair squealed when I pushed back from the table, and then I was hurrying through the cafeteria. I had nearly reached the exit when a boy I didn't recognize grabbed my wrist.

"Relax," he said as I tried to wrestle away. "I just want to see you up close."

"Let go." I pulled harder, but he held fast.

"It's not like I'd be the first," he added. He yanked me closer and put his hands on my sides, like we were dancing. One hand traveled up, stopped just by my left breast. The heel of his palm pressed there, not quite groping, not quite grabbing, but enough to show me what he could do. A suggestion of ownership, and maybe a promise of more to come.

He let go just as quickly, but I could still feel his hand on my body. I stood in front of him for a moment, sputtering. I couldn't breathe. I'd dropped my lunch bag in the tussle, and it lay smashed at my feet. The boy's entire lunch table—three boys, one girl—broke into laughter.

"I can't believe you touched her," the girl said. "You might have caught something."

I turned and ran from the cafeteria. I wasn't thinking, I was merely fleeing, so it came as a surprise that I headed straight for the principal's office. I burst inside, gasping, to find Mr. Radshaw drinking a cup of coffee. He calmly set it down upon my entrance, as though he'd been expecting me.

"I can't do this," I burst out. I stayed by the door, holding on to the doorknob as though it were the lifeline that could save me.

"Of course not," he said. "Those kids will make your life hell. But it was impressive that you insisted on trying. As I said, most girls don't."

"I wanted to graduate. I wanted to become a psychologist." I started to cry. "It's not fair."

"No, it's not. But there are other options for your diploma. You're a smart girl, and you'll figure something out." He reached for the phone. "Have a seat and try to breathe. I'll call your mother to come pick you up."

I let go of the doorknob and came over to his desk. "I'd rather you didn't. She was against me coming back to school in the first place."

"Then she'll be relieved you're leaving."

"Please don't call her. It's too embarrassing. I can walk home."

Mr. Radshaw hesitated. "I can't let you walk home alone in this state. But I suppose I could have my secretary drive you."

I shook my head. "You can call someone else."

I gave him Julia's number.

She arrived within the half hour, time I passed sitting quietly while Mr. Radshaw worked at his desk. He gave me a book to read, some fairy tale about girls who were really birds, or maybe it was birds who were really girls; I couldn't focus on it. When Julia finally arrived, Mr. Radshaw nodded to me.

"I wish you the best," he said, and held out his hand for me to shake. "And you can keep that book."

I didn't want the book. It had a hard cover made of aged blue cloth, and it smelled musty. But I took it with me as he asked, all the while knowing I'd never open it again.

"You should have called your mother," Julia told me as she guided me outside. She had hugged me hard when we met outside Mr. Radshaw's office, an enveloping, all-consuming embrace. I could still feel it. "You need your mother at times like these."

"I need a break from my family."

We reached a car that was unfamiliar to me—a copper-colored, slightly beat-up sedan. I'd later learn she bought it after my abduction, when she was overcome with guilt thinking that if her old car had been usable on First Friday, she could have driven me home.

Julia paused before getting into the driver's seat. "If you weren't going to call your mother, then I'm glad you chose me. You and I—we need to trust each other from here on out. Do you understand?"

As usual, I didn't understand Julia. But I nodded anyway.

"We were all so worried about you," she went on. "All of us, but especially your brother." She paused, her gaze landing on my exposed forearms. I was wearing a fitted black shirt with sleeves that stopped at my elbows.

"May I see?" she asked. I nodded again, and she took my arms in her hands.

A few remnants of bruising were still visible, but Julia looked past those to focus on my markings—my adult markings, the ones I hadn't let anyone see after I changed. How silly I felt for that attempt to hide myself. It had almost worked, too, up to that moment in the alley with Miles, after which I was taken and given these bruises. That was how I saw it, that the bruises were *given*, a monstrous gift.

Julia looked at my arms carefully, in a way that my mother and even Miles hadn't. Since I'd been in the hospital, they averted their eyes from my body, as if catching a glimpse of my skin would be shameful.

"You're all right," Julia said at last. "I'm so glad you're back, Celeste. Now get in. I'll take you to my place for the afternoon, but we have to hurry. I'm late."

"For what?"

She didn't answer.

During the drive, I considered unburdening myself to Julia. I could confess what had happened with the spit or the boy who grabbed me, but my mind was already cementing over those moments, sealing them off.

"I don't know what to do," I said. "I want to earn my diploma, but I can't go back there. I don't want to do correspondence classes, either." I turned to face the window, choking back tears. "It's impossible."

"There are other ways." Julia's voice was quiet. "The education at the Mountain School is stellar—better than anything you'd get here."

"My family can't afford that."

Julia paused, clearly too polite to agree with me. "Don't give up hope yet," she said eventually.

I didn't reply. Hope was another luxury I couldn't afford.

When we arrived at the townhouse, Miles was standing on the front stoop.

"We've been waiting," he told Julia. "You know I can't start without you. There's already a girl in your office."

I frowned at him. "Why aren't you in school?"

"I stopped going."

"You can't drop out. You're in your final year." I paused, shocked. "Do Mom and Dad know?"

"Not yet. But they'll accept it once they learn I'm bringing in an income."

I turned to Julia. "You can't possibly support this. What about his future?" The words came out of my mouth before I remembered that within a few years, that would be a moot point.

"This is my future," Miles said. "Working as an interpreter." He opened the front door and gestured toward the parlor.

Inside, we faced about a half dozen girls, all unchanged. Four of them crammed onto the couch, and the other two sat in the armchairs. The mood was that of a dentist's waiting area: no one was particularly happy to be there, and they wanted even less to be called for the appointment.

"Miles, you stay with Celeste," Julia said. "I'll call you if I need you."

Once she left, my brother led me upstairs.

"You can't do this," I told him. "The Office of the Future will never allow it." Back then I didn't understand much about the Office of the Future, or just how it might infiltrate our lives—but I knew enough to see it as a threat.

"They don't know about it. Besides, I'm more like Julia's assistant. For now, she does the readings and only calls me if she needs confirmation."

"Confirmation on what?"

He didn't answer. He took me to the guest bedroom and told me to have a seat on the bed. He sat at the desk, pulled open the top drawer, and took out a bag of bloodflower pills.

"You want one?" he asked.

I shrank back. "Definitely not. I'm surprised Julia allows bloodflower in her house."

"This is my stash. She lets me sleep in this room, sometimes, and she never comes in to poke around. She respects my privacy." He looked at me pointedly, as if he were too weary to bother telling me I had to keep his secret. All the while, he fiddled with the bag in a distracted sort of way. He looked half a second from removing a pill and popping it into his mouth.

"Miles, you can't take that. Not now." I heard the alarm in my voice. Fatal bloodflower overdoses were rare, almost unheard of, but I still worried. Any end was possible for my brother.

He sighed and tossed the bag into the drawer. "I never take bloodflower when I'm working, and Julia might need me to work today. So you can relax."

I pulled my legs up to sit cross-legged on the bed, trying to make sense of all that was going wrong. "I still can't believe you dropped out of school."

"Not everyone is a star student like you."

"Like that does me any good now." I paused, thinking. "On the way over here, Julia mentioned the Mountain School. It made me wonder if maybe they have scholarships. You know, for girls who are disadvantaged and have no other options."

"That describes every girl who needs that school, Celeste. It's only the ones with money that have a chance."

I frowned. "You might consider how frustrating it is for me to watch you throw your education away when I have nothing—no chance of getting into university, no way of becoming a psychologist."

"I had to drop out." He wasn't looking at me. "It's my only way to make up for what I did to you."

"What do you mean?" I asked, but he was silent. "Miles, what are you talking about?"

"Nothing," he said. "Forget it. Go on downstairs and join Julia for a little while. The girls won't mind having you around. Maybe you can even help them."

I was about to argue, but when I saw his expression—wounded, guilt-ridden—I agreed to leave him and go to Julia. He and I probably needed some space from each other anyway.

The girls waiting in the parlor raised their heads in unison when I came downstairs, but when they saw it was me, they looked down again and stared silently at their hands. Seeing them like that, vulnerable and uncertain, made me feel motherly. It made me feel old.

"Before I changed, Julia read my markings, too," I told them. "I was scared. But don't worry. Julia's very skilled."

"She is," one girl said. "But Miles is even better."

I was about to ask what she meant when Julia entered the parlor. Her face was pale.

"I need Miles. Now." She directed her words my way, but I had the sense she wasn't fully seeing me. "Celeste, hurry. Tell me where he is."

I blinked at her, startled. "He's upstairs. In the guest room."

Without another word, Julia turned and stiffly ascended the stairs. The girls were now visibly agitated.

"That's not a good sign," one whispered to another.

"What's going on?" I asked, but the girls only studied their hands again.

A faint sound drifted from down the hall. It sounded like crying. I followed the sound to Julia's office and pushed open the door to find a girl sitting on the chair next to Julia's desk, gulping back sobs. She had wide-set eyes and a smattering of amber-colored moles across the bridge of her nose. Like the other girls, she looked to be maybe fourteen or fifteen years old and unchanged. She was tall, her body wrapped in a pale blue hospital gown.

"Hi," I said softy as I entered. "I'm Celeste. I'm Miles's sister. What did Julia tell you that has you so upset?"

The girl looked at me, tears streaking her cheeks. "Nothing yet, but I saw the look on her face." She paused to take a strangled breath. "Julia wouldn't have gone to get Miles if she hadn't seen something."

I was still confused. "Like what?"

She lifted her left arm and pushed back the gown. "Here," she said, pointing to the markings near her elbow. "It must be those, right there."

Gently, I placed my fingers on her arm and traced her markings. All I could see was a vague indication of illness, like a bad cold.

"I don't understand."

Julia reappeared, pulling Miles into the room.

"Look," she told him, gesturing to the girl's arm. "Please tell me I'm wrong."

Miles pressed his fingers firmly to the girl's arm. Within moments, his face set in a grim expression.

"Yes," he said simply. The girl snatched at her hospital gown and started to cry harder.

Julia took a deep breath. "Try to calm yourself," she said. "Think of the other girls waiting out there. You don't want to frighten them, do you?"

The girl shook her head, the tears streaming down.

"What's going on?" I asked.

My brother's eyes skittered across the room instead of meeting mine. "It's her markings. She's going to be abducted after she changes."

"Markings don't reveal that type of information. That's not possible."

"It is," he said simply. "I learned how to do it. I can tell if a girl is going to be taken."

A rushing sound, like water or a train or another unstoppable force, flooded my hearing.

"You didn't see it with me," I said.

When Miles finally faced me, he looked stunned, his bottom lashes wet with tears. His eyes were entire worlds unto themselves, portals of our grief and lies, the secrets we kept and the futures we destroyed.

"That's the thing," he said, "the thing I never told you. I kept it from you to protect you."

"Miles, stop. This can't be true."

"It is. I could tell you were fated to be taken." His pupils looked huge, about to swallow him up and take me with him. "I never told you, but I knew the entire time."

STRATEGIES FOR REINTEGRATION:
A 7-STAGE GUIDE FOR RECOVERY AND REHABILITATION

Stage 7: Acceptance. This final stage is the most elusive. Indeed, many patients never fully accept what happened to them, but it is imperative to try. Acknowledging that you are powerless in the face of your newly changed future need not be distressing; instead, it can be liberating. Give yourself the gift of letting the past wash over you. Allow your trauma to be a part of your new reality.

Absorb it, accept it, let it set you free.

20

MILES CALLED HIS ability a gift. He said the prediction came to him like starbursts of color behind his closed eyelids: three sparks, all red. Then he knew to check more closely to confirm the girl was destined to be taken.

That was how he knew with me.

We left Julia with the ill-fated girl in the exam area to shut ourselves in the guest room. We sat on the bed next to each other, our shared weight creating a dip in the mattress, a bit of gravity pulling us closer.

"I don't believe this. I can't and I won't." I leaned forward at the waist, pressing my forearms into my thighs. I was so furious I was shaking.

"I first noticed something odd about the markings on your arm when we were kids, but I didn't understand what it meant," Miles said. "Later, when I found a similar pattern on Deirdre's arm, and then when she disappeared, I started to suspect it was a real prediction."

"If you'd said something," I told him, "maybe I could have been saved."

"I kept hoping I was wrong. I had no way to prove it, and not enough evidence to be certain."

My heart was pounding, and I felt ready for flight. But there was no-where to go, no way to escape what my brother had just revealed.

"I told Julia after Deirdre disappeared," he said. "She wasn't convinced, especially since it doesn't present as a regular pattern. The pattern itself varies, it's inconsistent, and interpreting it is partly based on touch. She thought it was a coincidence." He looked away, ashamed. "I was stupid. I made so many mistakes."

I took a deep breath, trying to reimagine my childhood through the lens of this new information. I saw Miles pulling at my shirt to look at my mark-ings, his hands lingering on my left arm—how he so deeply and openly anticipated my change.

"I kept telling myself that even if I was right, I couldn't do anything to prevent the prediction from coming true. If it's fated, it's fated. End of story," he went on. "But that doesn't excuse what I did that night. I wanted to get you alone to look at your markings. I thought they might give an-other clue, that they'd reveal exactly how you'd be taken. I planned the whole thing, you know. I told Cassie what to do beforehand, how she should go to Julia's so I could be alone with you. But I was reckless, and I'm sorry." His breath came out in a gasp. "I'm sorry," he repeated. "I swear I'll never forgive myself. That's why I left school, so I could try to help other girls. It will never make up for what happened to you, but it's all I can do."

I got up from the bed and grabbed *Mapping the Future*. I flipped through the pages so quickly they made snapping sounds. "If it's not in here," I said desperately, "then it can't be true."

"I'm trying. I've contacted the Office of the Future. I sent them copies of your childhood markings, plus copies of Deirdre's, and explained as best I could how to do the reading." He looked pained. "I thought they'd be grateful."

"No, you were showing off. You thought this could be your way into the profession." I dropped the book onto the dresser, where it landed with a hollow clap.

He flinched but kept going. "Imagine the change that could come, at some point in the future, if that prediction becomes an official part of

Mapping the Future," he said. "It might make things better for girls. For even just one girl. Julia says we can't change fate, but she also says our actions can have tiny, nearly imperceptible consequences. Think of what that can mean. Maybe fewer girls will be abducted, or maybe they won't be punished anymore for the crimes of men. Things could be different, Celeste."

All the pieces were clicking into place. My brother's contact with the Office of the Future, his revelation about this prediction—these were minor breezes that could shift his future in a new direction. Fate was a sensitive, complicated, evolving phenomenon, and maybe this was the catalyst pushing Miles toward the end of his life.

"Don't go through with this." I stood in front of my brother, summoning the will to plead with him even as I despised him, even as I understood his fate was set no matter how I tried to save him. "Don't try to get these markings added to the official record. Please."

"I have to, Celeste. Julia agrees. Girls should be fluent in their own futures, she says."

I laughed, the sound rolling out of me like pain. "Fluent in their own futures?"

"Yes."

I started pacing around the room. When I stopped at the dresser mirror, I confronted my reflection. I looked wild-eyed and furious. Feral.

Miles met my eyes in the mirror. His face was wet.

"Maybe this was the real reason I invented Did You Know," he said. "I thought it might help you, to be able to lie. I knew you'd have a hard time from here on out. If you could keep some things to yourself, to not reveal all your truths—that could make a difference."

"You might have done too good of a job," I said. In one swift motion, I grasped the hem of my shirt and pulled it over my head. Underneath I wore only a bra, solid black without a hint of lace.

Miles took a step back. "What are you doing?"

I wished I could say I was driven by guilt or compassion, the resolve to not let Miles live in the dark as long as I had. But in truth, I was consumed with anger. The horror of my own abduction was still all-consuming, and I wanted to exact a punishment. I wanted revenge.

Miles turned away. "Put your shirt on."

I took another step toward him. "I can't hide this anymore." I resisted the urge to cross my arms over my chest. I waited, cold and shivering and revealed. Agony.

At last, Miles faced me. He went directly for my left side, as I'd known he would, to the markings he hadn't been able to puzzle out from my father's photograph. A diagonal, an arc, a smattering of stars.

He lifted a finger and placed it on the markings. He traced them, gently, and in his touch I recalled all the other times he'd read my markings. How serious and insistent he'd been. Now I felt his hand shaking against my skin.

"Say something," I told him.

He closed his eyes. I felt, for a disorienting flash, that I was no longer in the room with him. He was alone, standing in silence, grasping at his own receding future.

Time slowed, stopped, held steady. I found myself swimming in a memory. It was a few summers back, out in the heat of our neighborhood, when Miles and I came across a group of boys tormenting a praying mantis. They'd tied a string to it, ripped off one of its legs, and were twirling it around. They were laughing. I started to turn away, but Miles inserted himself into the group and confronted those boys, speaking in low tones until they hung their heads and drifted away. We were left with the mantis lying at our feet, mangled and dismembered but still alive. Miles looked down at the struggling insect for a long moment before he lifted his foot and brought it down, hard, on the delicate green body.

I couldn't shake that memory. It had been a time I'd witnessed two parts of my brother at once: his mercy, his ruthlessness. How even his kindest intentions resulted in ruin.

Miles picked up my shirt and handed it to me, looking away as I slid it on. He wore a hardened expression, his body tensed as if bracing for impact.

"I'll tell Julia," he said. "She needs to know we're running out of time."

"Miles."

"Those markings on her ankle make sense now," he added. "I worked so hard to try to figure it out, and it turns out I'm the one she'll lose." He looked at me, his eyes sharp and daring. "Julia can know, but that's it. I'm serious. Don't tell anyone else, Celeste. Not your friends. And especially not Mom and Dad."

"I'm the one who's been keeping this a secret in the first place. But it's going to get out before long. This is too big, Miles. This is your entire life."

"Exactly. It's mine, and I don't want them to know. Not telling them is a kindness."

"Do you wish I hadn't told you?"

He wouldn't answer. He stepped to the mirror and studied his face up close, as if he could find a clue to his future there.

"It's not an easy secret to keep," I added. "It was the hardest one of my life."

When Miles looked at me again, I fell silent. Of course he would succeed in concealing his future, just as he kept my future from me. Not only was he a master liar, but he taught me his trade. Deception had become our shared language.

"Only Julia can know," he repeated. "At least until I'm ready."

I said nothing, refusing to offer him reassurance. As furious as I was, part of me understood that in his own way, he had been trying to protect me. Lying by omission was his gift to me—the very same gift I'd attempted and failed to give him.

The sound of approaching footsteps pulled our attention to the door, which Julia pushed open to face us. I could read everything in her eyes. She wanted to know if I was all right, if I could forgive her and Miles for withholding my fate. I couldn't stand to look at her.

"I'm sorry," I told Julia, and then I pressed past her and fled.

ON THE WAY home, I was determined to reveal everything. Now that Miles knew the truth, I couldn't imagine not telling our parents. I believed that to move forward, we all had to start from the same place. That meant they needed to know.

It was mid-afternoon, far too early for my father to be home from work, but his car was in the driveway. I let myself inside and heard my parents' voices drifting from the kitchen. I didn't pause to consider what that might mean. In that moment I was still thinking of myself—how I'd hidden the truth about Miles from them, how they'd react when they learned his fate.

I rounded the corner into the kitchen. My parents sat at the table, their hands open and empty in front of them.

"You're home early," said my mother.

The school day crashed around me, a minor catastrophe overshadowed by the rest of the day's horrors.

"So's Dad," I said.

My father shifted in his seat. "I was let go today."

A wave of vertigo hit me. "It was because of me, wasn't it."

My father wouldn't look my way. "Cutbacks were in the works for a while now, and it seems my department was bloated. That's the word they used. *Bloated.*"

"They could have let someone else go. You've been there forever." My legs were shaking. I sat down, heavily, at the table with my parents. "Now we won't have any money, and it's all my fault." I started to cry.

"Don't," my mother said. "This family is going to be fine."

They couldn't know I was crying not just for the lost job, but also for what would happen to Miles—for what I couldn't possibly tell them now.

"It's not your fault, Celeste," my father added. "We each played a role in this. All we can do is find a way to move on."

I shook my head. I was still crying. "I've tried to move on, and it was awful. Like school? I can't ever go back. I quit."

My parents took in that news with grim but unsurprised expressions.

"We'll figure something out," my mother assured me. "You can take correspondence classes, and I'll find work."

"No one will hire you now, Mom."

For once, no one argued with me. Then I remembered something. I jumped up and ran upstairs, dug a paper out of my bag, and brought it back down. I unfolded it and lay it delicately before my mother. She picked up the application with two fingers and held it at a remove.

"I know it seems extreme, but humanitarians make a lot of money," I said. "And you'd make an excellent humanitarian, especially with your teaching experience. Think of how gratifying it would be to help girls. This is perfect for you."

My mother allowed herself a small smile. "Maybe. But this job is serious. I'd have to leave home."

"Our expenses would be taken care of." I paused. "Plus, it would help me. You'd make enough to pay for tuition at the Mountain School."

My adrenaline was flowing, my solution big enough and wild enough to convince me everything was not yet lost. I felt defiant and determined, ready to fight for my own future. For the first time, I not only questioned but outright refused what I'd been taught about the nature of fate. Perhaps the future was not outlined permanently, in stone, but rather made of something more malleable. With enough time or pressure, markings could fade, shift their meaning, or represent something else.

My brother had known before I had the tragedy that awaited me. I was furious with him, but I was also struggling to see the future a bit more like he did: complicated, interlocked, prismatic. Perhaps capable of change. No more did I see the markings as little gods, the rulers of my life and the future. They were part of my body, but that was all—one single aspect of my larger, more brilliant life.

"It all works out," I went on. "You'll get a fulfilling career, and I can get my education."

"It's an outrageous idea," my father said, but my mother was quiet. Maybe she was already imagining the new life she could step into—something she could embark on alone before eventually retreating home, where she'd find her family intact again. We all needed some sort of fantasy.

"It had crossed my mind," she finally admitted. She looked to my father. "We have so few options. We're already in debt. With neither of us working, things will just get worse."

"But you can't leave. That will only tear our family apart more."

"It's a job. Not an abandonment." My mother seemed to grow more determined with every word. "And the job wouldn't last forever."

"It's the only way," I confirmed, and the way my parents sat sagging in their chairs, helpless, made me feel lonelier than anything else. I was sixteen, and I was feeding them the answers. I was right to think that my father was so ashamed that he found it trying to be in my presence. I was right that my mother longed to follow her ambitions. I was right about it all.

I left my parents to make the decision I saw as inevitable. Upstairs, I entered my brother's room. Two steps in and my fury was reawakened: how he'd known what would happen to me, and how he'd pushed me into a dark alley anyway. The scene replayed in my mind on a loop, always with the same result: Miles never able to save me, and the two of us destined to withhold the full truth from each other. It had all started when he wanted to record my markings, to put them down on paper as if they belonged to him instead of me.

I grabbed giant handfuls of Miles's practice drawings and began tearing them to shreds. I used my bare hands, working so quickly and roughly that I gave myself papercuts. I didn't care. I wanted to leave my blood in his room. I wanted, in that one small way, to leave him the evidence of what had happened to me. To give him a glimpse of what was one day coming for him.

LATER, AS I sat alone in my bedroom, I thought of the girl I'd seen roll blankly past in the hospital, and of the rumors that she'd hurt herself. I understood that girl better now. I sensed the dark temptation licking my own veins, calling out for something to change, and what was an ending but a change? Maybe I couldn't do what that girl had attempted, but I could still make a break. I could erase myself from my family, from my past mistakes.

And so, when Miles returned home from Julia's a few hours later, he found me dismantling my bedroom. I tore through my possessions, tossing armfuls of clothes and mementos into my suitcase. I was sweating, and excited, and sick, as if I were leaving that very night instead of waiting the weeks it would take to arrange for my departure. I tasted bile and blood and a deep thrumming energy as I grabbed the objects I'd soon display in my dormitory in the mountains. My brother found me like this. My brother— my weary, wounded, ill-fated brother—found me packing.

For the second time, he was forced to watch me disappear.

IV

Reclamation

The Mountain School: An Origin Myth

In the deepest reaches of the forest, a girl birthed herself from a rock that cracked open like an egg. Instead of yolk there was light. Instead of shell there was stone. A slice of stone slipped inside the girl's heart. The light seeped, glittering, into her skin. She unfolded her limbs and came spilling out into the forest, a lonely creature with no parents, no siblings, no past, and no future.

There in the pale filtered light of the forest, she blinked.

21

I HUDDLED WITH MY friends Bettina and Alicia on the bed in Bettina's room. It was late, but that didn't matter. We had no curfew on the mountain, no quiet hours or dress code or any of the stifling rules we were accustomed to in our hometowns. The three of us were young women of seventeen, eighteen, and nineteen years old, cloistered away far from the real world with the freedom to be ourselves. We dreamed it could be like this always.

It was the first of June, but the nighttime mountain air was thin and chilled. Across my shoulders I draped the blanket my mother had sent me the previous fall for my seventeenth birthday. It was handmade, crocheted in jewel tones by girls assigned the task as therapy. As a humanitarian, my mother met girls who faced infinitely more harrowing realities than any of us had before we came to the mountain. I pulled the blanket close and poured myself a fresh cup of tea, mostly so I could feel the warmth through the cup.

"It's easy to criticize the inspection ritual here, where we have the

perspective to recognize how wrong it is," Alicia was saying. "But to everyone back home, it's just part of regular life."

We were carrying on the conversation we'd begun earlier that day in
our Heritage and Rituals class. The lesson had focused on the father-
daughter inspection ritual, that shameful rite of passage we'd each endured
back home before we had the language to denounce its flaws. One of our
classmates was determined to give a public lecture about the ritual once
she left the mountain and returned home, but my friends thought her plan
imprudent.

"Nothing she can say will change the minds of fathers back in her
hometown, or anywhere," Bettina said. "To them, it's an honorable tradition. They see it as their right."

"Even mothers advocate for it," Alicia added. "People get sentimental
over anything they consider tradition."

I carefully placed my teacup on Bettina's bedside table. "You sound
defeatist. Remember what our professors say—while fate cannot change,
people can. If we go home and say nothing, the ritual will carry on as always. These traditions stick around for so long precisely because no one
tries to stop them."

"True," Bettina said, "but I don't see how we can change something that
big. It's not like people are eager to listen to returned girls. Besides, we have
to be careful not to call too much attention to this place."

She was right. When we eventually returned to the outside world, we'd
need to be subtle regarding what we'd learned on the mountain; our professors stressed that above all else. That was why I hadn't told my friends that
I wrote to Julia and Miles about all I was learning on the mountain, or that
I hoped to put this education to use with them in the future. In any case, I
was not in a hurry. I'd been on the mountain for a good stretch—five hundred and seventy days, to be exact—but I had another year remaining before graduation.

We were still debating the merits and risks of trying to upend the
father-daughter ritual when our friend Lena appeared in the doorway. She
was holding something behind her back.

"Celeste." She seemed nervous. "I need to show you something."

Lena was only fourteen—she'd changed younger than most, and she'd only joined us at the Mountain School a few months prior—but she was clever and courageous. She'd attacked her captor, pressing her thumbs into his eyes until he released her. Though she might have escaped without anyone knowing about her abduction, she went right to the police. Not that it did much good, since her abductor was eventually set free on a technicality, but the fact he was arrested at all was a victory.

Lena waited. I was starting to feel uneasy at the sudden change in the room, the way the air had grown heavier.

"Whatever it is, just tell me," I said. "You know I hate secrets."

Lena stepped forward. From behind her back she produced a plain green box. I knew what it was at once, even before she handed it to me.

A tarot deck—the newest erotic edition.

I swallowed, determined not to cry. In my nearly two years at the Mountain School, I'd rarely cried. I was happy there. My bedroom had a view of mountain peaks, plus a sliver of far-off river that blazed in the setting sun. Out back were horses to ride, and berries to pick, and friends to laugh with. It was a good place. It still was, even with that deck in my hands.

I opened the box. Inside, the top card showed a drawing of a brown-skinned girl, naked with small breasts, her markings dotted in iridescent ink. The deck I'd seen years ago, at Rebecca's house, had been of the style that drilled tiny holes for the markings. This deck represented the classic version, the predictions painted on in spots as tiny as needle pricks.

It was my turn, anyway. Most of the other girls had already endured this. Bettina was back in her hometown, still recovering in a Reintegration Wing, when she appeared on flyers tacked up in sex shops. A nightmare. Alicia had been in a comic book, which was even worse. In comics, you were given movement, plotlines, partners. You were acted upon.

The cards were cold in my hand. I could not bring myself to look. In addition to my naked body and all my predictions, my card would also include one key detail: the marking pattern on my ribs predicting Miles's

death. I had never told my friends about my brother's fate. Only Professor
Reed knew the full truth.

I considered, then, that I'd made a grave error. The mountain was not
the real world. It was a place of safety and trust, and I should have shared
the truth with my friends. Instead, I'd reverted to my old ways of secrecy
and solitude.

"I'm sorry." I covered my face with my hands.

My friends did not ask me to elaborate. They drew closer and curled
around me on the bed. I let the tarot deck fall on the bedspread and imagined retreating back in time, to when I still had those telltale markings by
my left elbow. Back to a time when Miles knew a secret about me while I
knew nothing of what was to come for him.

WHEN I FIRST came to the mountain, Professor Reed handed me a
copy of *The Mountain School: An Origin Myth*. Every girl received a slender
leather-back copy of this story when she arrived, and tradition dictated that
she sleep with the book under her pillow that first night. On my first morning on the mountain, I'd woken up feeling changed. Like I had absorbed the
story overnight.

I was a different person back then. I was frightened, and sheltered, and
hadn't yet untangled the ways girls and women were held back in this
world. It took a month until I acclimated to the rhythms of the mountain,
until I began to understand the other girls and their unfamiliar language.
They critiqued the rituals we'd all grown up with, and questioned why
things worked the way they did, and proposed solutions. They seemed, to
my young eyes, on the brink of changing the entire world.

After my second month on the mountain, after making new friends and
meeting with Professor Reed and absorbing my course work, I felt ready to
face what I'd avoided back home: the study of interpretation. I started by
asking Alicia if I could read her markings.

"Of course," she'd said, and slipped out of her clothes right there in her
dorm room.

It was a gift, that level of trust. I approached and ran my fingers over her skin. Instead of telling myself I had no talent, instead of turning away and giving up when I reached a complicated prediction, I kept with it. I waited for the hum in my fingertips. I closed my eyes and opened them again. I let the force of the future rise from my friend's skin into my hands.

"Are you getting what you need?" Alicia asked me. I nodded, pressing my fingers to her markings to silently convey, *Yes, thank you, yes.*

I wrote my first letter to Miles and Julia after that reading. I didn't explain how something had changed in me, that I was no longer the girl they'd known but rather a young woman with a new purpose—they could grasp that on their own. I simply offered my help, and asked for theirs in return. From that moment on we forged a partnership across hundreds of miles, across time and distance and betrayal and hurt. Across the past and into the future.

I RETURNED TO my room and tossed the tarot deck onto the nightstand next to *The Mountain School: An Origin Myth.* For a long time, I sat staring at those two items on the nightstand. One fairy tale and one horror story. Fantasies, both. Finally, I reached past the origin myth and picked up the tarot. I wrapped my fingers around its weight and told myself I could survive whatever I found there. I had to. Surviving was all I knew.

I fanned the cards on my bed, flipping past each girl quickly. I didn't want to see these girls, didn't want to participate in their exploitation. We had a whole class devoted to this matter on the mountain, where we learned that purchasing, possessing, sharing, or even casually viewing stolen markings contributed to the suffering of those girls. How we could refuse to participate in the systems that surrounded us.

I shuffled through the cards in a rapid blur until I felt a tingling in my fingertips, a desperate zip of alarm as if my body recognized my own card before I did. I steeled myself, and then I looked.

The image was stunning. The card featured a midnight-blue background with a border of gold stars. I stood facing forward but turned, slightly, to the side. My left hand reached to partially cover my right breast while the other arm trailed back in a graceful arc. My hair—my normal, everyday brown hair—was idealized, made to be long and thick and wavy, the curls cascading in gorgeous spirals. And yes, there was my body, my nakedness.

Ace of Stars, the card read at the bottom. A mere three words of text. Otherwise, my tarot-self existed purely as skin, limbs, future.

I brought the card closer. How strange, to see my markings illuminated in gold ink on my skin. They were minute and delicate, little needlesticks of gold. I had to squint to make it out, but I could, just barely: the markings on my left side. The pattern was readable even without a magnifying glass. If my parents came across this card—my parents, whom I had abandoned for the mountain to pretend this tragedy would not play out—they would finally know.

The tarot had a way of traveling, of ending up in the hands of more than just immoral men. Collectors, art enthusiasts, interpreters who claimed erotic cards were powerful, and regular people who bought the cards as gifts or gags or even romantic gestures. Some women bought erotic decks to honor the girls pictured there, to celebrate their beauty and their loss. Such tangled, misguided intentions.

My parents had never discussed the tarot with me, but that didn't mean they weren't looking. Perhaps my mother, off on a humanitarian mission, might hear about the newest edition. I could picture her scanning the deck with a hard-beating heart as she searched for her own daughter. It was too dreadful to imagine my father doing the same, that he would allow his eyes to rest on my naked body once more, but I couldn't dismiss it. By then I knew not to discount any possibility, no matter how unsettling.

I spread the crocheted blanket across my lap, as if it could protect me. Officially, my mother's humanitarian job dispatched her to foreign nations to meet with vulnerable populations of girls whose own governments failed to support them. But I learned on the mountain that humanitarians also worked within our own nation. It seemed at-risk girls could be found everywhere, the world churning with female oppression. In extreme cases, humanitarians were sent to help girls who felt so trapped they turned to self-harm. These girls might tattoo over their markings or dye their skin in an attempt to escape their predicted futures. One girl in a neighboring nation reportedly poured battery acid on her arms to obscure her predictions. Another girl lit herself on fire.

My mother negotiated with local leadership to encourage improved policies. She also provided domestic art therapy for the girls, such as crocheting, beadwork, weaving, and fabric dyeing—creative outlets that instilled a sense of autonomy. The single time my mother was able to visit me on the mountain, she brought me a gorgeous silk dress, its color an ocean of blues. A girl had made it while recovering from the burns she suffered when she tried to bleach the markings off her skin.

"How awful," I'd told my mother. I tried to give her the dress back, thinking the girl who made it could use the beauty in her own life. But my mother refused to take it.

"Once these girls make things, they want nothing to do with them. These items remind them of their grief." She held up the dress, fingering its silken fabric. "Besides, this dress will be glorious on you. You deserve something pretty."

During that visit, I'd tried to mine my mother for more information about her work as a humanitarian. I wanted to know that what she was doing could change the world. But she was reticent; she said her work required the utmost confidentiality. I, meanwhile, did not tell her about Miles. And so we circled each other, afraid to reveal ourselves.

I swept the tarot cards from the bedspread. Soon, I would have no reason to continue hiding my brother's fate. Once my parents discovered this card bearing my image, I'd stand exposed, the truth sliding from my grasp as easily as a swath of fabric pieced together by the hands of girls who struggled but nonetheless survived.

Dear Celeste,

You asked in your last letter if I'm being careful. I'm not sure how to answer that. You say you want the truth, but you and I have never been fully honest with each other, have we?

I can assure you that Julia and I are hard at work, and the bits of curriculum you send us are exceedingly helpful. But what we're attempting is difficult. You're not here to witness the work we're doing day after day, how futile it sometimes seems to try to influence the future, and how our personal concerns are so small in the face of all there's still to accomplish. So no, I won't say I am being careful. I'm just doing all I can with the time still available to me.

As always, I hope you are learning as much as possible. I hope you are happy, and able to imagine a new kind of future for yourself. Please don't waste time worrying about me. What will come will come. Isn't that what we've always known from the start?

Miles

22

In the chill of morning, I slid into a wool sweater and set off for class. I passed the dining hall, the administration building, the darkroom, and the performing arts center. Through clusters of trees I caught glimpses of the man-made pond we used for skating in the winter and swimming in the summer. If I proceeded to the outskirts of campus, I'd reach the stables, where we took weekly riding lessons, and then the cemetery, where the tombstones were engraved with marking constellations.

Of all the miracles I experienced on the mountain—the friendships, the safety, the academics, the love—it was the school's physical existence that seemed the most astounding. The campus had been built decades ago on a summit in the White Star Mountains, a place once slated for an observatory. The atmosphere was thin, the nights darker than the darkest any of us had ever seen. What a trial it must have been to haul the brick and stone all that way. Professors and staff made periodic trips down the mountain to town, but the other girls and I were content to stay behind. It was safe on the mountain, isolated, our lungs strengthened by the elevation. It was a place meant for viewing the stars.

The academic hall was located next to the campus nursery, where I found my friend Jenn on the bench outside. She was nursing her infant daughter, Sophie, who was wrapped in a thick blanket.

"Aren't you cold?" I asked Jenn.

"I needed some air. One of the toddlers vomited all over the playroom." She laughed a little. "I thought I'd bundle up Sophie and give her breakfast while someone else cleans up the mess. Is that wrong?"

I smiled and joined Jenn on the bench. "No. I would have done the same."

"Won't you be late?"

"I'll only stay a minute. Sophie always cheers me up."

Jenn nodded. "Yes, I heard about the tarot. I'm sorry, Celeste. That's awful."

I waved my hand as if the tarot were inconsequential, as if the most private part of myself hadn't been wrenched from me and into the hands of the public. "I'll be fine. Besides, it's something we all have to go through."

"Hopefully not all of us." Jenn nodded at her daughter, who was nursing blissfully, her eyes squeezed shut beneath a woolen baby hat.

"I didn't mean Sophie," I said quickly. "Or any of the children here." I paused. "May they all have brighter futures than we do."

"It's all right. I know what you meant." She shifted Sophie to her other side. "But it's scary to think what's out there, and what kind of fate my daughter or any other girl might meet."

I nodded. Aside from Jenn, several other friends of mine on the mountain had babies. Giving changeling girls birth control, the theory went in many parts of the country, encouraged promiscuity. I only grasped how backward and cruel that line of thinking was when I came to the mountain and found a nursery full of babies and toddlers, all of whom had been born to abducted teenage girls.

"I want Sophie to be free," Jenn said. "To grow up to be herself. You know?"

I did. More than anything, I wished for those girls to have the ability to command their own lives, no matter what was marked on their skin. I wanted them to be liberated, and unafraid, and brimming with potential and possibility. But that wasn't how the world worked for girls and women. Instead, we were made vulnerable through no fault of our own and held liable for the crimes committed against us.

We were born already broken.

I STAYED WITH Jenn for longer than I'd expected, and when I finally left her, I bypassed the academic hall and headed toward the cemetery. I felt drawn to the world of the dead, to the quiet landscape of lives put to rest.

We learned so much on the mountain, but sometimes this education seemed a waste. To avoid unwanted attention from the Office of the Future, we had to be careful. We couldn't lead public charges against the crisis of abductions or the weak protections girls had compared to their kidnappers. Instead, we had to work covertly, making incremental efforts toward change. Our professors told us to think of our work like planting wildflower seeds. The seeds themselves were tiny, innocuous, and invisible once tucked into soil, and the person who planted them would be long gone before the first sprout pushed to the surface. It took time for the seedlings to grow to maturity, but if granted the right combination of sun and rain and patience, they'd one day flourish, covering the earth with color.

It was a lovely image, but I didn't want to make gradual, minuscule changes. I wanted girls and women to have better lives. I wanted the impossible: to upend the powers of fate. I wanted my predictions gone, erased, so I could move blankly through the future. So I could unlearn the truth of what was coming for my brother.

When I reached the cemetery, I paused to take in the gravestones of past professors and staff, the silent stretch of the otherworld. Maybe I was looking at things the wrong way. In the end, what was marked on my body did not matter. One day I'd join the dead, my bones laid in the earth. Just like Miles. Just like everyone.

In the older part of the cemetery, the headstones were made of marble instead of granite. While some of the engravings had faded or discolored beyond recognition, the marking patterns memorialized on the stones were still visible. I approached a cracked tombstone and ran my hand over its cold surface. Eloise Bethany Jenkins, born in the springtime and only forty-one years old when she passed. Her memorial marking—two large star-shaped marks offset by a trio of smaller dots at the top—represented fidelity.

When a woman died, it was tradition for her family members to select a representative marking pattern to include on her gravestone. I touched Eloise's constellation, feeling where the stone had been chiseled away for its creation. *Fidelity* would follow her forever. As women, we understood our memorial markings would remain a part of us even after our deaths—as if they mattered more than our skin, our breathing bodies, our entire lives.

I remained in the cemetery for a long time, thinking about the passage of time, and fate, and failure. That long-ago night in the alley, Miles tried to save me by better understanding my fate. He was clumsy about it, and wrong, and he failed—but all of this could also be said of how I'd reacted to the prediction of his death. We were two siblings on the opposite sides of a coin, forever connected yet held apart. Brother and sister. Heads or stars.

BY THE TIME I doubled back to the academic hall, my International Texts class was nearly over, but I wasn't worried. Professor Reed surely knew about the tarot by then and would understand that I might need time to myself. I slipped into my seat as she wrapped up a discussion of a foreign edition of *Mapping the Future* that included an addendum relating to gender expression.

Gender expression was not a term the Office of the Future would ever deign to define, much less codify in an addendum. This edition, however, was from a far-flung country in the north, a country so liberal that people born in female bodies who identified as men could have their markings stricken from the official record. Likewise, those born biologically as men were free to tattoo marking patterns on their bodies to express their identities as women. Anyone whose gender expression was not strictly binary, meanwhile, could choose to what extent predictions played a role in their lives, if at all. This approach was so progressive, so vastly different from what I'd known growing up, that I was still absorbing its implications.

I'd taken many classes on the mountain, from criminal justice to statistics, geometry, and interpretation theory, but this class had proved the most challenging. Most of us had grown up only learning about the worst policies of other nations; the more progressive laws elsewhere were largely a mystery. This class showed us more definitively how the rest of the world didn't necessarily mirror the ways of our own nation, and that ideas that seemed frightening or confusing within our culture could have merit elsewhere.

"For same-sex relationships, it's simpler," Professor Reed continued. "In this edition, there is no mention of whether romantic marking patterns refer to one sex or another. This, too, is a departure from our authoritative text."

I glanced toward Carmen and Jacqueline, who'd begun dating the year before. Whenever I saw them together, happy and unconcerned with how the outside world might view their relationship, I thought of Marie. I wanted my friend to experience this same level of freedom and love one day.

Marie hadn't written me in months, and it had been even longer since I'd heard from Cassandra. This was the way of the mountain, we were told. Some friendships from home might feel distant over time, but that didn't mean they were over. Once we returned, our professors assured us, those relationships could resume with some time and effort.

I didn't want to think about going home, not even if it meant seeing Cassandra and Marie or living with my family again. Not even if I found a way to pretend that Miles wasn't dangerously close to leaving us for good.

"Celeste." Professor Reed was standing before my desk. "Are you all right?"

I looked up. The other girls were starting to mill out of the classroom—was class over already?—while my professor waited patiently before me. She wore a silk lavender blouse that brought out the honey-colored markings on her neck and clavicle, markings that glowed against the deep hue of her skin.

"I'm fine." I forced a smile. She obviously knew about the tarot, how my stolen markings had entered the market, and was worried about me.

Professor Reed did not smile back. Instead, with an air of gravity, she placed a piece of paper on my desk.

"Please, join me in my office," she said. "We'll have a chat."

I stared at her. As long as I maintained eye contact, I could ignore that paper—the formal business letter with the Office of the Future's embossed red square at the top. The kind of letter Professor Reed received from her network of sources and that she only showed me whenever she had news about Miles.

The letter that I understood might have the power to change everything around me once more.

The Mountain School: An Origin Myth

The girl journeyed out of the wood. Halfway across a meadow, she stumbled and fell to her knees. There in the meadow grass she found her: a sister, small as a teacup, curled inside the heart of a daisy.

She scooped up her sister and carried on. She found another sister in the muddy ditch along a dirt road, and then a pair of twins who came pouring out of a tin watering can. By the time the girl reached the sandy dunes of the sea, she was plucking up sisters faster than she could carry them.

The girl and her sisters made their home on a mountaintop. During the day they played in the glittering dirt, letting the wind catch and lift their bodies like paper. At night they spread stardust under their eyes and played firefly. They chewed the rubbery tentacles of mushrooms and brewed berries into wine, and at night they slept together on a speckled bed of lichen and moss.

One morning, the girl woke to find a raspberry thorn wedged into her thumb. She yanked it out, put the wound to her lips. In that taste of blood she caught a flash of her return to the woods. How her body was swallowed by the shadow of trees. How she was made to reckon with the place from which she'd come.

23

PROFESSOR REED RESTED her elbows on the desk and pushed her glasses onto her forehead. I sat across from her, facing the vast, arched windows that overlooked the orchard and hummingbird feeders.

"The timing is not ideal, I know," Professor Reed said. "First the tarot, now this. I apologize for that."

The letter was in my hands, but I was afraid to read it. If I ignored my brother's fate, that fate might never arrive. This kind of denial was the only way I could thrive on the mountain, the only way I could allow myself to be so removed from Miles while his life grew closer to its end.

Professor Reed nodded at the letter. "They're preparing to take action, I'm afraid."

I finally made myself look at the letter, to read every last one of its stiff, businesslike words. It was a photocopy of a cease-and-desist notice from the Office of the Future, addressed to Miles. It demanded that he stop conducting unlicensed interpretations immediately.

"That's just a draft," she continued. "I'm not sure when they'll finalize and send it."

As the head of faculty, Professor Reed was the only person at the Mountain School who knew all my secrets. She had copies of my full government file, including the maps of both my adult and juvenile markings. She knew about the prediction on my left side. She knew that Miles could tell when a girl was predicted to be taken. She knew it all, and yet she never shared it with anyone. Privacy was cherished on the mountain, as was trust—and I'd always trusted Professor Reed, as much as I trusted my own mother.

"They'll issue a separate letter to Julia, too, though my source couldn't obtain a copy of that one," she added. "I imagine they'll threaten to close her business if she continues to allow an unlicensed interpreter to work with her. Naturally, your brother will have no luck procuring a license."

Professor Reed pulled out the file on my brother. Inside, I knew, were copies of the letters he had sent the Office of the Future in the last year. In those letters, he explained his system for determining whether a juvenile girl was predicted to be taken. He requested an official revision to *Mapping the Future*, as well as special dispensation to conduct professional readings on his own. Every one of his requests was denied.

"My other contacts indicate that your brother's work is becoming known, at least regionally," Professor Reed continued. "The more girls he reads, the farther word spreads. He and Julia are attracting more and more clients."

I already knew this. Miles and I stayed in close contact through letters, and I tried, as best I could, to share what I was learning on the mountain and to give him a broader perspective of what life was like for survivors. On the mountain, we even went so far as to call it the afterlife, the years of our altered futures stretching out like the vast unknown.

My brother also needed to sharpen his skills, to hone his abilities to an art form. He conducted plenty of readings, but it wasn't enough—he wasn't enough. He was starting to come up against his limits as a man, in terms of both how much the girls trusted him and how he couldn't fully grasp what they were enduring.

I skimmed the cease-and-desist notice again. "I don't understand why the Office of the Future refuses to acknowledge Miles's work. It's as though they want girls to be hurt."

"Change is difficult, Celeste. Historically, the Office of the Future has been slow to acknowledge new findings. But it's also about control. They can better control what they already understand. When it comes to markings, any new information is a threat to everything—to fate, to how our world works. In any case, your brother's expectations regarding the rate of change may be overly ambitious. The future shifts gradually—so gradually it's hard to tell it's changing at all."

"Like glaciers." We'd been studying the ice age in geology class. What struck me was that despite the painfully slow movement of glaciers, they were heavy and forceful enough to change the face of the earth itself. It reminded me of Julia's metaphor of the tree, how subtle movements and changes could affect the larger shape. Even on the mountain, I couldn't escape Julia's philosophy.

"The problem remains that word about your brother's work is spreading. The Office of the Future won't hesitate to shut it down, but there's only so much we can do from here on the mountain. We can't call attention to our curriculum. It's too risky."

I handed back the letter. Professor Reed never allowed me to keep those bits of evidence. She only showed me in the first place because she said no girl should accept something sight unseen. We were taught to observe, to question, to think for ourselves.

"Do you think he's in danger?" I asked.

"The Office of the Future is mired in bureaucracy and inherently resistant to progress, but no, I wouldn't say anything malicious is at play."

Her words didn't ease my worry. I could only think of my brother's future, or lack thereof, and how surely his unsanctioned work was mixed up in it.

"What your brother has discovered is unprecedented," Professor Reed went on. "The ability to predict abductions has the potential to change everything over time. If an abduction was viewed as another marker of fate, something no one could avoid, that would shift the blame away from girls. Perhaps the stigma would begin to dissolve."

"In that case, men could use the same argument to say they were fated to take a girl," I said. "They'd never be held accountable."

"That's true, but they're not held accountable now. They never have been. Let me show you something." She pushed back from her desk and went to the mahogany bookcase in the corner. From the bottom shelf, she selected a heavy photo album. Its faded cover bore the school seal embossed in gold. When she opened the album, its spine made a cracking sound.

"This is our history." She pointed to the first photograph. It was black and white, its edges yellowed. A dozen solemn-looking teenage girls, flanked by a few women, stood before a cluster of pines.

"These were the first girls to come to the mountain." Professor Reed flipped the page to another old photo, then another. "We have a class picture from every year. Go ahead. Look."

I turned the page. Girls back then wore long dresses, their hair pulled back in simple buns or braids. No one smiled. I started flipping faster. With each passing year, the number of girls increased while their dresses and hair grew incrementally shorter. Every picture was different, and yet every picture was the same: a group of somber girls, and a set of women guarding them.

"There are so many," I said quietly. And each girl was taken by a man who faced few to no consequences.

Professor Reed nodded. "It's overwhelming, to think of how many girls have come to this place, and how many others needed us who couldn't afford it. That is my biggest regret, that we haven't yet found a more equitable way to operate. But everything we do here is so precarious, so close to being found out and shut down." I breezed past more photographs while thinking of Deirdre, who could have had a different life had she been able to afford tuition on the mountain. Instead, the last I'd heard from Miles was that Deirdre had moved again, this time to another city farther away, where she worked as a seamstress in a factory.

"In the end," Professor Reed continued, "our legacy is that of women helping girls. But this isn't isolated to the mountain. This is a tradition one can find anywhere—across the country, and across the world, too. You're part of it now."

I kept my eyes trained on the album. The girls and women in the photos stared up at me, serious as ghosts. "You're saying I need to leave."

Professor Reed took hold of my hands. "I didn't say that, Celeste."

"You didn't have to. I know it's right—not just because Miles has so little time left, but because I need to help him and Julia."

Professor Reed squeezed my hands and I turned my head away, blinking back tears. Out the window, I caught sight of a hummingbird approaching the feeder, its wings beating into a blur. Any other day I would have watched it feed, delighting in its luminescent throat and needled beak. But I no longer saw any point in lingering in the presence of such beauty.

"I never planned on this," I went on. "I thought I'd become a psychologist. I thought I had no talent when it came to interpretation. But being here on the mountain has shown me otherwise. Miles has a gift, but so do I." I gently pulled my hands away so I could wipe my eyes. "I'm scared, but I need to leave."

"You can do this, Celeste," my professor said. "You can. And don't worry about graduation. You've proven yourself here. I'll grant you an early graduation to ensure you leave with a diploma."

I looked at Professor Reed. She'd taught me so much on the mountain, had shown me a world of the mind and the spirit and the heart. I'd always suspected she was too good to last, had always known that I'd have to leave her one day.

I just didn't expect it would be so soon.

*   *   *

LATER THAT NIGHT, once the news of my early graduation was out, my friends knocked on my door. They ushered me from our dormitory and into the night air, where more friends surrounded me. Each carried a wild-flower garland to drape over my neck.

"You're graduating," someone kept saying, like this was a magical thing. The scent of flowers surrounded me. Above us, the moon was so bright it obscured the surrounding stars.

When I first came to the mountain, I felt detached from the others. While there were a few like me—girls whose mothers, aunts, or older sisters became humanitarians to raise the funds for tuition—most of my classmates on the mountain didn't come from the same universe as I did. They had grown up with nannies, housekeepers, and tutors. They played piano and violin, and they competed in horse shows and tennis matches. I had nothing in common with them—until I was taken, just the same as they were.

I'd once believed it was mostly disadvantaged girls who were abducted, but the shine of money and privilege on the mountain told me otherwise. Our ruin was our equalizer, at least for these few years. After graduating, we could return to work on the mountain as teachers one day if we wished, but the majority of girls scattered out into the world, buoyed by family money. The mountain experience was a singular moment in time, a period of won-der to remember fondly but never repeat.

My friends led me to the large rock that hulked in the shadows behind the dormitory. We called it our lodestar. Bettina and Alicia pushed me to sit on it while everyone circled me. They clutched snarled handfuls of twigs and grass and leaves that they raised high above their heads. When they opened their hands, everything rained down like confetti.

"On this day, on this rock and in this forest, it happened," Alicia said. She brushed her palms together, releasing the last bits of grass and dust. "You were born."

I turned my face to the sky. I thought of those who really were born on the mountain, the daughters in the nursery. They would grow up with this place inside of them. I thought, too, of the other girls out there who were marked to be taken, and how they didn't know. How I could use what I'd learned to find a way to help them.

"I miss it here already," I said, but the other girls weren't listening. Instead they flowed around me, circling, whispering, laughing. As free and whole as they'd ever be.

Humanitarian Global Alliance for Women
DEPARTMENT OF AMBASSADOR MANAGEMENT

MEMORANDUM

TO: Paulette Morton, Ambassador 186C

FROM: Officer Young

PRIORITY: Urgent

STATUS: Confidential

SUBJECT: New Assignment

ABSTRACT: Assistance needed in nation where local law requires detainment and quarantine of juvenile girls predicted to contract communicable disease.

DUTIES:

- Conduct outreach and therapy services for affected girls.

- Arrange goodwill meetings with local officials.

- Attempt educational intervention with authorities, if receptive.

- Foster and maintain diplomatic relations with government representatives.

- Complete fact-finding to determine local policy for adult women marked with comparable communicable disease predictions.

Contact your commanding officer directly via secure line for travel details and in-depth assignment narrative.

24

THE JOURNEY HOME lasted four days and three nights on a train that coiled through the highlands. We clung to the sides of mountains, took dizzying sidewinder turns, and crossed bridges that soared above crystalline water. We went through tunnels, six of them—pitch-black shoots of space that stole time. I spent those days on the train half remembering, half dreaming. Expecting, at the train's every jostle and heave, a spectacular crash.

When we at last pulled into the station in my hometown, my father was waiting for me on the platform. He was alone.

"Where's Miles?" I asked as we performed a stiff hug.

"At Julia's. He wants you to meet him there." My father swung my suitcase into the car. "Come on home and get settled first. I'll make you lunch."

At home, our front lawn was transformed into a vegetable garden. Kale and lettuce, plus a jumble of what I'd later learn were onions, garlic, beans, and squash, grew in raised beds. Tomato cages filled the northwest corner. I clutched my backpack to my chest and studied the garden in silence.

"You did all this?" I asked.

"Who else?" he said, and heaved my suitcase out of the car. "Not your brother. He's barely home, and when he is, he doesn't eat. I don't know what he lives on."

My father headed inside, and I followed. During the drive home, I'd been uneasy over how we'd spend our time together. I imagined him pouring a beer and sitting silently in the living room. Instead, he headed straight to the kitchen, where he sliced an acorn squash down the middle and rubbed a baking sheet with oil. I went upstairs to my old room to unpack, but within moments I lay down and closed my eyes. It should have been a comfort, to return to my childhood bed, but all I could think of was my dormitory back at the school.

After a while, I gave up trying to nap and went downstairs. The kitchen smelled like garlic and butter. The table was set for two. I eased into a chair and let my father serve me: salad, acorn squash, garlic bread, plus sparkling water poured into a wineglass.

"This is delicious." I took another bite of squash, which was stuffed with wild rice, mushrooms, and spices. "I remember when you used to say you were fated to be a bad cook. Guess you were wrong."

He laughed a little. "I suppose so."

Our conversation drifted into silence. I observed my father as he ate. He looked thinner, and younger, somehow, even though nearly two years had passed since I'd seen him. We couldn't afford train tickets for visits after my tuition.

After a few moments, he cleared his throat. "Your letters made it sound like you loved school."

"I did."

"An early graduation is unusual," he said. "I thought maybe something happened."

I avoided his gaze. "Professor Reed thought I was ready."

My father put down his fork and stared down at the table, as if steeling himself. Then he pushed back his chair and disappeared into the kitchen. He returned with the phone in hand, the cord uncoiling behind him.

"Here," he said. "It's your mother."

I was holding my fork so tightly it hurt. "Please, Dad."

He thrust the phone in front of me. "Talk."

I took the phone and pressed it to my ear. The cord had to stretch so far from the kitchen that it pulled taut; I could feel the tension in it.

"Celeste." My mother's voice sounded far away. "I'm so glad you're home safely. But your father is worried about you."

"I'm fine. I promise."

The connection sizzled like a firework. "I couldn't be prouder of you for graduating so quickly. You always were a star student." A sound like rustling papers drifting through the line. "I miss you terribly, but they need me here. If it's all the same, I think I'll carry out this assignment before coming home."

"How long will that take?"

"No more than a month or two."

Professor Reed had been right that time was too short. The tarot could reach either my mother or my father in mere weeks. And Miles—my parents deserved to have time with Miles before it was too late.

I took a breath. "I'm sorry to do this, but I need you to come home. Right away."

My mother paused. "Something's wrong," she said finally. "I knew it."

"I'll explain when I see you. Just come home." I was about to cry, and it came through in my voice. My father sat across from me, watching without a word.

"I'll have to request emergency leave to exit this assignment."

"Then do it." I blinked to hold in tears.

"All right, Celeste." Her voice was resolved. "I'll file my request today."

If my mother was grieving the loss of her career, she hadn't let her voice betray it. Maybe she believed she'd be able to return to her post. Surely no part of her saw it coming, how the time we had left with Miles was diminishing day by day. In a few months he'd turn twenty, and sometime within that coming year, he would be gone. To not know any more than that was agony. It was unfair. It was the way of fate.

*　　*　　*

LATER, I WEDGED the tarot deck the best I could into the back pocket of my pants and headed for Julia's. Everything along the way looked the same and yet smaller, less significant. Living at the Mountain School had skewed my perception.

Once in the interpretation district, I drew to a stop near Julia's townhouse. Chloe's storefront across the street was boarded up, the sign ripped clean off. I stared at it until a familiar voice called out behind me. I turned and there she was: Julia with her flyaway hair, her uniform of jeans and a fitted dress shirt. The sight of her made me long for my mother. I was so surprised by this desire that I started to cry, right there in the street.

"Oh, Celeste." Julia hurried down her front steps and embraced me.

"I'm sorry," I choked out. I wasn't even sure what I was apologizing for—for keeping secrets, for leaving, for not coming back sooner.

"You have nothing to be sorry for." She smoothed my hair. "You're home now. Come inside."

She guided me toward her townhouse. Inside, everything looked the same as I remembered, save for the cluster of girls and a few of their mothers waiting in the parlor. I turned my face from them. I could feel the tarot deck crammed too tightly in my back pocket.

"Our client list is growing. Girls from farther away are hearing what your brother can do, and they find their way here, whether on their own or with the support of a parent," Julia said. "But as long as the prediction isn't in *Mapping the Future*, it's unofficial, underground. I think for some of them, coming here for a reading is like a game. That's one of our challenges—convincing them it's real."

I understood, without Julia saying so, that my presence could help. I was living proof that juvenile markings had predicted my abduction.

"The three of us have a lot of work to do," I said.

"Four." Julia gave me a tense smile. "We have help from someone else, too."

She pressed the intercom button near the entryway and spoke into it. A moment later, a girl of about fifteen entered the room from the back hall-way. At first, I could only register that she was a changeling. I hadn't seen a changeling girl in a long time, not since before leaving for the mountain, and her presence was like a cold splash of water in my face. But she was not just any girl.

She was Angel, Chloe's niece.

My mouth felt dry. I couldn't speak.

"You remember Angel," Julia said. "Chloe's in the hospital, so Angel has been staying with me."

Angel approached, her eyes cutting straight to me. She held out her hand, but I didn't move. After a long moment, she dropped it.

"Chloe has cirrhosis of the liver," she said in a matter-of-fact tone. "She won't get better, but Julia says I can stay here."

I could feel Julia watching me.

"That's terrible. I'm sorry, Angel." My concern felt performative, and I could only think of how Chloe had helped trap girls like me. I had to re-mind myself that Angel was no longer Chloe's helper but a changeling—a young woman living through perhaps the most dangerous time of her life.

"Life's not fair, is it," Angel said. Her tone was flat. "You should know that more than anyone."

"Angel's been enormously helpful," Julia put in. "She takes reservations and joins Miles during exams to put the clients at ease. She's become vital to our process."

I felt an envious twinge, a fleeting belief that it should have been me working with my brother, not Angel. But I'd left without looking back.

"Where's Miles?" I asked. "I'd expected him to meet me at the train station."

"He's had clients all day, but he'll be done before long. He's excited to see you."

"It's true," Angel said, a touch of sourness in her voice. "He's been talk-ing about it for days."

I looked at Angel, really taking her in this time. As a changeling, she was beautiful, but she was also more than this radiant transformation. She

was a teenage girl, clear-eyed and certain. She was not that different from
my friends on the mountain. She was not so different from me.

"I have to ask," I began. "Did Miles check you before you changed?"

"Yes, of course, and I don't have the abduction marking." She seemed a
bit exasperated. "Most girls don't, you know. We're not all as unlucky
as you."

I fell silent. Angel didn't believe in luck, and neither did I. We believed
in fate.

"If you wait here, Miles will be out soon," Angel added. She moved to
the appointment book in the corner and began jotting notes in the margin.
I hovered for a moment, then took a seat in the parlor with girls still waiting
for a reading. They peered my way curiously, but did not engage.

Time passed. Behind me, I thought I felt the air change in the room. A
minor disturbance, a new energy entering.

"Celeste."

I hadn't heard him speak in so long. The sound of his voice was the
same, almost as familiar as my own. I rose from my seat and slowly turned
around. Miles stood in the doorway wearing a white lab coat. He was no-
ticeably thin—so much thinner than when I had last seen him. His skin
seemed pale, his eyes red-rimmed, damp. I barely recognized him.

He took a step toward me but stopped short. I did the same. We had let
too much time pass and didn't know how to be around each other. Our time
apart, how we'd aged, the guilt and secrets and regrets—I could see it all
on his face, just as surely as he could find it in mine. We were twins and
strangers at once, still trapped on opposite sides of a coin.

And the coin was in the air, turning over itself, dropping fast.

We were both waiting for it to land.

Dear Miles,

I'm writing this letter late on my last night on the mountain. The other girls just gave me the traditional graduation send-off—though I suppose you don't know what that entails, and I don't have the energy to explain it right now. I'm not sure why I'm writing this letter in the first place. Even if I post it in the morning, I'll arrive home before it reaches our house. I suppose I'll carry it back with me, though I don't imagine ever giving it to you. It's one more secret between us.

What would you think, I wonder, to know that I'm treating you like a diary right now? Maybe I'm preparing for the future, for when you aren't here—when all I'll have are these made-up conversations with you that I create in my own mind.

I've been thinking how strange it is that we know any part of the future at all. Imagine if we never knew when our loved ones would die! We'd never know when it's the final birthday or holiday or anniversary with someone. We'd never know to be on the lookout for the first sign of cancer, the initial ache of heart attack. We'd just live. That would be terrifying in its own way, to know nothing, but sometimes I think it would be better. Don't you?

These are the things I wish we could talk about. Like friends. Like siblings. So much is fraught between us just for knowing the worst of what the future will bring. But in this moment I'm writing to you alone in my single bedroom on the mountain, trying to delay the moment I must leave. I don't want to descend into the heavier air below, but that's where you are, Miles. And it's time for me to return to you.

Celeste

25

MILES FINALLY LEANED forward to hug me, but he hesitated at the last second. He was being cautious, like he worried he might lose me again if he made any sudden moves. Maybe he was right, because the sight of him spooked me. I had anticipated my brother's death so many times that it was a shock to see him standing before me, alive and in the flesh.

I pushed down those feelings and embraced him. I felt his ribs through his clothing, the rigid structure of his spine.

"Glad to have you back," he said, as if I'd been away on a mere holiday. He glanced at the girls in the waiting room. "Let's go to the office so we can talk."

He, Julia, and I headed down the hall to the office and shut the door behind us. I hadn't been in that office since that day I'd brought Cassandra for a reading. It reminded me of being young and frightened and uncertain of everything.

I took a seat as Miles paced in front of Julia's desk.

"You already know that Julia has learned to read the abduction marking," he said. "That means you can learn, too. It was all foretold in your juvenile predictions, how they said we'd work together. Well, here we are. I can't do this without you anymore." He started to rush, speaking faster with every word. "You're the one who endured the abduction. You're the one who knows what it's like to be marked with the future. Only you can help these girls in the end."

"Miles, slow down and listen to me." I took a breath. "I learned on the mountain that the Office of the Future is preparing to take action, to officially ask you to stop giving readings without a license." I turned to Julia. "And, Julia, if he doesn't stop, your license might be revoked."

Miles didn't seem fazed. "They're using the license as an excuse—they're upset because I'm offering readings as a man, and because I'm pushing for an addendum in *Mapping the Future*. But once you learn to read the abduction markings, you'll take over and then they'll have no lawful reason to shut us down."

"I don't have a license, either. Considering my transcript, it's not likely I'll be able to get one."

"You can serve as my apprentice without a license," Julia said. "By the time you're ready to apply for one, you'll have enough experience to pass the test. As long as you earn a high enough score to justify why I'd choose to hire you over others, your transcript might not matter as much."

As Julia spoke, my gaze drifted to a chart hanging on the far wall in her office. I left my chair and wandered toward it, drawn as if it held the energy of a changeling girl. In a way, it did—it was a chart listing all the clients Miles and Julia had seen since the beginning of that year. It contained hundreds of records listing the date, anonymous client number, and either a positive or negative result for the abduction marking. The vast majority were denoted as negative.

"What's this?"

"It helps us track." Julia approached the chart and drew her finger down the column of abduction findings. "We don't have enough data yet to be sure, but we hypothesize that the rate of girls who have the abduction marking seems to be incrementally decreasing. Right now, all we can do is record and observe."

"And hope that we're right," Miles added.

"I don't understand." I scanned the chart again. "The girls who come here for readings have the same juvenile markings they've had since birth. It's not as though they can change."

"No," Julia said. "But if things were fated to shift—if your brother's discovery of the abduction pattern is set to make a real difference—then the number of girls fated for abduction may begin to decline as we continue our work."

I felt like a child again, struggling to understand. "So we're not changing the outcome so much as the fact that Miles was fated to make this discovery, and we were fated to help him, all of which will be reflected over time as fewer girls are shown to bear the abduction marking."

"Yes," Miles said. "It's like that study you sent us from the mountain last year, about those scientists who tracked how fate evolved over time by analyzing the fated behavior in individual lives over many years. We don't have the luxury of studying a time period spanning decades, but this is a start."

I put my finger to one of the few positive results on the chart. The girl was identified only as Client 145, which made her results seem clinical and detached, but I knew the truth. She was a girl marked to be taken, to have her life wrenched apart. No matter how many outcomes we studied, we could never answer why such terrible things happened. It was something my friends and I discussed often on the mountain—why the overarching course of fate allowed tragedy, and why our free will wasn't enough to overcome it. How we acted the best we could within the confines of our own fate.

"With your help," Miles said, "we should be able to see more girls, and to earn the trust of others who don't yet believe in what we do." He nodded to the chart. "Soon enough, you'll be making your own entries."

"You're forgetting that I'm not like you. I'm not gifted at interpretation."

"You can do this, Celeste. You just have to learn."

Julia went to the door. "We can start right now," she said. "I'll get Victoria."

She slipped out of the office. When she returned, a pre-changeling girl, brown-skinned with amber markings, followed her. The girl perched on the edge of the exam table in the corner and crossed her ankles demurely.

"This is Victoria," Julia told me. "Miles identified the abduction pattern in her markings last month. She's agreed to help us by letting us practice reading her. Victoria, this is Celeste, Miles's sister."

Victoria and I nodded warily at each other.

"Is it all right if we show Celeste your markings?" Miles asked, and Victoria pushed up her left sleeve in response.

I was still trying to process the fact that I was standing before a girl predicted to be taken. I felt sick on her behalf.

"Go on," Miles said.

I held Victoria's arm gingerly and focused on the undefined smattering of markings by her elbow. I'd long been taught that women were the root of the future, the cause and effect all at once. But at that moment, the future betrayed me. I came up empty.

"I don't see it." I frowned. The markings on Victoria's arm did not match the juvenile markings I had in that place. Without a reliable pattern, I didn't understand how to read the prediction.

"It's not what's there." Miles hovered over me. I could feel his breath on my shoulder. "Look for what's missing."

He could explain it eighteen different ways and I would never grasp how to locate something that simply wasn't there. Even if this prediction was added to *Mapping the Future,* it would be a challenge to describe it. It wasn't like the other markings, which could largely be identified on sight alone. That was probably enough reason for the Office of the Future to dismiss it.

I continued brushing my fingertips over Victoria's left elbow. She watched me with interest, as if she were rooting for me. After a few moments, something came alive there—a tingling series of jolts, like Morse code. It faded just as quickly. Surely I'd imagined it.

"There," Miles said, nodding. "I think you're getting it."

"I didn't feel anything." I dropped Victoria's arm.

"You need to try harder," Julia said.

"I can't do this." I started backing my way to the door. "This is all wrong—I wasn't meant to be an interpreter."

Miles and Julia looked at each other.

"It takes time," Julia said gently. "Why don't you go home and rest. We'll be back at it tomorrow."

I couldn't look at either of them. I kept my eyes on the carpet as I left the office, where Angel was waiting in the hallway. She stepped in front of me, blocking my path.

"You can't leave us." She grabbed my arm and looked as fierce as I'd remembered her back in Chloe's waiting room. "Celeste, listen. Chloe's leaving her money to Julia. Part of it goes to me, part to fund Julia's business. So Julia can pay you like a real interpreter."

I shook her off. "I don't believe you. Chloe is a monster."

"No, she's just weak. She says the world was set up for her to do what she did." Angel loosened her grip on my arm and stepped closer, lowering her voice. "Those girls would have been taken anyway. We know that now, thanks to Miles."

"We're also working to change fate," I said. "You saw the chart. What you and Miles and Julia are doing here can make a difference. We're not like Chloe—we refuse to accept the world for what it is."

"But Chloe is helping now," Angel said. "She's leaving her money to Julia, and to you, too. You should be thanking her."

"I'd never thank Chloe." My voice was shaking. I wanted to hate Angel, to hurt her, to make her feel all that Chloe had destroyed—but I couldn't. She was a girl like the others, and she didn't deserve the world people like Chloe had helped create.

I pulled the tarot deck out of my back pocket. I was going to show Angel how serious this was, all the destruction Chloe had brought upon us. But my hands were shaking so badly that I sent the cards flying. They scattered across the floor, dozens of exploited girls splayed near Angel's feet.

The commotion brought Julia and Miles to the doorway. They peered out to see me crawling on the floor in the hallway, gathering cards. I was on the verge of crying.

"Mom is on her way home, Miles," I said. The tarot cards were slippery, slick like they'd been coated in something sinister. "We have to tell her and Dad about what's going to happen to you."

I finally found my own card, which I held up with shaking fingers.

"See," I said. "This prediction isn't just ours anymore."

Miles reached down and took the card. He might have anticipated this moment years ago, back when he was copying my markings in his notebook. Back then he knew what I did not—that I would be taken, and that my markings would cease to be my own. It had all come to pass just as he'd known it would.

"That prediction is going to come true either way," I said. "Keeping it from them won't prevent anything. You should know that more than anyone."

My brother looked at me. I was crouched on the floor, loose tarot cards in my hands.

"All right," he said. "We'll tell them together, once Mom is home. But in the meantime, we need to work. And that includes you."

He handed the card back to me. He gave me back myself.

The Mountain School: An Origin Myth

Across her cheeks the girl smeared lines of red mountain mud; on her thighs and collarbone she dotted the iridescent dust of crushed shells. So disguised, she began the long climb down the mountain. Behind her, the voices of her sisters drifted like mist.

Down to the foot of the mountain, across the rocky stream, through the valleys and meadows. When at last she entered the shadow of the forest, her body sang out for her old home. What beauty, what pain. She named every tree, every leaf, every patch of moss and liverwort. Every bluebell and fungus and poisonous weed. The stone in her heart was beating hard, so hard she could not ignore it. The girl sat on a rock much like the rock that had birthed her and reached into her own heart for the slice of stone. It slid out easily, a slippery beast. When she dropped it to the ground, the earth shuddered and groaned.

26

ON THE MOUNTAIN, I read a fantasy novel about a society in which markings didn't exist—no one could predict the future. The characters lived in a state of unknowing, waiting for everything to unfold before them without the benefit of fate or prediction.

I read that book straight through in one sitting. How bizarre, how breathtaking, to not know what would come. I'd placed a long-distance call to the humanitarian dispatch center that same day so I could talk to my mother about it. She could tell I was shaken. She kept saying, "It's only a book, Celeste. It's not real." But I was unsettled. In that book, both girls and boys grew up blank. They were the same.

My mother, at that time, was working with a group of girls in another country who'd been denied education because their markings indicated they'd become homemakers. What's the point in educating them, the teachers argued, if they won't use their schooling? As a humanitarian, my mother fought for those girls. She brought them books, pencils, notebooks. She sounded out words with them. She taught them how to write and thus gave them the whole world of literature.

After we'd hung up, I spent a long time thinking of what my mother was doing, how she'd altered the future even slightly. Those girls would grow up to be homemakers just as their markings predicted, but they'd also be changed by their ability to read. They could, perhaps, pick up the same novel I'd just finished and imagine different worlds out there, different ways to shape the same life.

I tried to imagine a new world of my own making. I tried to imagine it back then, after speaking to my mother, and again that first night home, when I left Julia's and walked back to my neighborhood alone. I envisioned a world where girls could go out at night, even as changelings, and where they could create their own futures without dishonorable transcripts holding them back. It was an outrageous dream, preposterous—but I lost myself in it anyway.

At home, my father was waiting for me in the living room. The lights were off except the reading lamp at the far end of the couch. He was cloaked in shadow.

"Are you ready to talk?" he asked.

I paused in the entrance to the living room. "Not yet. Not until Mom is here."

My mother was rushing toward us on a train at that very moment. She was growing closer by the hour; I could feel her approach in my body.

"All right." He looked hurt, or maybe irritated. "I suppose you always were more her daughter than mine."

His words stung. I wanted to shake him, to make him see what I was really trying to say, what useless repetition ran in a loop in my head: *I'm sorry, I'm sorry, I'm sorry.* But I wouldn't apologize to my father, not then and not in the future, either. I regretted hiding Miles's fate, but as for the rest of it—the guilt and shame I'd carried from my abduction—I was done. It might take the rest of my life, but I was going to shed that burden, wash it off my skin. That was what I wished for: a metamorphosis, the ability to wake up restored and transformed.

Or maybe that wasn't enough. What I truly wished for, what I could barely allow myself to imagine, was a full reckoning. To transfer the shame and responsibility from the girls who were harmed to where it belonged—to the men, and to everyone who defended those men in myriad ways. It was so much to want for the world, so much change and justice and mercy, that it hurt to dwell on it.

I left my father and went upstairs. In my bedroom, I groped around under the bed for the cardboard box sealed with thick silver tape. The tape had fibers inside, tough like tendons working to hold the whole thing together. I had to use all my strength to tear it apart.

A single piece of paper lay flat against the bottom of the box. It was my brother's charcoal drawing of the man who'd abducted me. I hadn't looked at it since I'd packed it away before running off to the mountain.

I held the paper at arm's length. Back when I compelled Miles to create this drawing, part of me hoped it could lead to justice, that a sympathetic police officer might use it to track down my abductor. After my education on the mountain, I understood that it didn't matter how compassionate any individual officer might be, or how unfair it was that perpetrators walked free while girls' lives were ruined. The whole system, the entire structure of our society, was built around protecting men instead of girls.

This man, I told myself as I stared at the drawing, didn't matter. He was one man, but he was also all of them, every last abductor who took liberties with a changeling. And I rejected them all. I wanted to tear this paper to pieces. I wanted to rip that man's face and reduce him to a pile of scraps, to go on tearing and tearing until I tasted only smoke, ember, rage.

But I couldn't do it. With shaking hands, I replaced the drawing in the box and sealed it up again. Even if no one believed me, this was my only bit of evidence. Holding on to it gave me hope that one day, things could be different. With enough time and analysis, maybe that chart in Julia's office would reveal a different kind of future for girls. Maybe, in the wildest version of the world to come, it could even open a new future for me.

*   *   *

I DREAMED ABOUT my mother all that night. In the morning, I went downstairs to find my father making breakfast: pancakes, scrambled eggs, toast sliced on the diagonal.

"Thanks." I poured a stream of syrup on my pancakes. "This is nice."

He nodded. His eggs were slathered in hot sauce, a taste I'd never taken to. The plate looked bloody.

"Miles left early this morning," he said. "He mentioned that he needed you."

"Yes. We're working on something."

I waited for him to ask a follow-up question, but he merely opened the newspaper in front of his face, cutting me off. I felt hurt that he wasn't curious, that he didn't seem to care.

Or maybe he knew us better than I thought—that Miles and I were siblings bound together so tightly that there was no use trying to break his way in.

I washed my dishes and set out for Julia's. As I walked, I listened to the sounds of the neighborhood—distant passing cars, a neighbor raking leaves—and tried to see everything through my younger eyes. There were the stone lions with their cracked-open mouths. There was the shop where Miles and I bought candy and gum. And there, if I turned left instead of right, was the street where Marie lived. I paused at that juncture, thinking of Marie, of Cassandra, of all we once shared and how we'd grown distant from one another. How I'd never told them the truth.

After a moment of consideration, I turned left instead of right and walked to Marie's house. She and her mother lived in a squat ranch house on the corner. Their yard was overgrown with weeds, the crooked stone pathway leading me drunkenly to the front door. The door knocker was shaped like Pegasus with a chipped wing. I rapped three times, hard.

Marie's mother opened the door. She wore a long, heavy skirt, a turtleneck with sleeves flaring like bells over her wrists, and delicate gloves. Her

hair was wrapped in a pretty blue-and-white scarf. Not a single marking
was visible.

"Celeste?" She took a step back, but then seemed to remember herself
and came forward to hug me. "What a surprise. Wait right here. I just put
some tea on."

When she reappeared, she brought a china teapot and two matching
cups to the rickety table set up in the corner of the porch. I lowered myself
into a chair, wondering if I wasn't welcome in their house because I'd been
abducted. That didn't seem likely, but then I didn't know what to think
about modest women.

"Marie's not here, I'm afraid," her mother said. "She's off for the weekend with her girlfriend. Are you home for a visit?"

I let the word *girlfriend* hang in the air. Did she mean it in the way I was
thinking?

"I just got back from the mountain yesterday. An early graduation."

Marie's mother congratulated me. She poured the tea—white tea, for
the antioxidants, she said—and told me that Marie was preparing to move
in the fall. She'd earned a scholarship to a university in a larger city a full
day away by train. And Cassandra, she added, was spending the summer in
a special premed program before beginning her own university studies.

"Cassie surprised us all," Marie's mother said. "Ever since she switched
to that private school, she's been focused on nothing but schoolwork. She
and Marie don't see each other much." She frowned, setting down her teacup. "But you were always special to Marie. She misses you. When she's
back, you'll have to meet her girlfriend, too. Louise. They've been together
for a few months now. I've never seen Marie so happy."

"I'm glad." I was trying not to stare at the gloves covering her hands,
trying to reconcile how she could be modest but also accept that her daughter was dating another young woman.

"Graduating early from the Mountain School is quite the accomplish-
ment," she went on. "What are your plans?"

"My brother and I are working with an interpreter to help girls." I'd meant to offer a white lie, but the truth came out instead. Still, I didn't care, didn't regret my indiscretion. I realized I wanted her to know. "Especially girls who have been, or who might be, abducted," I added. "We want to change things in the future. For them and for as many girls and women as possible."

A silence overcame our table. I didn't dare make eye contact.

"I've heard the rumors," Marie's mother said quietly. "People have noticed that girls from out of town are seeking out our interpretation district. I just didn't realize that you and your brother were mixed up in this." She paused, studying me. "But I want you to know that you have my full support."

I wasn't sure what to say. I wasn't even sure what her support might mean.

"When Marie gets back," her mother continued, "I'm going to send her to you. Maybe she can help." She paused, staring out at the empty street.

Was it really as simple, I wondered, as whispering the plan to other women and waiting to see how they responded? To give them the opportunity to be stronger and more determined than the rest of the world imagined.

"I wish I could help, too, but I don't think I'm capable of it." She held up her gloved hands and studied them, as if mystified by what she'd become. "But you are, and Marie, and Louise."

"I hope so." I picked up my cup of tea, which was rapidly losing heat. I could see it escaping in narrow threads of steam. Everything was so fragile, so susceptible to decline.

Marie's mother freshened my tea to heat it up. I raised my eyes and studied her, every covered inch of her being. She looked at me in return, considering my uncovered hair and neck and clavicle. We sat like that for what felt like ages—long enough, perhaps, for the world to change around us.

AS SOON AS I made it to Julia's, Angel ushered me back to the office, where Miles and Julia were waiting with a girl who looked to be about thirteen years old. I was meant to read the markings by her left elbow to determine whether she was fated to be abducted.

At first I felt nothing. I closed my eyes and pressed a little harder, but I felt only static, echo, rainfall. When I applied more pressure, the girl wrenched her arm away.

Miles guided her arm back to me. "Try again. Softer this time."

I held her arm again and focused all my attention on this girl's markings, on her future, and still I came up blank.

"I don't feel anything." I looked up helplessly. "I can read the markings, but nothing is jumping out at me related to that prediction."

"That's because she's clear," Miles said. "Nice work, Celeste."

I studied my hands. They were trembling slightly.

"Am I done?" the girl asked.

"You're free to go," Miles told her.

After the girl left, Julia walked over to the chart on the wall. In the prediction column, she wrote *negative* in careful lettering. When I scanned the list, all the negatives ran together, girl after girl assured of her freedom.

I thought of the fantasy novel. I thought of possibility. I held up my hands again and saw that they were strong, capable. They were instruments of the future, providing a way to continue my brother's work through my own body.

When I closed my eyes, I saw ice: the heavy, gradual advance of a glacier.

Addendum X:
Abduction Prediction in Juvenile Girls

Category—Abduction

Location—Elbow, left outer

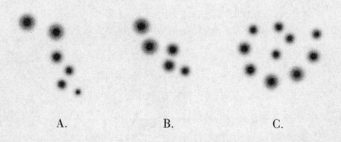

A.   B.   C.

Diagram Variations: This pattern can assume various forms. In some cases, individual markings will cascade from left to right while decreasing in size [**A, B**]. Other variations are possible, however, including a spiral pattern [**C**]. Please note that these pattern examples are not exhaustive.

Interpretation: This marking pattern is unlike others and, as such, relies more heavily on the sense of touch. To obtain an accurate reading, run the pads of your fingers over the marking in a clockwise motion, softly at first, then firmer. Exhibit care. Close your eyes if need be. Wait to feel it—sun flare, vibration, a quivering sense deep in the stomach. Be patient, be steady. If no sensation arises, the subject may be clear. Read again to be sure. Read again, and think of her not as a subject but as a girl, as a body holding breath, as a future independent of prediction and prophecy.

27

I WORKED FOR HOURS that day. All the while, my mother drew closer on the train. She was due to arrive that night, but I wouldn't let myself think about what would happen when that moment came. Instead I read girl after girl, and I came to believe my skills were improving, that I might have a future in this. I started to believe in something bigger, too—that the maps of fate were open to gentle revision if we only reimagined them. A road might be erased and redrawn a few degrees to the left, or an obstacle removed from the route. As girls, we were taught that our fates were set and any change was impossible, but that was a lie. I could feel the truth through my fingers as I worked.

The rest of the day passed in a haze. Eventually, Miles and I walked home together. We had dinner with our father, a meal he'd made from the garden. Then we waited. We'd planned on going to the station to meet the train, but it must have been ahead of schedule. Our mother showed up in a taxi, its headlights glaring through our front window as it pulled into our driveway.

I stood to the side of the window and watched my mother emerge from the car. Her heels made dull, jarring sounds on the paving stones as she walked toward the house. Miles and my father hurried to the front door to greet her, but I remained by the window.

"Home at last," my mother said as she crossed the threshold. She dropped her bag and embraced Miles. I witnessed it, the final moment before I cracked the world apart for her.

When my mother let go of Miles, I finally moved toward her, drawn by a potent combination of instinct and memory and love. She engulfed me in a hug and we clung to each other for a long time. I could feel her heart beating, which reminded me of hugging Cassandra as a changeling—two female bodies connected to each other and to the larger, mysterious forces of life.

"I HAVE TO show you something," I told my mother when we finally pulled away. "It's serious."

She and my father both faced me with weariness, patience, love. They waited as if they'd known this was coming. I steadied myself, then pulled up the hem of my shirt to reveal the prediction on my ribs. The marking pattern that foretold the death of their son.

I held my shirt and breath and waited. A long beat of silence followed. I closed my eyes and waited more. My mother was the one to step forward and trace my markings. She did so with caution, as if she thought they could spark into flame. My father did not touch my skin. He did not say a word.

After what felt like a long time, I lowered my shirt and wrapped my arms around my chest. I pressed hard, as if trying to contain the whole of the future inside my body.

LIKE MY ABDUCTION, like other traumas of its kind, the conversation that followed left me with few concrete memories. One minute our parents thought our family was whole, and the next, I tore it down by revealing Miles's fate. A family wasn't a static, solid thing as I had once assumed. Instead it was moveable, breathable, breakable. It would expand to make room for the coming loss, and it would also collapse on itself under the weight of grief.

"We're here now," our mother kept saying. We sat on the couch, all four of us, crammed together thigh to thigh. "This is not the future," she went on. "This is right now, this instant, and we're together."

She was right, but then time never stopped, and the future never ceased advancing. It was inescapable—and yet I continued to blame myself for the fate that awaited my brother and our entire family.

I apologized once and then again until my father asked me to stop.

"You had no control over this," he told me. "What is marked on your body, what is fated, is nothing you could prevent. You have no reason to be ashamed."

"But I separated Mom from Miles." I felt wrung out, emptied. My throat was scratchy, my eyes swollen. "I sent her off to become a humanitarian so I could go to the Mountain School."

My mother turned my way. Already she looked at me differently, like I was all she had left. "This is a shock," she admitted. "I wish I'd had the full story back then. But I don't regret becoming a humanitarian. My job didn't just benefit you, Celeste. I helped girls. I had a purpose."

"Exactly," Miles added. "Which is why we're working with Julia—we want to help girls. We want to change the future. That is our purpose."

Purpose wouldn't keep my brother with us. But as my mother had said, we were all together in that moment. Four bodies pressed on a couch. Hearts beating, lungs expanding. One day, Miles would be gone, my family contracted until I found my husband—because I'd marry eventually, just as my markings predicted.

In that moment, however, we were still a family. Mother and father, brother and sister. As it had always been. As it would never be again.

THE NEXT DAY, Miles and I took a brief break from our work to stay at home. Our father spent hours cooking for us. He made soups and casseroles and breads and a blueberry pie. He said, in fact, that cooking was the only way he could take his mind off the news about Miles—news he said he couldn't ever accept.

"You will," Miles told him. "It seems unbelievable now, but one day, the fact of my absence will be just that: a fact. One day you won't believe that you never knew it."

That was my older brother, so calmly philosophical about his own death, while I'd had nightmares all the previous night. I dreamed of Miles hit by a car, plugged into machines in a hospital, falling down a great crack that opened in the earth at his feet. My anxiety would only grow, I knew, as our shared birthday drew closer in the coming months. Miles was fated to lose his life sometime in his twentieth year—it could be only days after he turned twenty, or it could be months. We had no way of knowing.

My mother unpacked and delivered her suitcases to the basement. She didn't discuss the assignment she'd left behind when she resigned, other than to assure me that another humanitarian had taken her place, and that she hadn't abandoned the girls and women she'd been helping. When I found myself alone in the living room with her purse that first day, I peeked into it. I wasn't sure what I expected to find. A diary, perhaps, or notes from the girls she'd helped. The purse held nothing but her wallet and a new notepad, just waiting to be filled.

For most of the day, my family stuck close together. We ate meals in the kitchen and sat together in the living room. We talked, and we sat in long stretches of silence. Finally, by late afternoon, my mother went upstairs to take a nap. My father headed to the kitchen to scour the dirty pans. And Miles—Miles retreated to his room, and came out again with red eyes, and smiled at me loopily. I wanted to tell him that bloodflower took part of him away from us, made him feel already departed. I wanted to tell him I feared for not just his life but also the loss of our life together, as a family. But my brother was not clearheaded enough to listen.

I went to my own room. On the wall above my bed was the framed impression card my friends had given me for my sixteenth birthday. A black-and-red lick of fire. I stared at it until the image blurred and I started to imagine it into something else. Not a flame, but movement, like wind. Like coming change.

At my desk, I pulled out a notebook and a pen. I remembered what it was like to read Victoria's markings, that trembling, treacherous sensation when I came up against her abduction prediction. If I could only express what it felt like, what mix of instinct and magic led to that interpretation.

I sat at my desk and wrote for hours. I crossed out and recast and doubled back. I consulted the back of *Mapping the Future*, where the addenda were published. I recalled the revision requests Miles had sent the Office of the Future, how he'd tried but failed to describe the abduction marking. I also made lists of every class I'd ever taken on the mountain, every lesson that had been most important to me. I considered what other kinds of classes could be helpful—classes for boys, for instance, to help them understand how to interact with girls and treat them with respect. A class to prepare girls who were fated for abduction, and another to support those who returned. Unlike the Mountain School, these offerings would be available to girls of all economic classes.

Finally, I set down my pen. I had drafted a proposed roster of classes I envisioned creating. Some I could teach myself, but others, like gender theory, would require outside help. I'd have to write to Professor Reed to ask for her contacts. Perhaps we could receive materials or even host a visiting teacher from the northern country that published the gender expression revisions.

Aside from this course list, I'd produced one more document: an addendum for *Mapping the Future* that described how to read the abduction pattern in juvenile girls. It was a draft, an opening attempt in need of Miles's review, but it was a start. I titled it "Addendum X" even as I knew it stood little chance of ever being published in *Mapping the Future*.

"Celeste?"

I turned to see my mother in the doorway. As she stepped into my room, I held out my papers to her. I was tired of secrecy, privacy, holding my plans close. I wanted her to know everything.

She stood behind my desk reading, her face expressionless.

Finally, she looked up. "The Office of the Future will never publish this addendum."

"I know. Miles has already petitioned them to add this information, and he failed. But I thought—well, maybe we don't need to go through the official channels. We could print a whole stack of these and slide them into copies of *Mapping the Future*. In bookstores, libraries, schools. An underground way to offer people the truth."

My mother shook her head. "It's too risky. If you run around planting an unauthorized addendum, you'd surely be caught. And the penalty for tampering with an official document can include jail time, Celeste."

I was about to protest, to tell her we at least had to try, when she continued speaking. "If we're going to do this, we have to be smart about it," she said. "Fortunately, ambassadors know how to work without attracting attention." She paused, looking at me. "Do you understand?"

I stared at her. My mother, marked to marry and have children. My mother, marked for so much more.

WE CHECKED ON Miles, but he was still in his room, sleeping off the bloodflower.

"Once he's awake, I'll have a talk with him," my mother said. "I won't allow him to waste his remaining time like this." She closed his door. "But we can get started without him. Let's go to Julia's. You two can catch me up."

My mother drove us to the interpretation district. It had been so long since she and Julia had spoken in person—that open house Julia held years ago, back when Miles was still uncovering his gift—but once reunited, they fell into an easy rapport. In Julia's office, my mother spent a long time studying the chart on the wall. She was taken by this chart, obsessed with it, even. She recited the marking outcomes like a chant: *negative, negative, negative, negative, positive, negative, negative, negative.*

"You're detecting a decline over time?" she asked.

"That's the hope," Julia said. "We need to wait and see."

My mother had plans. She had connections. She talked of secrecy, of not attracting attention from the Office of the Future. Distributing the addendum locally, in a small and centralized area, would raise suspicion. But if humanitarian ambassadors could travel to us, to learn how to read the abduction prediction and take copies of the addendum away with them, the movement would be more difficult to track.

We were deep in this discussion when Angel came for us.

"Someone's at the door," she said. She looked worried. "Someone from the Office of the Future."

For a second it was like my high lucidity had returned. I felt all the blood rushing through my body, a series of rapids surging and falling.

"Man or woman?" Julia asked.

"A woman," Angel said. "An inspector, I think, based on her uniform."

Julia nodded. "Invite her in. We'll be there in a minute."

Once Angel had gone, my mother turned to me and touched my cheek. "Don't worry," she said. "This is good news, if they've only sent an inspector. It means they haven't escalated things too far, which gives us time."

"The three of us should go out there together," Julia said. "It's best that we appear transparent."

We walked as a group into the parlor, where a woman waited for us. She wore a navy suit and a tiny red pin glinting on her jacket lapel, and she carried a clipboard stacked with papers. Julia shook her hand, then introduced each of us in turn.

"What brings you to us today?" Julia asked.

The inspector held up her clipboard. "I'm meant to investigate this place of business. We've received reports of a young man offering readings without a license."

"I give the readings, and my license is valid." Julia nodded to me. "I've made Celeste my apprentice, it's true, but she works under my supervision."

"That's not a problem. What concerns me is the flood of recent reports of a male interpreter." She glanced at her paperwork. "It appears he'd be your son, Mrs. Morton," she said to my mother. She paused, her eyes flicking my way. "And your brother, Celeste."

Julia gestured to the empty parlor. "I'm closed to readings this week. If you were to return, I could assure you that you'd find me working alongside Celeste, not Miles."

The inspector lowered her clipboard. "The problem is that I might not be the one to return in the future. Someone else, someone who might dig a little deeper, might show up next."

No one said anything for a long stretch. I studied the inspector, the way she carried the weight of that red pin on her jacket. She was a woman. She was like Julia, like my mother. Like me.

"Will they hurt him?" I asked quietly.

The inspector looked surprised. "I don't know what you mean."

"Yes, you do."

The woman started flipping through the papers on her clipboard. As a government employee on assignment, she carried the files that contained my transcript and every official record of my markings, which meant all the Office of the Future knew about me and, by extension, Miles. She stopped when she came to my medical records from the Reintegration Wing, turning the clipboard toward me so I could glimpse the map of my skin. There were my adult markings, including the pattern predicting my brother's death. My secret was terribly kept.

"The Office of the Future has no reason to take such drastic action." She pointed to the markings drawn on my left side and gave me a sympathetic look. "Fate will take care of it for them."

I swallowed. "So you don't know how he'll die, or when?"

My mother put a hand on my arm.

"While it's true the Office of the Future wants to prevent your brother from working, they don't want to make a martyr of him," the inspector said. "They'll find a legal justification to stop his work. But these things take time—and it will take even longer once I report that I found nothing suspicious during my visit."

The inspector turned to the first page on her clipboard, checked a series of boxes, jotted down a few notes, and signed the bottom.

"There, now." She tucked the pen in her pocket. "Investigation complete."

I gave her a wary look. "What did you write?"

"That I've just completed a site visit at an interpreter's place of business. That I found no sign of a young man on the premises, just a licensed female interpreter, along with her female apprentice. No reason for suspicion or alarm."

She leaned in. She was so close I could see the beginnings of wrinkles around her eyes. "So long as you don't raise additional suspicion, it may be months before they send someone else to check my work. If that follow-up visit doesn't go well, it's over. They'll give Miles a choice: submit to being arrested, or have this entire business shut down. Julia's license will be revoked."

"He won't allow them to shut it down," I said. "I know he won't."

"Then he'll be detained."

"For how long?"

"It's hard to say. Long enough, perhaps. I recommend that you use the time until then to your advantage. And that you proceed with caution."

"Thank you," Julia said. "We appreciate your assistance and your discretion."

Before she left, the inspector shook my hand. Her skin was warm, and the back of her right hand was free of markings. That was considered auspicious, to not have markings in that place. As I watched her descend the front steps of Julia's townhouse, I dared to imagine a time when women could move through the world as if unmarked—absolved of the very future that once held them back.

PROPOSED COURSE LIST

Support and Action. Weekly meetings to provide confidential support, information, and preparation strategies for juvenile girls predicted to be abducted.

Parental Education. A class offering parents the information and tools to raise healthy, well-adjusted, independent girls without resorting to shame, fear, or avoidance. A special focus on protection, empathy, and understanding.

Sensitivity Training. A course specially designed to help boys and young men gain understanding surrounding the trials and challenges juvenile girls, changelings, and young women face.

Gender Theory. A class examining traditional and evolving gender roles and norms, domestic law, and international customs related to gender and gender identity.

Gender Expression. A gender theory course taught by guest instructors to help students of nonconforming gender explore their questions in a place of acceptance and understanding.

Return and Support. A class offering confidential coping strategies for returned girls who suffered abduction.

International Theory. A survey course providing an overview of the laws and customs related to markings in other nations, and the implications for girls and women here.

Body and Mind. A course providing creative exercises to encourage girls and women to expand their worldviews beyond their predictions and to consider other possibilities or realities.

Education Completion. High-quality, accredited curriculum to allow returned girls to complete their education post-abduction.

28

By LATE THAT summer, I was the one standing behind the glass doors of Julia's classroom. I was the one passing out textbooks, scrawling notes on a chalkboard, offering lectures in our newly created education program. In the beginning I taught girls exclusively, but soon my students included parents, then even some boys. In the confines of that classroom, our students were allowed to question the society that made them, to reconsider the taboo, and to ask: *Who am I?*

It was the same question I asked myself throughout those long summer months, especially during the Support and Action classes. A half dozen girls attended that class weekly, some traveling from as far as an hour away, to commiserate over the fact that they were each marked with the abduction pattern. I was constantly evaluating my role in helping these girls, trying to think of new methods to comfort, educate, and prepare them. Sometimes, the best I could do was roll up my sleeve to show my left elbow, how the skin there was free of markings in my adulthood. As if everything that had gone wrong for me was erased, scabbed over and healed.

"I know how painful it is to have your expectations for the future taken away from you," I told my students. "I'd always wanted to be a psychologist. Or, I should say, I always believed I wanted to be a psychologist." I paused. "I have a different path now. I get to be here, with you. I get to share what I've learned."

The girls listened. They asked questions, they cried, and they grew angry and yelled at the cruelty of fate. Some were not convinced, not wholly, that the markings on their left arms meant anything at all. They entered my classroom with doubt and denial. Those who had told their families—and not all of them had—were met with skepticism. Any marking pattern that did not appear in *Mapping the Future* was subversive, uncertain, perhaps deceptive. That was what we had been taught.

"One day, that prediction will be official," I promised. "Until then, we need to have faith."

In reality, I didn't believe in faith so much as I believed in connections, in covert operations, in my mother's ability to quietly summon humanitarian ambassadors. Whenever an ambassador showed up, Miles and I supplied her with copies of our new addendum. The ambassador would ferry this addendum away and deposit it in a range of untraceable locations, such as in bookstores in the towns she passed through on her travels. If each addendum reached only one person, maybe that could make a difference.

During this time, I lived in a state of near-constant fear. I looked at the girls marked for abduction and waited with dread for them to pass to their adult markings. But I also felt the same fear when I imagined a wider acceptance of this prediction. Once people accepted that some girls were destined to be abducted, I worried about how those girls might be treated. Perhaps they would be cast out even earlier, as children, before they could pass into their adult markings and become women. Perhaps things would get worse for these girls before they got better.

I couldn't say. I could only continue to work. So I showed up day after day in that classroom to stand behind a pair of glass doors that let in all the light, and all the darkness, of whatever was happening on the other side.

* * *

MY MOTHER HAD a marking on her stomach that denoted *daughter*. As a young girl I often studied this marking, marveling that the whole of my being had once been packed inside that tiny dot, like a miniature universe waiting to explode. Next to this marking was another that indicated an older sibling, a son. In this way my brother and I were born before our time, tied together in the body of our mother.

"Miles," I said. We were alone in Julia's parlor, long after the last girl had departed for the day. How difficult it was to be alone with him then, how easily I could imagine the time when he was no more and I was on my own. "Miles, when we were children, what did you see in my markings?"

My brother was on the couch, immersed in *Mapping the Future*. Perhaps he was envisioning how our addendum would look if it were ever to be published there. He couldn't know that eventually it would have its place in the official guide; that revision was years away, long after his time.

"I saw what everyone sees," he said. "The future."

"No. I mean the markings on my left elbow." I paused, remembering. The basement with its dirt floor. How his bedroom and mine were next to each other, how we shared a wall. How he studied my skin with a sense of awe, of reverence. "For as long as I can remember, you were fixated by that pattern. How early did you know what it meant?"

"I never knew, not for sure, not until you were taken. It didn't seem like something that could be true."

I wasn't convinced. I walked over and stood in front of him, looming, feeling the power of my body. I was nearly eighteen years old. I was a woman. I had a future—I had proof of that on my very skin.

"You suspected it for a long time." I tried to smile down at him, but it came out more like a frown; I could not control my expression. I felt everything inside of me was roiling, uncontainable. "There was always something different about you, Miles, ever since we were kids. You were beyond your years, beyond your gender, beyond yourself."

"No." Miles clapped *Mapping the Future* shut and looked up at me. "I was never the one who was different. It was you."

"I refuse—" I began, but then I stopped. His death could not be refused, my body's predictions could not be refused, our history and our future could not be refused. I knew this. Miles had known it already for years.

How unbelievable the future was, how vast. One moment I was gathering wild strawberries and the next I was allowing my brother to read my childhood markings. I was gazing with wonder at my newly changed body and I was riding a train into the mountains. I was holding a *MISSING GIRL* poster and I was being led into a dark basement. I was a girl and then I was a changeling. I was a sister and then I was not.

"Celeste." He waved a hand in front of my face. "Where'd you go?"

I blinked. Miles was still sitting on the couch, still studying me. Still alive.

"Please don't do that again," he said.

"Do what?"

"Abandon me. It's like you disappeared, even though you're standing right there." He balanced *Mapping the Future* in his hands, as if testing the weight of all the future, of every last possibility in the world.

The doorbell rang. We both glanced toward the entryway.

"It must be another girl for a reading," I said. "You should go upstairs, just in case."

We never knew when the Office of the Future might send someone else. We had to protect ourselves and our work. That meant my brother could never answer the door. He had to hide, which meant he had to leave me, again and again.

With some reluctance, he stood and headed upstairs. Once he was gone, I went to the front door and pulled it open to stare into the face of a girl so young and frightened she reminded me of myself.

I WAS FORCED to send the girl away that night. Accepting clients after hours could raise suspicion; the neighbors would notice if girls were coming and leaving after normal business hours, especially in the dark when changelings were not meant to be out.

Fortunately, this girl was local and could easily return another time. Sometimes, girls showed up late at night after traveling for days. It was too risky for us to host them, so we made a list of sympathizers who might help. Marie's mother was at the top of the list. She'd hosted three girls so far, giving them a safe place to stay while they attended our classes. She also remained true to her word by sending Marie our way once she was back.

Marie had arrived on her own the first time. When I entered the parlor and saw her, I could only stop and stare. She was different. She had passed to adulthood and was no longer the girl I remembered but a young woman, her future unfamiliar to me. I didn't know what to say, so I asked if I could touch the constellation of markings at her throat.

"If you'd like," Marie had said.

I came closer, my fingertips grazing her neck. The pattern there foretold of a temperament that would remain steady, honest, and kind.

"I don't need these markings to know who you are," I told her. "Even if we weren't friends it would be clear. Even if you were a stranger."

"But we are friends." She gently pulled away. "And we'll never be strangers, Celeste."

With time, Marie began bringing Louise with her, a slight girl who'd earned a full scholarship to study history. She and Marie had met the year before, during a university visit. Louise proved herself to be trustworthy, a calming presence for the most anxious girls, so she joined in on our studies. We were Miles's pupils, a small circle of women he could trust. We had to study in the evening, after hours, sometimes breaking our own rule by asking one or two girls to stay behind so we could read them.

On a humid August night, we all gathered in the examination room. Two girls waited there for us: one from my Support and Action class, and another who took the Body and Mind class. One marked for abduction, one not.

Miles looked at the two girls with disappointment. "This isn't a large enough sample size."

"We have no way of knowing whether we're being watched," Julia told him. "Keeping even two girls late is enough of a risk."

My brother was holding a copy of the new addendum, which he rolled into a tight tube. "The whole point of this is to train others to read. It's going to take forever at this rate, and we're running out of time. My birthday is six weeks away." He turned to me when he said this. We shared the same birthday. We operated on the same clock, our bodies ticking in the same rhythms.

"Better slow than not at all," Julia said.

"Then we need to widen our reach and teach others," he countered. "As many as possible."

At the time, Julia and I were Miles's best students. Our mother, Marie, and Louise were also making progress. Angel, meanwhile, was exploring other roles in Julia's business. Only days after Angel had passed out of her changeling period that summer, Chloe died, alone and in the middle of the night in the hospital. In the wake of Chloe's death, Angel's interest in interpretation waned, and she gravitated instead to the behind-the-scenes work. She made appointments, arranged our schedule, and kept our records in order in case we were audited. Julia told Miles not to push her, not to push any of us—that we each had a role to play.

"We're wasting time by arguing." I gestured to the examination table, where the girls waited. "Let's get started."

I began by reading the markings of the girl predicted to be taken. As usual, I felt compelled to close my eyes during the reading, as if I had to cut off one sense in order to bring the others fully to life. When I did open my eyes for a moment, I marveled that Miles was there, alive and next to me, and that we were working together as my juvenile markings had predicted. It seemed as impossible as the fact that our partnership, so newly formed, was already approaching an end.

"You're doing well," Miles said, glancing my way. "I know this isn't easy."

The abduction prediction was a complicated, subtle pattern with range. When I read juvenile girls, I waited to feel or not feel that tingling sensation. I waited for the hairs on my arms to stand up, for my breath to catch in my throat, but really I was waiting for the absence of these things, because I never wanted a girl to be marked to be taken.

What I wanted, instead, was for the chart in Julia's office to continue expanding as it had been for weeks: *negative, negative, negative,* over and over. In the last few months, we'd only found three additional girls marked to be taken while the negatives bloomed faster and faster. We attached new sheets to the chart every few weeks, taping it together until the data started running off the wall and onto the floor.

Meanwhile, the summer turned over into September. Cassandra surprised me by sending a letter relaying her first week at university. "I hear you're doing important work," she wrote near the end, her only cryptic reference to why I might have returned home. I accepted this opening and replied at once, and soon we struck up a correspondence in which I revealed to her what Miles and I were up to.

"I'm not surprised," she wrote in another letter. "You always were made for great things, Celeste."

It felt good to have Cassandra back, especially as I was about to lose Marie and Louise as they prepared to depart for university. At their joint farewell party, Marie's mother gave us each a handmade bracelet—to maintain our connection, she said. My bracelet was made of thin, soft strips of braided red and brown leather. I wore it on my wrist not only in honor of my friendships but as a reminder that Marie's mother was not quite the person I'd expected. While she was well versed in the domestic arts and could make bracelets and her own clothing and five-course meals, she also had a subversive streak. She sent her daughter off to university with a girlfriend. She looked for ways to help Julia, Miles, and me. She was so much more than I'd ever imagined.

Once my friends had left to further their educations, I remained behind with Julia and Miles. I conducted readings. I continued teaching behind the double glass doors. The days were ticking by, the sun rising and falling again, and October crept ever closer. October, the month of dropping leaves, wood smoke, decay. The month that would bring my brother's final birthday.

Course: Body and Mind
Assignment: Fill-in-the-Blank & Short Essay
Instructor: Celeste Morton

Label the diagrams below with the appropriate prediction groups as outlined in *Mapping the Future*. Next, select no fewer than three (3) of these areas to describe your own specific predictions, including all possible interpretations. Go deeper than what you might find in *Mapping the Future*. For every negative prediction, consider its positive. For every positive, consider its potential complications. Be creative. Consider not just what is marked on your skin, but what alternative interpretations might be possible. Imagine what it might be like if your body was not beholden to the future. Points awarded for creativity and imaginative display.

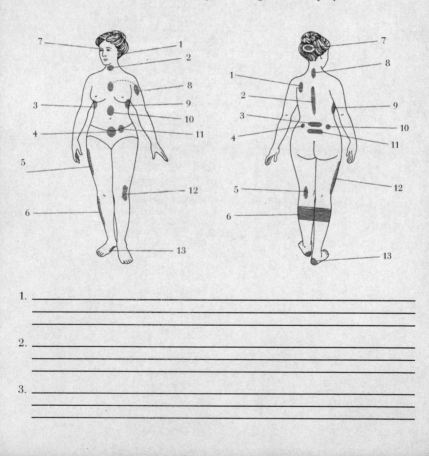

1. _____
   _____
   _____

2. _____
   _____
   _____

3. _____
   _____
   _____

29

ON THE THIRD of October, I rose from bed, my body moving automatically as if pulled by an unseen force. I grabbed the package waiting on my dresser and went to my brother's room. Miles was already awake and sitting at his desk, his hands folded over a wrapped package of his own. He was waiting for me.

"Happy birthday," he said, offering the barest of smiles.

"Same to you." I sat on his bed and we exchanged gifts.

Miles went first, ripping open the wrapping paper. Back on the mountain, I'd made him a journal in bookbinding class. Every bit was hand-crafted, from the paper, which I'd mashed in a pot, to the cover, which I'd dotted with wildflower seeds. I'd had a hard time deciding what to give him—no gift seemed appropriate for someone's final birthday—but it felt right to offer him something that had the ability to grow.

"You don't have to actually use it," I said. "You can tear the cover apart and plant it in the backyard."

Miles ran his hand over the cover's embedded seeds. "It's perfect."

It wasn't. The handmade paper was rough and bumpy, difficult to write on, and he might not have time to fill the pages anyway.

"Now open yours," he said. His gift to me was a broad flat rectangle, like a book. I remembered the astrology book he'd given me for my sixteenth birthday. I still had it somewhere in my room.

I carefully peeled away the paper. I didn't want to tear into it, to destroy what my brother had put together for me. When I finished, I was holding a notebook with a spiral binding and a worn cover of pale blue. It was instantly recognizable, as familiar as an old friend—the journal Miles had kept throughout our childhoods to map out my juvenile markings.

I flipped through the pages, astonished. It was like looking at old photographs of myself, or reading my own biography. My childhood markings had once seemed unforgettable, their patterns indelible in my mind, but now they struck me as foreign and strange.

I kept turning pages until I arrived at the juvenile pattern on my left elbow. Miles had sketched these markings again and again, drawing different lines to connect them as if to conjure new possibilities. The visual evidence of his obsession and his uncertainty.

"Check the back," he said.

Tucked inside the notebook's back cover were loose sheets of paper, mangled and torn but taped together in rough topographies. At first I wasn't sure what I was looking at, but then I understood: These were the practice drawings I'd ripped to pieces before I left for the mountain two years prior. These were ravaged drawings that my brother patiently put together again, using transparent tape to seal the wounds.

"I thought you should have all of this, especially after I'm gone." He paused. "It always belonged to you, anyway."

I clutched the notebook to my chest. On this, the last of our birthdays spent together, we'd given each other paper. Paper like the tissue-thin pages of *Mapping the Future*. Paper like the drawing of my abductor sealed under my bed. Paper like the letter I'd written to Miles but never sent. Paper like the tarot card revealing the truth of my body and my fate.

Breakable, burnable paper.

*   *   *

IN THE BACKYARD, my mother prepared a table for my birthday luncheon. She spread out a lace tablecloth, made a centerpiece of lilies, and set five place settings with a seating card tucked behind each plate: *Celeste, Marie, Louise, Angel, Cassandra.*

I stood barefoot in the grass with my arms crossed, watching her.

"I'd rather spend the day with you and Dad and Miles." I had to hold myself back from pointing out this was our last guaranteed day together as a family. No one needed that reminder.

"It's your birthday, too." My mother adjusted the vase of lilies, making sure it was centered. "You need time with girls your age."

I did miss the close company of other girls. My friends from the mountain sent me letters enclosed in pale violet envelopes, but it wasn't the same. Since returning, I'd spent nearly all my time working with Miles and Julia. Even my visits with Marie focused on work. Now, with Cassandra, Marie, and Louise each home from university for fall break, my mother was convinced the timing was perfect for a girls-only birthday lunch.

"They'll be here any minute." My mother checked the lilies one more time before letting her gaze rest on me. "You look lovely, Celeste. Like that dress was made for you."

I wore the blue dress she'd brought to me from her work with vulnerable girls. It was a dress envisioned and crafted as part of therapy, a dress of blues as deep and as complex as water.

Aside from putting on that dress, I didn't bother much with my appearance. I let my hair hang long and loose, and makeup wasn't even a consideration—I wasn't sure if I still had any, and I didn't care to look. Trying to find an appropriate pair of shoes felt like too much effort, so I remained barefoot. Besides, standing directly on the grass, the slight chill aside, was comforting. It made me feel grounded.

My friends began to arrive. Marie and Louise were first, carrying an overflowing bouquet of flowers between them. Angel was next, wearing a smart pantsuit that made her look older than her fifteen years. She gifted me a delicate silver locket, the space for a photo empty and waiting. I could already see my brother's image there, miniaturized and hanging close to my heart.

Only one seat was still vacant. I stood and paced, too nervous to relax, until finally she came. Cassandra. She stepped into my backyard in a fitted black dress, her kitten heels digging softly into the grass. She struck me as sophisticated, confident, adult. She was, I reminded myself, a young woman studying to become a doctor. She was going to live a beautiful life.

Instead of the flowers or jewelry I might have expected from Cassandra, she held a wreath of ivy leaves.

"Ivy for remembrance," she said. "And some say for immortality. May I?" She lifted the wreath and gently placed it on my head, adjusting my hair under it. I stood perfectly still, unsure of how to respond, and grateful when Marie and Louise came forward to help.

"Your hair has gotten so long, Celeste," Marie said, moving it gently around my shoulders. "It suits you."

I hadn't thought of my hair in ages, and I certainly couldn't remember the last time I'd cut it. It was a part of me, but it didn't warrant my attention—it just kept growing quietly in the background. Now I ran my fingers through the long strands and marveled at its length, its strength. How it would keep on growing even after Miles was gone.

We took our seats, and my mother served us the food my father was busy cooking inside. Only later would I understand that my parents were giving me a gift. They were showing me that life would go on, that I needed friends and normalcy, and that grief aside, there was beauty in enjoying a warm autumn day with people who mattered to me.

My mother brought out a bottle of dry white wine so my friends could toast my birthday. I kept sneaking sidelong looks at Cassandra until she met my eyes. She knew about Miles. She knew about my work with Julia. She knew, and yet she was so far away from me.

"Marie," Cassandra said, but her gaze was still on me. "Have you told Louise the story of the banner downtown? The one for the skin cream. Remember?"

"No one could forget that banner," Marie said with a laugh. In a flurry, she and Cassandra filled Louise in: how the banner showed a naked woman without markings, how the entire town erupted over it, how it was removed in only days. Louise sat listening with wide eyes. She was from a more cosmopolitan city, where she said such a banner wouldn't be quite as scandalous.

"Some people might have a problem with the nudity," she clarified, "but not to the extent that it would be removed so quickly."

"It was a simple line drawing, not detailed or graphic," Marie said. "Now I wonder what that was all about—why people got so violently upset."

But I knew. I'd had time to think about it on the mountain, to let the outline of that woman become part of my daily life.

"It wasn't that she was naked." I watched the sun sparkle against my wineglass. "It was the fact that she had no predictions. Think about it. If you walk into a museum, every last portrait of a woman includes markings. Even statues have them, chiseled right into the marble. But to show a woman who is blank—that's making a statement."

Everyone looked at me. I noticed Marie and Cassandra did not point out that my father had been the one to design the banner. We could have asked him what he'd done and why he'd done it, but I believed I understood better than he did. The implications of his work were so subtle that he probably hadn't been conscious of them at the time.

"It was a threat," I continued. "A woman unmarked, a woman not restricted by either her own future or that of others. No one knew what to do with that."

Louise leaned forward, her eyes steady on me.

"It sounds a lot like what you and Miles are doing with Julia," she said.

My friends and I sat in silence for a moment, contemplating our work as a threat, as a way to transform everything. We glanced around as if to pinpoint all that we might be able to tear down with our strength and our anger. The confines of my backyard, or perhaps the neighborhood, or the entire city. The sky, the earth, the whole of the world.

The Mountain School. An Origin Myth

The girl returned to the mountain thin and shaken. Her sisters swarmed her, anointed her, fed her a soup of bitter berries and leaves. The girl felt the empty slice in her heart, how the wound throbbed just as surely as the stone that had been in its place, but she did not tell her sisters. This pain was hers to bear alone.

For the rest of her life, the girl would feel apart. She lamented the stone in her heart, both its presence and its void. Sometimes she dreamed of the forest, of the smell of sweet decay. But on the mountain she was wild. She and her sisters taught one another, fed one another, and sparked blazing fires for warmth.

Time passed. The girl grew older and yet she remains a girl, the youth of her sisters keeping the light alive in her skin. On her best days, the forest flows through her like wind and she understands her history, how she was born of rock and stone.

On these days, she runs full speed across the mountaintop. From that height she sees it all: the great turning sky, the clouds rolling over themselves, the burning glint of sunset. From that height she knows her place. She is the world and the sea and the sky. She is cracked open like the rock that bore her, and the brightness that spills out is a gift she offers her sisters now and for all of time—luminous streams of loss and light.

30

ABOVE OUR MANTEL hung a large metal clock in a starburst design. It had been a fixture in our home since my childhood, but on that night, when I sat with Miles and my parents in the living room, I couldn't take my eyes off it, couldn't stop tracking the minute and hour hands as they both edged closer to the *XII* at the top. Once midnight struck, we had no way of knowing how long Miles might remain with us.

"Nothing is going to change after today," Miles said. "You know that, right?"

My parents and I nodded. We understood that lightning wouldn't strike our house at midnight. No alarms would sound. The stars would stay out, and the sun would rise again in the morning. He was right that the larger world would remain the same.

"Tomorrow," Miles continued, "we get back to work as usual." He looked at me as if awaiting confirmation.

"Of course," I told him. "I'm ready."

I was, in fact, already picturing the long line of girls waiting for their readings. We could tell those girls so much about their lives, but we couldn't tell them enough. Not yet. It would take years for the addendum to finally be published, and even longer for the stigma surrounding abduction to begin to fade. We were yet further removed from the first returned girl being admitted into university, or from the father-daughter inspections falling out of favor. At the time, I could only hold on to Julia's metaphor of the tree, a concept that remained so present and alive in my mind I could hear the rustle of wind through leaves whenever I closed my eyes.

"It's almost midnight," my mother said. We directed our attention to the clock despite ourselves. How indebted we were to time.

"It doesn't mean anything," Miles repeated, but his voice broke on the last word.

My father put his arm around my brother's shoulders. My mother held my hand. The clock struck midnight, and nothing changed. And nothing would be the same again.

THE NEXT DAY dawned warm and humid, and I woke up sweating. I remember the salt on my skin, how my hair stuck to the back of my neck. I remember almost everything about that morning and the strange hours to come: how my brother knocked gently on my door, how he nudged it open and peered inside, how he asked me to join him on a walk.

He led me through the outskirts of town, cutting through alleys and backyards, moving farther and farther from home. We walked together mostly in silence. I could feel an energy coming off him—anger, maybe, or resentment, or grief.

He cut to the right, taking us into a park.

"Where are we going?" I asked. His legs were longer than mine, and I rushed to keep up.

"I want to show you something."

He led me off the park path, through the athletic field, and along the edge of the woods. Where the field ended, we proceeded into a meadow overgrown with tall grasses.

"My friends and I spent time here when we were kids," he told me. "We made forts out of mud and weeds. A few times, we came late at night to set off bottle rockets."

I had known none of this. It was another of my brother's secrets.

"When I got older," Miles continued, "I brought girls here."

I ducked my head, embarrassed. "Why are you telling me this?"

"So you can know me better. So we can know each other."

Miles led me through the weeds and I followed, stepping in the trace marks he left in the grass. I watched as he bent down to retrieve something and hold it aloft.

It was a strawberry—a tiny, bumpy strawberry plucked from its sweet green leaves. The berries grew late that season, later than I'd ever seen them before.

"You remember these?" he asked. "We had them all over the yard."

"We tried to sell them."

"A business failure. We were hopeless." Miles brought the strawberry closer to his face, examining it. Then he popped it in his mouth and chewed.

We were quiet, as if waiting for something to transform. Finally, Miles bent to pick another berry, and then another. I would never forget that image of my brother standing with his hands cupped full of strawberries, a look on his face like triumph. As if he believed those berries could bring him life.

"You were afraid to eat these at first," he went on. "Remember? You thought anything wild was poison."

I joined him in gathering. We raked the grass clean, staining our fingers. We folded the bottom hems of our shirts and dropped the berries there. A cool wind snapped against us, hitting me so strong and sharp I felt I was being unzipped.

Miles reached into his pocket and pulled out a plastic bag. Bloodflower pills rolled around inside.

"You want one?" he asked.

"No. And you shouldn't take one, either."

"We all need a way to go on." He gazed into the field beyond, deep in thought. "You know, I took you into that alley because I was weak. I wanted answers, and I wanted to save you, but I was also afraid of not knowing the future. I felt helpless against what was coming."

"I understand, Miles."

He rattled the bag again, but I shook my head.

"Maybe bloodflower will be the reason, in the end," I said.

He made a face. "The reason?"

"You know what I mean. You should take care of yourself."

His expression was amused. "We both know how this ends. Let me do what I need to face it." He brought a pill near his lips and paused, meeting my eyes. "Take one with me?"

I pulled back. "Bloodflower made me remember."

"This time will be different. Especially if you just take half." He placed the pill between his teeth and bit down hard, cracking it in half. He withdrew one of the pieces and held it out.

"Half will be gentler," he added.

"Why is this so important to you?"

He blinked, as if the answer were obvious. "So we can be together. We don't have much longer, do we?"

With some reluctance, I accepted the sliver of bloodflower. I took this drug that had come from my brother's mouth and placed it in my own. I swallowed.

We lay next to each other in the grass. For a long while we watched clouds move across the sky. I was thinking how the world can open up in new ways if only you shift to view it from a different angle. Before, all I saw were weeds and wildflowers, but now I had the whole blue face of the planet to gaze into. There were so many layers to the world.

Miles reached over and took my hand. The bloodflower was working. We floated, skimming along the grass together. First I saw us as children, picking and eating those strawberries, but then I watched our current selves as if from above: brother and sister lying in the grass, holding hands. I felt, in that moment, a mistake had been made. We were meant to be twins, to share one fate, to live the same stretch of time on this earth.

"Miles," I said. My voice felt strange, a disembodied vibration in my throat. "Are you afraid?"

Silence. I felt the grass pushing against my back, the sun on my face. My brother was quiet for so long that I wondered if he'd fallen asleep. Finally, he spoke.

"You and Julia are going to work together for a long time. The two of you will help countless girls." He paused. "You're going to change things."

"We already are. We're changing things right now, with you."

"You have years ahead of you. Decades. I'll be gone soon, but you're so young, Celeste. You have the whole of your adulthood to come. You and Julia will be experts in the field. You'll accomplish things I couldn't even imagine."

I clung to his hand. It was impossible to imagine him being gone—no more body, no more voice, no more mind. Where would he go, I wondered, and what would be left of the rest of us?

"You and Julia will expand your curriculum," he continued. "Our parents will help the cause, as will Marie's mother, as will so many other people you haven't even met yet. That addendum will be published in *Mapping the Future*. Fewer and fewer girls will be abducted. All girls and women will gain more control over their own lives and bodies, bit by bit. It will happen slowly, but it's coming. And you'll be at the head of it."

"You can't know all this," I said. "Not for certain."

But I knew that Miles was right. I knew it as surely as if he had a direct line to all that was to come, a map of markings more complete and complex than any other. This future he described unfolded before me as clearly as if our mother was reading it to us as part of a bedtime story: There I was, an older version of myself, working side by side with Julia. There I was, handing out textbooks and teaching a class. There I was, making the same predictions my brother had once made. I was a teacher, an interpreter, someone who earned the respect and trust of girls the nation over. I moved, I married, I taught girls, I watched as the abduction predictions dwindled over time, until they stretched so thin they started to disappear.

In that wavering mirage of the future, Miles was by my side. Then he was not. Throughout the whole of my womanhood, I would carry not just my brother's life but his death. The slick patch of winter-made ground, the fall, the hematoma. The end of him, despite it all.

I came to with a start. The sun had moved in the sky. Miles was lying on his hip, glassy-eyed, watching me.

"What just happened?" I asked him.

His expression was serene. "I think you know."

I didn't. Or if I did, I refused it. Everyone knew the only true way to predict the future was through a woman's markings. The tarot, crystal balls, astrology, palm reading—all of that was a scam. Bloodflower was a drug for the past. It made girls remember. It couldn't tell the future, that was impossible, it just couldn't.

But I saw the future spreading before me regardless. I watched the un-spooling vision of girl after girl lining up outside Julia's townhouse, each more beautiful and true-skinned than the last. Miles was not there save for a strobing flash in my memory, the energy in my hands as I carried out our work. The taste of strawberry. The markings spelling life and the markings spelling death.

I lifted my arm tentatively into the air. The grass below my body prick-led. I was of the world and I was beyond it. Girls were being born all over, their cries beating a protest into the air. The vision was clear. I grew older, grew settled, grew skilled. Girls lined up to see me. In those young bodies I found the same thing, which is to say a lack, so many times that soon I was barely looking for anything at all. Instead I pressed my fingers to the mark-ings on the girl before me and thought, with wonder and intention: *You are free. You are wild. You are, now and in the future, entirely your own.*

Acknowledgments

Thanks first and forever to my literary lifelines: Huda Al-Marashi, Jennifer Marie Donahue, Liz Breazeale, and Jackie Delano Cummins. Jennifer and Huda have been there from this novel's beginnings and are, to steal Huda's term, my literary soul mates. Liz and Jackie made my years in the MFA rich in feminist energy, which surely infused the pages of this book, and their continuing friendship sustains me both creatively and personally. Each of these brilliant women lent her time, attention, and critical vision to help me become a better writer, and I'll remain forever grateful.

Huge thanks to so many other writers who helped me along the way. Charlie Oberndorf read parts of this novel in various early iterations, and Kathy Ewing, Mary Grimm, Lynda Montgomery, Mara Purnhagen, Tricia Springstubb, Sam Thomas, Susan Grimm, Bill Johnson, Amy Kesegich, Mary Norris, Jeff Gundy, Donna Jarrell, Susan Carpenter, Sherry Stanfa-Stanley, John Frank, Lawrence Coates, the late Wendell Mayo, and my cohort at Bowling Green State University's MFA program contributed advice, insight, and writerly camaraderie over the years. Thanks also to Bob Mooney and Kathy Wagner, who encouraged me in earlier days when I needed it most, and to Washington College for the gift of the Sophie Kerr Prize.

My eternal appreciation and respect to Erin Harris, my outstanding literary agent. I knew from the start that she'd make me work harder than any other agent, and because of that, she got the best book out of me. Erin, you were right: it was worth the wait.

I could not have dreamed up a better editor than Stephanie Kelly, who has been an enthusiastic advocate for this novel from the moment she read it. Her sharp editorial eye helped me see this fictional world more clearly and inspired me to bring renewed energy to its pages. All my thanks to Lexy Cassola, Natalie Church, Caroline Payne, Sarah Thegeby, Alice Dalrymple, Chris Lin, Kaitlin Kall, Erin Byrne, Tiffany Estreicher, and the rest of the Dutton team, as well as Alexis Seabrook and Mary Beth Constant, for putting such care into this book.

The Corporation of Yaddo, Art Omi: Writers, the Tin House Summer Workshop, and the former Writers in the Heartland offered invaluable support related to this novel. Thanks to Ramona Ausubel for teaching the craft class at the Bread Loaf Writers' Conference that sparked the genesis of this story back in 2012. I also extend my gratitude to the good people of Cleveland Public Library for giving me a flexible job that helped support my own writing, with special thanks to Tim Diamond.

My late mother, June Lois Walter, always believed in my writing, and I'll never stop being grateful for her support and influence. Thank you to Craig Walter and Scott Walter for the sibling experiences; to Emily Garver and Jenny Benson for embracing me as family from the start; to Kelly Moore for always championing my efforts to make the writing life a priority; to Megan Doyle, Amy Mescia, Adrienne Murry, Bethany Schrum, and Erin Snell for the long-standing friendships; to Matt Weinkam for all he does for local writers; and to the many writers, teachers, students, organizers, librarians, and booksellers who make Cleveland's literary scene what it is and for welcoming me into it.

Finally, to Peter Garver: thank you for challenging me, for supporting me, and for always encouraging me to pursue what matters most.

About the Author

Laura Maylene Walter is a writer and editor in Cleveland. Her writing has appeared in *Poets & Writers, Kenyon Review, The Sun, Ninth Letter, The Masters Review*, and many other publications. She has been a Tin House Scholar, a recipient of the Ohioana Library Association's Walter Rumsey Marvin Grant, and a writer-in-residence at Yaddo, the Chautauqua Institution, and Art Omi: Writers. *Body of Stars* is her debut novel.

Body of Stars

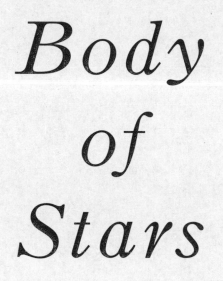

Laura Maylene Walter

Discussion Questions

BOOK
ENDS

DUTTON

Discussion Questions

1. Celeste's femininity is both a source of power and vulnerability. Her ability to predict the future is also marked by duality—it is a gift and a curse. How do these tensions play out throughout the novel? Do they appear in your own life?

2. The novel centers around two siblings, Celeste and Miles. How does a book focused on a sibling relationship differ from one that has a romantic relationship at its center?

3. Secrets have a lot of power in this book. Why do you think Miles didn't tell Celeste that he knew what would happen to her? Why did Celeste not tell Miles about what she sees in his future? If you were in their shoes, would you have told either of their secrets, or kept them? Did your opinion about what you would do change as you read?

4. Each character struggles with personal conflicts as well as broader de-
    sires to change the future and influence society. Do you think one is
    more important than the other? Do Celeste or Miles achieve their goals,
    and if so, how? How do you balance these concerns in your own life?

5. Tarot, crystal balls, astrology, and palm reading all play a significant
    role in the book. How do these practices relate to the way women's bod-
    ies are used to tell the future? Do you use any of these tools in your own
    life? Why or why not?

6. There is a constant tension between the dictates of fate and the charac-
    ters' free will in *Body of Stars*. How much agency do you think Miles and
    Celeste really have?

7. What is the relationship between the fate of individuals (like Miles,
    Celeste, Deirdre, etc.) and the fate of their society as a whole? How are
    they related?

8. The Office of the Future plays an enormous role in the lives of citizens.
    Do you think this reflects or distorts the role of government in real life?
    What made the Office of the Future such a powerful force in Celeste's
    world?

9. The Mountain School provides an important space for Celeste follow-
    ing the trauma of her changeling period. Do you think there are spaces
    like the Mountain School in our world? What value do you think they
    bring to society?

10. What did you think of the way the novel ended? Do you believe in
    Miles's bloodflower-inspired visions of the future?